Bella,
Discover new roads,
enjoy new adventures.
Nancy Moser 7/2017

THE JOURNEY OF
JOSEPHINE CAIN

NANCY MOSER

summerside
PRESS™

New York

The Journey of Josephine Cain

ISBN-10: 0-8249-3427-X
ISBN-13: 978-0-8249-3427-9

Published by Summerside Press, an imprint of Guideposts
16 East 34th Street
New York, New York 10016
SummersidePress.com
Guideposts.org

*Summerside Press™ is an inspirational publisher offering fresh,
irresistible books to uplift the heart and engage the mind.*

Distributed by Ideals Publications, a Guideposts company
2630 Elm Hill Pike, Suite 100
Nashville, TN 37214

Guideposts, *Ideals*, and *Summerside Press* are registered trademarks
of Guideposts.

Though this story is based on actual events, it is a work of fiction.

All Scripture quotations are taken from The Holy Bible,
King James Version.

Cover design and interior design by Müllerhaus Publishing Group,
Mullerhaus.net

Printed and bound in the United States of America
10 9 8 7 6 5 4 3 2 1

Dedication

To my father-in-law, Bill Moser
(1930–1996)

A hardworking man who
got his start working on the railroad

With malice toward none, with charity for all,
with firmness in the right as God gives us to see the right,
let us strive on to finish the work we are in,
to bind up the nation's wounds.

—ABRAHAM LINCOLN

Prologue

April 14, 1865

Life was good.

Josephine Cain beamed as she and her mother entered Ford's Theatre on the arms of her father, who smiled graciously at those offering congratulations and greetings.

An artillery sergeant approached them. "It is quite the celebration, is it not, General Cain?"

Josephine had become very good at recognizing a soldier's rank by his chevrons and sashes. This man wore the red wool of a noncommissioned officer.

Papa wore the buff sash of a general. This very evening Josephine had embraced the honor of wrapping Papa's sash twice around his waist and tying it over his left hip. She had been very careful to align the two tassels to hang just so.

"It is a celebration that comprises only five days of peace after four years of hell," Papa said to the sergeant. "There is still much to do to heal this nation. I simply pray it *can* be healed."

The man looked shocked, as if he had no doubt.

Josephine squeezed her father's arm while keeping her eyes upon the sergeant. "When my brother and cousin come home, *then* it will truly be over," she said.

The sergeant's eyebrows rose. "Of course. General. Ladies." He excused himself.

As soon as he left, Mother leaned across Papa and spoke to her. "The sergeant had no wish to hear your opinion, Josephine. He wanted to speak to your father."

Papa smiled down at Josephine. "It just so happens that in this, your opinion *is* my opinion."

So there.

"You simply want the boys home so you can go on your Grand Tour together," Mother said.

"That is not true. But can I help it if I'm eager to see Europe?" Josephine said. "We were all set to go, and then this stupid war—"

Papa pulled free of her arm. "Never, ever call this war stupid," he said under his breath. "To do so diminishes the sacrifices made on both sides."

Josephine hated having him cross with her—and she also hated that others might witness her scolding. She smiled at him prettily and said, "I am sorry, Papa. It *was* selfish of me to say such a thing."

"It most certainly was," Mother said.

If Josephine collected all the two cents her mother added to conversations, she would be independently wealthy.

"In fact," Mother continued, "I am not sure I shall let Thomas go anywhere after he returns home, and I know my sister will concur and keep William close too. The boys have been gone far too long already."

"But—"

Papa shushed them. He was right. This argument could be delayed—for a short time. Tonight Josephine wanted to concentrate on the most important man in her life. Papa was home, and though his military duties would likely drag on for a few more months, tonight she had him in her presence. She was going to savor every moment.

Josephine loved the attention they received as they meandered through the lobby of the theater and took their seats. She knew much of it was due to Papa's rank and station—after all, he was a confidant of President Lincoln's—but she hoped some of the notice was devoted to her appearance. She felt beautiful in her evergreen velvet gown. She hadn't had a new gown since the war began, but when Papa had confided that it would likely end soon, he had given permission to have this one made.

She had personally told the dressmaker to add short gold fringe along the wide, off-the-shoulder band, and longer fringe to accentuate the draped scallops along the bottom of the overskirt. For the occasion her mother had generously offered to let her borrow an emerald necklace. Josephine was grateful, but then she'd been bold. Could she please borrow the amber necklace instead? The tawny orange stones might be a striking contrast to the deep green of her dress *and* accentuate the ginger cast of her hair. It turned out Josephine was right—as she usually was in all things pertaining to fashion.

Their seats were front and center, just six rows back. The presidential box was raised and to their right, its railing draped in the stars and stripes. Two arches highlighted one extended seating area, and white lace curtains opened within each arch beneath heavy gold fabric swags. A portrait of George Washington hung on the centerpoint outside the balcony, as if the first president's job was to connect the two viewing areas. She had a thought that President Washington would be very relieved the war between the states that *he* had helped unite was finally over.

The president and Mrs. Lincoln sat to the right side of the box, and another couple sat in the archway to the left. The woman looked fairly young. "Who is that girl, Papa?"

Papa squinted. "Ah yes, that's Clara Harris. She is the daughter of Senator Harris, and the man with her is her fiancé, Major Henry Rathbone. A good man, Rathbone."

Josephine felt a twinge of jealousy. Clara Harris had a fiancé *and* had been invited to sit in the president's box? Josephine imagined herself in that spot, perhaps with Papa by her side.

But as for a fiancé? The absence of eligible men in Washington was another reason she was glad the war was over. She ached to be courted and taken to parties and soirees where she could enjoy a beau's company.

The play began. *Our American Cousin* was a comedy, but Josephine didn't pay much attention to it. Her eyes were on Clara Harris, admiring the lace on her dress and wondering what the play looked like from her vantage point.

Enough daydreaming. Josephine forced herself to be thankful for her own pretty dress and Papa's presence beside her.

But just as she chastised herself, just as Josephine decided she really *should* watch the play so she could discuss it later, she saw a man enter the box from behind the president. She assumed it was a servant, bringing refreshment, but then—

A gunshot rang out!

A scream.

Another scream—her own.

Josephine pointed to the box. "The president's been shot!"

The shooter tried to escape, but Major Rathbone struggled with him, adding his own scream to the uproar as he was stabbed and slashed with a knife.

The shooter jumped from the box to the stage and said something in Latin, then limped away.

The audience was on its feet. She saw the crowds in the two tiers of balconies vying for a view—or perhaps seeking a means for their own escape.

"Papa, what should we do?"

General Cain pulled his wife and daughter under the protection of his arms, but Josephine sensed from the twitchiness of his muscles that he struggled between chasing the shooter, helping the president, or herding them all to safety. She could feel the beating of his heart through his uniform. He yelled out, "Doctor! He needs a doctor!"

Help was already in motion with people rushing to the president's aid. One man came into the box from the door and another was lifted up from the stage. President Lincoln slumped in his wife's arms. The initial communal screams of fright had been replaced by wails of sorrow and disbelief.

"He'll be all right, won't he?" Josephine asked.

Papa's eyes were locked on Lincoln. She heard him murmur under his breath, "Please God, please God, please God . . ."

Josephine joined him in prayer.

PART ONE

I like the dreams of the future
better than the history of the past.

—THOMAS JEFFERSON

Chapter One

Frieda carried a black mourning dress into the bedroom. With one look, Josephine knew she could not put it on.

Not today.

Not on the day of Papa's homecoming. She would *not* greet him wearing black.

"Take it away, Frieda," she said. "And please bring me the green velvet."

Frieda put her hands on her hips and gave Josephine a well-honed look.

Josephine shook her head. "Take that horrible death-dress away, I say."

"I will not," Frieda said. "You are still in mourning. If you come downstairs wearing anything but black, your mother will faint dead away, and you'll have her to mourn too."

Josephine bypassed her maid and entered the dressing room that housed her many gowns—beautiful, lush dresses befitting the daughter of General Reginald Cain. She perused the line of gowns until she found the one that suited her mood. "Here. This one." It was an evening dress of lush velvet.

Frieda's head shook left, then right, in a stubborn *no*. "It is simply not proper, *Liebchen*. You are to mourn your brother and cousin a full year, and then wear a deep violet—"

"I *shall* mourn them a year," she said. "I shall mourn Thomas and William the rest of my life. But not today, please not today. I've just spent the entire afternoon sitting with Mother and Aunt Bernice, staring at the walls. I've done my duty. This evening is meant to celebrate Papa's return—even if he is leaving again." She looked back to the mirror, hoping Frieda would let her break the rule of etiquette just this once. "I won't complain about wearing black for a whole month."

"Well . . ."

Josephine kissed her cheek. "It will make Papa so happy. You'll see."

"You have always been your father's pet."

It was true. They shared a closeness that belied the time they had spent apart during the four long years of war, and this last year of postwar rebuilding. They both loved learning and adventure, and they shared an exhilaration about life's possibilities.

Unlike Mother.

Although Josephine loved her mother, their interests were as far apart as black and white, up and down, North and South. Always a homebody, Mother had planted even deeper roots since Thomas was killed.

Frieda interrupted her thoughts. "Come now. Since you have won the skirmish, let us get this gown on you."

Frieda Schultz was Papa's unmarried cousin. She had lived with the Cains for as long as Josephine could remember, first as her nanny and then as her lady's maid. Josephine loved her maid more than she loved her mother. She had certainly spent more time with Frieda, who had virtually raised her from birth and schooled her in reading, writing, and other important lessons of life. Mother might have run the household, but Frieda had run the children's lives, and both Josephine and Thomas had looked to her for maternal nourishment. It was backward to what she knew she should feel, but so it was.

But then a year ago the balance of the household had shifted permanently when they had received news that Thomas and cousin William had been killed in the final days of the war. Aunt Bernice moved in, and suddenly, daily, Josephine was asked to sit with her mother and aunt as they grieved. During those interminable hours, Josephine felt as if *she* were dying a slow death.

The dress on, Josephine relished the feel of the luxurious fabric against her skin. She walked up and back, enjoying how the weight of the skirt swayed back and forth like a bell when she walked, embodying the grace and elegance of womanhood. It felt so good to wear something pretty again. If only Mother would allow her to go out and socialize . . . How was she supposed to find a husband while held prisoner in her own home?

Or didn't Mother care? She often wondered whether Mother liked the notion of Josephine remaining by her side forever. *Till death do us part.*

That was *not* acceptable. Josephine wanted a husband, a house, a family . . . all the things girls her age dreamed about. Between the restrictions of mourning and the distressing fact that the pool of young marriageable men was sadly smaller, Josephine longed for something exceptional to burst into her life, take her breath away, and make her happy.

Happiness wasn't a bad thing, was it? Wasn't this country founded on the principle that its citizens had the right to the "pursuit of happiness"?

The clock on the mantel struck five. Papa's train was arriving in Washington this very hour, and he would be home for dinner. And then . . .

She was more than ready to talk with him about her plan.

Josephine turned to Frieda. "Will he be pleased?"

Frieda kissed her forehead. "How could he be otherwise?"

* * * * *

Josephine descended the stairs and braced herself.

As expected, her mother and aunt were seated at either side of the fireplace in the parlor, two she-bears enshrouded in dark mantles. Only their plump faces and short fingers provided Josephine's eyes some relief from the color of death. Even their palms were covered in black fingerless gloves. They existed in this state of near-hibernation, exuding an unspoken warning for others to stay away: *Do not disturb. Our growl is as fierce as our bite.*

Josephine paused outside the doorway in an attempt to ignite a spark of courage. She didn't wish to offend by her choice of dress, but the truth was, wearing mourning would not bring the boys back, nor would it erase the sadness that gnawed at her heart. Josephine prayed that someday sorrow's teeth would be worn down, lessening its sting.

She looked down at her dress, adjusting the neckline to properly cover her bosom so she would cause the least offense. Her gold bracelet sparkled in the candlelight, and she held her hand in midair, second-guessing her choice to dress up for Papa's homecoming.

Dowd, their butler, entered the foyer behind her left shoulder. "Miss Josephine?"

She was forced to follow through with her intent. "Papa should be here any moment, Dowd. Please make sure everything is ready for his arrival."

"We are well prepared, miss." His eyes traveled the length of her dress, as if to imply that *she* was not.

Hadn't Papa seen enough death and mourning? Surely he would be happy to see his daughter—his one and only surviving child—at her prettiest. Especially since he'd been gone for two months in the Nebraska territory working on an enormous new project, a railroad that would someday connect the East Coast with the West. She hoped he would appreciate her effort tonight. Even more than that, she hoped he would listen to her proposal.

Her future depended on it.

Josephine squared her shoulders and entered the bears' den.

As if by a common decision, her mother and aunt looked up from their tea, set their cups upon their saucers with a near synchronized *clink,* and opened their mouths to speak.

Mother's words came out first. "What *are* you wearing, Josephine? Where—"

"—is your mourning?" Aunt Bernice finished.

Josephine's heart fluttered in her throat. "I set it aside in honor of Papa's return."

"There is no *setting aside,*" Mother said.

"One does not set aside mourning," her aunt parroted.

Josephine moved to the apex of the womanly triangle, taking care not to venture close enough to be drawn into their lair. "I mean no disrespect for either Thomas or William. I love them and miss them as much as anyone."

"By this action you show otherwise," Mother said.

"Otherwise," Aunt said, shaking her head.

How could she explain? "What is in my heart doesn't need to be worn on my sleeve, does it? Besides, today is a day of celebration. Today, for a short while, Papa is finally ours again."

For the briefest moment, Josephine saw her mother's eyes clear, as if she had emerged from the well of death and glimpsed the sunlight.

Then the veil returned, and Mother sank into the pit of sorrow once again. "You must change your gown, Josephine. You will not disrespect our sacrifice."

Aunt Bernice shook her head. "No disrespect."

But before she could plead her case a second time, the front door opened.

"Papa!" Josephine ran into his arms, pressing her cheek against the wool of his coat. "I have missed you so much! I'm so glad you're finally home."

He wrapped his arms around her, and she felt his beard brush against her hair. He kissed her head. "My sweet girl. How I have missed you."

She closed her eyes and breathed deeply the scent of him: the musk that had always been his special scent, and the hint of cigar smoke and manly work that was Papa.

He gently pushed her back, taking her hands in his. "Let me look at you."

Her choice to wear the green dress was brought front and center. Would he chide her for her choice?

Papa spun her under his arm, allowing the wide bell skirt a full swirl. "You take my breath away, daughter. You are a vision of beauty."

"She is a vision of impropriety."

Mother had left her den and stood in the doorway.

"Lizzie," Papa said, extending his arms to her.

But Mother shook her head and took a step back. "I wish you would do something about your daughter, Reginald. For her to wear a party dress when we are in mourning, and more than that, the dress she wore the night the president was shot."

Josephine drew in a breath and looked down at the dress. Her memories rushed back. This *was* the dress she had worn on that dreadful night.

The president of the United States had been assassinated while Josephine watched, while she envied Clara Harris for sharing the presidential box. Josephine still suffered the guilt of her frivolous nature.

But more was lost that night than their president. With the assassination, Josephine's faith faltered. For how could the Almighty allow such a thing to happen to so great a man? Especially when peace had just been achieved.

The president's death had marked the beginning of her family's descent into sorrow. As the nation grieved President Lincoln, the Cains received news of the deaths of their boys. Thomas had died in the last days of the war at Sayler's Creek, and William had died in a Confederate prisoner-of-war camp. With that news, Josephine's mother and aunt had donned their bereavement black and had silently declared their own lives over but for the bothersome breath in their bodies.

Josephine was drawn out of her memories by Papa's voice. "Actually, I am relieved to see some color. With more than six hundred thousand dead, the entire nation is wearing black. Enough, I say. It is time to move forward."

Mother shook her head. "We must not forget the past."

"We must not forget, but we must not let it drown us." He looked at Josephine, as if his next words were mostly for her. "As I hinted at in my last letter, I have good news. I have been officially offered the position to oversee the construction of the Union Pacific rail lines as they head west across the Nebraska territory." His shoulders straightened as if his next statement were especially important. "Work on the railroad has already begun in California, heading east, and I am to supervise the construction heading west. I have some business to attend to here in Washington, but then I shall be leaving again."

Josephine took a deep breath. *If everything goes as I've planned, I shall be going with you.*

Mother shuddered. "You are a general, not a railroad worker."

"I am not a general anymore, Lizzie. That duty is done."

Aunt Bernice offered the next hurdle. "You are a lawyer."

Papa waved his hand. "I *was* a lawyer, as I was a general. There are enough lawyers in Washington. Besides, since the war, the soldiers have gone home to reclaim their lives, and many need jobs. The railroad will provide those jobs. I am used to soldiers, and they are used to me. It's a good match. And now, to be chosen to oversee such an important task . . . it is an honor. And it would be a continuation of the president's dream."

Mother shook her head. "But the West, Reginald. It is so very . . . west."

He looked to the floor. "That it is. The line starts in Omaha and will not end until it connects with the Central Pacific's line coming east from Sacramento. *They* have been laying track for eighteen months. We have barely started. There is much at stake for the line that lays the most. Compensation, land, property. And power."

Mother shook her head, her expression heavy with distaste. "So you're battling again? West versus East? Hasn't this country seen enough battles between North and South?"

He cocked his head as though he'd never thought of it in that manner. "This is not a war, my dear, but a competition. The United States thrives on competition. It brings out our best. And it brings about progress."

Aunt Bernice's eyebrows rose, as if she were considering his words. "The West always intrigued my George. The thought of unknown worlds . . ."

"Men," Mother said. Her tone suggested the species was deplorable.

Papa turned to look at his wife. "If it were not for the ambition and vision of men, this country would still consist of thirteen colonies under British rule."

"That is true," Aunt conceded.

Mother flashed her sister a look and then led her back to their chairs by the fireplace.

Good riddance. Josephine linked her arm in Papa's. "May I speak with you, please? I have something important to talk to you about."

His eyebrows rose. "Is everything all right?"

"Well, of course . . . actually . . . not really." She sighed deeply. "If we might go to your study? Alone?"

Before he could answer, Dowd announced that dinner was served. As they moved toward the dining room, Papa leaned close and whispered to his daughter, "We will talk after dinner."

"Good, because what I have to say is really important and—"

He put a finger to his lips, then left Josephine in order to escort his wife in to dine.

* * * * *

Throughout dinner, Josephine's thoughts strayed from the table conversation to the one she would be having after dinner. She *must* convince Papa to take her with him rather than abandon her to life with the she-bears.

Had they not been separated long enough? He'd already been gone for much of the war, and now he would be off again, his focus turned from battles to railroads.

They had always been close, closer even than Papa had been to Thomas. Josephine was the one to listen to Papa's stories and lessons, and her fondest memories involved sitting on his knee and playing with his beard while listening to his mellow bass voice. Thomas did not have the patience nor the interest to sit still and listen to anyone, much less Papa. When the South seceded from the Union and war was declared, Thomas had been in his element. She'd never seen her brother happier than when he'd stood before them in his Union blues, ready to leave for battle. Thomas was born to be a soldier.

And died one.

She shook the thought away, causing the footman to think she was rejecting another helping of yams.

So be it. She didn't feel like eating anyway. She wanted time with Papa. How would he respond to her idea? She set aside her fork and felt inside the waistband of her dress to assure herself that her list was still tucked away, ready to share with him. It was ready. She was ready. Beyond ready.

As she sat back in her chair, Papa gave her a questioning look. She grinned, and he offered a wink.

At the other end of the table, she caught her mother's disapproving stare. Mother subtly pointed her fork to her plate, indicating Josephine needed to eat. The stare did not dissipate until Josephine took up her fork, stabbed a yam, and brought it to her mouth.

But that still was not enough for Mother. She straightened her spine, pressing her shoulders back, wanting Josephine to sit up straight. Only after she complied did Mother relinquish her to her own volition.

* * * * *

Dinner dragged on interminably, but finally it was done, and the she-bears were safely ensconced in the parlor. Papa invited Josephine into his study, where he took a seat behind the desk.

She sat in the leather chair across from him, suddenly nervous. What if he said no?

She was glad when he initiated the conversation. "I know some of what you have been enduring, my girl. Before I left, I tried to help your mother and Aunt Bernice move forward from their grief. But the more I tried, the more they dug in their heels. I do think they find some kind of contentment in their lives—at least I hope they do."

"I have also tried to help them, but it is impossible when all they want me to do is sit with them in silence. They are suffering, but I am suffering too. The war ruined everything. And now I am stuck—"

"Careful, daughter. You cannot compare your loss to what the boys lost."

Josephine sighed. She hated when her selfishness slipped into view. Of course the boys had lost more than any of them. "I'm sorry."

"I know."

Josephine ran her hand up and down the nap of her velvet skirt, waiting for courage. *Up, back. Smooth, rough.*

"You wanted to talk to me about something?"

It was now or never.

Josephine removed the folded note from her waistband and opened it.

Papa laughed. "You have always been a list-maker."

She took no offense. But before she could get to the list, she had to tell him the core of her plan. "I want to go out west with you."

He sat back in his chair with a gentle outlay of breath. "Go with me. While I work on the railroad."

She held her list front and center. "Number one. I miss you—and you miss me. Out west we can be together."

"You hit the element of sentiment first, I see."

With good reason. "Number two, and I mean no disrespect, but I am suffocating here."

She did not like it when he only shrugged, so she pressed on. "Number three. Seeing new country will be an education. You have shared some of what you've seen in your letters, but it is not the same as experiencing it firsthand. You have always been the one to teach me about the world, Papa. All Mother seems concerned about is whether I wear the proper gloves at the proper time, whether I play Chopin without mistakes, or whether I read aloud her books of sermons to her satisfaction."

"Those are worthy pursuits."

Josephine stifled the urge to roll her eyes. "Not compared with seeing history being made. With you. Out west."

He smiled. "I am curious to hear number four—if there is a number four."

This was the weakest reason. "You were going to let me go to Europe alone."

"Not alone. With Thomas and William. And Cousin Frieda."

She had expected that response. "But out west I will be with you."

"The Nebraska and Wyoming territories are not Europe, Josephine."

"Of course not, but . . ." She set the list on her lap. "Please, Papa. I need to get away from here."

"*Need* is a strong word."

"It's an apt word. Please let me go with you. Let me witness some good being done in this country. Let me see people working together again."

He put a hand to his face, stroking his beard. She held her breath.

"I would love to have you there, but . . ."

But . . . ?

"But I simply cannot. The land and the people are too wild."

"I would take wild over tedious!"

"You must be reasonable, Josephine." He swept a hand to encompass the room. "You are used to lavish surroundings, servants, fashionable dresses, and people with manners. Life in the Nebraska Territory is as straightforward as the people. Manners lose their importance out there."

"I don't need manners! And yes, I complained about wearing mourning, but I would wear those clothes forever if I could be with you."

He moved around the desk and cupped her cheek with a hand. "What we have here is an impossible situation. You wish to be saved, but by saving you I put you in a volatile situation where your safety might be jeopardized."

"But Papa, I will be all right because I will be with you."

He dropped his hand. "Thomas was with me at Sayler's Creek, and I could not keep him safe."

Sorrow aged his face, and Josephine stood and wrapped her arms around him. Would they ever rid themselves of this awful grief and regret?

"Will you think about it?" she asked. "Please?"

He put his finger under her chin and looked into her eyes. "My answer is no, Josephine. I am sorry, but . . . no."

Stunned, she took a step away from him. Hot tears pricked her eyes. "Please don't look at me like that."

She ran out of his study, hiked her skirt, and raced up the stairs to her room. Once inside, she slammed the door and rushed to the fireplace where she proceeded to tear her list into little pieces and feed them to the flame.

Within seconds, Frieda came in. "What's wrong? What happened?"

When the last piece met its death, Josephine stared into the fire.

Her life was over. Completely and utterly over.

Chapter Two

Omaha, Nebraska

Every muscle ached.

Hudson Maguire groaned as he sat up in bed and let his feet touch the floor of the boardinghouse.

"Don't groan so loud," came a complaint from the other bed.

Using his foot, Hudson shook the neighboring mattress. "Get up, Raleigh. Time waits for no man."

Raleigh sat up on his elbows. "All work and no play makes Raleigh a dull boy."

"Dull but rich."

"Hardly."

Hudson tossed a pillow at his little brother's face. "Hurry up or they'll run out of ham again."

That got Raleigh out of bed. Working fourteen hours a day in the rail yard of the Union Pacific caused a man to need some hefty fuel to get going: eggs, ham, bread and butter, potatoes, and coffee strong enough to eat through metal. But at the boardinghouse it was first-come, first-served, and with every room occupied with two workers—with a few sleeping in the halls besides—there had been a few mornings when he and Raleigh had been left with only bread and butter. Live and learn.

Hudson washed in the cold water in the basin. He looked in the mirror, wishing he had a pair of scissors to trim his beard. Even though it occasionally itched something crazy, he'd grown used to it during the war. Besides, there was never time or hot water to shave. He ran a comb through his hair, which touched his shoulders. He had no idea where there was a barber in Omaha. And who had the time and money to waste on vanity?

Not him. Every nickel Hudson earned was for his girl, Sarah Ann, back in Pennsylvania. He'd gone home to Allegheny City after the war, and checked in on the cotton mill where he and his entire family worked. Their oldest brother, John, had been killed in battle, moving Hudson to the top of the hierarchy of the remaining three boys. As the new eldest, it was his responsibility to do everything he could to keep the family stable. But for that they needed more money than the mill could provide.

When Hudson heard General Cain was going to head up the work crews on the new Transcontinental Railroad—and was going to pay good wages—he'd known it was the best way for him to earn seed money he could plant for the rest of his life. So he and his youngest brother, Raleigh, had left their middle brother, Ezra, to work at the mill and take care of their mother, father, *and* Sarah Ann, who lived nearby with her family. Once the railroad was completed, Hudson would go home, marry Sarah Ann, move away from the Pittsburgh area, and find another way to make a living. Maybe carpentry. He liked building things.

Sarah Ann had promised to wait for him, and he'd vowed not to disappoint her.

The West held so many possibilities that he considered bringing his entire family out to join him. Anything to be away from the stagnant and difficult life in the mills. He'd build them their own houses with plenty of windows, and a porch where they could all gather in the evenings to watch the sunsets. There was something about the prairie sunsets that fascinated him.

He heard the thunder of feet going downstairs to eat.

Sarah Ann might wait, but breakfast wouldn't.

* * * * *

Raleigh ran a finger across the front of his teeth while he and Hudson walked to the work site. "I think that butter was rancid. I feel it coating my teeth."

"You could consider brushing them."

He held up his index finger. "This'll be fine. Back home a stick or a feather did the trick."

"You make us sound like hicks. We had toothbrushes. That you chose never to use one is your problem."

"Yes, it is," Raleigh said, stretching his arms high. "I like being on our own." He pointed west. "We've got the whole world in front of us."

Hudson hooked his thumb over his shoulder. "*And* our responsibilities back in Pennsylvania. The family's depending on us to earn enough to make their lives better too."

Raleigh shrugged. "I'm not going back."

Hudson stopped his brother, shoving his shoulder to confront him face-to-face. "Neither of us wants to go back there for good. But we can't forget about them. You know Da's back makes it hard for him to work like he used to."

"That he ever thought he could load that barge like he was still twenty . . ."

"See? He needs us. So does Mum and . . . Mum."

Raleigh grinned. "Mum and Sa-rah-ann." He sang her name.

Which was fitting because Sarah Ann was like a song, a gentle melody that hung in the air.

Hudson pushed his brother to get him going again. "It might do you good to find a woman to tame your mangy hide and get you to settle down."

Raleigh shook his head. "I'm only eighteen. You had your time for adventure during the war while I was stuck at home with Mum and Da. I'm not near ready to settle for anything."

"I'm not settling. I'm working toward a goal."

Raleigh rubbed his fingers together. "So am I. I'm aching for the dough. The greenbacks. The silver." He slapped the pocket of his coat. "I can't wait to be weighed down with the money."

"Money to send home."

It was Raleigh's turn to stop. "Not all of it. Right off the top the railroad's going to keep twenty dollars a month for room and board, so that's already near seven days a month we're working for free. A man deserves to keep a decent amount for all his trouble. Don't he?"

Hudson felt bad for his little brother. He understood the attraction of being off on his own. When Hudson joined the Union Army with John and Ezra and they'd first marched off to battle, he'd felt puffed up inside, like he was finally a man. They were doing something noble and good by fighting for their country and the cause of freedom.

The lofty feeling only lasted until the first shots were fired and he actually saw a Confederate killed by *his* bullet, and then saw John killed, right there beside him. A few seconds was all it took. Their first battle had been John's last. How unfair was that?

Hudson and Ezra had nearly given up and gone home, right then. If it hadn't been for General Cain riding through the stunned and hurting ranks that evening, pausing to offer his special condolences for the loss of their brother . . . And so he and Ezra had managed to stay on and fight—for John's sake. They didn't want him to have died for nothing. And Maguires were not quitters.

Fighting never became second nature, though Hudson *had* become numb to the blood. He'd had to. A soldier couldn't be heaving behind every bush. Dysentery caused enough problems.

Hudson was thankful the war was over so Raleigh would never have to see such violence, never smell death, never be scared into thinking that it would be better to die rather than to endure the constant fear.

A swat to Hudson's hat brought him back to the present. "Ah, don't worry about me," Raleigh said. "I ain't as dumb as I pretend to be. I know what's what with saving a little money. As a spiker we'll get three dollars a day—which is ninety dollars a month. Even after the room and board, we'll have seventy."

"Glad to know you can add."

They weren't alone in their trek to the work yard. Hundreds of men swarmed forward like ants converging on a crumb. The crumb was work. The crumb was money. The crumb was hope. Many were soldiers needing work after the war, but many were immigrants from the East— and even Europe beyond—lured by the promise of steady work, decent pay, and the adventure of experiencing the mythical "West." There were even ex-slaves working right alongside the men who'd fought to keep them enslaved. An odd thing, all around.

Hudson wasn't as starry-eyed as some. There *was* fighting ahead. He'd heard awful tales from both sides of the Indian issue. There'd been Indian raiding parties and scalpings of railroad men. There'd been the Sand Creek massacre, where soldiers killed 150 Indians, including women and children. And the retaliation of a thousand Indians killing whites, pulling down telegraph wires, and burning Julesburg, Colorado, to the ground.

There seemed to be a lot of wrong going on, and very little right.

That's what lay to the west, along with the hopes and dreams of a better future. Raleigh might still see the horrors of a different kind of war.

Hudson nudged his brother to get to the front of the group. There wasn't work enough for every man, at least not until they got underway laying track. Hundreds had been waiting in Omaha, waiting for the Missouri River to be free of ice so supplies could come across. But finally the ground was thawed and they could get laying. The land ahead of them was mapped out and grading was underway. They had deadlines to meet or the Union Pacific wouldn't get paid.

And if they didn't get paid, all these men wouldn't get paid.

Hudson and Raleigh shouldered past the crowd and settled right in front of the foreman. Hudson knew Boss had seen how hard they worked, so he was hoping—

"You and you," Boss said, pointing at Hudson and Raleigh, then a couple dozen others. "I want these bunk cars finished by the end of the day."

The men who weren't chosen grumbled, but Boss yelled after them. "There's a new shipment of ties to be loaded into the Burnettizer."

The men ran toward that work, yet the Burnettizer was a mystery to Hudson. Somehow putting soft cottonwood railroad ties into a long cylinder, then taking all the air out and putting some chemical in, made soft wood hard. Supposedly. Hudson couldn't help but think somebody at the railroad had been sold a bill of goods.

It wasn't his problem. Hudson had to assume that Dr. Durant and Mr. Reed and all the others who were in charge had the best interests of the project at heart.

Boss interrupted Hudson's thoughts with his usual, "Get on it, men!"

* * * * *

Hudson was not surprised that the bunk cars were General Cain's invention. The general had always put his men first.

Up until these cars were built, the workers who'd laid the first forty miles of track had been forced to bring their housing with them. They'd slept in tents or shanties and moved their shelter as the work progressed. It was not entirely efficient. But these bunk railcars would let the workers move with the work without having to set things up from scratch at every stop.

Hudson climbed on top of the first car, which was taller than a normal railcar. There were three rows of windows mirroring stacks of three bunks. Both ran the length of the car, which was eighty-five feet long. Hudson knew. He'd measured and cut the floor planks to fit. Today, they were installing skylights on the roof.

"Catch," said a worker on the ground. He heaved a rope up to Hudson. At the ground end, the rope was tied to a large pane of glass. "Careful now. Pull 'er up."

They installed the glass and continued the process many times across the top of the bunk cars. After repeatedly squatting down to nail the mullions in place, Hudson stood and arched his back.

Raleigh laughed at him, though he also stretched. "What is it Da always says?"

"That which does not kill us makes us strong."

Raleigh pointed his hammer at him. "Yeah, that's the one. I hate that saying."

Maybe so. But it was true. And Hudson knew that this work was nothing compared to laying rails.

Chapter Three

The clock on the mantel was an instrument of torture.

Tick-tock. Tick-tock. And the occasional *tock-tick.*

Aunt's snorting snore interrupted the incessant reminder that time was passing. Josephine's youth was passing; her life was passing.

Mother seemed unaware as she read a book, her chin occasionally bobbing against her chest.

Was this *it*? Was this all there was? Spending day after day in a luxurious parlor that had been decorated for gaiety and society? It wasn't fair that Josephine's coming-out years had paralleled those of the war. What should have been the sunniest years of her life had been rained on with worry, and then drowned with mourning. Those years had slipped away, never to be recovered. The bloom of her youth had been left untended and was shriveling before her eyes.

This parlor, which should have held musical soirees, parties, and flirtatious conversation, had instead been used as a place for women to roll bandages and listen to abolitionist lectures.

And now that the war was ended? The country was trying to rebuild.

The *rest* of the country. The Cain residence had its foundation fully mired in the past. There would be no rebuilding here. That Josephine was barely twenty . . .

She glanced at the clock and saw it was past six. Papa should be home by now. Although he'd remained firm in his decision to bar her from traveling west with him, she was not about to surrender. He'd always—always—given in to her wishes before. That this particular request was more substantial than her previous desires (which admittedly had

33

tended toward the frivolous) only meant that persistence was needed. Father *would* cave. Family history said so.

When she heard his voice outside and his footsteps upon the stoop, she rushed to greet him.

Dowd opened the door to Papa—and another man. He was shorter than Papa, with dark eyes. After removing his hat, he ran a hand through longish black hair, making it bow to his will.

Josephine kissed Papa's cheek, then turned toward the man. "You've brought home a guest?"

"Indeed I have." He motioned the man forward. "Josephine, I would like you to meet Mr. Lewis Simmons. Mr. Simmons, this is my dear daughter, Miss Josephine Cain."

He offered her a neat bow, and she nodded.

"So nice to meet you, Miss Cain," he said, putting his gloves into his hat and handing them to Dowd. "Your father has spoken of your beauty and gracious nature."

"Oh, has he now?" she asked, giving Papa a look. For they both knew that "gracious" was not one of her attributes.

Papa ignored her and instructed Dowd to have another place set for dinner. By now, Mother and Aunt had awakened and joined them in the foyer. Josephine let the introductions recede into the background. Her eyes were glued on Lewis Simmons.

My, he was a handsome man. Perfect actually, with just the right length of nose, and square of chin. The only flaw seemed to be the hint of danger in the way he handled the moment, as if he had a winning hand but wasn't about to show it. Yet.

But perhaps that wasn't a flaw at all.

As Papa took Mother's arm and led her in to dinner, Mr. Simmons offered his arm to Josephine. "Shall we, Miss Cain?"

* * * * *

Please help me say the right thing.

Lewis Simmons took a seat at the table next to Josephine Cain. He saw the tablecloth move above his lap, and realized it was his very own leg causing the movement. He slipped a hand atop his thigh and pressed it into submission.

He was so nervous he wasn't sure if he could eat. An unexpected dinner invitation from General Reginald Cain, when Lewis had just promised himself that he *had* to meet the general's daughter . . . He wasn't used to having things go his way.

He'd been watching Miss Cain for months—not that she went out much. He'd wanted to meet her but wasn't sure how to scale the tall wall of mourning that surrounded the Cain household. He'd heard from the Cains' coachman that the general was coming home for a visit, so he'd planned on finding a reason to call. But today when he'd seen the general enter the offices of the *Washington Chronicle*, a better plan had hatched in his mind. Lewis had a valid excuse to also be in the building, as he was trying to sell some of his illustrations to the editor, so meeting the general there was a pleasant happenstance. And then, when the general had remembered a published sketch Lewis had drawn of President Lincoln . . .

That one sketch, plus a little charm, had led to this invitation to dinner, and now he was seated next to the general's daughter. That one open door caused his mind to swim with possibilities. Lewis was nothing if not an opportunist, a trait that had saved his life more than once.

Now he was in. Now, his plan could proceed.

Winning the heart of Josephine Cain would not be a hardship, as she *was* a beauty, though the reddish tint to her blond hair was a color more unique than fashionable. He found her freckles pleasant—though he knew society looked upon them otherwise. He liked her voice too. It was strong yet feminine. He could already tell she was spirited, a girl who knew what she wanted and was used to getting it.

He could already tell she was her father's prize.

Which made everything quite perfect.

Lewis saw the others put their napkins in their laps. Yes, yes. He remembered now. It had been a long time since he'd *dined*.

A footman ladled soup from a tureen on the sideboard. It smelled delicious, and his stomach calmed. The ladies were served first, then the men. It was cream-of-something. He didn't much care. It was hot, and he knew it was only the first of many courses. He would not go to bed hungry tonight.

"I hope you like cream of asparagus, Mr. Simmons," Mrs. Cain said.

"It is a favorite."

He waited until she took the first spoonful, his mother's teachings coming back to him.

"Tell us about your family, Mr. Simmons," she said.

"My father was in transportation—steamships, to be exact. He worked with Cornelius Vanderbilt up in New York."

"The Commodore?"

"You have heard of Mr. Vanderbilt?"

"Of course we have. Everyone has." Mrs. Cain seemed properly impressed. "Your father's name?"

Lewis hesitated for only a moment. "Thomas Simmons."

"Thomas!" Mrs. Cain said. "That was our son's name."

"It's a fine name," he said with an inward smile.

Mrs. Cain touched a finger to her lips, thinking. "I believe we may have met your father when we were in New York before the war. Don't you think so, Reginald?"

"It could very well be. The name Simmons sounds very familiar."

Lewis suppressed another smile. This was going better than he could have hoped.

"Are you involved in shipping too?" Miss Cain asked.

"That would be my father's wish, but he's given me permission to pursue my dream."

"Mr. Simmons is a wonderful artist," the general explained.

Lewis was happy for the praise—and the designation. "Artist" sounded better than "illustrator" and far better than the truth.

Miss Cain's interest must have been piqued. "What sort of artist?"

He hesitated, then risked saying, "A good one."

They all laughed. An encouraging sign.

"I meant, what medium do you use?"

"A few. But I prefer pen and ink."

The general added more explanation. "Mr. Simmons's illustrations have been seen in many East Coast periodicals. Do you remember the drawing of Lincoln's assassination in Ford's Theatre that was in the papers?"

She looked to her plate. "I do not need a drawing to remember."

Lewis set his hand upon the table between them. His voice was soft. "I was there too, Miss Cain."

"You were?"

He pointed a finger to his temple. "The entire scene is pressed indelibly upon my memory."

"And then upon paper," the general said.

"But why would you immortalize such a horrible moment of our history?" Miss Cain asked.

"Josephine!" her mother said.

"No," Lewis said, " 'tis a fair question. As an artist, I feel a responsibility to capture historical moments for all time." *That I was working backstage as a stagehand need not be mentioned.*

"But such a horrible moment—"

"Must be remembered. The turning points of a nation—good and bad—must not be forgotten."

When no one spoke, he wondered if he'd been too bold. "I am sorry. I shouldn't—"

"No," Miss Cain interrupted. "You are right."

"But on to happier thoughts," the general said. "When I was at the newspaper office, the editor there, Mr. Wilson, offered me two extra tickets to the opera. *The Marriage of Figaro* is playing. Your favorite, Josephine."

Lewis saw her blush, and with another glance at her father, he knew that now was the time to do what he was expected to do. "Your father has been kind enough . . . I would be very honored if you would accompany me, Miss Cain."

Mrs. Cain interceded. "I hardly think the opera is appropriate while we are in mourning."

"Most inappropriate," the aunt said.

"And you two most certainly cannot go unaccompanied," Mrs. Cain continued.

Lewis wasn't pleased that the general had created this faux pas. "Of course. Forgive me for bringing up such a frivolous subject."

"Opera is not frivolous at all," the general said. "Such magnificence of sound from voice and orchestra is heaven-sent." He looked at his wife. "And they will not be without chaperone, my dear. Mr. Wilson's brother and his wife have offered to meet them there. You remember Robert and Edith Wilson?"

The girl flashed her mother a pleading look, but Mrs. Cain shook her head vehemently. "No, Josephine. You may not attend."

"But our year of full mourning is over."

The older woman's chin hardened. "Our mourning is never over."

"Of course not, Lizzie," the general said. "But I see nothing wrong with Josephine going to the opera."

"Thomas always loved the opera," Miss Cain said.

At the mention of this memory, tears formed in Mrs. Cain's eyes. Her daughter pushed back from the table and rushed to her side, kneeling before her.

"I am sorry, Mother. I shouldn't have said that and reminded you . . ."

Mrs. Cain retrieved a handkerchief from her sleeve and dabbed at her eyes. But then she nodded, and even smiled. "Thomas adored *The Marriage of Figaro*."

Miss Cain nodded and touched her arm. "He especially loved the duet '*Che soave zeffiretto.*'"

"He said it sounded like two angels singing."

Miss Cain leaned her head against her mother's arm. "I remember sitting beside him at the opera and watching him as he listened to the duet. His eyes were always closed, his face tilted upward as if sensing that the majesty of the music came from God."

Lewis looked to the general, wishing for help to make things right.

But then, Mrs. Cain touched her daughter's cheek. "You may go to the opera, Josephine. Remember Thomas through the music."

"I remember him with every breath I take."

In that moment, Lewis could imagine how Mrs. Cain used to be before grieving had become her occupation. But then she looked away, and the mask of mourning dropped into place. "Well then," she said, looking out over the table.

Miss Cain stood, but before she returned to her place, she kissed her mother's cheek.

"Very good," the general said. "To the opera you shall go."

Lewis was delighted.

And petrified. Although the tickets were complimentary, there would be other expenses. A carriage, and perhaps dinner after the opera . . .

It would require money he didn't have.

But money he could get. He had his ways.

* * * * *

"Thank you for the delicious meal, Mrs. Cain," Lewis said as he gathered his hat.

"Of course, Mr. Simmons. You are welcome in our home anytime."

She offered him a shy smile, which surprised him. Obviously dropping his fork on the carpet hadn't offended her too badly.

Lewis nodded to Miss Cain. "Shall I fetch—come for you—at half past seven?"

"That would be perfect," she said. "I look forward to it."

"Very good," the general said to him. "I will see you out."

Once the two men took the steps to the street, the general reached into the inner pocket of his coat. He pulled out the two tickets. "For you."

"Thank you, sir."

"I know you must think me very presumptuous for pressing you to escort my daughter, but after speaking with you at the *Chronicle* offices, and getting a nod from Mr. Wilson . . . I am not usually so impulsive, but everything seemed to fit into place."

"As if it were meant to be, sir." Lewis couldn't have expressed it better himself.

The general hesitated but a moment. "*That,* we shall see. But the truth is, my daughter's desire to go out has been weighing heavily on me. When the opportunity arose to make her happy . . ." He sighed. "I *am* very glad to see a spark between the two of you."

He'd seen a spark? "Thank you, General. I find your daughter very lovely and charming, and I shall look forward to spending time in her company." It felt good to be able to speak a truth.

"Then you don't take offense at my using you as a knight in shining armor to rescue Josephine from her prison?"

"Prison?"

"Mourning is a prison, my boy. One that can sap the life out of a person as sure as any torture."

Lewis nodded. He knew this firsthand.

"It is time my Josephine was set free, time she was occupied with the pleasures of life. Time she was distracted."

Lewis found the last word odd. "Distracted?"

"Never mind. Show her a pleasant time. Perhaps the opera can lead to other outings."

"Perhaps it could." Gaining the approval of the Cains had been far easier than Lewis had hoped. Mentioning Mr. Vanderbilt had been a good idea, as was changing his father's name to Thomas. That his father *had* worked with the mogul made the story easier to maintain.

The general turned toward the front door. "Very good then. How lucky we ran into each other at the newspaper office."

"Yes, indeed." Lewis smiled as he turned away, remembering one of his father's favorite sayings: *You make your own luck.*

* * * * *

Lewis Simmons's gasp was just the reaction Josephine had hoped for.

On the night of the opera, Josephine floated down the stairs to the foyer, feeling her confidence grow with each step. She couldn't remember the last time a man had gasped upon seeing her—if one ever had.

She watched Mr. Simmons's eyes as he took in the sight of her.

"You take my breath away," he said in a near-whisper.

That was what she had been aiming for. The joy she felt in putting on her ivory evening gown filled a place that had been empty too long. Yes, it was prewar fashion—for Mother would never have considered ordering something new while in mourning—but the dark gray stripes created from satin ribbon, and the oversized bows parading up the skirt to the bodice . . . she felt pretty. Luxurious. And very, very female.

It gave her comfort to notice that Mr. Simmons was also wearing evening fashion a few years too old. As such, he wouldn't be quick to judge. When he moved to the bottom of the stairs, she placed her gloved hand upon his and let him draw her toward the door.

Their butler, Dowd, smiled. He held her shawl, but Mr. Simmons took over and wrapped it around her shoulders. "The evening is cool," he said near her ear.

On the contrary. Josephine felt very warm.

* * * * *

Josephine was surprised that nearly every seat in Grover's Theatre was filled. She had no idea life had moved on in DC society.

She enjoyed the company of Mr. and Mrs. Wilson, who were very at ease in the setting as they greeted those around them.

Josephine recognized a few people. She saw Mrs. Wiggins and Mrs. Doolittle. They had both lost husbands in the war, and yet they were here at an opera. Perhaps it was as Papa said—with the entire country in mourning, it was imperative people looked forward instead of backward.

"Can you see well enough?" Mr. Simmons asked as the orchestra conducted its final tuning.

"Perfectly," she said. "And I wish to thank you."

"But the opera hasn't started yet."

She shook her head in a short burst. "They could be playing 'Dixie,' and I would thank you."

He smiled his understanding.

The gaslights dimmed, the orchestra began the overture, and the curtain opened.

The curtain of her new life opened.

As the opera began, she let herself escape to a land where wars were absurd and emotions keen, deep, but ultimately, happy. And then, finally . . .

Josephine knew what was coming next. The duet. Her brother's favorite song.

She leaned close to Mr. Simmons. "It's next."

He nodded. Josephine drew in a breath, readying herself for the music that had so entranced Thomas.

The flute and the violin began the soft arpeggio, and then the soprano came in. Josephine closed her eyes, blocking out everything but the sound. The rhythm made her want to loll her head back and forth in a gentle lullaby.

Then the other woman joined in, melding her voice with the first until Josephine couldn't tell where one voice began and the next ended. Two became one, mimicking each other, trilling back and forth, wooing each other to heights beyond the ability of a single voice. The words weren't important. It was all about the music, the marriage between melody and harmony.

Yes, Thomas, I understand. Do you hear the music with me? Is God letting you look down from heaven to share this? Oh please, Lord, let us enjoy this music together.

And then the song ended.

Josephine opened her eyes and noticed that her head was tilted upward, just as Thomas's had been on that long-ago evening. And she knew, just knew, that tonight they had both heard the music.

A handkerchief appeared in view. From Mr. Simmons.

Only then did she realize she had been crying.

She dabbed at her eyes and the opera continued.

Mr. Simmons drew her hand around his arm.

She did not move it away.

* * * * *

"How was your evening?" Frieda asked as she unbuttoned the back of Josephine's gown.

"Perfect."

Frieda spun her around. "The music, or the companion?"

"Both."

Frieda's eyebrows rose. "You like him, then?"

"I do."

"I caught a glimpse of him out the window when he helped you into the carriage. He is very handsome."

"He is."

Frieda returned to the buttons. "I still cannot believe your mother let you go."

"Neither can I. But I hope the freedom will continue." It was Josephine's turn to face Frieda. "She *will* let him court me, won't she?"

"Is that what he's going to do? Is that what you want him to do?"

Josephine thought for a flicker of a moment. "Yes."

"What about going out west with your father?"

She had considered this. As the evening progressed, and the old feelings of romance and hope and possibilities wove a warm cocoon around her, she'd thought, *What about going with Papa?* She hadn't allowed herself an answer then, and only reluctantly allowed herself an answer now. "I think—I think I would be all right staying here."

"Now aren't you the fickle filly," Frieda said, as she drew the dress over Josephine's head.

Free of its weighty encumbrance, Josephine tried to untie the petticoat in back. "I am not fickle. I had no reason to stay before now."

Frieda batted Josephine's hands away and unfastened the petticoat and the hoop, allowing Josephine to step out of them. "So this man, Mr. Lewis Simmons, has given you cause to be reasonable in one short evening? Does he know how much power he has over you?"

"He does not have power over me. He has simply shown me a glimpse of the way things used to be and could be again." She sat on the edge of the bed and removed her garters and stockings. "I was never allowed to enjoy the perks of a proper young lady. I was on the verge of all that when the war started and ruined everything."

Frieda flashed her a look.

Josephine cringed at her own tactlessness. "Oh pooh," she said. "You know what I mean. I understand the cruelty of the war, how necessary *and* how costly. I know all that. But am I not allowed to grieve the loss of my young womanhood? Everything I looked forward to and planned for was put on hold. Tonight Mr. Simmons helped me see that it wasn't dead, just sleeping. I can have a life again. I can see people and have friends and enjoy myself *and* get out of this house. I can look forward instead of back. That is not against some moral law, is it?"

Frieda placed Josephine's coral necklace and earrings in their velvet box. "It is not." She pointed a finger. "Who loves you best?"

"You do."

"Exactly. So if this courting proceeds, I only ask that you don't try to pretend things are what they are not. I have been living with this family since before you were born. I know you, Josephine Cain, and love you in spite of it. Be true to yourself, and not to some imagined image of courtship and love."

Josephine smiled and draped a stocking over each of Frieda's shoulders before kissing her cheek. "What would I do without you?"

"You would be one muddled and befuddled young lady."

"So . . . do you approve of Lewis Simmons?"

"I know nothing about the man, but I approve of your being courted. I will leave it to your parents to decide his worthiness."

"Good, because—"

"But what I approve of most is having that Wild-West notion knocked out of your head. You? On the plains amongst Indians and ruffians? I think not."

"But you would have been with me."

"I would not!"

"Would you not follow me anywhere?"

"Anywhere civilized." She brought Josephine her nightgown. "That you have found a reason to stay here in Washington is fine by me."

* * * * *

Lewis removed his top hat and cape before he turned onto his street. He knew it was best not to stick out when walking along the canals at night.

Luckily the shops were all closed—except for the barroom on the corner. Once he got past the drunks there, he would feel safe. Safer.

He hugged the shadows and walked quickly.

"Hey! You! Got a spare coin for a needy sod?"

The man staggered off the curb and only missed falling face-first onto the street by the saving arm of his friend. "Come on now. Want to share a pint, fancy man?"

Lewis hurried away, just short of a run. Only a block more.

But then he tripped, falling on his hands and knees.

The cause of his fall moaned and curled around his bottle.

The butchershop was just a few steps away. Lewis reached in his pocket and retrieved his key, readying it for the door to the right of the shop. He heard laughter farther down the street, and then a scream.

He opened the door, spilled inside, and slammed it shut. He locked himself in. Only then did he allow himself a breath.

The landing at the foot of the stairs was void of all light, but he didn't mind. This was his place, his flat. No one could touch him here. He waited until his heart calmed, then felt his way up the narrow flight. Once inside his room, the moon supplied enough light until he lit a lamp.

Not that there was much to see. A bed, a dresser, a chair, and a tiny table. A stove in the corner for heat and to make coffee. Water retrieved from a pump outside.

He could do without water until morning.

Lewis carefully removed his evening coat and hung it on the only hanger. The entire ensemble had belonged to his father, who'd bought it just before he'd been killed. Lewis was relieved it wasn't too out of style and even more glad that the rules of etiquette had eased a bit due to the war. He never would have been able to afford new evening attire.

He placed the top hat on the table, removed the frilly shirt, and smelled beneath the arms. He'd wash it in the sink at work tomorrow. Mr. Connelly, the butcher, didn't mind sharing a bit of soap and water with his best worker.

Work. He had to be at work by seven. He had to sleep.

Lewis fell upon the bed and let the memories of the music fall upon him.

Seeing Josephine's face in utter rapture, lifted to heaven, totally engrossed in the music . . . she had looked like an angel.

Somehow, someway, he had to make her *his* angel.

Lewis Simmons married to the daughter of a Union general.

What an ironic and satisfying coup that would be.

* * * * *

Josephine awakened to two thoughts: *Papa is leaving today without me.* And, *that's all right.*

It was the addendum to the first thought that was the most shocking. She had been so sure going west was what she wanted and needed, so sure it would happen—in spite of Papa's initial objections.

The reason for her change of heart was simple and could be expressed in one word: Lewis.

Was she in love?

Don't be ridiculous. Even she knew love took time. There was no such thing as love at first sight. But the possibility of love was a mighty incentive to stay put and see what happened.

Yet for now . . . she needed to dress quickly so she could see Papa off on his journey.

Chapter Four

Upon arriving in Omaha, General Reginald Cain stepped onto the platform at the back of one of the bunk cars, and called the workers to gather 'round.

Hudson was glad to see the general again. He hadn't changed much since the war, though he did look a little older.

Didn't they all.

Although Hudson had worked with the other men every day, seeing them all gathered together in one place emphasized their disparity. There were men of every size and color, from fair-haired Irishmen with their lilting voices, to men with olive-toned skin and black hair who spoke Italian. There were dark-skinned Negroes and towheaded Swedes. There were men wearing the remnants of Union uniforms *and* Confederate. They all had two things in common: they needed work, and they thirsted after a new life.

The general raised his arms, and the men quieted. "Men of the Union Pacific! It is finally time to march forward, to leave Omaha and move this railroad west!"

A roar erupted. Cheers.

"I look across this rail yard and see heady evidence of intricate planning and work. Hard work is the fuel that will move this railroad west. Upon your backs a fresh nation will be born!"

More cheers.

"It is clear that the workers of the Union Pacific are ready, willing, and able to lay track across prairies, rivers, and mountains until we come nose-to-nose with those men of the Central Pacific working their way east from Sacramento. Without men like you, the dream dies. But with you . . . are you up to the task of connecting this great nation from ocean to ocean?"

More cheers and affirmation, then a chant of "U-P! U-P! U-P!" Hudson joined them, pumping his fist in the air for the Union Pacific.

Raleigh leaned toward him, beaming. "This is what we needed."

"*He* is what we needed."

* * * * *

Josephine swept into her dressing room. "Thank you for coming over, Rachel. I have scant notion of what is in fashion after a year in mourning." Rachel Maddox was the perfect advisor since her father owned a large mercantile. As she was also the perfect chaperone for tonight's dinner, being a married woman. Josephine was ever so glad to be invited along—with Lewis, of course.

"I am happy to oblige." Rachel perused the gowns. She pulled out the skirt of a grayish-black dress and raised an eyebrow at Josephine.

"It used to be light blue. We dyed it black for mourning, but it has faded."

"It is frightful."

Josephine had to agree. She pulled out a white satin with red bows. "How about this?"

Rachel put her hand to her cheek and studied the gown. "The skirt is too wide. Fashion is leaving the crinoline behind."

"In favor of what?"

"A lot of petticoats." She smoothed her hand against her abdomen. "A smoother front is becoming the fashion."

Josephine despaired. She didn't have anything that owned that silhouette.

"Perhaps if you wore the white without the cage?" She sat on the tufted ottoman. "Put it on and let me see."

It was worth a try. With Rachel's help Josephine stepped out of her day dress, removed her crinoline undercarriage, and added additional petticoats. Then Rachel helped her lift the satin gown over her head and buttoned a few of the buttons that paraded up the back.

"Without the hoop, it's a little long," Josephine said, looking in the mirror.

"That is not a problem," Rachel said. She took Frieda's pincushion and began to pull portions of the skirt into draped flounces, drawn toward the back. Her work finished, she stepped away to measure the effect. "Add a few rosettes or bows at the top of the flounces, and you have a new gown."

It was really quite nice. But then Josephine thought of Frieda, and the fact the dinner was tonight. "I don't know if Frieda can alter it by then."

"You will never know if you do not ask." Rachel walked out of the dressing room and called out, "Frieda? We need you."

Not a minute later, Frieda came into the room. Her eyes swept over the refashioned gown as Rachel explained the adjustments that needed to be made.

Josephine felt guilty for putting Frieda on the spot. "I apologize for the haste of it all."

"But it is very important," Rachel said. "We are both going to a dinner at the Wilsons'. Mr. Wilson is the editor of the *Washington Chronicle*."

"I know very well who he is," Frieda said as she fiddled with one of the flounces. "Josephine went to the opera with his brother and wife. This one is a little too far to the left."

"You have my gratitude in advance," Josephine said. As soon as Frieda collected the gown in her able arms, Josephine kissed her cheek. "As always, you're wonderful. Thank you."

"You can thank me by having that Simmons fellow propose marriage."

Josephine immediately looked to Rachel, whose eyebrows rose.

"I told you the name of my escort," she explained. "And despite what Frieda says, we are not near to getting engaged." Josephine stepped out of two of the extra petticoats and handed her day dress to Rachel, needing help to get it on.

"Why have I not heard much of him?"

"We have known each other for only a few weeks."

Rachel tapped her chin with a finger. "Simmons, Simmons . . . I don't know of any Simmonses in Washington society."

Josephine's defenses rose. "You wouldn't know him because he comes from a wealthy New York family. His father worked with Cornelius Vanderbilt. Father introduced us."

"I am so weary of hearing about New York society," Rachel said with a sigh. "Vanderbilts, Astors, Guggenheims. It is as if Washington society does not exist." She flipped the thought away. "What is he doing in Washington?"

"Mr. Simmons is an artist. He sketches important events."

"Oh? Did he create illustrations during the war?"

That was a good question. "I don't think so. He said he was in Europe for a time."

"How convenient," Rachel said, buttoning the dress.

Josephine turned 'round to face her. "What do you mean by that?"

Rachel shrugged, took Josephine by her shoulders, and spun her back again, returning to the buttons. "I am sure many of our boys would have liked to be overseas instead of fighting." She patted Josephine, signaling she was finished. "I know I have never been more glad that I did not have brothers." She looked into the air between them. "I do miss your Thomas. I might have fallen in love with him had I not met my Clark. I just know it."

The thought of Rachel marrying her brother did not bring Josephine pleasure. She was a good enough friend, but her frivolousness combined with Thomas's impulsiveness? It would have been a marriage without a rudder.

If he had lived. Which he hadn't.

Josephine felt sorrow rise from her toes to her heart. She must not let it reach its target, or she would never feel up to dinner. To quell its progress, she linked arms with Rachel. "Now tell me the latest gossip."

Sometimes there were advantages to having a frivolous friend.

* * * * *

The two couples stood at the door to the Wilsons' brownstone. Lewis fidgeted, pulling at his vest, fingering his tie.

"Are you nervous, Mr. Simmons?" Rachel asked.

"A little."

"Nonsense, my man," said Rachel's husband, Clark. "You have already been to the opera with Wilson's brother, so you're *in*. Relax and enjoy yourself. I plan to."

Rachel patted his arm. "You never have trouble with that."

Lewis looked down at Josephine. "Have I told you how ravishing you look?"

"Once or twice." But she didn't mind hearing it again.

Nervous or not, he lifted the doorknocker and let it drop. A butler let them in and took the men's hats and gloves and the women's shawls.

The parlor was ablaze with gaslights, a fire, and candles. A handsome middle-aged woman came to greet them, and she—Mrs. Wilson—led them to her husband. "Darling, the Maddoxes have arrived, along with a Mr. Simmons and . . . ?"

"Josephine Cain," she supplied. Why hadn't Lewis introduced her? And hadn't Rachel told Mrs. Wilson they were coming? It was horribly awkward, as though they were simply a couple called in off the street.

"Cain?" Mr. Wilson said. "Might you be a relation to General Reginald Cain?"

She was thrilled to be able to say yes. "He is my father."

"Ah yes. Now it is all falling into place. Robert and Edith so enjoyed their time at the opera with you. And as for your father, I know of no finer officer, and no finer man to take over the construction of the Transcontinental Railroad project."

"The railroad?" said another man.

Mr. Wilson filled him in about Josephine's father and his position.

The other two couples gathered close, and Robert Wilson asked how the railroad project progressed.

"Come in and have a seat, my dear," Mrs. Wilson said. "Tell us all about your father's special work out west."

"Indeed," Rachel said with a wink. "Tell us."

Josephine was led to a sofa she shared with Mrs. Wilson. The others stood nearby, placing her in the center of their attention. Josephine noted the look on Lewis's face. His jaw was tight and his brow furrowed.

But she couldn't worry about that now. The company was full of questions, and she answered them the best she could. She was glad for her father's detailed letters.

After her discourse, Mr. Wilson looked at Lewis for the first time. "You must be very proud of Miss Cain and her family, Mr. Simon."

Lewis's face flashed just a moment before he said, "Simmons. And yes, sir, I am."

But he didn't look proud. He looked oddly afraid.

* * * * *

Josephine wished she could take lessons from Mrs. Wilson on gracious hospitality. The woman had a talent for making everyone feel involved and welcome. And the food: a mushroom soup, turbot, braised leg of mutton, new potatoes, Virginia brown bread, and upcoming, strawberry custard tartlets.

Josephine didn't have another smidgen of space left in her stomach, but upon seeing the luscious dessert, she knew she would have to find some.

As they were being served, Rachel piped up. "I hear you spent the war in Europe, Mr. Simmons. Drawing?"

Lewis rearranged his napkin, then said, "I—I traveled to many countries sketching the points of interest."

"Which was your favorite city?"

He hesitated a moment, then said, "Rome."

"I adore Rome," Rachel said.

Mr. Wilson nodded. "Did you visit the Pantheon? That's a favorite of mine."

"No, I did not travel to Greece," Lewis said.

There was a moment of silence, and Josephine didn't know whether to save him or let it pass.

Another guest did it for her. "The Pantheon is in Rome."

"Yes, yes, of course."

Josephine offered a little laugh. "Pantheon, Parthenon—they sound so similar, it *is* hard to keep them straight."

"Where did you earn your artistic training?" Mrs. Wilson asked.

A pause. "The—the Louvre," he said.

Again, a spat of silence. The Louvre was a museum. Was it also an art school?

Mrs. Wilson picked up her fork. "My, the strawberries are lush this year. Enjoy."

Josephine had lost her appetite.

* * * * *

Lewis slammed the door of the carriage, plopped into the seat across from Josephine, making the entire carriage sway.

"He did not say one word about my drawings," he said.

"Mr. Wilson?"

"Yes, of course Mr. Wilson. The reason I was happy to go to this dinner was to impress him so he'd buy more of my drawings for the newspaper."

"But Mrs. Wilson showed interest. She asked you about your training."

"Quizzed me. Interrogated me." *Tripped me up.*

"They were showing interest. Is that not what you wanted, what anyone wants at such a soiree?"

Maybe. But what he really needed was some decent income as well as praise for his art. Courting a socialite was a drain on his meager wages from the butcher shop.

He gave his attention to the passing buildings.

Josephine leaned forward and touched his knee. "I am sure Mr. Wilson simply didn't want to discuss business at a social gathering. He will likely contact you tomorrow."

Lewis knew the odds of that were slim. Yet all he needed was a chance. What good did it do to have talent when he couldn't make a living with it? And how could he keep Josephine's interest when he was a nobody, with no prospects? She thought he had family money. If only . . .

Once they were married and his plan was fully implemented, he'd have plenty of money. Her money would be his. But until then, if she ever found out who he really was . . .

Frustration trumped his common sense, and he said, "You certainly were the belle of the evening, being the daughter of the great General Cain."

"I did not seek attention."

"But it found you nonetheless. Some people get all the luck, all the time."

"There was no *luck* involved in my being asked to talk about Papa and his work on the railroad. I received nothing from the attention, except perhaps pride in being his daughter." She touched him again. "As I was proud to be your companion. Please, Lewis. Don't be angry. I thought the night was very pleasant."

"That does not surprise me."

Josephine leaned away, creating distance.

After a few moments, Lewis reached for her hand. "I am sorry. I'm a selfish lout. Forgive me?"

She nodded.

He had to be more careful. Lose Josephine and all was lost.

* * * * *

Josephine tossed her earrings on the dressing table and one jumped to the rug. "He is the most exasperating man I have ever known."

In the mirror, she saw Frieda smile as she removed the pins from her hair. "You must like him very much."

"How can you say that?"

Frieda held her hand palm-up, which was a reminder for Josephine to hold out her own hand for the pins. "It is just that young ladies seldom waste their time and protests against a man for whom they have no feelings. You are upset at Mr. Simmons because on this particular evening, he did not fit into your image of the perfect man."

She harrumphed. "Hardly perfect at all."

Frieda leaned forward and whispered in her ear. "It would not bother you unless you cared for him."

Somehow the logic seemed skewed, but Josephine was too tired to sort it through. "He was really quite insufferable, making it my fault that the host and hostess engaged me in conversation about Papa and the railroad."

"*He* wanted to be the man in your life this evening."

Oh.

But then she thought of something else. "He confused the Pantheon with the Parthenon."

"He should be shot."

Josephine got the point. "He *was* nervous. He wants Mr. Wilson to buy his drawings for the paper."

"There you go. He has ambition and wants to use his talents. Both of which are attributes."

Josephine saw her own shoulders relax. Frieda was right. She must focus on the evening's pleasures and forget its shortcomings.

And what were its pleasures?

Her mind went blank.

Chapter Five

Hudson and Raleigh took their places on top of a bunk car, legs dangling over the side.

"We're hardly riding first class."

"But we do have the best view." Hudson pointed to the west, to that point on the compass that owned such a huge responsibility to all those who contemplated it. *The West* elicited feelings of adventure, hope, danger, thrills, and promise. That he was sitting on top of a train that would take him there, that he was poised to lay the track that would bring the West close to anyone who wished to see it, was a heady thought.

"We're riding on the cusp of history," he whispered to the wind.

A deafening whistle announced it was time to leave.

Then the sound of metal against metal and a jerk as if the train had awakened and was stretching its muscles. Hudson joined the other workers as they cheered. He couldn't have remained silent if he'd wanted to as the immensity of the moment demanded release.

The train moved forward, inching, then sprinting, then finding its stride in a full-out run.

Black smoke and sparks flew past, making Hudson glad the bunk cars were a few back from the locomotive.

"We're going, we're really going," Raleigh said.

"That was the goal," Hudson said with a laugh.

Yet this was not just any train ride, nor any train. This was *the* ride of *the* train that would be the prequel of hundreds and thousands of trains to come.

The Omaha rail yard grew smaller behind them.

"It's a new beginning," Raleigh said.

Hudson nodded, and together they watched what was past and what was known move faster and farther away.

* * * * *

Lewis opened the lid of the trunk that held what was left of his parents' belongings. He removed a small box and set it on the table. Inside were his mother's jewels, though perhaps "jewels" was too strong a word. They were pretty trinkets, but he had no idea if they were real or paste. He guessed the latter. The valuable pieces had been sold long ago, after his father and Vanderbilt parted ways.

He fingered through the lot, freeing a pearl necklace from the tangle. He held it to the light and saw that the outer layer of a few pearls was peeling off. "Apparently an oyster didn't make these."

A pair of earrings was next, two gold baubles hanging from thin wires. But he overruled them as he'd never noticed whether Josephine had pierced ears.

Then he saw the bracelet. He let the gold chain sit in his hand. Its only ornament was a single teardrop of a red stone. Could it be a ruby? He gave it closer inspection. It *was* pretty. And the weight of the piece made him think it could actually be of real worth.

Then keep it. If things get worse, you might have to sell it.

He shook the thought away. By finagling a meeting with General Cain, he'd set in place something more precious than jewels: a chance to set his destiny in motion. That he liked the general's daughter and she seemed to like him—well, that was an added perk leading to a goal he was determined to achieve, no matter what.

"She'll love it," he said to the room.

And more than that, it might go a long way toward making amends and keeping his plan alive.

* * * * *

Lewis entered the butcher shop.

"It's about time ya showed up," Mr. Connelly said. "I was gettin' ready to bang a broom on the ceiling to rouse ya." He swung the cleaver into the back of a pig then peered at Lewis over his spectacles. "Yer not wearing that fancy suit to work. We got a side of beef to break down, and two—"

"I can't work this morning. There's something important I have to do."

Connelly wiped his bloody hands on his apron. "More important than working for me? Or has you come into a stash of money so's you don't have to work no more?"

Lewis was going to argue, then changed his tactic. "I'm working on the latter." He yanked at his lapels. "How do I look?"

"Like yer wearing your da's old suit."

Really? "It doesn't look that bad, does it?"

Mrs. Connelly came in from the back room and eyed him. "You look right handsome, Lewis. Though me and the mister don't know squat about what's in fashion. But who does anymore? People have more to think about now than the width of a skirt or the length of a coat."

He felt a little better for her words. "Thank you, Mrs. Connelly. I appreciate that."

"Care to share the name of your stash o' money? I assume it's a she."

"I think I'll keep that bit to myself, if you don't mind."

Connelly pointed the cleaver at him—though not in a threatening way. "I don't begrudge you trying to better yerself, but I do begrudge you not being at work. How long you gonna be gone?"

"Just a few hours. I'll work late tonight. I promise."

"You'd better." He emphasized his words by hacking the feet off the pig.

* * * * *

Josephine heard the knock on the door and set her reading aside.

Mother looked up from the pillowcase embroidery. "Dowd will get it."

Yes, he would. But Josephine was eager for any diversion from another afternoon spent in the bears' den.

She heard men's voices, then the butler slid open the doors of the parlor. "Mr. Simmons is here to see you, Miss Cain."

Before she could fully respond, Lewis entered the room carrying a bouquet of magenta peonies.

The three women gasped. Josephine felt her heart melt. Any animosity she felt toward Lewis dissipated at the sight of the gorgeous flowers, which she had never seen in any florist shop. Where had he found them?

"Oh Lewis, they're—"

He sidestepped her and walked toward her mother. "Actually, if I may . . . I brought these for you, Mrs. Cain. I thought they might brighten your day."

Mother blushed like an ingénue accepting her first tussie-mussie. "Oh Mr. Simmons. They're beautiful." She pressed her nose into the blooms to inhale, and a look of contentment softened her face.

"Peonies symbolize healing," Aunt said.

"Really?" Lewis asked.

Mother and Aunt exchanged a look. "You are not familiar with *The Language of Flowers*?"

"I am afraid I'm not."

"Let us go find these a vase," Mother told Aunt.

Surprisingly, they both left. Josephine and Lewis were alone. During all of Lewis's visits to court her, they had never spent time in the parlor without her mother, aunt, or Frieda present.

"That was very nice of you," she told him.

"My mother always liked flowers."

He had not spoken much about his family. "Liked?"

"She died a few years ago, of yellow fever."

"I am so sorry. Is your father still living?"

He hesitated a slightest moment. "He lives in New York."

She'd had the impression they both were alive. But when he didn't elaborate, she let it go. "Come, sit down."

Lewis avoided the ladies' chairs and moved to the end of the sofa. He waited until Josephine had taken a seat at the other end.

"Well then," he said.

"It is nice to see you," she said.

"I'm surprised to hear you say that after the abominable way I treated you at the dinner last night, and afterward."

"It's all right."

He reached for her hand. "No, it isn't. I can blame nerves or frustration or any number of things, but nothing gives me the right to treat you in any way but with the highest respect. For I do respect you, Josephine. I do prize you highly." He reached into the inner pocket of his coat and removed a small drawstring bag. "This is for you."

He handed her the velvet bag, which was little larger than her palm. It felt a bit weighty, though not overly so. "You did not need to do this."

"I wanted to. Open it."

She emptied the contents into her hand, then *ooohed.* "It's beautiful," she said, picking up the bracelet of gold chain. At the clasp there was a single red stone, hanging as a teardrop.

"It's a ruby. Or at least that's what my mother always said it was. I'm afraid I don't know a gemstone from a piece of glass."

She held it to the light. It certainly looked real. And if it was his mother's? That made it extra-special. "Help me on with it."

He fastened the clasp with an expertise unusual for a man. She turned her wrist this way and that, loving the movement of the teardrop. "Thank you ever so much. I am honored that you trust me with something of your mother's."

Lewis stopped her movement with his hand, and drew her hand to his lips, where he offered the lightest of kisses. "Thank you, Josephine, for being the woman I can never deserve."

The past was quickly forgotten, and Josephine's thoughts focused on the future.

Her future with Lewis.

* * * * *

For the second time that day, the train slowed to a stop. The first time they had stopped at Fremont, Nebraska, where supplies had been cached all winter.

"What're we stopping for now?" Raleigh asked.

Hudson carefully got to his knees atop the railcar and looked west. He saw a line of graded land and ties stretching forward—ties waiting for rails. "It's the end of the line, men! We're here!"

When they climbed down he wasn't sure if what surrounded him was a foreign netherland or hell. For they had indeed come to the end of the track. What happened next was a muddle of confusion and chaos. The men tumbled out of the boxcars like fleas jumping off a dog. No one knew where to go. They had been told what their jobs would be, but none of them had laid any actual track. Rumor was that up until now, when no one knew exactly what to do, the men before them were lucky to lay a half mile a day. Now with the new reinforcements and the general's organization, the bosses expected nearer to two.

Two *miles*. It didn't sound like much, but when he broke it down to laying one rail at a time, hitting one spike at a time . . . Hudson could feel his muscles aching already.

The men wandered around until hope stepped forward. General Cain stood atop a crate and directed them this way and that.

"Don't we get no time to check out the town, to take it all in?" Raleigh asked his brother.

"Guess not."

All was Columbus, Nebraska, an odd assortment of buildings and tents, scattered on either side of the track. Crude signs announced their purpose: *Saloon, Railway Office, Sawmill, Store.*

But there wasn't time to explore, as the general and Boss gave directions. Everyone had a purpose. Months before, another Union general, General Grenville Dodge, had scoped out the best route. His surveyors had marked the way, and graders smoothed the land, while other crews laid the wood ties like a ladder stretching toward tomorrow. Now it was the tracklayers' turn. Hudson had heard it was General Cain who'd come up with the idea of giving each group of men a specialized job.

Two generals who were used to getting men to do what needed to be done. Somebody was mighty smart putting them in charge.

Raleigh and Hudson were handed their spike mauls. Raleigh ran a hand along the foot-long head with two tapered ends. "I bet we'll go through a few of these before we meet up with the Central Pacific."

Hudson weighed it in his hands. "It's not so heavy, about the same weight as a sledgehammer—ten, twelve pounds?"

"Not heavy just holding it, but swinging it from dawn to dusk?" Raleigh squeezed Hudson's biceps. "You may even get yourself some real muscles."

Hudson could've argued with him, saying something about Raleigh's build, but the truth was, his little brother already had the physique of a spiker. He seemed to thrive on physical labor.

Hudson was fine with labor, but he preferred a mix of mental and physical. He enjoyed the chance to plan and organize, to think of what things *could* be.

But there was no call for thinkers here. Though they were all men, they were hired to work like machines. Or animals. He only hoped they would become neither.

"Here we go," Raleigh said as he headed to the end of the line. "Another day, another dollar."

"Three dollars," Hudson corrected. "Come on. Let's do this."

Within half an hour, the work began in earnest. A horse-drawn lorry car filled with iron approached the end of the line. Four men removed each rail and trotted forward, laying it on the ties. When the lorry was empty, a man unhitched it from the horse, and it was pushed off the rails, into the ditch, making room for another one to move forward.

The men who'd been assigned to be "bolters" and "gaugers" stepped forward. The first group fastened the rail sections together, the second aligned them.

Then it was Hudson's turn. As a "spiker," he hammered the rails into place. The feel of the heavy maul racing through the air and hitting the spike made his muscles ring, as if the sound itself became physical. The music of metal hitting metal sounded like an anvil chorus.

"Come on, men," the general yelled. "Spikers, keep the handle horizontal or you'll bend the spike and ruin the head. Three strokes to a spike, ten spikes to a rail, four hundred rails to a mile that runs over three thousand ties. It should only take you thirty seconds for each section. In twelve hours we should lay three hundred tons of rail."

One of the rail layers yelled out, "Yer making me tired just listening to you, General."

Hudson saw two young boys run past, dumping the iron spikes on the ground on either side of the track. They were in constant motion, dumping and running back for more. The way everybody was working together made Hudson want to move faster.

But by the end of the day, the music of the anvil chorus had turned into a dirge of moans. Two hundred men sat shoulder to shoulder on the benches in one of the dining cars, their shoulders slumped, their heads hanging heavy. A hunk of meat and a pile of cubed potatoes lay on each plate, and each plate was nailed to the table.

"I can't even pick up my fork," Raleigh complained as he flexed his raw fingers.

"It's my arms that are a'hurting," said another man, who'd had to carry the rails into place with tongs.

"Shoulders," was all Hudson could manage. He focused on the meat. He'd never been so hungry, because he'd never worked so hard. Back at the mill they worked long days, and though it also involved repetitive movement, it wasn't backbreaking work. Tedious and boring, but not backbreaking.

A man across the table pointed his fork at Hudson's plate. "You want yer potatoes?"

"I believe I do." He stabbed a chunk to claim them.

"Did you even chew, Oscar?" Raleigh asked the man.

"I chewed," the man said. "But I need more."

Just then a kitchen worker came into the car carrying a platter and bowl.

Second helpings were had by all.

* * * * *

"Come on, Hudson. There's whiskey to be had."

Hudson settled in the empty dining car with his paper and pencil. "I need to write to Sarah Ann."

Raleigh shook his head. "You're one strange man, choosing letter-writing over whiskey."

"So be it. Don't you think you should write Mum and Da?"

"You say my howdys for me."

Hudson looked up at his brother, his little brother who was a man. "Behave yourself, all right?"

"I most certainly will not." Raleigh winked and hurried away, joining the throng of men who were finding solace in the saloons of Columbus.

Sarah Ann. She was Hudson's solace.

He smoothed the page and wrote the date and salutation: *June 4, 1866. My dearest Sarah Ann . . .*

But then he hesitated. What should he tell her? If he was truthful about the grueling work, she'd worry. So he looked out the window and wrote about *that*.

> *The Nebraska plains go on forever, a softly undulating tan spotted with low-growing grasses and fields of wildflowers, bowing in the breeze. The sky is a bowl of blue, rimming the land on all sides. Periodically we pass piles of construction debris, proof that the line is stretching out before us, waiting for the rails.*

He read it over, nodding. She'd like to hear about wildflowers. Back home she was so proud of the zinnias and asters that she'd planted in a rickety window box.

> *General Cain says we've reached the 100-mile mark. That's a nice round number, but it's more important than that. Congress gave us a deadline. We needed to measure 100 miles of track by July 1—with watering facilities, fuel facilities, and sidetracks, all good enough to have passenger and freight run out of Omaha— or the Union Pacific would lose its charter. And we've made it. I'm hoping my back and shoulders hold out for the next hundred miles.*

He hadn't meant to mention his aches and pains and considered crossing it out. But he left it. It didn't hurt to have her know how hard he was working.

For her.

Chapter Six

"*Le Grand Isle?*" Raleigh asked, as the track they laid reached an existing town that was just sitting on the prairie, waiting for them to arrive.

"That's what some French fur trader called it seventy years ago. We're supposed to call it Grand Island," Hudson said.

Oscar added, "It's a forty-mile island in the Platte River."

Hudson liked the sounds of that. He missed water. Pittsburgh was built on a river. "I wouldn't mind doing a bit o' fishing at the end of the day."

Another worker shook his head. "We all need to be careful with that river. It's not like most. I've heard it said that it's two miles wide and will have six inches of water sitting over six feet of dangerous sand. It's too thin to walk on, too thick to drink, too shallow to put a boat on, too deep for safe fording, too yellow to wash in, and too pale to paint with."

Hudson laughed. "Sounds pretty useless—as rivers go."

"Which makes me wonder why we're following it all the way to Wyoming."

Hudson shrugged. But he'd heard a reason. "It's a path. Along with the wagon ruts of the Mormons who've come before. When you have hundreds of miles of open land, some path is better than starting out from noth—"

"Indians!"

Every eye looked to the south. There, near the river, was a band of more than a dozen Indians on horses.

"Guns! Get the rifles!"

Workers scrambled back into the bunk cars where a cache of rifles was stored by the ceiling. Within seconds a line of men formed from inside the car to out, handing the guns down the line into eager hands.

Some men climbed on top of the rail cars, lying low with guns pointed. Every man put the train between them and the Indians.

Someone up top yelled out, "General! Come back!"

Hudson and Raleigh hopped over the coupler between two cars, needing to see.

General Cain was riding out to meet the Indians. "What is he doing?" Hudson asked.

Raleigh crossed himself, mumbling a prayer. "He's one brave man." *Or stupid.*

As one moment moved into the next, it became apparent that these Indians were not going to attack. And even more surprising was the fact that the general seemed to know the lead man. They spoke back and forth, and . . .

They shook hands.

Then they all rode toward the end of the line, toward the place where Hudson and the others would be laying track.

When General Cain turned around and saw the workers and the guns, he raised a hand. "At ease, gentlemen. Spotted Tail is a friend. He and his men would like to see how we lay track."

"Well, I'll be," Raleigh said.

Hudson watched the Indians surround the track on their horses. "They've told us not all the Indians are dangerous. The Pawnee are friendly, and the Sioux. It's the Cheyenne we have to worry about. And the hotheads in every tribe."

"How can we tell them apart?" Raleigh asked.

"I have no idea," Hudson said. "But I think we'll have to learn."

* * * * *

Hudson tried not to stare at the Indians, but as this was his first look . . .

They were darker skinned than all but the Negros, and he let a quick question enter his brain: was that because they were outside all the time? Their hair was coal-black and straight as a horse's tail, and not one had any facial hair—or hair on their chests. Most were without shirts, and their muscles were impressive. The clothing that covered them from waist to feet was more of a legging than a true pair of pants, and they wore soft shoes without hard soles. He hoped none of them stepped on a stray spike, lest their pain cause some commotion.

He didn't have time to ponder more, as the general started the rail-laying demonstration. When it was Hudson's turn to hit the spikes, he did his duty. It only took him two hits to get the spike in, and it occurred to him he was showing off.

No one would blame him. Showing strength to Indians was a good thing, wasn't it?

Yet was it wise to show these Indians how track was put in? Would they use the knowledge against the railroad and tear it up?

Such questions were not his to ask. He'd trusted the general with his life before; he would do so now.

A length of rail laid, the general invited the Indians to see a bunk car. Spotting Hudson, General Cain said, "Show them inside."

Hudson lost his breath for a moment but followed orders, getting in the car and even helping the Indians step up into it.

One Indian paused a moment after Hudson helped him in, looking at him eye-to-eye. His eyes were nearly as black as his hair, which hung down his back. He had a scar on his cheek. A ripple of fear sped through Hudson's gut. "Welcome," he said, then felt stupid for it. For the Indians weren't welcome. If he had his way, they'd never have gotten close to the train, much less come inside a car.

And did they speak English? He certainly didn't speak their language. "This is where we sleep," he said to the group as they stood between the bunks.

One Indian seemed to understand, for he immediately translated. A few of the Indians lay on the mattresses, marveling at the pillows, making comments to each other. A few others held their noses. The stench left behind by hundreds of working men *was* hard to take.

But then one of them looked upward and pointed to a goodly number of rifles stacked horizontally along the roof. Their joviality left them, and they slid off the bunks. They whispered to each other, and one Indian put his hand out the window, measuring the thickness of the car's wall. As he looked to another, Hudson could imagine him saying, "I wonder if a bullet could go through the walls." Or an arrow shot from the other side?

He quickly led them outside. Was their motive friendship—or were they on a scouting mission?

"Now the butcher's and baker's cars, Maguire," the general said.

Again, Hudson wasn't sure it was wise to show them the store of meat and food supplies. But he did as he was told.

The Indian interpreter spoke for the group when he said, "Much food. Hard winter."

Hudson could only nod. He knew that it *had* been a hard winter on the plains. Were the Indians hungry?

By now there was a crowd of hundreds of workers watching the Indians step out of the food cars. One of them said, "Let's see how accurate they can shoot their arrows."

Hudson thought that was a horrible idea, but other men hopped to, and soon there was a shovel placed in the ground, and the Indians were steered to a point fifty feet away.

The general spoke to Spotted Tail through the interpreter. Then Spotted Tail instructed each brave to try to shoot through the shovel's handle. The first arrow sliced through the air and went through the hole, to the appreciative shouts of the workers.

Then another.

And another.

"They're good," Raleigh whispered.

"Too good," Hudson said.

Others nodded.

As the show continued, the encouraging shouts dimmed as every arrow was successful. Hudson could feel the nerves of the workers tighten, for in proving their accuracy, the Indians were also proving that if their mark was a railroad worker, they wouldn't miss.

Finally, the seventeenth Indian shot his arrow—and it hit the handle, knocking the shovel down. He looked to the ground, disgraced. But Hudson and the workers were relieved, and he heard more than one mumble of "Good" and "It's about time."

"I don't think it's wise to give them confidence," he said.

"It's just a game," Oscar said.

Hudson was not alone in shaking his head. "This may look like a game, but I assure you, it's not."

"Let's have a race!" someone yelled. "Ponies against our locomotive!"

A cry of assent rose up. Hudson hated the idea. This day couldn't end soon enough.

He saw the Indians mount their ponies and get in a line. They seemed eager for the race.

Hudson looked upon the scene, feeling wary. Then he heard the general's voice from near the cab of the locomotive.

"Come, ride inside," the general said to Spotted Tail.

At first the chief seemed reluctant, but he climbed on board. The Indians lined up even with the front of the locomotive, ready for the signal.

Hudson felt his gut grab. "This will not end well—either way."

One worker went out in front of the line of riders, raised his arm, then lowered it. "Go!" the workers yelled.

The ponies sped forward, ahead of the train. The Indians were thrilled with their certain victory and let out a whoop that made Hudson shudder.

But then the engine gathered speed and easily passed them. Victorious, the engineer blew the whistle full blast. The sound so startled the Indians that they bodily swung to the off-side of their ponies, hanging on with their legs over the back.

And then, it was over.

"We won! We won!" the workers yelled.

Hudson shook his head. There might be a price to winning.

The Indians returned, their heads down, clearly crestfallen at their defeat.

"Now they can leave," he said.

"Are you really afraid of them?" Raleigh asked.

"I'm cautious. I just know if I had strange people building across the land my ancestors had held for centuries, I'd be upset and want them *gone*."

Raleigh stared after the Indians, as if taking this in. "Surely the general knows what he's doing."

I hope so.

Spotted Tail was talking with General Cain, making arm gestures to include his braves and . . . eating?

"Oh no," Hudson said. "They're wanting food."

Sure enough, the general ordered the cook to set out a meal.

This was getting out of hand.

But General Cain asked a few of the railroad men to eat a meal with the Indians—Hudson included.

When they sat around the tables in the dining car, the Indians tried to pick up the plates but found they were nailed to the table. Yes, it *was* odd, but necessary. Otherwise the jostling of the train would bounce them all over the place.

Food was served. Immediately, the braves ate it with their eyes. But they hesitated and looked to Spotted Tail. He, too, held back. Did they think it was poisoned?

General Cain filled his plate then passed the bowl around. "Eat," he said.

The rest of the workers did just that, and as soon as they did, the Indians dug in, shoveling food into their mouths with their fingers.

Hudson felt sorry for them. It was clear they hadn't eaten in a long time. No one spoke, which was fine with him. The sooner they were done eating, the sooner they'd be gone.

When the serving bowls were empty, the braves picked them up and swiped the last bits with their fingers.

Spotted Tail stepped over a bench. He said something to the translator, who told the general, "He says you are to fill our horses with sacks of flour and quarters of beef."

The general also stood and freed himself of the confines of the bench. "No. We let you eat with us here, but you can't carry any food away with you."

Spotted Tail let off a long discourse, his brow stern. The translator said, "If you don't give us what we want, we will come at night with three thousand warriors and clean you out."

The general's chest heaved and Hudson held his breath. "Tell Spotted Tail exactly what I say." Then he put his doubled fist against Spotted Tail's nose and let out a string of oaths such as Hudson had never heard.

Spotted Tail didn't answer but quickly led his band to their horses. They rode away.

"Will they be back?" Hudson asked the general.

He stared after them. "Double the night patrol."

"Yes, sir."

Time would tell whether the Indians would come back—as friend *or* foe.

* * * * *

Dowd entered the parlor carrying a silver salver. "The mail, Mrs. Cain."

"Set it down. I shall look at it later."

Dowd did as he was told, but said, "There is a letter for you, Miss Josephine."

She popped out of her chair and retrieved it. "It's from Papa!" She broke open the seal and began to read, "'*Dearest Josephine and family. I—*'"

Mother lifted her hand. "Please do not read it aloud. You may inform us if there is anything of interest after you have read it through silently."

Josephine stared at her mother. *It is all of interest.* But she read it to herself, voicing the highlights. "Papa had Indians visit the train!"

Aunt Bernice made use of her fan. "Indians!"

"They were friendly," Josephine said, realizing she should have made that clear. "They just wanted to have a tour. Papa had a meal with them."

"He's lucky *he* wasn't the meal," Mother said.

"Indians don't eat people."

"Then why are they called 'savages'?"

Josephine went back to the letter. Her heart began to beat wildly— and not for more mention of Indians. "Papa has invited all of us to come west for a huge celebration they are having when they reach the one-hundredth meridian!"

"Median?" Aunt asked.

"Meridian." Josephine found the explanation in the letter. "'It is a point of longitude measured from Greenwich, England.'"

"England?" Mother asked. "I thought they were in Nebraska."

Josephine resisted the urge to roll her eyes. "They are. It is only a measurement, a milestone." She consulted the letter. "It is two hundred forty-seven miles west of Omaha."

"I thought they passed the hundred-mile mark," Mother said.

So she *had* been paying attention to Papa's letters. "One hundred miles is not the same as the hundredth meridian. And they will not reach it until October, when they will host a grand celebration."

Mother gave her head a little shake. "I do not care when it happens. We shall not be going."

Josephine was stunned. "Of course we shall! We must go." She shook the letter. "Papa says Dr. Durant, the head of the Union Pacific, is leading a promotional excursion. Three hundred invitations have been sent out, and we three have one of them. It is an honor."

"An honor to be put in harm's way? Did he not just mention Indians?"

Josephine wondered what Papa had been thinking, putting mention of Indians in the same letter as the invitation. And why had *she* read that part aloud? "We would not be alone. Hundreds of people will be going west. Hundreds of dignitaries. They would not let us come if it was not safe."

Mother's head began its slow back-and-forth. "We are not going."

"But—"

"Go see if lunch is ready."

Josephine was incredulous. "You think about lunch when we have just been offered the most thrilling excursion of our lives? And we would see Papa! Don't you want to see your own husband?"

Mother's face reddened, and Josephine knew she had gone too far. "Lunch, Josephine. And not another word about the excursion."

She turned on her heel. "I'm not hungry." Then she ran upstairs, slammed her bedroom door, and flung herself on her bed.

She knew it was childish, but she couldn't help herself. The chance to see Papa! The chance to see the West!

Frieda came in to check on the commotion. "What's wrong, Liebchen?"

Josephine sat up and told her. "I have to go see Papa. I have to!"

Frieda smoothed a stray strand of hair, tucking it behind Josephine's ear. "There is not much you can do if your mother says no. Take solace in the fact Lewis is here to provide you some diversion."

Josephine drew in a breath and held it as an idea formed. "Lewis! He could take me!"

"Your mother will not allow you to travel across the country with a man who is not your husband."

True. But then she thought of the solution. "You can come with us! Papa invited me, Mother, and Aunt Bernice. Three people. And three people can accept: you, me, and Lewis."

Frieda put a hand to her chest. "Me? See the Wild West?"

"Why not? You are Papa's cousin. Your family and Papa's came over from Ireland when you both were young. That was a much longer voyage than an expedition to Nebraska."

Frieda sat on the edge of the bed, staring into space. "We did, didn't we?"

Josephine saw her chance and sat beside her. "See? You have adventure in your blood. The itch to see new worlds . . ."

"Indeed. My husband and I had planned to homestead in Ohio."

"What?" All thoughts of Josephine's plight left her. "You have never mentioned a husband before. I thought Schultz was your maiden name, and the 'missus' was just a courtesy."

"My maiden name was Cain." Frieda took a few steps away from the bed before turning around. "My husband was Karl. Karl Schultz. He was from Germany. We met shortly after we both arrived in America."

Josephine was embarrassed by her ignorance. "What happened to him?"

"We were living in Boston at the time, but he went back to Hamburg to settle some business with his father's estate so we'd have the funds to homestead. But while he was back in Germany, a fire destroyed much of the city, and he died trying to save his family home."

It was Josephine's turn to offer comfort. "Why didn't I know this? Why have you never mentioned him?"

Frieda pulled a handkerchief from her cuff and dabbed at her eyes. "I try not to think about him and all that could have been." She shook her head as if wanting to dispel the memories. "I was carrying Karl's child when he left, but after I lost him, I gave birth too soon. My baby girl died."

Josephine clapped a hand to her mouth, stifling a sob. "Oh, my dear Frieda. What you have endured." All she had known about Frieda's past was that she was Papa's cousin. She had never met Frieda's parents, never bothered to ask the woman much about her life before she'd come to live with the Cains, and just assumed . . .

Assumed too much. And not enough.

Frieda blew her nose, then lifted her chin in an act of strength. "After Karl and my baby died, my parents died too, so I was all alone. I remembered your father was in New York City, so I sought him out, and he kindly took me in. He was recently engaged to your mother, and they were moving to Washington. Grateful for the support, I became your mother's lady's maid. And then you were born. You became the little girl I lost. . . ."

Josephine pulled Frieda into her arms. "I love you like a mother. I always have."

They rocked each other until their tears abated. Frieda was the one to pull away. "Just know that wherever you go, I go. If you want to go west for the celebration, I will go with you."

"Indians and all?"

"Indians and all."

* * * * *

Convincing Lewis to accompany her west was easy. But convincing Mother?

Josephine had a plan. It was manipulative, but Mother wasn't giving her a choice.

She slipped her hands around Lewis's arm and whispered in his ear. "Use all your charm, Lewis. Make her see that it is imperative we go to the meridian celebration. It is an honor, and as Papa's daughter, I—"

"I know what to say. Leave it to me."

She kissed his cheek and let him enter the parlor alone. But then he surprised her by giving a wink and closing the doors.

Josephine hadn't expected to be in the room with them, but she *had* wanted to eavesdrop. She put her ear to one of the sliding doors and found the voices muffled. Too muffled.

The butler came in the foyer and gave her a look. "It is all right, Dowd. I promise."

He raised an eyebrow and left her alone.

"Psst!"

Josephine was distracted by Frieda, standing on the landing above. "What's he saying?"

"I'm trying to hear!" She waved her off and went back to the door to listen.

But then she heard a very foreign sound.

Laughter. Her mother's laughter. And Aunt's too!

They hadn't laughed in over a year. Then she heard Aunt's snort—which meant she was laughing hard. It had been even longer since she had heard that.

What was Lewis saying to them?

She put her hand on the door handle, aching to join the merriment. Thankfully, she didn't have long to wait. The doors opened, and Lewis said, "Come join us."

She looked to his face, wanting answers, but he simply drew her toward the ladies. "Would you like to tell your daughter the good news, Mrs. Cain?"

Mother nodded and even stood. "After speaking with Mr. Simmons, I have changed my mind about the one-hundredth meridian celebration. You may go, with Mr. Simmons as your escort and Cousin Frieda as your chaperone."

Incredulous, Josephine felt her mouth open. "Really?"

"Yes, my dear. Really."

She did not risk asking how or why Lewis had managed it; she just stared at him in wonder. Then she embraced her mother and her aunt. "Thank you, thank you. Papa will be so pleased."

When her mother's smile faded, she realized she had not chosen the right words. "I mean, he would rather that you and Aunt Bernice accompany me, but at least one of us will see all he has accomplished."

Mother offered a conciliatory shrug. "Go on now, you two. I am sure you have many preparations to make. Gather Frieda, and then you may use your father's study for your planning."

Josephine kissed each woman's cheek and left quickly, still fearful they would change their minds. Once in the foyer, she whispered to Lewis, "What did you say to them?"

"That's between the ladies and me."

"But—"

He put a finger to her lips. "Let's make a list of what we need to bring, shall we?"

* * * * *

Mr. Connelly ran out of the butcher shop when he saw Lewis walk past. "You ever coming to work, Simmons?"

"Right now. Just let me change clothes."

His boss's eyes gave him a good once-over. "You always dressing in fancy clothes makes me wonder what you got cooking."

"Just trying to better myself, that's all." He unlocked the door that led up the stairs to his apartment. "I'll be right down."

"The chickens won't wait," Connelly said.

Or the cows. Or the sheep or pigs or ducks or . . . If Lewis could get by with never eating meat again, it would be fine with him.

Once upstairs, he carefully hung his coat on a hook, put the shirt over the back of the chair, and smoothed the trousers on his bed before draping them across the table. His new boots—pinched from a shoe-maker's shop—were wiped of the day's dust and set at attention near the door. Only then did he take up his work pants and shirt, and pull on the boots he'd been given when he'd joined the army the first time.

He looked in the cracked wall mirror as he buttoned his work shirt. "Congratulations," he told himself. He couldn't believe his good fortune. To go west with the rich and illustrious notables of society? With Josephine? Finally, his luck was changing.

Luck. He didn't believe in luck. *He* was making this happen.

He gave himself another congratulations for winning over her mother and aunt. Telling them he wanted to ask the general for permission to marry his daughter . . . It was a stroke of genius.

And a central part of the plan. She was a prize—and a means to an end.

Although she was an expensive one to woo, he'd reap the spoils after the wedding. If not immediately in money, in the satisfaction of fulfilling a promise he'd made to himself after seeing his father murdered.

He heard a broom banging on the ceiling below.

Off to work.

Chapter Seven

"Sergeant Maguire. If you please."

Hudson was not surprised to be singled out by General Cain, because ever since he'd helped the general during the Spotted Tail visit, he'd successfully handled some other special assignments.

They had not gone unnoticed. By anyone.

He set aside his spike maul and followed the general back to the railcar that housed his office.

"Yankee favoritism, that's what it is," said a Confederate who seemed intent on keeping the war alive. He spit on the ground, barely missing Hudson's boots as he walked past.

"Why don't he ever give a Reb special duties?" asked another Southerner.

"Because everybody knows you Rebs don't have the brains of a prairie dog," said a former Union soldier from Maine.

A fistfight broke out, but Hudson didn't stay to see who won. No one ever *won*. Boss would break it up, and the men would go back to working side-by-side until the next time. He couldn't blame them for getting testy. He wasn't too keen on working with ex-soldiers from the South who would have shot him on sight eighteen months ago.

Of course, he would have shot them too. War was strange that way. Men shot each other, not seeing the man but the uniform of an opposing philosophy. Seeing his brother John get shot, knowing how impersonal the bullet was . . .

The general was waiting for him to catch up. "I hope my singling you out isn't causing many problems."

"None I can't handle."

"Good, because I need someone I can trust, and you've proven your-self that man—during the war, and now."

"I appreciate that, General."

They reached the last car on the train, which was exclusively the general's. They entered at the back along a small landing. The car was outfitted with furniture like a parlor, but with a desk at the near end, along with a table set up with a telegraph machine. As they added more track and moved on, the telegraph line was the first thing they set up. It was their link to civilization.

Hudson spotted two open doors at the far end, one revealing the edge of a bed and the other showing a washbasin on a stand. The perks of being in charge.

"Have a seat, Sergeant."

"If you don't mind, sir, I'd rather you just called me Maguire."

The general hesitated the smallest moment, then nodded. "Of course. I should have realized that. Maguire it is."

Hudson sat in an oak slatted chair, and the general sat behind his desk. The man took a deep breath, as if needing to fuel his words. "The vice president of the Union Pacific, Dr. Durant, is eager to show off the progress of the railroad and has sent out three hundred invitations to important people back east—including President Johnson and all the members of Congress. Two excursion trains are going to meet up in Omaha, and the guests will head west to witness what we've done to reach the one-hundredth meridian."

"But we're not there yet."

"We will be by early October. Because the land is flat, we're moving along nicely."

"Flat and hot." Sometimes the air was too thick to breathe.

"It *has* been a scorcher of a summer. Nonetheless, I have been authorized to offer bonuses if we are able to reach the milestone by mid-October, when the guests arrive."

That was only three weeks away. Yet September had brought slightly cooler weather, and they *were* making good progress.

"What do you need me to do?"

The general shook his head. "It all sounds so theatrical and inane but . . . Durant is arranging the excursion's first stop in Columbus. Hundreds of tents must be set up for the guests, and—"

"The president is going to stay in a tent?"

"I doubt President Johnson will come, as he's been quite indifferent to the railroad. It was Lincoln who had the vision."

"I didn't know that."

The general nodded. "Tale's told that before he was president, Lincoln stood on a bluff east of Omaha and pointed west, seeing the endless plain just begging for a railroad. He was in Council Bluffs, Iowa, to check on some land that someone was using as security for a three-thousand-dollar loan. Sometimes I think that loan was God-sent, a means to get Lincoln in the right place to see the possibilities. General Dodge was there too, sharing the dream." He turned to Hudson. "Things like that are not coincidences."

There was such intensity in his eyes. "No, sir."

With a shake of his head, he moved on. "But if President Johnson does come . . . perhaps Durant will give up his fancy Lincoln car."

"Lincoln *car*?"

"President Lincoln's funeral railcar. The one that carried his body from Washington to Illinois. Durant bought it for his own use." He repeated the words again. "His *own* use."

"That sounds kind of . . ."

"Blasphemous?"

"Disrespectful."

"Between you and me, that's a good word to describe Thomas Durant. He has the clout and power we need to get this job done, but in the meantime, it is best to know that Dr. Durant comes first to Dr. Durant."

"I'll remember that, sir." He had another question. "This Durant is a doctor?"

"An eye doctor."

It seemed ridiculous. "An eye doctor is heading up a railroad?"

The general shrugged. "All that aside, I need someone I can trust to go to Columbus and make sure things are set up right—someone who won't be tempted by the abundance of whiskey there."

"Most whiskey tastes like turpentine."

"Bad whiskey certainly can." The general shook the subject away and got back to the work. "Will you handle it for me?"

And get away from spiking for a few days? "Of course. You can count on me." Then he had an idea. "I probably could use some help. Even one other man."

"You have someone in mind?"

"I do."

* * * * *

"Yee-ha!" Raleigh said, waving his hat in the air. "When do we leave?"

"We'll have to ride horses back to Grand Island where we can catch an east-bound train. How's *now* sound?"

Raleigh tossed his maul to the ground with a loud *thump.* "Let's go."

They walked away under a bevy of questions, which Hudson didn't stick around to answer.

Most men didn't handle envy well.

* * * * *

Lewis checked their itinerary. "It says to meet the other guests on Track Three, the train heading to Pittsburgh and then Chicago."

"What about our luggage?" Josephine asked. Although she was used to big-city crowds, the number of people who were passing through New York City's Grand Central Station was daunting.

Frieda gripped her arm, clearly unsettled. "What if we board the wrong train?"

"We will be fine," Josephine said, even though she suffered the same concerns. "Lewis will take us where we need to go."

As if in response to her confidence, Lewis stopped staring at the itinerary, accosted a conductor, and asked questions. The man pointed to their right, then took their baggage claim tickets, handing them to a porter.

Lewis returned. "Down there. Look for two locomotives decorated with flags."

"Shouldn't we eat something before we board?" Frieda asked.

"I asked about that, and the man said there was no need to eat in the station. There is a refreshment saloon in one of the cars—an entire car dedicated to feeding us."

Josephine took Lewis's arm and rewarded him with a smile as they made their way through the crowd.

The conductor was right. There was no way they could have missed the excursion train. American flags adorned the locomotive's every appendage. Once the train was on its way, a man came through the cars, greeting everyone.

"Who's that?" Lewis asked Josephine.

"I don't know, but he is evidently important."

It was their turn to be greeted. "Hello there," the man said. "My name is Grenville Dodge and I'd like to welcome—"

"General Grenville Dodge?" Lewis asked. "Of the siege of Atlanta?"

The man stood more erect and swiped a hand over his beard. "You know your history, sir. And you are?"

"I am Lewis Simmons, an illustrator for the *Washington Chronicle*."

Josephine felt her eyebrow rise but let the white lie go. To her knowledge, Lewis had not heard back from Mr. Wilson at the newspaper.

General Dodge turned his bright eyes on her. "And you, young lady. Are you Mrs. Simmons?"

She felt herself blush. "Oh no. I am Josephine Cain. My father is—"

"General Reginald Cain." He nodded appreciatively. "I have heard him boast about you. Your father and I are working together on the railroad. He on the track, and I as the consulting engineer."

"And what does a consulting engineer do?" she asked.

"As little as possible," he said with a laugh. Then he added, "I plan the route and sort out anything in our way."

"He means me," said another man, coming up behind him.

This man had a longer beard and a devious gleam in his eyes.

General Dodge stepped aside and made introductions. "Dr. Durant, I would like you to meet Mr. Simmons, Miss Cain—"

"General Cain's daughter," Durant said. "I've heard about you, my dear."

Somehow the way he said "my dear" made Josephine uncomfortable. She responded, "Nice to meet you, Dr. Durant." Then she turned to Frieda, who had been left out. "I would like both of you to meet Mrs. Schultz, my father's cousin, who is accompanying us."

Frieda's eyes were large, and she was clearly uncomfortable with the attention. "Nice to meet you."

They gave her a quick nod, and Dr. Durant rested a hand upon Josephine's shoulder. "Do let us know if there is anything we can do to make your experience more . . . pleasurable."

Although his touch was ostensibly innocent, Josephine wanted to move out of his reach. There was something discomfiting about Dr. Durant, even if he was an executive of the entire railroad project. Her feeling propelled her to ask, "Are you married, Dr. Durant?"

He pulled his hand away. "I am. With two beautiful children."

"How nice for you." Whether it was nice for *them* was another matter.

He moved his hand to Dodge's back, propelling the two of them toward the next group of guests.

"My, my," Frieda said. "That doctor seemed important."

"He *is* important," Lewis said. "Were it not for him, there would be no Transcontinental Railroad."

"I think my father and thousands of workers would beg to differ."

He gave her a teasing smile. "I meant no offense."

When Josephine didn't answer, Frieda jumped in. "None taken."

* * * * *

Lewis had never been on a train.

He knew how ridiculous that sounded—how ridiculous it was for a man of twenty-two to be devoid of that experience—but it was the truth.

Just after Lewis joined the Union army in a fit of ridiculous patriotism, his father cut ties with Vanderbilt and decided to move the family to North Carolina, where they had relatives. So Lewis was stranded up north while his mother and father moved south, into a state that had seceded from the Union.

"You fight for yourself first, and your country last," his father had written to Lewis, begging him to reconsider his choice and join them. After a short while, North or South no longer mattered to Lewis, and the army mattered even less, so he eventually ditched his Union blues, headed south, and began working with his father—for the other side.

So he had experience. Plenty of it. Just not with trains.

He knew that the key to this trip was to act as if he belonged. Finding himself in a situation that a normal man-of-bearing should know about, he needed to act at ease. Once they got west—when it would be new to everyone—he might be able to let down his guard and be himself.

It had taken five days to travel on the excursion train from New York City to St. Joseph, Missouri. In Chicago they'd picked up the Great Western Light Guard Band. Their specialty seemed to be polka tunes, which gave him a headache.

Lewis enjoyed meeting the myriad of important people on board: President Lincoln's son Robert; George Pullman, who designed opulent sleeper cars for trains; a congressman from Ohio named Rutherford B. Hayes, who, with five war wounds, had plenty of entertaining stories to tell; three senators; a Scottish earl; a French marquis; and all sorts of railroad bigwigs with their families. Two hundred guests, all told.

Lewis was glad that Frieda and Josephine enjoyed talking to the wives and playing with the children, leaving him free to make himself known. With such an opportunity before him, he felt like a hungry stallion in a stall of golden oats. He would flit from one conversation to the next, milking the contact, eagerly telling people of his artistic ability.

He felt a bit guilty for doing so and knew his professional ambition had to remain secondary to his central objective. Yet he couldn't help himself. Surely his parents would have understood. Mother had always encouraged his art.

His father, less so. He'd always wanted Lewis to join him in the shipping business, and for a time, Father had gotten his way. Lewis first learned about steamers working with him in New York. His life would have continued in that direction if the war hadn't mucked everything up.

But that was the past. Life was giving him a chance to use his art. He'd be stupid not to take advantage of it.

During the second day of their journey, Lewis had taken out his paper and pen and started drawing portraits for the rich and famous. Today he was sketching the duo of Mrs. Dodge and her daughter.

"Sit still, Lettie," Mrs. Dodge said to the ten-year-old. "We brought you along because we thought you were a big girl. Perhaps we were wrong and should have brought your sisters."

Lettie was immediately still, allowing Lewis to get back to work.

"How many children do you have, Mrs. Dodge?"

"Three girls. Lettie, eight-year-old Eleanor—"

"Ellie," Lettie corrected.

"We call her Ellie," Mrs. Dodge conceded. "And finally Anne, who's only seven months." She looked around with only her eyes, being careful not to move her head, then lowered her voice. "I am sure my husband would like a boy, but—"

General Dodge strode up the aisle and rested a hand on Lettie's head. "Girls are fine with me, Ruth Anne. I wouldn't give them up for a battalion of boys."

Lettie beamed, and Lewis had no further problems with her fidgeting.

When the sketch was finished, Mrs. Dodge gushed over the result, "How much do I owe you, Mr. Simmons?"

He wished he could let her pay—let any of them pay—for he was out the cost of the supplies, but he repeated what he'd told all the others, "Consider it a gift."

Mrs. Dodge held the drawing like a delicate masterpiece. "Bless you, sir. Lettie and I will cherish this always."

Which was something. If he couldn't get paid in coin, he'd take accolades. They would remember him for his art.

And, perhaps, for his less admirable future achievements.

It was unfortunate he couldn't accomplish both, and Lewis struggled with a desire to let the latter go. Leave the past in the past and focus on the future. A normal future, married to Josephine, expanding his art, and making an honorable name for himself.

But his name was the issue. He could never make a fictitious name honorable.

He shivered as a cold gust of two images returned to him like ghosts haunting his soul: the image of his mother dying in his arms, and the image of his father hanging from a gallows.

Injustice demanded a price—from others, and from himself.

As did judgment.

* * * * *

In St. Joseph, they left the train and were met by Mr. Herb Hoxie, who led them to two waiting steamer ships, the *Colorado* and the *Denver*. The Rosenblatt Band joined them, which played with more ability and restraint than the brass band from Chicago.

As they boarded, Josephine heard Senator Wade's wife say, "This is surprisingly delightful—and astonishing."

"Why is that?" Josephine asked.

"To come a week's journey out of New York and still be among people of wealth, refinement, and enterprise. The excursion even has its own newsletter." She shook her head. "Who would have thought?"

Josephine nodded, yet the woman's snobbery offended on two accounts. First, the guests aboard the train had not ventured far from its tracks, so their society was self-contained. And second, the woman seemed to imply that everyone who lived west of the large cities back home was ignorant and unworthy. From what Josephine could see, the people who had been courageous enough to leave what was known and tackle new lands—with no guarantees—owned attributes of far more import than wealth and refinement.

Nevertheless, they were on a new leg of their journey, a two-day trip on a steamboat, up the Missouri River toward Omaha.

She stood on the upper passenger deck of the boat. Lewis joined her. "Another adventure," he said.

Josephine nodded as the paddle wheel on the side of the ship made *whoop-whoop* sounds. "I must admit I felt safer on the train." She pointed down to the muddy river. The branches of fallen trees reached out of the river like murky hands wanting to grab the boat and take it under. "This ship is barely in the water."

"Because the water isn't very deep," Lewis said.

"It feels like we could tip over on a whim."

He wrapped his arm around her waist. "Perhaps if we stay very still . . . "

She appreciated his levity—and his arm. "Then there are those fingers of sand that protrude into the river."

"Sandbars."

She didn't care what they were called, only that they made her nervous. "I heard from one of the workers that hundreds of riverboats sink every year. It is not the branches you *see*, it is the ones you don't see that are the problem."

He whispered in her ear. "I'll keep you safe. You can always depend on me."

She leaned her head on his shoulder, wanting to believe him.

* * * * *

It was exhausting. There was no getting around it.

Five days on the train, then two days on the steamer paddle boat, which finally arrived safely in Omaha. But then a caravan of carriages and stagecoaches took them from the dock to the Union Pacific rail yard. There they boarded a very special excursion train, all dolled up like a belle at her first ball. There were two locomotives festooned with flags, followed by nine cars: a baggage and supply car, a refreshment car, a cooking car, four passenger coaches, the "Lincoln" car for Mr. Durant's personal use, and finally, a magnificent directors' car.

Josephine fell into a seat with Frieda beside her. "Now what?" she asked.

Frieda consulted the itinerary they'd been given. "Next stop is Columbus, Nebraska, where we'll camp."

"Camp?"

"Tents will be provided."

What had she gotten herself into? "How I long for my own bed."

"Nonsense," Frieda said. "You can have your own bed for the rest of your life, but who gets the chance to do what we're doing?" She pointed to the itinerary. "Who gets a chance to see a war dance performed by real Indians?"

That got her attention. "War dance? Is that safe?"

Frieda shrugged. "It must be, or they wouldn't do it."

Josephine hoped so. She spotted Lewis making chitchat with Senator Hayes. "He is certainly enjoying himself."

"Hmm."

"What does *hmm* mean?"

"He's taking great benefit from this trip."

"So? Should he sit on his hands and not speak to anyone?"

"Of course not, but . . ." Frieda shook her head, looking at Lewis.

"I thought you liked him. Liked him for *me*. You have always stressed what a perfect gentleman he is."

"So I have," she said, but still sounded wary. "There's just something *suspekt* about him, that's all."

"Define *suspekt.*"

"It's a word my husband used to use. Lewis says all the right things at all the right times. He's kind to you—and me." She smiled and touched Josephine's hand. "I have to thank you for introducing me as a cousin, not a servant."

Josephine had never considered the latter. "You are family. And my most trusted friend in the world."

Frieda squeezed her hand. "You are a dear. But because we are so close, I bring up my doubts."

Doubts? Now she had doubts about Lewis?

A waiter brought around a tray of teacakes, and all doubts were forgotten.

For now.

Chapter Eight

Hudson pulled the tent rope taut, tied it around a stake, then flexed his aching fingers. "That's the last of them."

"Finally," Raleigh said. "I thought arranging for the excursionists was going to be easy work."

"Different work." Hudson looked out over the sea of tents they'd set up just past the station buildings. They covered several acres. A wonderful aroma wafted out of the large dining tent, igniting his hunger.

He took the last name tag from the pile and pinned it to the right of the tent opening: *Miss Cain & Mrs. Schultz.* "Cain. I wonder if she is a relation of the general's."

"At the moment I don't care who she is. We're done."

And none too soon. A train's whistle cut through the early evening, and they felt the ground rumble with its approach.

"I hope the Indians are ready," Raleigh said, gathering their tools.

"Hiring Pawnee . . . only Durant would think of such a thing."

"I just hope they cooperate."

"And do only what they've been hired to do."

"Amen to that," Raleigh said. "Either way, it's showtime."

* * * * *

"Tents? We're sleeping in tents?"

If Josephine heard that complaint one more time, she was going to scream. Yes, it was unconventional, and she had suffered her own apprehensions. But now, being out on the Nebraska plain, she surprised herself by feeling thrilled with the prospect. Ever since they'd left Omaha, she had been glued to the view of the Great Platte Valley. She was not alone, as many exclaimed in wonder and admiration. But just as many had complained about the miles and miles of nature, pining for their cities and the comforts of home.

Now in Columbus, they had been instructed to find their tents and gather at the dining tent for food to rival that of eastern hotels.

Lewis stepped to the ground and extended his hand to Josephine and Frieda. "Watch your step," he said, his smile charming. As they followed the surge toward the tents, he said to Josephine, "You seem content with the accommodations."

She lifted her skirt to keep it above the dusty ground. "Surprisingly, I am. I cannot imagine seeing this land without having the chance to truly be out in the middle of it."

"In the middle of it," he said with a laugh. "We are that."

A few men stood with lists that directed the guests to their tents. Lewis approached them, and Josephine watched as he seemed to grow perturbed by something. When he walked back to Josephine and Frieda, his head was shaking, his scowl deep. "You two are over there, to the right."

"And you?"

"Apparently, I'm off with the men, sharing a tent with a Mr. Rosewood. I think I met him briefly. He's a tradesman of some sort."

Josephine gave him a measured look. "Are you satisfied with your pairing?"

"Why shouldn't I be? I'm hardly equal to a congressman or railroad executive." There was a pull in his voice. But he shrugged it off and patted her hand. "It's fine."

* * * * *

It was not fine.

All of Lewis's efforts to hobnob with the rich and famous were apparently moot. Whoever was in charge of the tent assignments obviously considered him an underling. A nobody, even though he *had* been mentioned twice in the excursionist's daily newsletter. The name tag on the tent could just as easily have said, *Man 1 and Man 2*.

Mr. Rosewood had already arrived and was stretched out on a cot with his hands behind his head. He did not rise when Lewis entered. "Mr. Rosewood, I presume?"

"Sam. Yup, that's me. You're Simmons?"

Lewis knew he should have offered his first name, but he didn't. "Yes."

Rosewood sat up, setting his feet on the ground. "You're that fellow making the drawings, aren't you?"

The artist creating the art. "That's right."

"So you're my competition."

Lewis stared him. "Competition?"

Rosewood pointed to a stack of boxes. "I'm a photographer, you're a sketcher."

Suddenly Lewis placed Rosewood. He'd seen him taking a photograph of the steamboat before they left St. Joseph.

"You make any money sketching?" Rosewood asked.

Not when I've given them all away for free. "Enough. And you?"

"More than enough. I have a studio in DC. I sell the photos to the subject, on the spot, or I send them back to the studio where I'm setting up a gallery. Plus, I expect an influx of income once the Union Pacific understands how important it is to get all this chronicled. I plan on making a killing on that."

Lewis set his portfolio behind his cot. "You make that much?"

"I will."

"But you can't reproduce your photographs. It's one and done. I can have my drawings made into engravings that can be printed over and over."

"What's worth more, a rare diamond or a river rock?"

It took Lewis a moment. "I beg your pardon?"

"That was rude. Sorry. There's enough work for both of us. At least for now."

But was there?

Just when Lewis finally seemed to be finding a market for his art, there was something newer? Better? He glanced at the man's photography equipment. "Is it . . . difficult?"

"Not if you follow the science of it. Getting people to be still is the hardest part."

Lewis sat on his cot and heard straw in the mattress. He ran a hand over a brown fur cover. Buffalo? He faced Rosewood, their knees almost touching. "Perhaps if we have time, you might show me how it's done." What would it hurt? His father had always stressed the need for a backup plan.

"I don't need that kind of competitor."

Maybe Rosewood wouldn't have a choice. Lewis chose his words carefully. "How about an assistant?"

"Mmm. That's possible." Rosewood lay back on his cot, then rose up to his elbows. "I saw that pretty thing you're traveling with. Is she your girl?"

"That's the plan. She's the daughter of General Cain, the man in charge of the crews."

"Now there's a match that should make your life easier."

That was the goal.

He would marry Josephine, gain access to her money, then abandon her and break her heart. Hurting General Cain's daughter would hurt the general. It would never equal Lewis's pain, of course, but it would help.

But then there was his art, the thrill of creating something from nothing.

Could he achieve both goals? Or would he have to choose?

* * * * *

"But you cannot run off by yourself, Liebchen," Frieda said. "There may be people around, but we are still in the wilderness, and it is nearly dark."

"I am not *running* anywhere. I am simply going to take a stroll. I will be fine. Besides, this is the West. The rules of Washington etiquette do not apply here."

"Of course they do. Rules follow the people, not the land."

Josephine hoped this wasn't true. As they traveled west, she had felt a loosening of the bonds of home, as if with each passing mile the stifling tether that held her captive was being strung taut. Was it close to breaking?

Did she want it to break?

Frieda looked into a hand mirror and tucked away some stray hairs. Since they'd been on this excursion, she had taken more interest in her own appearance. "Don't you want to eat?" Frieda asked. "It smells delicious."

"Bring me back a roll or something. I have eaten enough this past week to last me till Tuesday. My corset is feeling far too tight."

"At least put on a hat or a bonnet. A lady must wear a hat when out in public."

Josephine laughed. "But I don't want to be in public. That's the point."

"At least take your shawl. The evening's crisp."

Josephine relented and wrapped the shawl around her shoulders. Then she walked away before Frieda could continue the argument. Josephine loved the woman dearly, but being with anyone for a solid week was bound to take its toll. She needed some time to be alone, without chatter or obligatory smiles.

She walked to the westernmost tents and stopped. The town of Columbus and civilization was behind her. In front of her was nothing but prairie. Endless miles and miles of open land, stretching to the horizon and beyond.

Without making a conscious decision, she walked forward a few tentative steps, then moved more swiftly. Only when the sounds of the festivities became an indistinguishable hum did she stop.

She heard her own breathing and found the sound of it astonishing. "I am alone," she whispered. "Completely alone."

Josephine made a full turn, quickening through the sight of the camp, and slowing to relish the solitude during the rest of the turn.

And then the sun hid behind the evening clouds. It was as though an artist had swept his brush across the sky, dipping into his palette of pink and blue and purple.

"Oh my . . . oh, God . . ." She lifted a hand to her mouth and let the tears come. The beauty wrapped around her like a heavenly embrace, and her heart overflowed. "Thank You for letting me see this. Thank You for creating this."

But then she started as she heard a sound coming from in front of her. To the right.

A wolf? An Indian?

What was she thinking, wandering so far from the camp? She turned to leave.

"No. Don't go."

A man came toward her, his form a silhouette against the setting sun.

"Isn't it beautiful?" he asked, pointing over his shoulder to the sunset. "I can't get enough of it."

Only when he came close could she see his features.

It was an odd first impression, to see someone walking out of the twilight, but judging by his countenance, he was a thoughtful man whose eyes were used to looking for the good in things. And though his build was that of a man who worked hard, there was also a grace in his walk.

His hair was brown like Papa's, but long, skimming his shoulders, and he wore a beard and a mustache. She didn't generally like beards—not even Papa's—but this man's seemed to suit him, creating an interesting and rugged frame for his gentle face.

"Sorry to alarm you like that, miss," he said. "Are you all right?"

She pressed a hand against her chest, letting out a laugh as her heart beat double-time. "I suppose I am as fine as a person can be who has just found her heart tossed into her throat."

He smiled. "Maybe I should've walked around you. But I saw you enjoying the sunset and thought I'd join you, since that's my reason for being out here too."

She was taken aback by this admission. "I have never seen anything like it," she said, looking past him. But then she gasped. The sky had changed again as the sun touched the horizon, burning it up. "We can't see this in Washington."

"It happens every night," he said. "Or so I've heard."

"Are you making fun of me, Mr. . . . ?"

"Maguire. Hudson Maguire, Miss . . . ?"

"Cain. Josephine Cain."

"Nice to—" He stopped. "Are you the general's daughter?"

"You know my father?"

"He's the one who sent me here, to get this shindig set up. I pinned the name tag on your tent just before you arrived, but I suppose I didn't put two and two together. Your father is a very good man. Now *and* during the war, when I fought under him."

"I am very proud of him."

She wanted to talk with Mr. Maguire more but couldn't take her eyes off the sunset. "I can't believe I have never seen this before. I wish it would slow down."

They were silent for a few moments before she heard his voice again. "'The sacred lamp of day, now dipt in western clouds his parting day.'"

She looked at him. "How beautiful. Did you write it?"

"I wish I could take credit. It's by the Scotsman William Falconer from his poem, 'The Shipwreck.'"

"You read poetry?"

"I can blame or thank my mother, who read poetry *to* me."

"I would thank her," Josephine said.

"I'll do that. Next time I see her."

"And when will that be?"

He shook his head, looking upon the sun. "I don't know. My youngest brother and I are out here working to help the family."

"That is commendable. Where is home?"

"Allegheny City. Near Pittsburgh. Pennsylvania."

"You are a long way from home."

"Everyone here is a long way from home. There are a thousand men with a thousand stories of what brought them here. A thousand reasons why this train is our hope for the future."

"You sound like my father."

He nodded. "It'll be pitch-black soon. Once the sun goes down, it's *gone.*" He pointed toward the tents. "Would you like me to accompany you back, Miss Cain?"

She smiled. "Yes, please."

* * * * *

As they neared the dining tent, they heard horrible screams and whoops. And drums.

Josephine stopped and grabbed Hudson's arm. "What is going on? Have we been attacked by Indians?"

He hated that she was afraid. "Everyone's fine. Dr. Durant hired some of the friendly Pawnees to put on a war dance as entertainment."

He felt her grip relax. "That's right. I saw it on the agenda. He has thought of everything, hasn't he?"

"Thought of too much."

"What do you mean by that?"

Should he tell her and ruin the surprise? "It's a secret."

Even in the low light he could see her face take on a coquettish smile. "Oh, do tell, Mr. Maguire. 'Tis not polite to tease me like that."

Her flirtation annoyed him. "I wasn't teasing, it's just that I was sworn to secrecy, and . . ." He made a decision. "I think it's best if you're as surprised as everyone else."

She let go of his arm, and they resumed their walk toward the bonfire. Once they were close, a dark-haired man came to claim her. "Josephine, I'm glad you're back. Come and see."

He glanced at Hudson, and Miss Cain made introductions. "Lewis, I would like you to meet Mr. Maguire. He works for my father—and fought under him during the war. Mr. Maguire, this is my friend, Mr. Simmons."

Simmons eyed Hudson warily, as though they were rivals.

Which was ridiculous.

Then he nodded once, dismissing him. He extended his arm to Miss Cain. "Let's get back to the festivities, shall we?"

But as they walked away, she looked back at Hudson.

His stomach danced.

Which was ridiculous.

Really, it was.

* * * * *

Where is he?

Josephine pretended to watch the Indians, who were decked out in elaborate feathered and animal-skin regalia, dancing in a circle around the bonfire to the beat of a drum, chanting and yelling odd syllables. Their faces were painted, and they carried axes, bows, and spears in their hands, shaking them at the sky. It was quite impressive. But her interest lay elsewhere.

She scanned the fire-lit faces of the onlookers, seeking Mr. Maguire. When there was a gap in the crowd, she tried to see past it, but the night was too dark.

Frieda tugged at her sleeve. "Looking for someone?" she asked.

Lewis—who stood on her other side—looked her way. Josephine offered him a reassuring smile and answered Frieda. "No one in particular. I was just taking it all in."

* * * * *

Hudson watched the war dance from a distance.

Raleigh stepped beside him. "They seem to be enjoying it."

Hudson shook his head. "I can't believe the Pawnees agreed to it." He had mixed feelings about the Indians providing entertainment. There were influential people in the crowd, and they were going to go back east and tell their constituents about the friendly Indians they met.

The Pawnee were generally peaceful, and some of the Sioux. But other tribes were not. Hudson had heard stories of Indian raids and horrific scalpings. No man could think of such a death without a shudder and a prayer.

Peaceful or hostile—such labels didn't make much difference to Hudson. He knew there were young hotheads even among the friendly Indian nations who could cause plenty of deadly trouble. And hotheads on the white man's side too. Men who wanted a fight always found a way to pick one.

Hudson wished the railroad would pay for more protection from the military. Becoming lax or too at-ease could be lethal. Sometimes it felt like the railroad was racing west with blinders on, merely hoping for the best.

He spotted Miss Cain in the crowd. Her companion drew her hand around his arm, and she left it there for a few moments before withdrawing it with the pretense of adjusting her shawl. And she only pretended to look at the Indians. Her eyes were clearly scanning the faces, looking for—

"Who is she?"

Hudson let his gaze move to the anonymous crowd. "Who?"

Raleigh leaned close and pointed to Miss Cain. "That pretty girl with the blue shawl and the eager eyes?"

Eager eyes? But it was best to answer. "That's Josephine Cain, the daughter of the general."

"How do you know that?"

"I was out looking at the sunset and met her."

"She was walking in the dark?"

"It wasn't dark yet." He thought a moment, then added, "She seemed to really like it."

"Just remember *you* didn't make the sunset, brother."

"I never suggested—"

"Don't you have a letter to write to Sarah Ann or something?"

Hudson didn't like the implication. "Can't I talk to a girl without you accusing me of something. . . ."

"Inappropriate?"

"I was not inappropriate. I would never be, never do—"

"Glad to hear it," Raleigh said, putting his hands in his pockets.

But as they ended the discussion, Hudson had to force himself to look elsewhere.

Anywhere but at Miss Josephine Cain.

Chapter Nine

"Why are we stopping so soon?" Josephine asked as the train slowed.

Lewis looked out and saw that they were on a high embankment. He stuck his head out the window and saw a bridge coming up. Was there a problem on the bridge?

But then he saw a large group of Indians riding fast toward the train. "They're going to attack!"

The railcars echoed with screams both male and female, and the men called for guns.

But once again General Dodge walked down the aisle of the car, telling them that a Pawnee reservation was close by. "I have arranged for your enjoyment a mock meeting of the grand and terrific, with the Pawnee fighting against the Sioux."

"So now we have two tribes around us?"

"Just one," the general said. "Both sides will be played by our friends, the Pawnee."

"Can we go outside in order to see better?" Josephine asked.

"Josephine!" Frieda said.

But the general smiled. "You may, Miss Cain."

She turned to Lewis and said, "Let's go."

He had no wish to be outside. Friend or no friend, he didn't trust any Indian.

"Lewis?"

He saw Sam Rosewood exit the train, carrying his equipment. Lewis *should* go sketch. The lure to capture the moment on paper stirred him. . . .

"Lewis?" Josephine said again, nearly at the door.

He grabbed his art supplies and went with her, but in his opinion, Josephine was too bold for her own good.

* * * * *

Like the sunset the night before, Josephine wished the battle of the Indians would slow down so she could take it all in. "Isn't this astonishing?"

"It seems a bit excessive," Lewis said. "A war dance *and* a mock battle?"

"Oh pooh," she said. "It is glorious."

Horses reared and plunged against each other as Indian grappled Indian. Rifles, revolvers, and arrows shot out, and people fell from their horses, leaving riderless steeds roaming over the plain. There was even a mock scalping that made her gasp and other ladies scream. All was confusion and turmoil, until the Pawnee were victorious and brought their beaten enemies into camp, shouting in celebration of their triumph.

Her heart beat in her chest, and she felt her cheeks grow warm in exhilaration. "Isn't it wonderful?"

"It is *not* wonderful," Frieda said. "Pretending to kill is near as bad as real killing."

"No, it isn't. No one was hurt." She pointed to the scalped victim, who now stood in full health. "See?"

"It's not ladylike to be exhilarated, Josephine. Death is not exhilarating."

No it was not, and Josephine had a hard time justifying her feeling. "Death isn't, but truth is. If this is the truth of the West, I am glad to see it."

Dr. Durant rode out among the Indians and threw presents and trinkets into the band. They scrambled for the gifts as if they were gold. Durant returned to the guests like a conquering hero. "And there you have it, folks. The Wild West played out right before your eyes." He bowed to the applause. "Now, all aboard! Off we go to the one-hundredth meridian!"

As they boarded the train, Josephine caught sight of Mr. Maguire. He tipped his hat.

She felt herself blush with another kind of exhilaration.

* * * * *

Josephine looked out the window as they passed a town called Plum Creek. "I never knew there were so many towns out here. Silver Creek, Lone Tree, Grand Island, Elm Creek, Kearney."

Senator Hayes heard her remark. "Many of the towns were planted nearly twenty years ago with the expectation that the train would come someday."

"But what if the train hadn't come this way?"

He shrugged. "The towns would have died." He pointed out the window. "Many still will. In the West, only the strong survive."

Frieda gripped the armrest of the seat. "Aren't we going too fast?"

General Dodge—who always seemed close at hand—answered her. "We're making up for lost time. I've told the engineer to get us there fast. We're traveling at upwards of forty-five miles per hour."

Another man stood to join in the discussion. "Isn't that against railroad operating rules?"

Dodge leaned close. "It is. So, *shh.* I won't tell if you won't."

Lewis spoke up. "Wasn't there a massacre at Plum Creek?"

His words elicited a round of murmurs from the other passengers.

"That was two years ago and involved a wagon train," Dodge said. "*Not* the railroad."

"I remember that," said a man. "Weren't a lot of pioneers killed and some of the women and children captured?"

For the first time, Josephine saw the jaw of General Dodge clench, as if he were struggling to control his anger. "Yes. There were nearly a dozen innocent people killed, and a few taken captive."

Josephine looked out the window, remembering the mock Indian battle they had witnessed just hours earlier. The Pawnee were friendly— now—but were they . . . "Excuse me, General, but were the Indians that attacked the pioneers Pawnee?"

"Oh no," he said. "They were Cheyenne. You have nothing to fear from the Pawnee."

"But much to fear from the Cheyenne?" Lewis asked.

He received a glare from the general before the man put on his host-face again. "Now, now, ladies and gentlemen. Enough ancient history. Today we celebrate a magnificent moment. We are making our own history." He looked out the window and pointed. "And here we are! The one-hundredth meridian!"

The train stopped, and they dutifully got out. But all that was there was a wooden arch with a sign above two posts, announcing its importance:

100th Meridian
247 Miles from Omaha

"I need to make a sketch," Lewis said.

As he went off to do his work, Mr. Maguire came near. "Are you impressed, Miss Cain?"

"By the accomplishment, certainly. But the exact spot is a little . . . anticlimactic." She looked across the prairie, which stretched long and far in every direction. "I am not sure of the significance, except that it is a nice round number. Why are we measuring from a point in England?"

"Ah," Mr. Maguire said with a glint in his eye. "I don't have an answer to your last question, but I assure you, the significance is great. By reaching this milestone, the Union Pacific is guaranteed the irrevocable right to keep laying track westward."

"So it is about money."

"Of course."

Why did everything have to be about money? She looked to the west, where the track continued to the horizon. "I thought this was the end of the line."

"We've gone more than forty miles farther. We got to the one-hundredth on the sixth of October, weeks ago, before you even left New York."

"So the work never ends."

"Not until we meet up with the Central Pacific." He must have spotted someone giving a signal, because he nodded and said, "It's time to move on. Just a few more miles to milepost 279, our next camp."

The thought of being able to lie down was appealing. "No more Indian raids?"

"Don't tell me you've had your fill?"

"Actually, yes."

He opened his mouth to speak, then closed it.

"What are you wanting to say, Mr. Maguire? I insist you say it."

"I don't mean to alarm you, but the camp tonight is purposely located near Fort McPherson. Soldiers will be camped close by to . . . to . . ."

She let one thought lead to another. "To protect us from real Indian attacks?"

"There *have* been bands of hostiles roaming the area."

"Knowing this, how am I supposed to sleep?"

His brow furrowed. "I just want you to be aware. And safe. I'm sorry, I shouldn't have said anything."

"No, no," she said. "I insisted you tell me the truth."

"But the truth has caused you to worry, and for that I'm sorry."

She was warmed by his concern. "I will be all right. I am tougher than I look."

Josephine was glad her words made him smile. He touched the tip of his hat and left her.

Left her feeling very much alone.

* * * * *

They arrived at camp after dark and were told there was a grand meal awaiting them. But most of the passengers opted to go straight to bed.

Each tent was lit with a lantern, which made Josephine feel both safe—and targeted. She stood at the tent flap, looking out into the night. How many Indians were waiting in the darkness for the group to turn in?

"Enough looking around, Liebchen," Frieda whined from inside the tent. "You said you wished to retire, so retire."

She considered telling her about the Indian menace but decided against it.

It was bad enough *she* knew. Ignorance would have been bliss.

And yet . . . she was honored Mr. Maguire had told her the truth. She knew she was being two-faced, enjoying her knowledge of the truth but regretting the unpleasant reality it exposed. She couldn't have it both ways.

Either way, sleep would not come easily.

Chapter Ten

"I'm not looking forward to working on the line again," Raleigh said as the train neared the end of the tracks.

Neither am I. Setting up the two camps had been a relief from the backbreaking work of laying track. And the highlight of Hudson's respite had been meeting Miss Cain.

The train slowed and Hudson rolled up his sleeves, ready to resume the role of spiker. They both jumped down before the train came to a complete stop. He spotted General Cain on his horse and hurried toward him to offer a report.

"Did everything go well, Maguire?" the general asked.

"Yes, sir. No problems at all."

He looked past Hudson, toward the train. "Did you happen to meet—?"

"Your daughter? Yes, sir, I did. I think she enjoyed the journey."

"Papa!"

Josephine hung out a window and waved. The way the general's face lit up at the sight of her spoke volumes about their relationship.

The general rode toward her, reaching for her hand. "Come out here, daughter. I've missed you."

Josephine nudged her way to the front of the line of people making their exit. The general dismounted, and she ran into his arms.

There were many appreciative sighs and murmurings. Hudson heard someone say, "Too bad she'll be going back east tomorrow."

He didn't want to think about it.

* * * * *

Josephine knew they were getting a show, and she didn't mind one whit. Watching the railroad men fully synchronized as they lay eight hundred feet of track in a mere thirty minutes was exhilarating.

Of course there was one worker who caught her eye more than the others.

Mr. Maguire . . . the way he swung the hammer in a wide arc, over and over and over, with power yet also with grace. There was a rhythm to the work that mesmerized both visually and audibly.

Lewis sidled up beside her. "I'd like to say that I could do that, but I'm not sure I could."

She was positive he *couldn't*. Lewis was not a man of muscle, but of mind.

Which wasn't a bad thing.

Necessarily.

* * * * *

Lewis hadn't been this nervous since he'd joined the Union army—for the second time. Of course it didn't help that Josephine's father was a general—*the* general who had ruined his life. Men like Lewis didn't feel comfortable with Union officers.

He waited until the general was finished talking to General Dodge.

Two generals. Great. Luckily, Dodge moved on.

"Mr. Simmons," General Cain said upon seeing him. "Have you enjoyed the excursion?"

"Greatly, sir. I'm very impressed with all the progress you've made."

"Not just me," he said, stretching an arm toward the track. "The workers are the ones who break their backs to accomplish the dream and build our common destiny."

"You are very gracious." Lewis thought the general's penchant for speaking in such lofty terms as *dreams* and *destiny* was overblown. He really doubted the men who *were* breaking their backs were thinking too much about *dreams* except in reference to getting a good night's sleep, and *destiny* beyond getting their next paycheck.

But who was he to have an opinion about that? He had his own dreams and his own destiny, and they both involved the general and his daughter. Possess the one in order to harm the other.

A man was walking toward them, which meant Lewis's time was short. "If I may be so bold, sir . . . one reason I wanted to accompany your daughter out west was so I had the opportunity of speaking to you in person about . . . in regard to . . ."

"Do you wish to marry my Josephine, Mr. Simmons?"

Lewis drew in a breath and let it out. "Yes, sir."

"Do you have good assurance that she will accept your proposal?"

Not yet. "I hope to. Actually, I don't have an exact plan about when I might ask her, but I wanted to make sure I had your blessing when the time does present itself."

The man who'd approached now stood a dozen feet away, awaiting his turn.

"We have not yet met your family, Lewis."

You've met my father. "My mother has passed, but my father lives in New York. He is very busy working with the Commodore to rebuild the steamer business. Those pesky Confederate blockade-runners during the war, using a Northern invention for ill-gotten gain . . ." Lewis smiled inwardly, for his family had benefited from that gain. "Father has given me this time away to nourish my passion, my art."

"So he approves of it?"

Lewis nodded. "My mother was my patron, and my father wishes to respect her memory."

"Ah."

"I do know the steamer business, sir. And if my art does not prove of benefit financially, I am prepared to rejoin my father in his work." Lewis sensed that he was beginning to sound too eager, and he moderated his tone. "You are in the business of railroads, and my family is in the business of waterways. Both modes of transportation are needed for trade and profit, don't you think?"

"Of course." The general stroked his chin. "I do appreciate your family's roots and high connections. I would not have allowed you to court my daughter had I not approved or felt assured that if your relationship ripened, Josephine would be able to live in the manner to which she is accustomed."

"As expected, sir."

"How is your art doing—as far as providing a living?" the general asked.

"Very well," Lewis lied. "I have the highest hopes." *That* wasn't a lie.

"Then I give you my blessing." He raised a finger. "But the final decision will be Josephine's. She is a woman who knows her own mind."

Don't I know it.

"Thank you, sir. I appreciate your trust."

* * * * *

The excursion was leaving.

Miss Josephine Cain was leaving.

Hudson leaned on his spike maul and watched as she made tearful good-byes to her father. All this way, to see each other a few hours.

You'd travel that far to see your loved ones for a few hours.

The image of Sarah Ann and his parents flitted through his mind but didn't linger. He couldn't go back to Pennsylvania and visit yet. His place was here with the railroad, undertaking the work that would assure his future. Their future.

His thoughts traveled from Pennsylvania to Nebraska as he saw Miss Cain leave her father's side and walk toward him.

Raleigh nudged him in the side. "Uh-oh. Here she comes."

There was a chorus of hoots as the other workers realized that her destination was Hudson.

He left Raleigh's side to meet her halfway. "Are you ready to leave, Miss Cain?"

"No, I am not. But I have no choice." She looked at her father longingly. "I miss him already."

"He misses you too."

She nodded once. "I told him how good you were to me, how you gave me special attention and made sure my journey was a good one."

"I didn't do that much," he said.

She looked him squarely in the eyes. "You did more than you know."

She rested her gloved fingers on his arm. "I shall never forget the prairie sunset, Mr. Maguire." She pointed to her temple. "It is etched in my memory forever."

He touched his own temple. "As it is in mine."

She sighed, and he sensed there was more she wanted to say.

There was more *he* wanted to say, yet the feelings were hard to form into words. "I—I hope we can meet again, Miss Cain. Perhaps you can visit a second time."

Her eyes lit up. "I . . . Perhaps I can." She looked back at her father. "Though I doubt it." She offered him a brave smile. "May God keep you safe, Mr. Maguire."

"And you, Miss Cain."

With that, she left him.

* * * * *

Tonight's my chance.

Fireworks on the prairie. What could be more romantic? If only Lewis could get rid of Frieda for just a few minutes.

This trip wasn't working out as well as he'd hoped. He wasn't being accepted as a member of the elite set that populated the junket, and he wasn't making romantic inroads with Josephine. He'd thought they would grow closer on the long journey. He'd thought they'd be on kissing terms by now.

But every time he thought the time might be right, Frieda was there, or one of the other passengers. Or Josephine popped out of her seat, wanting to see something out of a window on the other side of the train. They had not enjoyed a single minute alone.

He tried to think of diversionary tactics—like tying her in her tent—but in regard to non-forceful means, his mind was blank. As the dinner ended, and the group moved their chairs to the edge of an open field, he decided that perhaps the direct approach was the only way.

As Frieda finished the last of her dessert pastry, Lewis whispered in Josephine's ear. "Can you come with me a moment?"

She looked at him curiously. "Of course." She left Frieda and followed Lewis. "Is something wrong?"

It was the opening he needed. "Actually . . . yes. During this entire excursion I've longed to spend time alone with you."

"That's nice to hear."

"It's been special to experience all this with you. In fact, I can't imagine experiencing it with anyone else."

She touched his arm. "Thank you, Lewis. I agree."

"So . . . I was thinking that perhaps tonight, during the fireworks, we could sit together, perhaps away from the rest? If that would be agreeable to you?"

Her smile offered him relief. "That would be very nice." She looked to the west. The sun was just beginning to set. "Perhaps you'd like to . . ."

"Like to what?"

"Never mind." She turned her back to the sunset and gave him a smile. "Until later then."

He couldn't wait.

* * * * *

As it grew dark and the fireworks were imminent, Josephine saw Lewis beckoning her toward a chair slightly apart from the others.

Frieda was on immediate alert. "Where are you going, Josephine? It's dark."

She suffered a sigh. "I am off to California to pan for gold." Then she flashed Frieda an impatient look. "I am going to sit with Lewis to watch the fireworks display. Right over there, not twenty yards from your prying eyes."

"Prying? You're going to give me reason to pry?"

"Yes. So leave us alone."

Frieda opened her mouth to say something, then closed it. What could she say? Josephine and Lewis had traveled hundreds of miles together, and he hadn't even tried to kiss her.

Had she wanted him to kiss her?

Absolutely.

That wasn't completely true. During the journey from Washington to Columbus, she had longed for a bit of romance from Lewis, yet since then . . .

Since Hudson Maguire . . .

Since saying good-bye to the latter, she had suffered a mental and emotional war. There was no doubt she was attracted to Hudson—what female wouldn't be? He was a virile, striking, thoughtful man. But beyond the attraction, she had to be practical. It did her no good to think of him. He was heading west and she was heading east. They would never see each other again.

Adding a lock to that door were Papa's comments when they had said good-bye. "I see you and Lewis are still close. Yes?"

"Do you want us to be close?"

"I am agreeable to it. If you are."

With Papa supporting her courtship with Lewis . . . she had to think of the future. She would be twenty-one at the end of February. It was time to marry.

There was no time for silly daydreams about Hudson Maguire.

Frieda interrupted her memories. "After the fireworks, two men are going to read the bumps on our heads. They are phrenigists."

Josephine had heard of such people and understood that most presented the readings with a good dose of humor. "Phrenologists."

"That's it. You should let them give you a reading."

"No thank you." She was confused enough. She didn't need some stranger reading her cranial bumps.

Impatient from waiting for her, Lewis approached. He offered her his arm. "Shall we, Miss Cain?"

With one last look to Frieda—who gave her a final warning by raising a finger—Josephine let Lewis lead her to two chairs set apart from the others.

"There now," he said as they settled in. Then he shivered. "These clear October nights are chilly. Are you warm enough? Would you like me to fetch a buffalo skin?"

The thought of sharing a buffalo skin seemed a bit scandalous. "I will be fine," she said, and changed the subject. "Where are the fireworks going to—?"

As if in answer, there was a loud explosion to the south, near the Platte River. A spray of red stars lit the night. Then another. And another.

"I have seen fireworks displays, but never anything that felt so close. With the land so flat, I wonder what the Indians think of it. Are they afraid? Are they in awe? Are they—?"

Suddenly, Lewis's lips were on hers. Soft lips. Insistent lips.

When he pulled away, she felt regret.

"I've been wanting to do that for weeks. I hope I didn't offend."

She took his hand. "I'm not offended. It was very nice."

Amid the glow of a hundred sparkles, he said, "May I kiss you again?"

"You may."

While kissing Lewis, the mental image of Mr. Maguire appeared, and the memory of *nearly* asking Lewis to go see the sunset with her. She had backed down from that invitation. Like it or not, logical or not, the sunsets would always belong to Hudson Maguire.

But for now . . .

She concentrated on Lewis.

PART TWO

Ideas must work through the brains and arms of men,
or they are no better than dreams.

—RALPH WALDO EMERSON

Chapter Eleven

Hudson leaned over the edge of the roof. "Hand it up, Raleigh."

Raleigh handed Hudson a board for the roof of the general store, then immediately put his hands in his pockets, his shoulders up to his ears. "It's freezing out here. Can't we finish fixing the roof tomorrow?"

"Sure we could, if it didn't look like a storm was coming, and if you're willing to shovel the snow off Mrs. Reed's sacks of flour. Of course then she won't have flour to make the cinnamon bread you take every chance to buy. If you're willing to sacrifice your bread supply then—"

"Fine, fine," he said. "But hurry it up."

Gladly. Although Hudson wouldn't complain about his current duty in Raleigh's earshot, he resented having to rebuild and repair buildings that were only a few months old. *Faster, faster* was the mantra of everyone in the new town of Cheyenne, Wyoming, and of everyone he'd met out west. The buildings were standing insults to every wind that blew through town.

When the ground had grown too cold to lay track, the settlement had burgeoned from a few hundred to over four thousand people, waiting out the winter. But those four thousand could dwindle to a handful as the railroad moved on. Nothing and no one was guaranteed to last.

Ever since the 100th Meridian excursionists returned home and started talking about their grand adventures, all sorts of easterners had come west. Their reasons were varied. Some prospective settlers wanted to buy lots and build houses and businesses. Lots selling for $150 a few months ago were now going for $2,500. But the God-fearing folks weren't alone. Scam artists, drifters, people who didn't fit in back east, and those running from something made up a good portion of the population.

It was hard to tell the good people from the bad. And no one was in charge. They'd tried to form a government, but the criminals had threatened the officials until they quit.

Hudson had assumed the army soldiers at Fort Russell, two miles north, would keep things under control, but they were there to protect the railroad from Indians, not to deal with civilian problems—which were many and varied. In fact, soldiers were told to stay away from the town for their own safety. There was something terribly wrong with that.

"Come *on*, Hudson," Raleigh pleaded. "There's a new game at the Grubstake I want to try."

Hudson stopped his hammering and peered down at his brother. "If you're wanting me to hurry, that's not the way to do it. How much have you lost to those shysters?"

"Just a little. But the new game is called Mexican Monte, and the odds are supposed to be in the players' favor."

Was he really that dumb? "Gambling odds always favor the house. Always."

Raleigh's pout made him look ten years old. "You're no fun."

"Never claimed to be."

"It's not like I'm going to spend my money on the girls at Miss Mandy's." He looked longingly in the direction of the whorehouse that had sprung up alongside the saloons and gambling houses.

Hudson climbed down the ladder, the work finished. "Raleigh . . ."

With a dramatic sigh, his little brother turned his gaze away. "Everyone's going—"

"Not everyone."

"But it's so close."

Hudson nodded in the opposite direction. "That new church is just as close."

Another sigh. "Why's it so hard? Every sort of temptation is right here, and Mum and Da are a thousand miles away and . . . and no one's watching."

"Except God."

"Yeah. I've thought about that."

"Good for you." Hudson felt for his little brother and all the men on the line. "But even I admit it *is* hard."

Raleigh looked surprised. "You're . . . tempted?"

"Don't make me out to be a saint, because I'm far from it."

"So you want to . . . ?" He tilted his head toward the temptations.

"True character is what you do when no one's watching."

Raleigh rocked his head back and forth. "And God's always watching." He moved the ladder from the edge of the roof to the ground by the wall. "But didn't President Lincoln say that folks who have no vices have very few virtues?"

Hudson had to laugh. "So that's why you're wanting to try a few vices on for size?"

He shrugged. "Well . . ."

Hudson put a hand on the back of his brother's neck and squeezed. "The vices are there so you can develop the virtues needed to avoid them. You shouldn't purposely sin and then say, 'Oops. I'm sorry.' It's supposed to be a struggle, one you conquer by tapping in to God's strength and not giving in to your own weaknesses."

"Oh."

"Come back to our room. I'll play you a game of double solitaire."

"If only *that* were tempting."

* * * * *

Josephine paused outside her mother's bedroom door before knocking. Today was her twenty-first birthday, and she was not in a mood to listen to another complaint.

But to go out with Lewis and *not* check in with her mother would have caused worse repercussions.

So she knocked.

"Come in," came Mother's sickly voice—which Josephine had learned could be turned on and off at will.

Josephine didn't mean to sweep into the room, but the intrinsic qualities of the nubbed silk of her gown created a distinct *shwoosh* sound.

Which caused Mother to open one eye. "Another new gown?"

"Not new. I've had it months." A month. "Do you like the rust color? It's called Havannah. Frieda says it brings out the copper in my hair."

Mother gave the gown a good study and ignored the question about its color. "I don't like this new fashion of trains. Dust-catchers, that's what they are. And what are you going to do with all the lovely gowns you have?"

"I told you. Frieda and I are refashioning them. We're attaching tapes to draw the front of each dress to the back in a drapery. Of course I *have* had to get new crinolines and petticoats to support the new silhouette, but the expense is not excessive."

"Hmm."

Lately, any expense was excessive to Mother. Josephine hadn't asked about it, but she had noticed that Cook was serving meat less often, and the fires in the grates were kept ablaze for fewer hours in the day. "Papa is proud of our ingenuity about the dresses. And I asked him if it was all right to spend the money on the underthings and he assured me it was."

"Of course he did."

Josephine regretted bringing up her father. Since he hadn't come home for Christmas, Mother had decided she was ill. Dr. Bennett had been called on multiple occasions, but he'd found no true cause. Yet the elixir he'd instructed Mother to take did help her sleep, which was of some benefit.

To Josephine at least.

And Aunt Bernice. For with Mother indisposed, Aunt Bernice had come out of hibernation and had joined a bridge club. The ladies took the card game quite seriously, but Mother drew the line at ever having them come to the house to play. Which meant Aunt was absent on many afternoons.

Which suited Josephine just fine.

And Lewis.

With the she-bears moved off to other lairs, the parlor was free for courting and put to good use by Lewis and Josephine, with only Frieda present. They had passed many an afternoon and evening there, and had even enjoyed an occasional rousing hand of three-person dominoes.

Though Frieda was lenient enough to let the couple have their private conversations, she never left the room. Which meant nothing untoward ever occurred—not that Josephine would have allowed such a thing anyway. But in spite of the limitations, their relationship had definitely blossomed.

Actually, Lewis seemed very content to stay at home, and he made a concerted effort to amuse her with his sketches, singing, and poetry reading. Yes, it would have been nice to go out, but who was she to complain about love poems? Especially when they led to talk of a future life together. And especially when the winter had been so fierce. Lewis was the one who'd had to brave the weather to come to *her*. He was a true gentleman.

"Where are you off to in such a dress?" Mother asked.

"As it is a special day, Lewis is taking me out to dinner with the Maddoxes."

She waited to see if Mother would take the bait and offer her a birthday greeting.

"But you're wearing long sleeves. A proper dinner dress shows the shoulders, the décolletage, and arms."

"It's the twenty-fifth of February," she said, giving her mother another chance to remember. "I refuse to wear such a dress when it's freezing outside."

"Since when do you defy fashion?"

It was meant to disparage. "Since I am old enough to choose gowns that combine fashion and common sense."

Mother pointed to the train. "A train is not sensible at all."

Perhaps not. Josephine kissed her mother's forehead. "Sleep well." There was no need to add, "Don't wait up," as her mother valued her sleep more than Josephine's well-being.

Or birthday.

Oh well. Hopefully Lewis would make up for it.

* * * * *

Tonight was the night.

Lewis stood on the stoop outside the Cain residence and patted the engagement ring in his pocket.

He'd wanted to propose at Christmas—with General Cain there to give his approval. But when the general had remained out west . . .

Actually, the main reason he hadn't proposed then was for the lack of a ring. Josephine had made it very clear she would not accept any proposal without all the proper accoutrements. As the holidays passed, he could tell she was getting antsy and knew she wouldn't wait for a proposal forever. Besides, he wanted to get on with it.

And so, he'd done what he had to do, and . . .

Tonight was the night.

* * * * *

Lewis handed his menu to the waiter after giving his order. He'd purposely chosen the least expensive items offered. But at the Willard, nothing was *in*expensive.

Alas, Josephine had not chosen with cost in mind, and neither had Rachel or Clark Maddox. Lewis had wanted to have a dinner at the Cain home tonight, but the Maddoxes had invited them out, and as it was Josephine's birthday, he'd agreed.

As if reading his mind, Josephine said, "I am so glad we went out tonight. It has been so long." She looked around the Willard Room and sighed. "Papa often talked about taking me here a second time."

"A second time?" How silly of him to think this would be a new experience for her.

She patted his hand. "I was very young during my previous visit. The Swedish Nightingale, Jenny Lind, was staying here and had some sort of reception in the hotel during her American tour. She sang a few songs. I don't remember anything about the hotel, but I do remember sitting on Papa's lap, and Miss Lind's voice lulling me to sleep."

"So you never returned?" Rachel asked.

She shook her head. "By the time I was old enough to care, the war was upon us." She gave Lewis the most disarming smile. "Actually, I'm glad Papa never got around to it, so Lewis and I could experience it together."

"Look at you two," Rachel said. She tapped her husband's arm with her closed fan. "Perhaps we should leave and give them their privacy."

"No, no," Josephine said. "Mother would have a fit. She had to be convinced to let me go out to a restaurant at all and agreed only because you two are here."

Rachel fluttered her fan. "You make me very relieved to be married, just so I could leave all that silly rigmarole behind. Aren't you glad, Clark?"

"Immensely," he said, though he seemed horribly bored by the whole thing.

Josephine looked around at the other diners and whispered to Lewis, "I am glad to be here, yet I've also enjoyed our times in the parlor, just us two."

"And Frieda. And sometimes your aunt and mother."

"Such are the rules," she said with a pretty smile.

Lewis found the rules of etiquette daunting. And annoying. The sooner he could get her back to the house, the sooner he could propose, and the sooner his stomach would stop its awful churning.

The sooner the better.

* * * * *

Josephine led Lewis into the parlor. "It's getting late. I'm not sure Frieda is even awake. Dowd has gone to fetch her, but you may have to leave." She sat on one end of the sofa, looked up at him, and smiled. "I will say it was a wonderful evening. Dinner was delicious, and—"

"Josephine." Unable to wait any longer, he slid onto the sofa and took her hand in his. "I care for you deeply. Would you do me the honor of being my wife?" He pulled the ring from the pocket of his jacket and held it for her to see.

In the flicker of the candlelight her eyes were as green as the ring's emerald.

"Oh Lewis. Of course I will marry you," she said.

He put the ring on her finger and was relieved it fit.

He ran his thumb across her knuckles. "Are you happy?"

"Completely," she said.

She looked at the ring, turning it in the light. Her forehead furrowed for just a moment, and he worried she was disappointed.

"It—it was my grandmother's."

Her face softened. "Which makes it especially dear. It is very striking. You have exquisite taste."

Beggars can't be choosers.

He drew her to standing and pulled her into an embrace.

"Ahem," Frieda said from the doorway.

Josephine ran to her. "Look! We are betrothed!"

Frieda gave the ring a good looking-at, then said, "What do your parents say?"

"I haven't—"

Lewis intervened. "I asked General Cain for permission when we were out west, and he gave it. Mrs. Cain gave her approval even before the trip."

Frieda's eyebrow rose, and she seemed only partially satisfied.

"You arranged all that?" Josephine asked him.

"I did. For I knew early on you were the one for me." He kissed her hand.

Josephine linked her arm through his. "So you see, Frieda, it is not a complete surprise—to anyone," Josephine said. "You have heard us speak of the possibilities, right here in this room."

"I suppose." Frieda took up her usual position in Aunt's chair near the fire and opened a book.

Josephine drew Lewis back to the sofa. "Where will we live after we're married?"

Whatever your dowry will buy. "I don't really know."

She shook her head, making her earrings bobble. "It doesn't matter. I will live anywhere with you."

He kissed her hand. "And I you."

"I simply pray we will be blessed with love, prosperity, and many children," she said.

Children? He didn't want children.

But prosperity sounded good.

* * * * *

After Lewis left, Frieda held Josephine's left hand under the firelight in the bedroom. "It's quite a large emerald," she said.

"Very large. And the setting is both delicate and intricate. I couldn't be happier with it. Besides, it was his grandmother's. In my eyes, that makes it perfect."

"I suppose you're right." Frieda pulled Josephine into her arms. "Congratulations, Liebchen." She shook her head, looking at Josephine from top to bottom. "I can't believe it. You're all grown up. And engaged. Where did the time go?"

Josephine sighed. "It has been a wonderful birthday," she said, as she removed her amber earrings.

"Now, to tell your mother and aunt."

She froze. "Not tonight."

"Pish-posh. You're not going to bed without telling them."

"But they are sleeping. And Mother is unwell."

"*You* will be unwell if your mother discovers you accepted Mr. Simmons's proposal tonight and didn't tell her. Besides, she apparently gave her permission already, so she'll be pleased. Go on now. You can tell your aunt tomorrow."

Josephine handed Frieda the earrings and walked toward her mother's room. Why was she so reluctant to tell her the good news?

Because I don't want her to say anything to ruin it.

The person she really wanted to tell was Papa. She would write him a letter this very night. He would be pleased. He had been the one to introduce her to Lewis.

Josephine reached her mother's bedroom and put an ear to the door. There was no sound, which was not surprising. Even though Mother approved of Lewis, she would find many negative things to say: *You are not marrying and leaving me alone without your father.* Or, *We don't have the funds for anything lavish.* Or, *I hope Lewis doesn't expect a large dowry.*

Bracing herself for the worst, she entered the room. Mother's bed could be seen in the firelight. She was clearly sleeping.

Leave. Just leave now.

But as Josephine decided to do so, her mother stirred, looked toward the door, then sat up. "Josephine! You nearly scared me to death. What's wrong?"

It was best to just get it done. She walked toward the bed. "Lewis proposed. We are engaged."

To Josephine's surprise, Mother clapped her hands together and beamed. "Finally! I thought he would never get around to it."

She was dumbstruck by her joy. "So you are truly pleased?"

"Of course I am. Your father and I have exchanged many letters over it, and we agree it is a good match."

She held out her arms and wiggled her fingers. "Come here, girl. Let me give you a hug."

Josephine couldn't remember the last time her mother had hugged her—or added a kiss for good measure.

"Go on then," Mother said. "Sleep if you can. We shall start making wedding plans in the morning."

Josephine turned toward the door. Would wonders never cease?

"Josephine?"

She turned back. "Yes?"

"Happy birthday, my dear."

Happy birthday indeed.

* * * * *

The snow fell heavy and hard outside Hudson's room. Tomorrow there would be no work on the buildings, but plenty of work clearing the track so trains could keep coming in from the east. With the railroads temporarily providing free freight there were stockpiles of supplies all over Cheyenne. Last time there was a blizzard it had taken a hundred men ten hours to clear the track.

Raleigh was readying for bed, tucking his long johns into his socks before getting under the freezing covers. "Get some sleep, Hud. You know the general is going to work us to death tomorrow."

"I will. I'm just finishing up a letter to Sarah Ann."

Raleigh pulled the covers up to his ears. "How long has it been since you heard from her?"

"A little bit." It had been three months. Since before Christmas.

"We've got letters from Mum and Da since then."

So I can't blame it on the mail. Actually, Hudson guessed why Sarah Ann's letters had stopped. "She's just mad because I didn't come home for Christmas."

"Rightly so, I'd say."

Hudson swung around in the chair to look at him. "You agreed it was best if we stayed here and kept working."

"For money reasons it makes sense, but for love reasons . . . you should've gone home."

"Now you say this?"

Raleigh turned toward the wall, adjusting the blanket over his shoulders. "Don't blame me. You knew what you were doing. Now hush. I want to sleep."

Hudson returned to the letter. *Dearest Sarah Ann . . .*

Raleigh was right. Hudson *had* known there was a risk in not going back to Pennsylvania for Christmas. But the thought of traveling all that way and entering that *before* world made his stomach clench. Yes, it would have been nice to see Sarah Ann, to hold her and kiss her. She was such a bitty thing that holding her close was like embracing a child.

But having to hear his parents and his brother Ezra talk about working at the mill . . . he felt like an outsider. He'd been away fighting the war for years, and had only been home a few months before he'd heard of the opportunities on the railroad. Allegheny wasn't home to him anymore. It held his childhood memories, but when he thought about the future he found it hard picturing himself there. The mills were a job, not a life.

He looked outside at the huge wet flakes flying by the window. His thoughts of the future were out *there*. Probably not in Cheyenne, but somewhere in the west that was to come. There was something exhilarating about the newness of the plains. Not that *they* were new, but until now only Indians had lived here, only fur trappers had tapped in to their potential. But both of them were transient sorts, and even the wagon trains were just traveling through. To stay put, to have *this* be his destination, not just his route to somewhere else . . .

It was easy for the idea to consume him, and so he finished his letter to Sarah Ann, sending it eastward.

Into his past.

* * * * *

Josephine turned over in bed. Again.

Realizing her eyes were wide open, she sat up. "This is ridiculous."

She rearranged her pillows, creating a comfortable throne. She drew her covers 'round and plopped her arms on top. "There," she said. "Now figure it out so you can get some sleep."

Figure what out?

Problems? Worries? She had neither. She was a happily engaged woman. Yet her sudden sigh spoke volumes she didn't want to hear.

There was a tap on her door, and Frieda stuck her head inside. "You're not asleep."

Josephine shook her head.

Frieda pulled a chair over to the side of the bed. "Tell me."

Right to the point. "Marriage is the next step. I am grown now. It *is* time I marry."

"So you've become betrothed because it's 'time'?"

Not exactly. "I became betrothed because . . ." *Because I was asked by a man who has done nothing to make me* not *love him, a man my parents approve of. How could I refuse?* "It is time I am a wife and start my own family. It is time I have my own house, and get out of this—"

"Yes?"

"Get out of this house for good."

"And?"

"Get away from Mother and Aunt Bernice."

"There you go. The truth is always best."

Josephine looked toward the window. A branch tapped lightly on the pane. "With Papa away, I still feel trapped here."

"If he were home, would you be so eager to marry Lewis?"

Josephine pursed her lips, not liking the answer that came to her. "But all my friends are getting married—or have married. It is my turn."

"So it is a contest?"

"Of course not. But I have dreamed of my wedding all my life."

"So it is the wedding you want, not the marriage."

"No, that is also not true."

Frieda looked at Josephine through her lashes. "You haven't shared the most important reason for marrying Lewis."

Josephine hesitated. "I do love him."

"Do you?"

"Of course I do."

Frieda moved to the bed, pulling her into an embrace. "Oh Liebchen. Having doubts is natural. Every big decision comes with doubts clinging to its side."

"Really?"

"Really." Frieda tucked her in. "Now go to sleep. Tomorrow is a fresh day."

Josephine liked the sound of that.

Chapter Twelve

Lewis walked through the cold with his shoulders raised to his ears. He was weary from working at the butcher shop every day then rushing over to spend time with Josephine. The trouble was, he couldn't ask her for sympathy. He'd told her he was working on some drawings for Mr. Wilson, which was hardly physically exhausting work.

If only it were true. Since the Wilson dinner party, he'd repeatedly approached the man but had been told they'd hired another artist to do their illustrations.

No one shut the door on Lewis Simmons. Not without consequence.

"Simmons? Is that you?"

He turned around and was shocked to see the photographer from the meridian trip. He shook his hand. "Rosewood. How are you?"

"Very fine actually. Come into my studio and tell me what you've been up to."

Only then did Lewis see that he'd walked past a new shop. Two men were inside, painting the name "Rosewood Photography Studio" on the windows in gold letters. Very impressive.

Inside was a photo-taking area complete with intricate, painted back-drops and props such as velvet settees and potted ferns upon Corinthian pedestals. The opposite wall was a gallery of very small photographs, two-and-a-half inches by four. Lewis moved forward for a better look.

"These are wonderful. You got some good ones of the Indians."

"I'd love to get more, but I'm kept busy here—busy enough to open this larger studio. The small *carte de visites* are all the vogue here and in Europe. Queen Victoria is quite a collector."

Lewis had never heard of them.

Rosewood explained. "Visiting cards. Instead of leaving calling cards, some of the upper crust like leaving these small photographs of themselves."

He'd seen such photographs of Josephine's brother and cousin in the Cain parlor.

"They're also small enough to send through the mail." He pointed at the studio area. "I'm getting a steady traffic of people wanting to see pictures of the West, or wanting me to take their own photographs. As you probably know, people are vain."

"Thank goodness."

Rosewood chuckled. Then he froze a moment and peered at Lewis. "Are you going out west again?"

"I wasn't planning on it."

"Because if you were, I could teach you the photographic process, and you could be my legs out there, taking photos, selling them on the spot, and sending plates back to me."

"So you can develop the plates away from a studio?"

"I'd set you up with a traveling darkroom."

It was intriguing. Ambition collided with his plan to marry Josephine. Yet, perhaps the two could be melded. The West . . . He *would* need a new place to settle himself after he carried out his revenge on the general, abandoning the man's daughter and humiliating the Cain family. Or—what if he could hurry up the plan? "How much would I make?"

Rosewood clapped him on the back. "Now we're talking."

* * * * *

"You are doing what?"

Lewis took a step back. "I'm going out west to take photographs."

Even after he'd repeated himself, Josephine couldn't believe what she was hearing. "Since when are you a photographer?"

"Since I crossed paths with Sam Rosewood, the photographer I met on the meridian trip. That's why I'm late coming over here. He was teaching me how to do it."

She remembered the man. Vaguely. "You are leaving me here for weeks? Alone?"

"Actually, I'm going to be gone for quite a while."

"Meaning . . . ?"

"Perhaps a few months."

This was getting worse.

She took her own step back, needing space between them. "What about our wedding plans? And setting a wedding date?"

He grinned and pulled her close, a hand at the small of her back. "How about today?"

She pushed free of him. "Today."

"Then you could go with me." He paused, then said, "I'm leaving tomorrow."

Josephine threw her hands in the air. "Tomorrow? You come here to say you're going off to *my* father's railroad project for a few *months,* and you're leaving *tomorrow*?" She let her hands come to rest on her hips. "This is not the way it's supposed to work, Lewis. We are engaged. We are planning a life together. To-geth-er."

"Yes, we are, and we'll fulfill that plan, we *can* fulfill it by marrying today."

Suddenly, the absurdity of the idea transformed into something palatable. The solution came as a flash, but she was quick and didn't let it pass without her catching it. "I know the answer to all of this. We will not hurry the wedding, but I shall come with you."

The words hung in the air. Outrageous words. Rousing words.

Yet Lewis looked anything but roused, which made her wonder whether he really wanted her along at all.

She slipped her hand around his arm. "I belong wherever you are."

He just stood there, his face blank, as if his thoughts were requiring all his attention.

"Come now, Lewis. It will be wonderful. There is nothing I would like better than to see Papa. Besides, I'm curious about the railroad's progress and how they are going to cross the mountains in Wyoming. I have never seen proper mountains."

A face beyond Lewis's and Papa's flitted through her thoughts. One she had very purposefully nudged aside since last October.

She shoved it aside once again.

"Telegraph your father," Lewis said with a sigh. "Tell him the two of us are coming. And Mrs. Schultz again, I suppose."

"*Tell* him?" She was close to Papa, but even she knew better than to *tell* him something.

"Ask him, using all the pretty words of a loving daughter. Tell him you miss him and—"

She raised a hand, stopping his words. "I know what to say." Then she looked toward the stairs—toward her other hurdle. "Mother will never agree."

"You are an adult. You do not need her permission."

"She *has* been feeling better lately. I'm not sure I could leave her if she were sick."

Lewis took her hand and strode toward the door. "Let's go to the telegraph office. Contact your father first."

"But you were leaving tomorrow."

"I shall postpone my departure." He held her cape. "I shall wait for you."

"*If* Papa says yes."

"He will say yes. He wants to see you as much as you want to see him."

Josephine could only hope that were true, as the anticipation building in her chest was the first she'd felt in months.

* * * * *

Hudson stood in the Cheyenne railway office, waiting for further instructions from General Cain, who was busy going over a map with one of the surveyors. The general glanced up, acknowledged Hudson with a nod, then looked back at the map.

Hudson didn't mind the wait. He had good news to report about a shipment of ties. They'd be ready to begin laying track soon. Although it was backbreaking work, he enjoyed seeing the constant progress, the *knowing* that what he was doing was vital to one of America's dreams. To his dream.

He trembled at the notion that he was a part of something so important. No one would ever remember his name, and history would go on without notice of him, but the people he was working for—General Cain, Thomas Durant, Samuel Reed, General Dodge—these were men that history would embrace. To think that he talked to these men, followed these men, worked with these men . . . that was a fact no one could take away from him.

"Excuse me, General? This just came for you." The telegraph operator sidestepped around Hudson and handed him a note.

The general read it, shook his head no, then said, "Well . . . why not?" He turned to the operator. "Write back, 'I miss you too. Travel with Lewis and Frieda at your convenience.'"

Lewis? Lewis Simmons? Was the note from the general's daughter?

As the operator left to send the message, the general chuckled to himself. "She is a spirited thing."

The surveyor said, "Sir?"

"My daughter." He looked at Hudson. "You know my Josephine."

"Yes, sir. I had the pleasure."

"It appears her fiancé, Mr. Simmons, has found himself an assignment taking photographs out here. And she is coming with him."

Hudson's mind stuck on the word *fiancé.* They'd become engaged? To the general he said, "I'm happy for you, sir. I can only imagine how you've missed her."

"Not going home for Christmas . . . that was hard on me, and on my family. You didn't go home either, did you, Maguire?"

"No, sir. My brother and I decided to stay here and keep earning our nest egg."

"Nest egg?" he asked with a smile. "So you have a sweetheart back home?"

He hesitated, then hesitated some more when he realized he'd hesitated. "Yes, sir. Sarah Ann."

"I'm sure she misses you greatly."

"Hopefully, sir."

The general's eyebrows rose.

"I haven't heard from her since before Christmas."

He stroked his beard. "Letters can be slow in coming. You know that."

"I know that."

Then the general nodded toward the telegraph. "Wire her right now. Tell her you love her. Tell her . . . whatever you want to tell her."

The idea that Sarah Ann could receive a note from him on this very day was almost too much to fathom. But the bigger question was whether she would welcome it.

"You're not going to even try?" The way the general looked over his reading spectacles was a challenge.

"No, sir. I mean, yes, sir. It is worth a try."

The general called out to the operator, "Frank, send Mr. Maguire's message."

"Yes, General."

He shooed Hudson away. "Go tell your girl you love her, and by the time you're through, I'll be ready to listen to your report about the supplies."

Hudson took his time crossing the room. He'd never had a chance like this. He didn't know exactly what to say.

Frank looked up at him, pad and pencil in hand. "Where's it going to? And to whom?"

"Allegheny City, Pennsylvania. To Sarah Ann Daugherty."

"Keep it short. That's the key."

Short. Short was good.

His first inclination was to send: I love you. But somehow, those intimate words sent across the country, over some wire-whatnot . . . it just didn't seem right.

And you aren't sure the words are true, either.

"Come on, man," Frank said. "I have work to do."

"Just write, 'I miss you. Hudson.'"

"That certainly is short."

"Too short? Because I—"

But Frank had already tapped out the message. "All done."

Yes then. All done.

* * * * *

Hudson helped himself to the mashed potatoes, then handed the bowl across the table to Raleigh. He wasn't sure he should say anything to his brother, because if he did, he'd get teased, yet if he didn't—

Suddenly, he heard himself saying, "She's coming."

Raleigh's helping was twice the size of Hudson's. He passed the bowl to the next boarder. "Who's coming?"

Hudson regretted starting this, but he couldn't stop now. "You'll never guess."

"Pass the gravy." Raleigh poured two ladles full on the moat of his potatoes, and another over his meat. Only then did he look at Hudson. "Surely not Sarah Ann."

Surely not.

"Josephine Cain. The general's—"

"I know who she is." He took a bite of potatoes, breaking the levee, allowing the gravy loose. "Why is this any business of yours?"

"It isn't. I was just—"

Raleigh pointed his fork at him. "You're *just* getting yourself into a heap of trouble."

"What trouble? I was stating a fact, a bit of news."

"Yeah, she's some bit-of-news, all right. A five-foot-nothing, perky, freckle-faced bit-of-news."

Hudson wasn't sure how to respond. To get defensive would just egg his brother on. "I simply enjoyed talking to her."

Raleigh leaned close across the table. "Are you sure that's all you did?"

"Are you accusing me of being disloyal to Sarah Ann?"

Raleigh backed off. "I'm just saying. You told me about showing her the sunset. Sounds romantic, that's all."

It *was* romantic.

"I think she could be a convert to the West."

"Is that your goal? Converting her to liking . . ." He swung his fork around the cramped dining room. "The grand life of the Wild West?"

"There's more to the West than what we've had to endure this winter." It was Hudson's turn to point his fork, and he pointed it toward the western point of the compass. "There *is* something grand about what's out there, beyond *here*."

Raleigh went back to his roast, dragging a piece through the potatoes. "The trouble is, neither you or me know if *beyond* here is better than *here*. You're thinking it's heaven, but it could be hell."

It could be. "The thing that intrigues me the most is that we're getting a chance to find that heaven."

"Even if you have to travel through hell to get there?"

It was complicated. This life wasn't easy. Heading through the Wyoming Territory, water would be scarce, the terrain a challenge, and the days interminably long. The months ahead were totally unknown, with only one guarantee: the work was going to be grueling, as bridges and tunnels would have to be built. Yet Hudson felt a spark in his stomach, as though something was burning there, just waiting for the right time to fire up.

"Now you're not so sure about that heaven, are you?" his brother asked.

"I am sure. Just because I can't articulate it—"

"Ar-tic-u-late." Raleigh laughed. "I'm guaranteeing that no one in this entire town can ar-tic-u-late much of anything." He turned to the room. "Right, men?"

Grumbles all around. No one was listening.

Was anyone feeling what he felt? Or were they just going through the motions, doing the work, waiting for a paycheck so they could blow it at a saloon or Miss Mandy's?

Some words came to him. "'Let us run with patience the race that is set before us.'"

Raleigh dug a piece of meat out of his teeth. "Race? Yeah, there *is* a race between the two railroads. But is it *our* race, Hud? Or are we merely pawns in someone else's chess game?"

There had to be more to it than that. He felt it deep inside.

He also felt that somehow Josephine Cain was part of it. Not romantically—she was coming out here with her fiancé—but somehow she was the key to . . . to . . .

The heaven that lay ahead?

It did no good to speculate. God's ways were unfathomable. And talking about any of this to Raleigh or anyone else was not the way to go. But that didn't mean he would stop thinking about it.

* * * * *

Cousin Frieda stood before Josephine, her hands on her hips. "Did you ever consider asking me if I wanted to go? Did you, girl?"

Josephine didn't have time for this. She'd asked Dowd to bring her trunk down from the attic and was already busy packing. "When Mother first said I couldn't go, I had to think of something. And so I reminded her that you would be going with me. And it worked, because she agreed."

"*She* agreed, *she* agreed," Frieda said, pacing back and forth. "I don't want to go west again. I don't want to sleep in a tent and worry about Indians and wild animals and, and . . . and whatever other dangers they have out there now. You used me to get your way."

Josephine stopped folding her nightgowns. Frieda was right. "Yes, I did. And I apologize."

Frieda stopped her pacing and took the nightgowns from her, refolding them *her* way. "At least you admit it."

Josephine ran a hand along her back. "It's just that with Lewis going, and Papa saying yes, I couldn't *not* go."

Frieda's face softened. "You couldn't *not* go. But . . ."

"But what?"

She looked at Josephine, then away. "I was just wondering if there was someone else involved in your desire to go west."

Her stomach clenched. "Someone else?"

"Don't act coy with me."

Josephine was about to deny everything, but just as Frieda knew *her*, she knew Frieda would never give up until she admitted it.

"If you are talking about Hudson Maguire, then—"

Frieda touched the tip of her nose. "He's the one."

She busied herself by going through her jewelry box. There would certainly be no need for much jewelry except for a few ear bobs. "I admit it will be nice to see Mr. Maguire—if he is still there. Papa has written that worker turnover is a huge problem."

"Oh, he'll be there," Frieda said.

Really? "How do you know?"

She shrugged, then said, "'Tis the way God does things."

"What has God got to do with this?"

"The Almighty is very adept at getting people to the right place at the right time."

It was an intriguing thought. "But Mr. Maguire is not the *right* people. He is simply a man I met in Nebraska."

"Who showed you the sunset."

"A sunset. He showed me *a* sunset." But she mentally corrected herself. There was no denying it was *the* sunset. "And I am engaged. I am planning my wedding. To Lewis."

"Planning a wedding is not the same as being married."

No, it wasn't. But Josephine defended herself. "I thought you liked Lewis. I thought you wanted us to marry."

Frieda took the bracelet Lewis had given her out of the jewelry box and pressed it into Josephine's hand.

"Of course. I was planning to bring this."

Frieda sighed. "I do like Lewis, and I do approve of your upcoming marriage. Yet underneath this plump body and wrinkled face, I'm also a romantic at heart. I saw Hudson Maguire looking at you, and I saw you looking at him, and . . . well . . ."

Josephine wanted to hear more. How had Hudson looked at her? "I don't know what you're talking about."

"Deny it all you want, but a spark flashed between you two. A big one."

I know. I felt it.

"I didn't think any more about it because you came home and he stayed out there. Some sparks die. But others . . ."

"Others?"

"Smolder, ready to flame again if circumstances allow."

Circumstances like my going out west again.

"Enough of such talk," Josephine said. "I am engaged to a wonderful man, a budding artist. Besides, Papa *and* Mother approve of the match. And they would never approve of Mr. Maguire, an Irish spiker from who-knows-where."

"Pennsylvania. You told me he was from Pennsylvania. And you're Irish too."

The memories of Hudson rushed back.

"Enough talk. We have packing to do."

Luckily, Josephine was adept at doing two things at once.

* * * * *

Mother did not come to the train station, suffering another bout of avoidance of all things that took effort. Or were her episodes of illness caused by the need for attention, or simply boredom? Josephine supposed it was a little of each.

And so once again, Josephine, Lewis, and Frieda left Washington with no one to see them off.

They watched as the porter loaded their trunks. "It's thrilling to visit Nebraska just weeks after its statehood."

"I doubt much has changed," Lewis said, slipping their tickets in the inner pocket of his coat. "And if passing through Nebraska isn't wild enough, we shall be slipping into Colorado before we end up in Wyoming. Neither of those are states yet."

"I am not looking for anything wild," she said, "just interesting."

"You may get both." He took her arm. "Come now. Let's board. We have a long journey ahead of us."

"But since we have done it before, it should be easier this second time."

He shook his head and checked the number of the car before entering. "Should be, but probably won't be. The first time we had General Dodge and all the others taking care of things for us. This time we're on our own."

She squeezed his arm. "You will take care of us and keep us safe, won't you?"

"I'll do my best." He looked for Frieda. "Mrs. Schultz? You first."

"Don't mind if I do," Frieda said. With one step to go, she turned back to them. "Do you think they'll have those delicious teacakes aboard like last time?"

"I don't think so," Josephine said.

"We're on our own," Lewis repeated.

He did not sound confident.

Chapter Thirteen

Eating was always a production. This trip was *not* like the one on the meridian train at all, with wonderful railcars fitted out with a chef and a dining car. Traveling west this time meant meals had to be found in the depots—quickly. With the mass of passengers disembarking for food and the sanitary facilities, one had to move fast, choose with little consideration to appetite, and eat almost without chewing.

In Chicago the lines were monumental, forcing them to take their food with them and eat on the way back to the train. Josephine ate a sandwich as they walked. The crumbs rained down on her skirt. "I am making a mess," she said.

"We could wait until we get back to the car," Lewis said.

"Too late now," Frieda said. "Besides, I'm famished."

So was Josephine. "Though a ham sandwich is my last choice. Isn't this the third one we've had this trip?"

"Fourth," Lewis said.

"Does no one have any creativity at these food stops?"

Frieda agreed. "If I had a café in such a place, I'd make my mother-in-law's recipes of bratwurst, schnitzel, sauerbraten, sauerkraut, dumplings, and *Bratkartoffeln*."

"Which is?"

"Fried potatoes with bacon." She finished the last of her sandwich. "And *Springerle* biscuits. I still have her mold."

"You are making me hungry *while* I'm eating," Josephine said. A dollop of mustard fell from her sandwich onto her skirt. She stopped walking. "Where is my handkerchief?"

As she managed the rest of her sandwich in order to get into her reticule, a man ran past and grabbed it away from her. "Stop!" she yelled. "Stop him! He stole my bag!"

She glanced at Lewis, but he just stood there. "Do something!"

Again he hesitated.

What is wrong with you?

"Come on!" she said to Frieda.

Because the crowd was so dense, the man hadn't been able to go far. And because they were women, the two of them carved a path. "Let us through! He stole my bag!"

Finally a man grabbed the thief and held him until Josephine caught up.

She was out of breath. "Thank you," she said, taking hold of the reticule.

But the thief wouldn't let go, and when she tugged harder, he broke free.

Until Frieda tripped him, making him fall. And then . . . she sat on him.

Josephine rushed forward with the man who'd first caught the thief, and snatched her reticule back. But before she let him up, she poked the tip of her parasol into his back. "How dare you steal from me!"

A police officer appeared. "Good work," he said to Josephine, his eyes wide with surprise.

"Mrs. Schultz was the heroine."

Frieda smoothed her skirt. Her hat was askew. "I couldn't let him get away. The ingrate."

As the officer took the thief away, the crowd applauded, and Frieda took a bow. Josephine was so proud of her. Of both of them. She thanked the first stranger who'd helped just as the train whistle blew, announcing its departure.

They hurried to their car, only to find Lewis standing outside, looking for them.

Waiting for them.

"Where were you?" he asked.

"Capturing a criminal. Where were you?"

"I . . ."

She pushed past him, up and into the car.

* * * * *

"There he is! There's Papa!"

Josephine waved out the window of the train and was thrilled when Papa waved back. And smiled. Oh, how she had missed that smile.

The farther they'd traveled west, the fewer passengers remained on the train, allowing Josephine to be the first to disembark. Papa didn't even let her feet hit the ground before he put his hands around her waist and lifted her off the step. Then he wrapped her in an embrace. "My darling daughter. I am so glad to see you!"

Josephine let the tears come. Happy tears were always welcome. To hold him, to smell the musky scent that was his alone, to feel his whiskers against her cheek . . . In spite of all the aggravation she had experienced on the trip, being here in his arms was worth everything.

He spread her arms wide, looking her over. "You have not changed a whit. Still the pretty girl with the flashing eyes."

She took offense. "But I have changed, Papa. I'm not a girl anymore. I am a grown woman, an engaged woman." For the first time, she thought about Lewis. He stood with Frieda nearby.

"Lewis," Papa said, extending his hand. "How good to see you. Thank you for bringing my daughter safely to my side."

To his credit, Lewis looked to the ground. Would he mention how brave Josephine and Frieda had been in Chicago? How they had taken care of the thief while he'd idly stood by?

"I'm glad to be here, sir. I'm looking forward to getting started with my photography."

Photography? He mentioned photographs and not their remarkable feat?

Papa tipped his hat toward Frieda. "Nice to see you again, Frieda. These two lovebirds give you any trouble on the trip?"

"I kept them in line."

"Then let's get your luggage and I'll show you where you are going to stay."

Josephine took Papa's arm and walked away with Frieda close behind.

She assumed Lewis followed.

* * * * *

Josephine and Frieda were staying in Papa's personal railcar that sat alone on a siding. The four of them entered the car from a back platform and saw that it was outfitted with furniture like a parlor. "This is where you'll stay," Papa said. He looked at Lewis. "I am afraid you will have to stay in the bunkhouse in town, with the men. There is a boardinghouse and hotel, but they are full at present. I hope that's all right."

"It will be fine, General." Lewis said. But Josephine could tell it wasn't fine. She often felt that Lewis was pickier than she was. He certainly was less adaptable.

Papa stopped at a desk. "This is also where I work when we're on the move. During the winter I stayed in a room off the railway office as the cars were too drafty—not that my room was much better."

Josephine ran her fingers along a narrow table abutting a wall. It was set with three chairs. Then she sat upon a sofa sporting navy upholstery. The car was nice, but cramped. Thinking of all three of them living here was a stretch. She wanted to say something nice, but she also knew that Papa admired her habit of telling the truth. "It is very . . . functional."

He let out a snicker. "That it is." Then he crooked a finger at her and opened the left-most of two doors at the end of the railcar. Inside was a man-sized bed wedged between three walls. On the wall at its foot were hooks for clothing, and at its side was a narrow table with a kerosene lamp. There was enough space to stand beside it, but Josephine's skirt touched both bed and wall.

"Your bedroom," Papa said. "You and Frieda shall have to share. I am sorry it's so small, but we are restricted by width and—"

She kissed him on the cheek. "It is more than I expected. Thank you."

Frieda popped her head in the room, then pulled it out. "It's very nice, General. We'll manage just fine."

He stepped back and offered her the right-hand door. Once opened, it revealed a covered commode, and between it and the doorway a wash-basin on a stand.

"It's a tight fit," Papa said, "But at least you'll have the essentials."

She was very impressed. For him to have thought of every detail was just like him. But then she started. "What about you? We are taking your room. Where will you sleep?"

"In the railway office, where I've been all winter. When we move on, your visit shall be over, and I'll take over this space again."

Papa went out to the landing and instructed some men to bring Josephine's trunk inside. It took up what little free space there was. She hated that their visit was causing him discomfort. But before she could comment, he said, "Now. Let me show you Cheyenne."

* * * * *

Josephine enjoyed being on Papa's arm as he showed her the town. "Once the ground froze and we couldn't lay track, we got to work building the town itself. There are railroad offices, a bunkhouse, washhouse, and mess hall. The windmill pumps in water needed for the trains. We even figured out a way to keep the water from freezing by having it warmed by a stove."

"That's quite ingenious, General," Lewis said.

For some reason Josephine found Lewis's compliments annoying, mostly because there were too many of them. He'd found the mess hall "of good size," the offices "well organized," and the water tower "of beautiful proportion."

He was trying too hard to impress. Had he always been so fawning? Or had she not minded it before because *she* had been the beneficiary of the compliments?

"And this is the most important building for the railroad," Papa said, bringing them to a large, round building constructed out of brick. "This is the roundhouse. Eventually it will hold forty engines, though currently it holds about ten." He pointed to the stone of the foundation. "No wood here. At least we're building this to last."

"To protect your greatest asset, the locomotive," Josephine said.

"Exactly."

Frieda walked along the circular track in front of the building. "I don't understand."

Papa left Josephine's side to explain. "The locomotive travels to this circle in order to turn around so it can rejoin the main line and head east or west, or it can enter the roundhouse for storage or repair."

"How ingenious," she said.

Why didn't Frieda's compliments grate?

In the distance, Josephine saw numerous tents and wagons huddled together. "Are those pioneers?"

"Mormons mostly. Hundreds of them headed west. They're also about to head out now that the rivers and streams are running and the grass is growing for their livestock. They pretty much stay to themselves and away from town."

It seemed an odd comment until Papa led them to the main street of Cheyenne. It boasted a gun store, general store, café, hotel, land office, and around the corner, a gambling house, more than one saloon, and a place called Miss Mandy's. The latter was an odd building with a mixture of wood and dirty canvas tents. A half dozen scantily clad women lolled outside, their wares apparent.

Lewis saw the direction of her gaze. "You're not the only woman here, but I will say you are the only lady."

Josephine tried to act nonchalant, but it was difficult. She had never seen such blatant, immodest, carnal . . .

Frieda yanked on her arm. "Look away, Liebchen. There's no need for you to see such filth and decadence."

Saloons and whores. If Mother could see her now.

"I agree with Frieda," Papa said. "But you came to see it all firsthand. This is the truth of the West, of these hell-on-wheels towns."

"Hell on wheels?"

"During the war, whiskey and women followed the soldiers, and now they've latched on to the railroad. When we move on, they move on."

One of the women, who was greatly endowed in bosom, stepped toward them. "Care to rest awhile, gentlemen?"

Neither Papa nor Lewis responded, but Josephine saw Lewis's eyes linger on the woman's—

"Lewis!" she whispered.

He did not apologize but covered his action with another comment to her father. "I'm sure it's difficult to keep the men in line. You should be commended for it."

"I am commended for nothing. It's impossible to keep them in line," Papa said. "There is no law. And without their families close by to remind them of their morals, the weak men succumb."

Josephine gripped Papa's arm. "It seems most of the men carry guns."

"They got used to guns during the war, and unfortunately those experiences carry over here. Many are battle-scarred." He pointed to his head. "Those are the dangerous ones. The ones who can blow up without warning."

To think of Papa living in such a place all winter . . . "Will you be glad to move on?"

"To get working again, surely. But the people of vice will follow us. There is no escaping them. I wish there—"

Suddenly, a Negro man spilled out of a saloon and ran past them. A second man followed, brandishing a gun. "You get back here, you cheater!"

A shot rang out.

The Negro fell.

Josephine and Frieda screamed and Papa herded them behind himself, shielding them.

But their screams were the only screams. The whores looked on as if nothing was amiss, and one fiddled with the laces of her high-top shoes. Others who walked along the street hurried along, but no one came to the man's aid.

And no one tried to apprehend the killer. He simply walked back into the saloon—to shouts of congratulations. Job well done.

The man on the street groaned. Papa pointed to the general store nearby and told Josephine and Frieda, "Go in there. I'll take care of this."

The women scurried inside—only to find Lewis already there. In the melee, Josephine hadn't seen him take cover.

And leave her out in the open.

"I . . ." he said.

"Why don't you go out there with Papa and help that man?"

"I don't know anything about medicine."

Josephine didn't know what to say. But she did know what to do. "Frieda, stay here." She went to the counter. "Towels? Cloth? Bandages? Do you have anything like that?"

The clerk handed her a towel and a roll of bandages.

Josephine took them outside.

* * * * *

Hudson ran to the general's aid. The injured man had turned onto his back, and Hudson could see a hole in his shoulder. "I'll help you move him," he said.

General Cain looked up and nodded. "Let's get him to my office."

Miss Cain came running out of the general store. She hesitated just a moment upon seeing him, then said, "I have some supplies."

"Good girl," the general said.

The men carried the victim back to the railroad office, and Josephine ran ahead to open the door. There was a large table with papers and maps on it, but she quickly gathered those up to clear it.

The man groaned.

"Get the basin and pitcher."

Josephine brought them close. The two men removed the man's coat, vest, and shirt. With a glance, the general said, "If you're squeamish . . ."

She looked pale but shook her head. "Just tell me what to do."

The general poked his finger in the wound. "Help me see his back." Hudson helped turn the man over. The man screamed at the movement.

"The bullet went all the way through."

"Is that good?" she asked.

"It can be. It means we don't have to do any digging."

She made a face and dipped the towel in the water. "Here."

The general cleaned the wound with a gentle hand. Hudson remembered seeing him help a soldier on the battlefield with the same authoritative but calming touch.

He nodded at Hudson. "There's whiskey over there."

Hudson retrieved the bottle. Once the wound was clean, he offered the man a swig, then poured a goodly amount on both front and back.

The man's scream was primal.

Hudson saw Josephine close her eyes and take a deep breath. He was impressed she'd held herself together. The sight of it made his own stomach roil a bit, though unfortunately, he'd gotten far too used to bullet wounds and blood.

The general took the bandage roll and wrapped it around the man's shoulder while Hudson held him up off the table.

Finally it was done, and they all took a step back. The patient's eyes were closed. The general was breathing heavily. "I think he'll be all right. Thank you for your help. Both of you." He gave his daughter a wink.

"Is he really a cheater?" she asked.

"It doesn't matter. He didn't deserve to be shot."

Her forehead furrowed. "So sorry. I didn't mean to imply that we shouldn't have helped him. I was just . . ."

The general washed his hands in fresh water, then touched her cheek. "I know, sweet girl. It *is* a logical question. Unfortunately, Mr. Maguire and I have become hardened to the guilty and the innocent out here. The line gets blurred by the conditions and the varied histories of the men. We have to go back to the basics of what *any* human deserves and needs."

Her forehead lost its tightness, and Hudson could see how much her father's opinion meant to her. Mutual respect was evident.

Hudson took the bloodied water outside and emptied it on the ground to the side of the building. When he returned, father and daughter were locked in an embrace. "I am so proud of you, Josephine. But I am also sorry you had to witness such a thing."

Hudson started to leave to give them privacy, but the general called him back. "Once again, Mr. Maguire, you have proven yourself indispensable."

"I'm glad I could help." He tipped his hat to Josephine, then turned again to leave.

"Will you join us for dinner tonight?" the general asked. "I have asked the cook to put together something special to commemorate my daughter's visit."

"I'd be honored."

Sometimes good deeds earned a very good payout.

* * * * *

General Cain ordered a table set outside, near his railcar. It was covered with a tablecloth and set for five.

One too many, in Lewis's opinion.

Everything Hudson Maguire did or said was like a needle jammed beneath Lewis's skin. The man was being treated like a hero. All he did was be in the right place at the right time. Running to help that man who'd been shot . . . Maguire was used to this wild, awful place. Lewis was not. So it was logical that when he'd seen the man shot right in front of them, he'd run for cover.

That was only common sense.

But to make matters worse, the general and Maguire knew each other from the war. Soldiers. Bonding. All that rot. The soldier life was *not* for Lewis. The army was the cause of all his family's problems.

"Remember before the Battle of South Mountain, when the cook tried to make raccoon, and a bunch of the men threw it into the bushes?" Maguire said.

"It was foul—at least the way he made it."

"Lieutenant Hayes said he'd rather get shot than eat it again."

"And then he got shot."

Lewis perked up. He'd heard this story before. "Rutherford Hayes?"

"That's the man," the general said. "He was shot at Fox's Gap while leading an attack on Lee's flank."

For the first time, Lewis felt involved. "Hayes was on the meridian excursion." He looked to Josephine. "We heard his stories about the war."

"He was wounded five times," Josephine added.

Point one for me.

"Were you ever shot, Mr. Maguire?" Josephine asked.

He shook his head but looked to his plate. "My brother John was. He was killed at Gettysburg."

Josephine reached across the table toward him. "I am so sorry. I lost my brother too."

The two of them locked eyes, and Lewis didn't like what he saw. Yet it was when they both looked away that he knew the gig was up. They had *forced* themselves to look away.

He hated Hudson Maguire.

Then Maguire looked directly at Lewis. "Which regiment did you fight with?" he asked.

Lewis tried not to hesitate, but his throat was completely dry. "I was in Europe during the war, studying art."

Maguire's right eyebrow rose.

"Where did you study?"

He remembered his faux pas at the Wilson's party. "All over. I traveled to the great cities of Europe and studied the masters." He'd learned it was best to remain vague.

Josephine cocked her head, her eyes on him. "Not the Louvre?"

She knows I was lying about that. He was appalled when he felt himself redden. "I certainly spent a lot of time in the Louvre, sketching the work of the masters, but the Louvre itself does not have a school."

"How handy of you to miss the entire war," Maguire said.

"You have no right to condemn me, Mr. Maguire."

He shrugged. "Sorry to offend."

Lewis *hadn't* missed the entire war, but he couldn't very well tell them that. He looked to Josephine, waiting for her to come to his defense by saying how she was glad that he'd been safely ensconced in Europe during all the fighting.

But Josephine remained silent.

This wasn't good. He *had* to do something to regain her favor. But what?

* * * * *

The dining table had been cleared and removed, and Papa had gone back to the railway office for the night. Lewis and Hudson were off to their respective lodging, and Frieda was preparing for bed.

But Josephine wasn't ready to sleep. Not even close.

She realized she should be exhausted from the day: the arrival in Cheyenne, the tour of the town, the shooting.

Images and sounds flashed through her mind, but not surprisingly, the sound of the gunshot took precedence.

She walked away from the railcar, on the side away from the bustle of the town. She needed to be alone. She needed to let the memory of the sound of President Lincoln's assassination merge with the sound of today's gunshot. A mere second where the air split with a blast and flash. The descriptive word *bang* was not sufficient. She could *bang* two pans together. But she could not create a *blast*. An explosion. That killed.

She drew her shawl tighter and closed her eyes. The memory of the president slumping over into his wife's lap merged with today's image of the man falling to the ground right in front of them.

And then the imagined picture of her brother being shot on the battlefield. Away from his family. Gone forever in an instant.

Josephine shivered.

"Are you chilled, Miss Cain?"

She turned around and saw Mr. Maguire approach. An impulse to say yes so that he might put his arm around her was quickly usurped by the truth. "I am chilled by the memory of today's shooting—and the one I witnessed the day President Lincoln was shot."

He took a place beside her, the two of them facing west where the sun was making its last stand against the day. "Life is precarious."

"And dangerous."

"It can be."

"I used to think otherwise."

"Until the war?"

She hated to admit the next to anyone. "Not even the war could change my penchant for seeing life through rose-colored glasses. The war was going on, and Papa was off leading soldiers to battle, but I was too young, too naïve, and too self-absorbed to let it color my ridiculous view of life."

"Believing life is good is not ridiculous."

"It seems so now, in hindsight. My brother and cousin were killed, and I saw the president murdered. . . ."

"You were actually there?"

She drew in a breath, trying to curb the tears that usually accompanied the memory. "I was there with my parents, watching the play, but not watching it, because I was too busy being jealous of the young woman who had the honor of sitting in the box next to the president." She faced Hudson, letting a tear fall unimpeded. "I was looking right at the box when Booth came in and shot him. I saw the flash. I saw the president fall into his wife's arms. I saw Booth stab Rathbone, the young woman's escort, before leaping to the stage."

"I'm so sorry."

"I'm sorry too—for the president, for the country, but also, selfishly, for me. Because that night was the beginning of the end of my ridiculous optimism."

"Optimism is never ridiculous. Optimism is hope. And hope is essential. Without it, we might as well dig ourselves a hole and crawl inside."

She gave him a smile. "Somehow it doesn't seem appropriate to pair the talk of hope with a grave."

"It's very appropriate. For the opposite of hope is apathy and despair."

Perhaps he had a point. She changed the subject. "Do you think the man who was shot today will be all right?"

"Until the next time."

She was taken aback. "You are implying he'll be shot again?"

"If he takes risks by gambling with crooks, yes. If they win, they get shot. If they lose, they shoot. And if they cheat . . . you saw the results of that." He pointed west. "There are enough risks ahead of us that we can't control. I don't choose to risk death when I don't have to."

"You sound very wise, Mr. Maguire."

He shrugged, then pointed to the sky in front of them. "Look. Another day is done."

The last sliver of the sun fell beneath the earth. Rays of pink and blue shot upward, marking the sun's passing with fanfare.

"You should get back to the train. It's not safe out here at night."

"But I feel very safe with you." She immediately realized how presumptuous and intimate that sounded. "Yes, I should get back."

He led her to the platform of her railcar. "Good night, Miss Cain. I hope I will see you tomorrow."

"That would be nice."

Once she got inside, Frieda was in her bulwark position, staring at her. "Off with Mr. Maguire? In the dark?"

"I took a short walk and he . . ." *Found me? Sought me out?*

"Joined you?"

"Yes." That was a good word. A safer word.

"What are you doing, Liebchen?"

Josephine tossed her shawl on the sofa. "I am not *doing* anything."

"But you're thinking about it."

Yes. Yes, she was.

Chapter Fourteen

Raleigh yawned and put on his shirt. "For your information, the early bird does not get the worm."

Hudson shrugged on his coat, then grabbed his hat. "Are you sure about that?"

"Honestly, Hud. What's up?"

"I simply have an idea of how to spend my time today."

Raleigh's eyebrows rose. "Does it involve a certain daughter of a general, whom you have no right to see because you're virtually engaged to Sarah Ann?"

Yes, there was that.

"What are you doing?" Raleigh asked as he skipped a button and had to start over. "You come back here last night, all puffed up like a kid with his first whisker. That girl has riled you but good."

He didn't want to answer, yet maybe it would be good to hear it from his own mouth. "She's earned my interest. I can't deny it."

Raleigh yanked him hard and pushed him onto the bed. "What about Sarah Ann?"

"She hasn't been writing to me."

"That you know of."

True. Yet best to get down to it. "Being apart like this for months and months, if not years . . . I'm not having the same feelings for her that I had before."

"So the first woman who comes along grabs your attention and makes you forget a girl back home? A girl you made promises to?"

"Miss Cain is not just any woman. She's . . . special."

Raleigh finished buttoning his shirt. "They're all special. At first."

Not all. As the older brother, Hudson had more experience with women—though not *that* much—and he'd met quite a few who weren't special enough to make him want to share more than a *hello*.

But Josephine Cain *was* different. She had interesting thoughts and opinions. Not that most women didn't own both, but he'd never met a woman who was so open to sharing what she was thinking and feeling. Good or bad. It was refreshing.

So much so, that when he'd awakened this morning, he'd known that he had to arrange to see her today—or at least try.

"I gotta go. Wish me luck."

Raleigh shook his head. "I don't think I can do that."

* * * * *

Hudson knew he was being presumptuous, but nothing ventured, nothing gained. . . .

General Cain looked up from his desk. "Yes, Mr. Maguire?"

"I was wondering, since your daughter and Mrs. Schultz are here, if you'd like me to . . . I don't mean to get out of work that needs to be done, but I just thought—"

The general's eyes revealed his understanding. "You're offering to entertain them?"

"Yes, sir. Because I know you're very busy."

The general waved his hands over the stacks of paper on his desk. "That I am." He sighed and sat back in his chair. "I left the ladies finishing up their breakfast in the railcar. Keep them occupied and happy." His face clouded. "But also keep them away from the seedier factions of Cheyenne. Once seen is enough."

"Will do, sir."

* * * * *

Josephine and Frieda finished breakfast. Papa had joined them for a cup of coffee, then left to go to work.

She had no idea where Lewis was.

Or Hudson.

"Now what?" Frieda asked.

Josephine had thought about it. "Now, I want to go watch the preparations for the train heading west. Papa said they were loading carloads of supplies that have been accumulated all winter."

"You can't go out alone."

Actually, she *could*, but she said, "I assumed you would come with me. Surely you're not going to stay in here all day." She stood, grabbing her shawl. "Let's go. The day's a'wasting."

"Wherever did you hear that awful saying?" Frieda asked, shoving the last corner of toast in her mouth.

Josephine ignored the question, picked up a royal-blue hat that matched her dress, then hesitated. "I feel rather haughty wearing a hat like this. Out here."

"You're not haughty, you're showing yourself to be a lady of bearing and breeding. I insist you wear the hat."

Josephine plopped it on her head, stabbing the hatpin in place.

"And take your parasol. I will not have you get more freckled, or heaven forbid, tanned."

She fingered the lace around its edge. "*I* did not pack this."

"*I* did."

"But it's utterly ridiculous. I'm here to see Papa and the men at work, not to go for an outing in the park."

Frieda set her feet with a quick *plop-plop* and stood. "I won't go with you unless you're properly attired."

Josephine knew the battle was lost. She waited for Frieda to put on her own hat, and they exited the train. She popped the parasol open against the morning sun.

But then she saw the sun glimmer off some water a short distance to the south. Judging by the string of trees, it looked to be a stream. The whole setting seemed so peaceful. She headed toward it.

"Where are you going?" Frieda asked as she hurried to catch up.

Josephine pointed ahead. "Just a little detour. Isn't that idyllic?"

"It's just a stream."

She stopped and flashed Frieda a look. "And when was the last time I saw a stream?"

Frieda hesitated. "Never?"

"I am through with the nevers in my life. I am here, the stream is inviting, and so, we are going." She set out again.

"You are the most headstrong—"

"Yes, I am."

The stream was edged by scrub trees, lying low in order to survive the harsh weather. The path of the brook meandered west, varying from narrow enough to wade across to formidable.

"There," Frieda said, glancing back toward the train and civilization. "Now you've seen it. We'd better get back to—"

Josephine heard a baby cry.

She whipped toward the sound and saw an Indian woman bent over her child, who was lying on the ground as if it had fallen.

The woman saw them and grabbed the toddler into her arms. She eyed Josephine, then Frieda.

Frieda ran back a few steps. "Josephine! Come! Run away."

Josephine shook her head, then smiled at the woman. "Don't be afraid." She held out a hand to show it was empty. But her other hand was gripping the opened parasol, so she lowered it.

The woman bounced her baby to comfort it, and Josephine was struck by the universal gesture of all mothers and their children. She stepped closer.

"Josephine, no!" hissed Frieda.

Josephine, yes. Go to her.

As she slowly walked toward the woman and child, Josephine became aware of the tassel on the handle of her parasol. She slowly unwound its string and held it free. "Maybe your baby would like this?"

The woman eyed the tassel, then Josephine's face, then the tassel again. When it seemed as though she wasn't going to flee, Josephine smiled at the baby, who must have been a little over a year old. She held out the tassel. "See the pretty toy?"

The baby did see it and squirmed out of her mother's arms,

insisting on being set down. Then the little one stood and stared at Josephine.

Josephine knelt down to her level. "Hello there, sweet baby." The child's gaze moved from Josephine's face to the tassel. "Would you like this? You can have it."

Both women watched as the baby toddled and teetered her way from mama to tassel. Her dark eyes were intent on the prize.

A dimpled hand reached out and got it. The baby smiled at Josephine. Then back at her mother. *See what I got?*

Josephine smiled. And the mother smiled. And the baby sat on the ground between them shaking the tassel, making the fringe dance.

But then . . . a train whistle shrieked, and both women turned toward the track and the town.

The moment was ended.

"Josephine, come. We need to go," Frieda whispered.

The woman scooped up her child and snatched the tassel from her, handing it back toward Josephine. But Josephine shook her head. "It's yours now. A gift from me to you."

The baby happily took it. Josephine made eye contact with the mother, nodded, and received a nod in return. Then the woman scurried away with the baby on her hip.

Josephine stood still a moment, stunned. Had the exchange really happened?

She looked in the direction that the woman had gone and saw nothing.

All that was left behind was a tassel-less parasol.

And the knowledge that the memory would never leave her.

* * * * *

As they walked along the length of the train, Josephine had never felt so out of place. She had felt more at ease with the Indian mother and child than among this throng of rough men. She was used to turning heads back in Washington—and had relished it. But here, with all these men from such different walks of life, from all parts of the country and the world . . .

She wished she wasn't wearing one of her prettiest dresses: a royal-blue moiré with black trim on the shirred bodice, the cuffs, and along the pleated ruffle around the bottom. Her parasol was a peachy ivory with a black lace overlay. She felt for the tassel and found it gone, and immediately remembered that it now belonged to an Indian child.

Frieda whispered out of the side of her mouth, "You have admirers. Ignore them."

Josephine looked down, avoiding the heat of hundreds of eyes as she picked her way along the muddy path. Some men removed their hats and bowed, some whistled their appreciation, some called out to her, others laughed, others chatted behind upraised hands, and others simply stared.

"Hey there, fancy lady," one called out.

Josephine looked up and drew in a breath. Fancy lady? It could be taken as a compliment, but judging by the grins of the other men, she realized it might be otherwise. So she stopped walking, pulled her hand free of Frieda's arm, and faced the men. "Who said that?" she asked. "Who called me a fancy lady?"

The men were clearly taken aback, and it was hard for Josephine not to look away or start walking again. But then a wizened man with a beard to his waist stepped forward. "I did. And what about it?"

Frieda pointed at him. "Watch yourself, mister. Do you know who this girl is? She's—"

Josephine didn't want Frieda making the introductions. "I am General Cain's daughter, and I am ever so glad to be here."

There were nods, and a few chuckles. The old man stepped back, looked from side to side, then said, "Sorry to offend, Miss Cain. I didn't mean nothing by it. Your father's a good man."

"He were a good general," another said.

"Still is a good general."

There was verbal affirmation, which made Josephine much relieved. "What's your name?" she asked the man.

"Sweetin, miss. Sweet to everyone but my mother."

Josephine smiled, realizing his comment could be taken two ways. "Mr. Sweetin, would you accompany us to where the supplies are being loaded? We would like to see the process."

His smile made a delta of lines appear at the corner of his eyes. "I'd be honored."

Unfortunately, as he led her toward the work, the rest of the men followed.

"Now you've done it," Frieda said. "Your father will *not* be pleased."

It was too late now. She couldn't very well retreat.

* * * * *

"Miss Cain?" Hudson knocked on the door of the railcar a second time.

There was no sound. Was she out and about already?

He left the landing and looked up and down the line. He heard men's voices sounding from the supply yard. Surely she hadn't . . .

Surely she had.

Hudson approached the gathering and saw that work *was* being accomplished—with fervor. It seemed that Josephine's presence was making them work harder, like a thousand suitors vying for her favor.

When a group finished loading a railcar in record time, Josephine applauded. "Bravo, men! I have no doubt such hard work will make the Union Pacific victorious over the Central line."

A cheer rang out.

Hudson stepped beside her. "You certainly know how to rouse the men to work."

She pointed to her head. "It's the hat."

He laughed. "The hat and other things."

She looked adorable when she blushed.

"So, Mr. Maguire, why aren't you working?"

"I am. I have been assigned as your escort for the day." He made a deep bow, playing the cavalier. "Your wish is my command."

"Can't argue with that," Mrs. Schultz said.

He gave the older woman a smile and gave Josephine another. "So? How would you two like to spend your day?"

Josephine pointed past the town. "I have heard there are Mormon families coming through on their way west. I want to visit them. Talk to them."

He admired her choice.

* * * * *

Lewis cracked open one eye and was surprised to see it was morning. He sat up and hit his head on the ceiling. He cursed at the bunk beds.

The room that housed twenty men was empty. He remembered hearing commotion earlier and knew that men were getting up, but then he'd fallen back to sleep.

He dropped to the floor and gathered his clothes. Why hadn't someone awakened him? Now he was late, for surely Josephine was up. He'd told her he would join them for breakfast.

Maybe if he hurried . . .

Ten minutes later, washed, dressed, and carting his photography equipment, Lewis found Josephine's railcar empty but for a man cleaning up the dishes. "Where did Miss Cain go?" he asked.

The man shrugged as he stacked the plates. "I dunno."

"How long has she been gone?"

"I dunno."

Lewis ran out the door. "You're no help."

The man called after him. "You're welcome."

Lewis saw commotion at the other end of the train, so he walked in that direction. Dozens of railcars were being loaded with supplies. General Cain was on his horse, making the entire process run with the precision of a military exercise. He saw Lewis and waved.

The wave changed Lewis's plan. Forget about Josephine. He'd impress her father.

And so he set up his equipment to capture the moment.

* * * * *

"There are so many of them," Josephine exclaimed, as they neared the tents and carts outside of town.

"The Mormon church is bringing four thousand from Europe and England to Utah. We heard that five shiploads crossed the Atlantic and are making their way west. But they want nothing to do with the town. Too bawdy and sinful. Yet it's said that two Mormons were the first inhabitants of Cheyenne."

"So they *do* having something to do with the town."

"Not really. Those two are dead," Hudson said. "They were killed by an Indian attack as the line was being graded, so General Dodge buried them and declared them Cheyenne's first inhabitants."

"That's horrible," Frieda said.

"That's reality."

Two little boys ran out from between the tents, playing tag. A happy dog skittered between them. Clean clothes hung on lines strung between tent posts, and dancing fingers of smoke lifted skyward from cooking fires.

"So," Josephine said, as they came close. "Who do you know here?"

"No one."

She stopped walking. "I assumed you did."

"You assumed wrong."

She lowered her voice. "Then why are we here?"

"You wanted to come."

Frieda shook her head. "You'll quickly learn that it's not always wise to give Josephine what she wants."

Josephine swatted her arm. "Be nice."

But Frieda just shrugged.

Then the little boys detoured toward them, stopping in their path. "Who are you?" asked the taller one.

"I'm Josephine. Who are you?"

"I'm Caleb. And this is my brother, Joseph."

She shook their hands. "Nice to meet you."

"You want to meet our parents?"

Josephine gave Frieda and Hudson a satisfied look. "We would love to."

They had to duck under a clothesline to gain entry into a circle of twenty tents. Other circles were spread around the area, encompassing many acres of land. The boys ran toward their parents, who immediately looked toward the intruders.

The father came forward and tipped his hat. "Caleb announced we had visitors." He nodded toward the town. "You've come from Sodom and Gomorrah."

Hudson seemed to take offense. "There are good people in Cheyenne."

He nodded. "I apologize for my generality. And we do—on occasion—go to town to get supplies." He extended a hand to Hudson. "Jonathan Deever." He looked over his shoulder as three women approached. He opened his arm to include them. "And these are my wives, Mary, Anna, and Martha."

Wives. Josephine had heard about polygamy, but she had never met anyone who practiced it.

Frieda took a step back, but Josephine linked her arm and pulled her forward again. "I'm Josephine and this is my cousin Frieda."

"And I'm Hudson Maguire."

There were nods of acknowledgment all around. Then Josephine saw Martha eyeing her parasol. "It's mighty pretty," she said.

Josephine handed it over for their inspection. Anna approached and touched the sleeve of Josephine's dress. "This fabric is so fine. And ours . . ." She looked down at her faded cotton dress that probably used to be a deep blue.

It was a bit embarrassing.

"May we help you?" Mr. Deever asked.

"We're just here to say hello," Josephine said. "My father runs the railroad crews, and Frieda and I are visiting from Washington, DC."

"We understand what it is to be a long way from home," Deever said. "Mr. Maguire, let me introduce you to the rest of the men."

Hudson looked back at Josephine, his expression asking if she was all right.

She flipped her hand at him. *Go on.* That handled, she returned her attention to the three women—who were being joined by a dozen more, many with babies on their hips or in their arms.

"Look at the sheen of this fabric," Anna said, as if Josephine's dress were hers to promote.

The ladies oohed and ahhed and spoke a few languages Josephine didn't understand. They touched Josephine's dress from drapery to hem, collar to cuff.

One of the women of Josephine's age eyed her hat. "Very smart."

Josephine was glad she'd worn the hat, yet she was also uncomfortable with the attention.

"It's completely impractical," said one of the older women, who stood along the edge of the group. Her arms were crossed, her face sour.

One woman put her hands on her hips and faced her. "Oh, stop being so stodgy, Esther. Our lives are full of *practical*. Sometimes women just want something pretty."

The rest of the group nodded, and one took Josephine's hand. "Your skin is so soft." She put her own hand next to Josephine's. "We're of the same age, yet mine looks old."

"Vanity is a sin," the old woman said.

"I put lard on my skin," another said.

More than one woman made a face. "It smells horrible."

Josephine thought of the jars of face cream and lotion she had back at the railcar. She touched the cheek of a baby, knowing that her own skin was as soft as this child's.

"And these awful freckles," a redheaded woman lamented. "Being in the sun all the time . . . You have my coloring, yet your skin is so fair."

Josephine's first impulse was to advise the woman to stay out of the sun, but she realized that would not be appropriate. So she thought of a second tactic. "If you mix some lemon juice with Venice soap, oil of tartar, and almond oil, you can bleach your freckles. To some extent."

The redhead's eyes grew large. "Really?"

"We don't have any of those ingredients, Rana, so it does no use to think about it."

"Can't the general store get you what you need?" Josephine asked. "Or supply you with face cream or rosewater?"

"Rosewater?"

These women were very ignorant. "Rosewater can be used as a skin toner and makes a delightful hair rinse." More than one woman eyed Josephine's hair. "Of course it also smells delightful."

"We could use a few delightful smells around here."

The women laughed.

"God created people to smell," said the old woman. "That's just the way of it."

Her comment received its own round of giggles and a comment from Martha. "I can guarantee that some smells are from the devil." She nodded to the group. "Our Jonathan is proof of that."

Anna and Mary nodded.

One of the babies started to cry, which made another one wail and the older ones fuss. The women were pulled out of their own concerns and brought back to the needs of their children.

"We'd better go. The children are getting hungry."

As they departed, the redhead touched Josephine's hand and said, "Thank you kindly for the information about the bleach. Maybe when we get settled on the other side of the mountains, I'll mix myself some of that." Then she hurried away.

Watching them, Josephine felt frustrated. "I can't imagine being without the basic comforts of womanhood."

"Certainly you know you've led a privileged life," Frieda said.

She felt herself redden. "Of course I know that. But a few creams and oils are basic. I cannot believe the store in town doesn't carry them. I have a mind to go talk to the owner and convince him to see the advantage of stocking such items. In fact . . ." She looked around for Hudson and saw him talking to some men. She strode over, causing the men to stand and doff their hats. "Gentlemen," she said. "I am afraid I must take Mr. Maguire away from you."

Hudson raised an eyebrow. "Apparently, I've been summoned. Mr. Deever. Gentlemen. Thank you for the conversation."

As they walked back toward town, Hudson asked, "What adventure would you like next, Miss Cain?"

"No adventure. I want you to take me to the general store."

"Is there something you need?"

"Many things."

Chapter Fifteen

"Let's go around, Miss Cain," Hudson said, trying to steer her to a side street.

"But isn't the general store straight ahead?"

"Yes, but your father asked me to keep you away from the bad parts of town."

"Oh pooh," she said. "I have already seen a man shot in front of me. Take me the shortest route, Mr. Maguire—and one that avoids as much mud as possible."

If Josephine thought she gained appreciative attention walking among the workers in the rail yard, within the boundaries of Cheyenne, she was treated like a pariah.

The men setting up the saloon for the day eyed her, hat to shoe. "Care for a drink, Miss Cain?"

She ignored them but whispered to Frieda and Hudson, "They know my name?"

"Word spreads," Hudson said.

"It's rather unnerving."

"Not much you can do about it."

She passed the brothel. The women's blouses were open low, revealing their corsets and more bosom than Josephine thought possible. One stopped and gawked. "What're you doing out of your cage, girlie?"

Cage?

Hudson pointed a finger at them. "Behave yourselves."

They made disparaging motions at him.

"Sorry about that," he said, moving to Josephine's other side to put himself between her and the prostitutes.

"Not much you can do about it," she mimicked. But she pulled Frieda along ever faster.

They entered the general store. Seeing them, the proprietor ran a hand over his oily hair. "Ladies."

Hudson stepped forward. "Mr. Benton, I would like you to meet Miss Cain, the general's daughter, and her cousin, Mrs. Schultz."

He made a little bow. "Pleasure to meet you. Fred Benton, at your service." Then he stopped. "Hey now. I recognize you. You came in here yesterday and took away a towel and bandages. Without paying."

Josephine was shocked. "Thank you for asking after the shooting victim, Mr. Benton. He is recovering nicely."

The man reddened. "Is there something you need? Specifically, I mean?"

"Not specifically. We simply thought it was time we checked your wares."

He stepped back to showcase the few shelves that were stocked. "A little of everything and a lot of nothing, I'm afraid. I stock up when a stagecoach comes through, or a shipment on the train, but it's slow going, and what I do get in gets snatched up pretty fast."

She perused the shelves. "Why don't you have more items that women would like to purchase?"

He made a *harrumph* sound. "Not enough women around to matter."

She pointed in the direction of the pioneers. "What about the pioneer women? I just talked to them, and I know they would appreciate some products to make their lives easier."

He moved to a counter of bowls and spoons. "I got kitchen stuff."

She shook her head. "Your vision is too narrow, Mr. Benton."

A little girl of about ten or eleven slipped into the store. At first Josephine wondered if one of the Mormon children had followed them here, but judging by her dirty appearance, Josephine guessed she wasn't one of theirs. Was she Benton's daughter?

Benton ignored the child and strode toward a china cup and saucer. "Perhaps this would interest you? It's hand-painted in London."

It seemed completely out of place among the more practical offerings of tin plates and cups, leather straps, rope, tent pegs, tobacco, beef jerky, blankets, and knives. Plus, it contradicted his objection to womanly products. "I would bet the women out in the camp would much prefer a few face creams and pretty-yet-practical lengths of fabric to teacups."

He shrugged.

Seeing no other such cup in the store she said, "It seems one of a kind."

"Oh, it is. I don't know why they sent it to me, 'cause I sure ain't gonna sell it to one of the workers, but . . . it seems suited to a fine lady like you—if you don't mind me saying."

She didn't mind. And actually, it was very pretty, with purple violets splayed along the golden rim and around the saucer. "I will take it."

He beamed. "That'll be a dollar, miss."

"That seems excessive, Mr. Benton." Or perhaps it was a way to get paid for the towel and bandages.

"It is excessive," Hudson said.

"You find another one within five hundred miles, and I'll pay you the difference."

Josephine knew he was right. Besides, she wanted him on her side. If she could convince him to stock a few items for feminine sensibilities, it would be worth it. If not for the ladies at the camp, for the ones who were certain to come after them.

She dug into her reticule and handed him a coin.

He looked around the store. "I'm afraid I don't have nothing to wrap it in, Miss Cain."

"No need. Mrs. Schultz and I can carry it safely back to the train."

The little girl was taking things out of one of the boxes and setting them on the shelf. "Is this your daughter?"

Benton shooed her away. "No, miss, she don't belong to me." He raised his voice so she could hear. "And I wouldn't have her. She works at Miss Mandy's and needs to go back where she belongs. Right now."

Surely this sweet young girl wasn't . . . didn't . . .

"Go on now, Nelly. Git."

"But the ladies sent me to—"

"Come back later."

Nelly eyed Josephine, then ran out.

"She is . . . isn't she a little young to be . . . be there?"

"And I'm a little old to be here. Is there something else I can interest you in, Miss Cain? A new blanket perhaps?"

She couldn't imagine needing one of the heavy and itchy-looking blankets. "No thank you. We will be on our way."

"Come again soon."

Not likely.

Hudson fell in place beside her. "I'd offer to carry your cup and saucer, but I think it's best I don't."

She smiled. "It *would* make for an interesting sight."

Frieda looked around nervously. "Around here you might get shot for it."

They walked toward the railcar, but Hudson said, "Let's take the detour I first intended."

Josephine was weary and just wanted to get back using the shortest route possible. "This shorter way will do just fine. Once more, through the gauntlet."

When they passed Miss Mandy's, Josephine couldn't help but look in the open door for the girl. The brothel was bad enough, but using a child . . .

It made her stomach churn.

One woman, tying back a tent flap, nodded at Josephine. Then she mimed drinking tea from a cup. "Keep yer pinky up, missy." The other women laughed and lifted their own pinky fingers.

Josephine realized she was carrying the cup and saucer at chest level, her finger through the handle, as if ready to take a sip. She lowered the pieces to her side and hurried even faster.

Then she saw some movement to her right and spotted Lewis quickly walking around a building, his camera in hand. Had he been photographing the prostitutes?

She didn't want to think about it, so she walked faster.

* * * * *

Hudson hated to see Josephine upset, though he wasn't sure if seeing the girl, Nelly, was the cause, or seeing Lewis near Miss Mandy's. When they reached the general's railcar, he stopped, ready to say his good-byes.

"Oh no, you don't, Mr. Maguire. You must come in. I need your ear."

"Of course," he said, though he wasn't sure he wanted to hear what she had to say.

Once inside, she ripped her hat off her head and threw it on the sofa. Stray hairs found freedom, making her look as wild as her mood.

"That poor girl. How can they use . . . I cannot even imagine such debauchery."

"So don't," Mrs. Schultz said, removing her own hat. "'For as he thinketh in his heart, so is he.' Or she. Or you. Don't let such thoughts come into your mind."

"My thoughts are nothing compared to the reality Nelly faces." She paced up and down before stopping in front of Hudson. "This kind of thing has to be stopped."

"I'm afraid that's going to be difficult, Miss Cain. Prostitution is the oldest profession."

"But it doesn't have to be tempting these men in every spare moment." She looked toward the town. Was she thinking of Simmons? If so, she didn't let on, but continued her rant. "And it should never involve a child."

Mrs. Schultz was nodding. "Never should, but apparently does."

Josephine seemed to consider this a moment. "Then I shall speak with Papa. He'll be able to do something."

She was being naïve. "I'm not sure there's much he *can* do about it. He doesn't have jurisdiction over the town."

"Then who does? Tell me his name and I shall go to the sheriff or the constable or . . . or whatever he is called."

Hudson turned his hat in his hands. "Like we said before, there is no sheriff. There's no law here at all."

"There has to be order and morals and . . . and . . ."

He softened his voice. "There should be, but there isn't."

She sighed heavily.

"I'm sorry. I also wish it were different."

Her jaw clenched. "Do you?"

He was offended. "Of course I do." *Does she really think so little of me?*

Mrs. Schultz put a calming hand on her shoulder. "Josephine, really. You shouldn't attack Mr. Maguire. He's been nothing but kind to us, a real gentleman."

Josephine shrugged her touch away. "But he's a man, isn't he? There would be no prostitutes, no gamblers, no drunks, and no killings if it weren't for men."

She had gone too far. "Don't go lumping all men together, Miss Cain. Should I lump you with—"

Her lips tightened and she pointed toward the door. "Out. Go. Thank you for your time, Mr. Maguire."

This was how she wanted to end the morning?

Her arm remained pointed toward the back of the railcar. Hudson put on his hat, adjusted it, then touched its rim. "Good day, Miss Cain."

As he left the car, Frieda ran after him. "We both thank you, Mr. Maguire. She's just upset. She doesn't mean it."

He nodded to let her know that he'd heard.

And hoped she was right.

* * * * *

"Sit!" Frieda told Josephine.

Josephine fell onto the sofa, feeling as if all strength had left her body. "I know, I know."

"Do you?" Frieda nailed her fists into her hips. "You are rude to Mr. Maguire, accusing him of being as bad as those men who partake of the temptations, when he's been nothing but kind and considerate to us."

Josephine hung her head. "I feel horrible."

"As you should. You're not mad at him. You're mad about seeing Lewis and about that little girl's situation. Neither of which are Mr. Maguire's fault."

Frieda was right of course. But admitting she was wrong . . .

Frieda upped the ante. "If you don't set this right, I will tell your father about you wandering off and meeting the Indian woman."

"I didn't wander off. I merely went for a walk. And you were with me. It was wonderful. I wouldn't take that back for anything."

"You put both of us at risk, Liebchen. You seem to have a penchant for that."

Right again. Josephine had no choice. "Fine. I will go after Mr. Maguire and apologize." She paused at the door. "You won't mention the Indian woman to Papa?"

"We'll see."

"Frieda . . ."

The woman flipped a hand at her. "Go. Make things right. And hurry up about it."

* * * * *

"Mr. Maguire, wait!"

Hudson turned around and saw Josephine running toward him, her skirt grasped in both hands, the edges of her white petticoat dancing. He guessed she was coming to apologize—he hoped she was. The despair he'd felt just moments before began to lift.

She reached him and put a hand to her chest and another at her waist. "I am . . . so . . . sorry," she said between breaths.

You should be was kept to himself. Instead he said, "Good."

She did a double take, obviously expecting him to be more gracious. "I said I was sorry."

"And I said *good*. It doesn't mean I don't accept your apology, because I do." He set his feet solidly before her and pointed toward the town. "I am sorry about all *that too*, but I know better than to blame the entirety of mankind for it."

She blinked. "We are all sinners."

"That we are. And we are all tempted. That's part of being human. But that doesn't mean all of us succumb. Some of us awful men choose to forgo the pleasures of the hell-on-wheels, your father and I being but two. As I started to say . . . should I lump you and Mrs. Schultz into the same group as the women at Miss Mandy's?" He cocked his head and raised his eyebrows, waiting for her to concede the point.

"You win."

That was easy.

He was mesmerized by the curved line that formed in her brow when she was concerned. "I know I was wrong," she said, "and as soon as I said what I did, I wanted to take it back. It was unfair to you. And Papa."

"And other men who choose right over wrong."

She cocked her head. "Are there many of you?"

He wanted to encourage her by saying yes, but couldn't lie. "Not enough."

"Oh."

Now he had *dis*couraged her. He pointed toward the end of the line where the track would soon be laid. "These men who create the railroad from nothing are hardworking men who are doing the work so thousands and tens of thousands of people can come after them. They are sacrificing months and years of their lives, sacrificing their health and the life they left behind . . ." He thought of Sarah Ann and his parents. They seemed to inhabit a different world. As did he. He was no longer the Hudson they knew and loved. He'd changed. This disgusting, awful, inspiring place had changed him.

Forever? Could he ever go back?

"Mr. Maguire?"

Hudson realized he'd momentarily left the here-and-now. "Sorry, I was just thinking."

"Of . . . ?"

"Of what I left behind."

"And who?"

He felt himself redden and hated himself for it. "And who."

"Does she have a name?"

He didn't want to talk to Josephine about it. "Sarah Ann. And I accept your apology, Miss Cain. Now, I'd better check in with your father and get further instructions."

He tipped his hat and walked away.

It took everything in his being not to turn back to look at her.

* * * * *

Papa came back to the railcar for dinner, and Josephine could see he was exhausted. She knew it wasn't a good time to talk to him about much of anything, yet she couldn't help herself.

As soon as he'd washed up and sat down to eat, the words spilled out. "I met a little girl today, at the general store."

"Oh?"

"Her name is Nelly."

"That's nice."

"She works at Miss Mandy's."

His fork stopped in midair. "What do you know about Miss Mandy's?"

"We walked by it—with you. I know it's a brothel. I know it is no place for a little girl."

"I told Hudson to keep you away from the seedy part of town. I—"

"It's not Mr. Maguire's fault. We met Nelly in the general store, and I was the one who insisted on taking the shortcut back, through the bad part of town."

"She's right," Frieda said. "Mr. Maguire tried to steer us 'round it."

Papa sat at the table and cut a piece of chicken. "You need to follow directions, daughter. This is no place for a young lady like yourself to go wandering around at will."

Josephine set her fork down and pushed her plate away. "This is no place for those women either. Whether they chose that life or had it thrust upon them, it is wrong. And it should not be associated with the railroad."

"It's not. It's a private enterprise."

"But it is here because of the railroad. And it is immoral. It's disgusting."

"So is the liquor they serve in the saloons, and the cheating that goes on at the card tables, and the high prices we're charged for supplies."

She hadn't thought about any of that. "Then close them all down. Make it against the law for those places to even exist."

He ate a piece of meat, chewing slowly. Thinking. "I would like nothing better than to do just as you say, if not for the morals of it, for the work time lost. I cannot count the number of men who don't show up because they've partaken of those vices the night before."

"Then talk to Dr. Durant, or General Dodge, or *somebody*. The railroad is all about money and productivity. They will agree."

"I have talked to Durant and other higher-ups. In Columbus—which already had saloons—Durant had us build a sidetrack, away from the saloons, and put our materials over there, hoping to keep the men confined. But the whiskey sellers delivered the booze to the men. Here at Cheyenne, having to be here all winter, the full contingent of temptations has caught up with us and set up shop." He nodded toward the town. "It's bad, it's deplorable, it's disgusting. All those words and more, but there's nothing that can be done about it. If I was able to shut them all down, I'd have a mutiny on my hands. When we're laying track, the men are working sixteen-hour days in atrocious conditions. When we have no work, they are bored. Either way they have to let off a little steam. And not all men partake."

That's what Hudson said.

"I'm sorry you have to witness it, and to even know about it. But there's nothing I can do—"

"But what about Nelly? Grown women selling themselves is one thing, but a little girl . . . there is no excuse for that, no justification."

Papa closed his eyes and scratched his head. "No, there isn't. And I wasn't aware there was a child involved. I'll see what I can do."

"When?"

"When I have time. When I get the supply situation worked out, when I find a way to inspire the men to work as hard as they did last fall, when the spring thaw is over so we don't have to put up with the mud, when I have one day when I don't get a wire from Durant, pushing me to work harder and faster."

"You're a good man, General," Frieda said. "You have the weight of the railroad riding on your shoulders."

"It does feel that way sometimes."

Josephine agreed, and she did appreciate her father's hard work and the issues that weighed on him. "But, Nelly—"

Frieda kicked Josephine under the table and gave her a pointed look. "Nelly will be very appreciative of any help you can give her, General."

But, but, but . . .

Josephine let the subject go, yet the thought of little Nelly in that awful place did not let *her* go.

* * * * *

Lewis walked toward the general's railcar. From the lamps inside he could see the general eating dinner with Josephine and Frieda.

They hadn't invited him.

Not that they had to, but Lewis feared he wasn't invited because of what Josephine had seen this afternoon. More than once he'd thought about approaching the railcar to talk to her about it, about his photographing the whores, but . . .

Was she telling her father about it? That very thought propelled Lewis toward the car. The general's good measure was essential for his future.

He purposely made his boots sound upon the landing, then knocked on the door.

"Come in."

Lewis removed his hat and entered. "Evening, General. Josephine. Mrs. Schultz."

He'd expected Josephine to look away, to ignore him.

She did no such thing.

"Care to explain yourself, Mr. Simmons?" she asked.

The general looked to his daughter, then to Lewis. "What's going on?"

"Would you care to tell him, or would you like me to?" she said.

What had gotten into her? He knew Josephine could be high-spirited, but he never thought of her as openly confrontational.

"Or are you going to deny it?"

My, my. She was on a roll.

"I think you'd better explain yourself," the general said.

"This afternoon I was taking photographs of some of the townspeople—"

"The prostitutes."

He nodded. "It's part of my job. They are a part of the western experience that Mr. Rosewood hired me to photograph."

"If you were so secure in your right to photograph them, why did you slink around the building when you saw us?"

Because he was enjoying the task a bit too much. "I apologize," he said, then thought of an excuse. "I'm as uncomfortable around such vices as you are. I hated being there, and when I saw you I didn't want you to think I was there for . . . for prurient reasons."

"That area of town is bad news," the general said. "I suggest you stay away."

Even if they were good customers and bought a dozen prints?

He turned back to Josephine. "I'll do that. But do you understand now? Am I forgiven?"

She flipped a hand at him, then took up a piece of bread to butter. "So be it."

"Josephine!" Frieda said.

"The man apologized," the general said. "Where are your manners?"

With a sigh, she glanced at Lewis and said, "You are forgiven. Now if you will excuse us, we are in the middle of dinner."

He left quickly but was pleased to hear Josephine being scolded for not inviting him to join them.

* * * * *

Josephine sat at the window of the railcar, looking out at the prairie but seeing nothing.

"Penny for your thoughts?" Frieda asked.

"Before this trip, Lewis and I were making wedding plans."

Frieda sat nearby and gave Josephine her full attention. "Are you having second thoughts?"

Maybe. "*You* like him."

"I liked him." Before Josephine could let this sink in, Frieda added, "I think you need to answer the most important question."

"Which is?"

"Why are you marrying him?"

A laugh escaped.

"It's not a laughing matter, Liebchen. You should be able to list the reasons, and the list should be long."

She was right, and yet the reason that came out first was, "He took me out to the theater and parties and—"

"He got you out of the house."

Well, yes . . .

"Now that you are free from your mother's home, do you still have a good reason?"

"He's generous. Lewis gave me the beautiful ruby bracelet and my engagement ring."

Frieda snickered.

Josephine didn't understand. Frieda was the one who had encouraged the courtship.

"What else makes him good husband material?" Frieda asked.

She thought for a moment. "He is a talented artist."

"Then buy his drawings and photographs. Appreciating his talent doesn't mean you have to marry the man."

What was going on? Josephine shook her head, incredulous. "Why this sudden turnabout?"

Frieda raised a finger. "Everything you've said about Lewis is factual—"

"Thank you."

"But something is missing."

"And what is that?"

"Love."

Why hadn't she even thought about mentioning love? Every point Josephine had made was a cold fact, not an emotion or a desire. Josephine knew her feelings for Lewis had changed, but now she began to question what she had *ever* felt for him.

Frieda put her hand upon Josephine's, her voice soft. "I didn't mean to make you sad."

"I'm not sad, but I am a bit mixed up."

"About?"

Everything.

* * * * *

Hudson pulled his heel across the metal boot scraper outside the boardinghouse. The owner was having a fit about all the mud the men were tracking in. Especially at dinnertime. "Mud and meals don't mix" was her oft-repeated saying. If someone was a repeat offender, he would end up hungry.

Hudson was using a stick to scrape the worst of it off the side of his heel when Lewis Simmons approached.

"Hey, you. Maguire."

He glanced up but kept working on his boot. "Simmons."

The man moved close enough that Hudson could see his shoes. Threateningly close. His work complete, Hudson stood, glad he was a good three inches taller and fifty pounds heftier. "You need something?"

"I need you to stop carrying on with my woman."

The phrase *my woman* struck Hudson as funny, making him smile. "I didn't know Miss Cain was anyone's woman."

"Well, now you do. We're engaged."

"Are you now."

"We are. Ask the general."

"Actually, it was the general who asked me to show them around."

"Only because I was busy with my photography."

"Yeah, I saw you busy with your . . . photography."

Simmons's head drew back an inch. "I'm earning good money for my work."

"Are you selling copies to the women at Miss Mandy's? Or to their customers who want a memento?"

Simmons started to take a swing, but it was so pathetically accomplished that Hudson had plenty of time to see it coming and grab his wrist.

"You really want to start this?" Hudson squeezed. Hard.

Simmons winced. "Let go!"

Hudson did let go but gave Simmons a push in the process. "Stay out of my way."

Simmons regained his footing, massaging his wrist. "You stay out of *my* way. With Josephine."

Hudson tossed the muddy stick on the ground between them. "I think it's up to Miss Cain to decide that."

He walked inside the boardinghouse and was greeted with cheers and a few slaps on the back, as the men who'd been listening from the dining room offered their endorsement.

* * * * *

Lewis stood in front of the building across the street from the boarding-house, and stared at it.

Glared at it.

Hated it.

Hated a certain man inside.

If Hudson Maguire ruined his plan to exact revenge on General Cain through his daughter, he'd be the next victim on Lewis's list.

Chapter Sixteen

Josephine slipped out of bed, being careful not to awaken Frieda. She took her clothes into the main part of the railcar and got dressed as best she could without help. She was in such a hurry that she shunned her corset completely and fastened as many buttons as she could on the back of her dress. She swept her hair into a quick twist and secured it with a few pins, then donned her short cape—which thankfully hid the undone buttons.

The sun was just beginning to rise as she left the railcar and hurried to Papa's office. She found him just sitting down to his desk.

"Josephine. What's got you up so early?"

She had decided to say it straight out. "Nelly."

It took him a moment to comprehend. Then he said, "I told you I'd look into it."

"Would—would today be a good day for that?"

He took the top page from a stack. "Not today."

"But—"

He pointed to piles of papers. "All of these railroad problems need to be handled immediately. I have hundreds of men awaiting my direction." He pointed toward the west. "Out west where the surveying crews are working, a hundred Sioux raided the camp and stole all their horses and mules."

"Was anyone hurt?"

"Not this time. They just wanted the animals. But earlier this spring they attacked a work train and killed three workers. The Indians are a constant threat. The issue of Nelly will have to wait." He rubbed his eyes. "In fact, I'm having second thoughts about your even being here."

"But Papa, I'm fine. I am here with you. I am safe with you."

"Perhaps. But you see why I don't have time for one girl? Please remember that patience is a virtue."

Patience *was* a virtue. One she did not own.

* * * * *

Back at the railcar, Frieda was still asleep, clearly enjoying having the bed to herself. Josephine hated to wake her, but . . .

She gently jostled the bed. When she got no response, she did it harder. And harder.

Finally, "Get up!"

Frieda sat upright, panicked. "What's wrong? What time is it?"

Negotiating the limited space in the tiny sleeping area, Josephine plucked a brown calico from a hook and tossed it on the bed. "Plenty is wrong, and it is time to fix it."

Frieda rubbed her eyes. "What are you talking about?"

"Get dressed."

* * * * *

While Frieda dressed, Albert brought them breakfast. Josephine took a few bites of dry toast. A few minutes later, Frieda emerged, still pinning her hair into a bun. "Oh good. Breakfast."

"We can eat later."

Frieda lifted the lid on a serving bowl of oatmeal. "It will be a leaden lump later."

"So be it." Josephine handed her a hat. "We need to go now, catch them unawares."

"Catch who?"

Josephine tied her own hat beneath her chin and strode toward the door. "The ladies at Miss Mandy's."

Frieda grabbed a fistful of skirt and yanked her back. "Oh no, you don't."

Josephine pulled herself free. "Oh yes, I do. Just this very morning Papa said he didn't have time to deal with Nelly. But I can't wait for when he *has* time. I can't go about my day with that little girl being mistreated a stone's throw away. God won't let me."

"That's all well and good, though I don't presume to know what God wants you to do at this very moment. But the Almighty repeatedly tells us to be wise. This is not wise. It's impulsive."

"But it's right. It is on the side of good. There is nothing good about that girl being brought up in a brothel."

"I agree with you." Frieda took her hand and led her back to the chairs. "Sit."

"But—"

"Indulge me."

Josephine sat, hating that her zeal was being squelched.

Frieda spooned the oatmeal into two bowls. "We will eat and be fortified."

"But I don't want to eat."

"We will eat." Frieda pushed the bowl in front of her and handed her a spoon.

She reluctantly took it and started to take a bite.

But Frieda stopped her with a hand. "But first, we will pray for God's direction and protection. You want both, don't you?"

She hadn't thought about it until now. "I suppose I do."

"I suppose you do." Frieda bowed her head and began to pray aloud. "Let us be strong in the Lord, and in the power of His might. Help us put on the whole armor of God, that we may be able to stand against the wiles of the devil. . . ."

Josephine hated to admit it, but Frieda was right. They needed God's help in this.

* * * * *

Josephine stood near Miss Mandy's and put a hand to her churning stomach. "I shouldn't have eaten."

Frieda put a hand to her own midsection. "Remember, we've put on the breastplate of righteousness—for Nelly."

Her words were strong, but Josephine could tell she was nervous too. The workers were in the rail yard, but people in town were stirring. It was best to do it now, before they risked too much of an audience.

Josephine took Frieda's hand and stopped before the front door-flap of the brothel. If she knocked on the wooden frame, would they answer? She didn't dare just go in. Who knew what they might see.

And so, she knocked, then cleared her throat and said, "Excuse me? Ladies? Anyone?"

She heard voices and shuffling inside, then someone said, "Whatcha want?"

"If I may speak to . . . to Miss Mandy, please?"

There were some half-asleep voices, then a middle-aged woman pulled open the flap. Underneath the blanket wrapped around her shoulders, she wore a chemise and pantaloons. She squinted at the full sunlight. "Well, if it ain't the general's daughter. Bored so soon? Lookin' for some diversion? I could keep ya real busy."

Frieda stepped between Josephine and the madam. "You watch what you say. You are speaking to a lady."

"Beggin' yer pardon I'm sure." She dug sand out of one eye, then glared at Josephine. "Enough of this chitchat. You woke us up. What do you want?"

"Nelly."

Her painted eyebrows rose, and Josephine noticed one was drawn higher than the other. And they were smudged. "How do you know Nelly?"

"I don't know her. I just saw her at the store the other day, and . . . and I want her to come with me."

"Just like that? You ask and I'm supposed to hand Nelly over?"

"She will be safe with me."

Mandy looked up and down the street. "Looks like she's safe with me."

A man stepped out of the saloon across the street. "What's up, Mandy?"

"Seems I'm in the presence of a real, live do-gooder."

He put his hands on the small of his back and arched it. "I hates do-gooders."

"They're not my favorites neither," Mandy said. She looked directly at Josephine. "You've come and made your case, now go back where you belong."

"And don't forget your teacup," a female said from inside, which, of course, elicited giggles.

Frieda tugged on her sleeve and whispered, "Come on, Liebchen."

"Yes, go on, *Liebchen*," Mandy said, shooing her away with her hands. "Leave us women alone."

But then Josephine saw Nelly through the opened doorway. She was standing there with a pile of clothes in her hands. Without thinking twice, Josephine pushed past Mandy, grabbed Nelly's arm, and pulled her out to the street.

"Hey!" Nelly said, dropping the clothes.

Mandy tried to grab her back, but Josephine drew the girl close, wrapping her arms around her torso. Once again, Frieda stepped between. "Let her come with us. It's the right thing to do."

"Letting you steal Nelly is the right thing? How's that the right thing?"

The saloonkeeper came over, along with a dozen other men who'd heard the commotion. Added to that were six of Mandy's girls. . . .

Mandy took advantage of the audience. "She's trying to steal Nelly from us!"

"Stealing ain't right," said a man. "Not even if you's the general's daughter."

Others shouted their agreement.

Josephine was in trouble. Big trouble. *Breastplate? Armor? God? Where are You?* "I am not stealing. I just think the girl would be better off with me, with us."

"She belongs at Mandy's."

That got her ire up. "She most certainly does not!" Josephine scanned the crowd. "You should be ashamed of yourselves. She is a little girl. She does not deserve . . . that."

Suddenly, Josephine saw Hudson Maguire make his way through the crowd. He stood close and addressed them. "Hold on, now. I'm sure this can be rectified to everyone's satisfaction."

"I don't know how," Mandy said. "Miss Priss here is interfering with business. We need Nelly."

The other women nodded, a few winked at Nelly, and one waved.

Nelly waved back.

Hudson pressed his hands downward, quieting the crowd. "Come on, Mandy. What kind of compensation will you need to let Nelly go with Miss Cain?"

Mandy's objections seemed to lessen with the mention of money. "I dunno . . . she's worth a lot to all of us."

Josephine shuddered at her words.

Hudson reached into the pocket of his vest and pulled out some coins. He placed them in her hand. "That enough?"

She quickly palmed them. "Almost . . ."

He pulled out a few more. And with that, the deal was done. Mandy's women retreated into the tent, and the crowd moved along.

Nelly looked up at Josephine. "I'm yours now?"

Josephine hated her wording, but she would clarify the situation later. She put a finger to her lips, then called out, "Miss Mandy? One more thing, please?"

The woman appeared at the flap. "Yes, your highness?"

"Would someone please gather up Nelly's belongings?"

Mandy shook her head. "We'll bring 'em over later."

"Now, please."

Mandy put her hands on her hips. "I gotta give you credit, Priss. You got gumption. Hang on."

"I don't have much," Nelly said.

"But you deserve to keep what you do have."

A minute later, another woman with jet-black hair came out with a small pile of crumpled clothes and a blanket. She pressed the pile into Frieda's arms, then touched Nelly's cheek. "You be okay, Nell?"

"I think so."

The woman thrust a finger in Josephine's face. "You take care of her, or the whole lot of us will make you regret it."

As if *they* had been taking care of her? But Josephine nodded.

When they walked back to the railcar, Josephine felt prickles go up and down her spine, as if any minute someone would rush after them.

It helped that Hudson came along.

"I have to thank you for your help, Mr. Maguire. And for your expense. I will see that you are reimbursed."

"I don't want your father's money."

Josephine felt herself redden, for any repayment *would* come from Papa.

As they reached their railcar, Frieda showed Nelly the view from the back platform of the train. It gave Hudson and Josephine a moment alone. "Now that you have her, what are you going to do with her?"

"I . . . I have no idea."

"Good intentions are sometimes costly."

"I said I would pay you back."

"I wasn't talking about money." He tipped his hat and walked away.

Josephine didn't have time for second thoughts, as Frieda said, "Come on, Josephine. Nelly wants to see inside, and I promised her some breakfast."

* * * * *

Nelly declared their railcar "fancy," though actually, it wasn't. Yet compared to a ramshackle structure made of canvas and scrap wood . . .

As the girl ate the rest of the breakfast food, Josephine and Frieda talked.

"Where is she going to sleep?" Frieda asked.

There was little extra space in their railcar, which already slept two adults.

"She will have to sleep out here on the sofa," Josephine said.

Nelly rose from the table and headed toward the door.

"Where are you going?"

"I need to pee."

"In here, girl," Frieda said, leading her to the washroom. "And we don't say 'pee.'"

"Whatcha call it then?"

"We talk about it as little as possible and if we must, we ask to use the facilities."

"That's an awfully fancy word for pee."

Frieda showed her the covered commode, shut the door on her, and leaned against it. "What are you going to tell your father?"

"I have no idea."

* * * * *

Josephine and Frieda sat outside, watching Nelly pick spring wildflowers. Josephine spotted some men riding toward the river. She recognized the brown coat and hat of Hudson Maguire. "I wonder where they are going."

Frieda fanned herself. The ostrich-feather fan looked ridiculous considering their location, but in their haste to leave, it was the only one Josephine had brought along.

Frieda tapped the closed fan on Josephine's arm. "He's gone now," she said. "You can quit ogling him."

"I am not ogling him. Or anyone."

"Whatever you say."

Had she looked at him longer than necessary? What was there about Hudson Maguire that captured her interest—besides the obvious?

Josephine wrapped her shawl tighter around her shoulders. The spring sun felt wonderful, but the air was still cool. "We owe him so much. If it weren't for his intervening this morning, Nelly would not be with us."

Frieda shook her head. "So having Nelly is a good thing?"

"Of course it is. We saved her from a horrible fate."

"Keep telling yourself that—until your father gets home."

"It is the truth I am going to stress when I talk to him."

Frieda looked up at the sun. "Which will be soon. It's nearly noon."

"Good. Because I'm famished." Josephine took a deep breath. *God, please help this go well.*

As if summoned, they saw Albert approach with their meal.

The hitch in her stomach propelled her to stand. "Nelly, come on back. It is time for lunch."

Nelly came running. "We get to eat again?" She handed Josephine her wildflower bouquet.

"They are very pretty."

"But look at you, girl," Frieda said, brushing off Nelly's skirt. "Dirt all over you." She turned over Nelly's hands. "You need to wash up and make yourself presentable. The general will be home soon."

Josephine lost her appetite.

Chapter Seventeen

They sat at the table in the railcar, which Josephine had moved in front of the sofa, creating a fourth seat for Nelly. Josephine sat at the table to Nelly's left, with Frieda across the table, on Nelly's right. They had her surrounded.

"When the general is here, remember to say *please* and *thank you*, and chew with your mouth closed," Frieda said.

"I always do. Miss Mandy hates hearing people chew."

"Good for her," Frieda said. She took the napkin and handed it to Nelly—who proceeded to tuck it into her collar.

"On the lap will be sufficient." Then Frieda turned to Josephine. "Anything you'd like to add?"

A thousand things. And nothing. What could she tell Nelly when Josephine herself didn't even know how to act when her father came in?

Footsteps and men's voices. He was home.

But when Josephine looked toward the door, she was surprised to see Papa was not alone.

"Look who I brought home for lunch," Papa said, removing his hat. "Hello, lad—"

When Lewis's eyes fell upon Nelly, he faltered, and that break in "ladies" caused Papa to look too.

"Hello," Nelly said.

"Hello, indeed." Lewis looked at Josephine. "Who's she?"

Papa answered for her. "Let me guess. Nelly, is it?"

She nodded. Then she lowered her eyes and pulled her knees up to her chest—or tried to, as the table was in the way.

"Sit up straight," Frieda whispered.

Reluctantly, Nelly sat up properly. But she still didn't look up.

Papa's head made a deliberate turn toward Josephine. "So much for patience."

Josephine would have explained the entire thing if it weren't for Lewis's presence. "The time seemed right."

"For you," he said. "Seemed right for you." He walked past the table. "I need to wash up."

Lewis set his hat on the rack near the door, then took a chair at the table. Papa returned from the washroom. Unfortunately, the only remaining seat was beside Nelly on the sofa.

Too late, Josephine thought of offering her own chair.

"May I sit beside you?" Papa asked the girl.

Nelly scooted over. Way over.

"Thank you," Papa said. He sat on the sofa and looked for a napkin. With Lewis's unexpected arrival they were short a place setting.

Josephine was horrified. "I will go tell Albert to get—"

"No need," Papa said. He spoke to Nelly. "Shall we share some dishes? I will take the plate and you can have the bowl. Will that be all right?"

Nelly nodded.

Then Papa picked up Nelly's fork and spoon. "Which do you prefer, the fork or the spoon?

She took the spoon from him.

"Well now," Papa said. "Shall we say grace?"

Josephine was relieved when Nelly bowed her head.

Papa gave the blessing. "Bless us, O Lord, for these, Thy gifts, which we are about to receive from Thy bounty. Help us to be mindful of all our blessings, and the needs of those who have less. Amen."

"Amen," they all said—including Nelly.

Then he lifted the lid on the bowl. "Yum. Roast beef."

Her eyes wide, Nelly nearly drooled.

"Do you like roast?" Papa asked her.

She shrugged and spoke for the first time since the men had arrived. "I don't get no meat at Miss Mandy's. The ladies do, but she says I don't need none."

"Need any," Josephine said. She immediately felt foolish for it, for Nelly's grammatical failings were the least of the girl's problems.

"She's from Miss Mandy's?" Lewis asked.

Josephine passed him the bread. "Not anymore."

Papa spooned some sliced carrots on Nelly's plate. Nelly pushed one onto her spoon and ate it. "Miss Josephine came and took me."

"So I see," Papa said. "And how did that go, daughter? Did Miss Mandy agree with your opinions and your plan?"

Frieda let a "humph" escape.

"It did not go without incident," Josephine said. "But I didn't expect it would."

"More than one man tried to stop her," Frieda said.

Nelly pointed out the window with her spoon. "You shoulda seen the ruckus."

"There was nearly a riot," Frieda said under her breath.

"There was no such thing," Josephine said. "Really, they exaggerate. Yes, I encountered some resistance, but my goal was accomplished and—"

"Once Miss Mandy got the money . . ." Frieda said.

Nelly nodded, trying to cut a piece of roast with her spoon. "She likes money."

Papa cut it for her. "What money?"

"I didn't pay any money," Josephine said. "Mr. Maguire was kind enough to—"

"So she rightly belongs to him."

Josephine couldn't believe Lewis's words. "She does not belong to anyone. Did we not just fight a war to end slavery?"

"I seem to remember that," Papa said.

Josephine buttered a piece of bread and laid it on Nelly's plate. Nelly set the roast on top and folded the bread over, making a sandwich. Josephine admired her resourcefulness.

"Mr. Maguire rightly concluded that Miss Mandy's objections might be quelled by a few coins."

"She *is* used to being paid for her favors," Lewis said.

"Enough," Papa said to him under his breath.

Lewis looked at his plate.

"Where are you from?" Papa asked Nelly. "Originally."

She looked at Josephine, as if asking whether she should say.

"Go on. Tell us."

"I lived in Council Bluffs. In Iowa, with my parents. But they died."

Josephine's heart melted. "I am so sorry."

"How did they die?" Papa asked.

"Pa pushed Mama down the stairs, then shot himself."

Josephine sucked in a breath, which made her cough.

"That's terrible," Papa said. "I'm sure you miss them very much."

"Not really," Nelly said, taking a bite of her sandwich. "Pa beat me, and Mama used to be a whore till she had me. Miss Mandy and the other ladies are much nicer than they ever were."

Josephine felt tears threaten.

"Can I have some more carrots, please?" Nelly asked.

"Of course." *Anything you want.*

Papa patted his mouth, then set his napkin aside. He said to Josephine, "If I could have a word outside, daughter?"

Josephine followed him, her stomach tight. They stepped away from the railcar. "I am so sorry—"

Papa stopped her words with a hand. "I don't object to having Nelly with us, as it is—"

"You don't?"

"Let me finish. I don't object to having her with us, as it is clear she needed saving. What I do object to is your taking matters into your own hands. You might have been assaulted or shot or who knows what else. This is not Washington. These are not cultured people, nor are they people with high morals or even much common sense. They are out here in the wild because they have a wild streak within them. You yourself witnessed a man shot for far less reason than what you did today, taking Nelly."

"I'm sorry, Papa. But the thought of her spending another day or night at Miss Mandy's made me sick to my stomach. I know you are busy. But I couldn't wait until you had the time. I had the time, so I just did it."

"You always just do it. You're too impulsive. What you want, you take. So far there haven't been any consequences, but your good fortune cannot last forever. One of these days, your impulsive behavior will get you in trouble. And just because Nelly is here with us, it does not mean she's completely safe. There are those who might not take kindly to her absence." He put a finger beneath her chin. "You are the light of my life, sweet girl. I cannot bear the thought of anything happening to you."

She nodded, feeling the same way about him. And now she was doubly glad he didn't know about her meeting the Indian woman. Or the Mormons.

"That's why tomorrow I am sending you back home. To Washington."

"But I don't want to go home yet. I just—"

"We are ready to lay track again. We'll be leaving Cheyenne, heading west into untamed country—as if anything is tamed out here." They both turned toward the sound of a coyote in the distance. "You remember what I told you about the Indian attacks?"

She nodded.

"General Dodge is determined to clean up the Indians and has asked for more troops. Things could turn nasty. You and Frieda *and* Nelly are going home."

"Nelly too?"

He gave her a peeved look. "Wasn't that your plan? You certainly didn't expect me to take care of her."

"No, no," she said. "Not you. I suppose I thought one of the pioneer families would take her in."

"Mormons?" He gave a little laugh. "Mormons who have shunned the town because of its decadence? You thought they would take in a girl from a brothel and make her one of their own?"

It did seem ridiculous. But in truth, she hadn't thought much beyond *taking* Nelly. It was a huge oversight. "But what will Mother say? And Aunt Bernice?"

He held a finger beneath her chin. "You made this bed, so now you must lie in it. Unfortunately it is not just your problem. It will affect Nelly, and Frieda, and those at home. Now do you see the disadvantage of acting impulsively?"

"I can't very well send her back to Miss Mandy's."

"No, you cannot. And so, as a consequence—hopefully as a lesson against future impulsive acts—you must cut short your visit and take Nelly to safety."

She thought of the way they had arrived, with Lewis to accompany them. "What about an escort? Frieda and I cannot travel that far by ourselves. And I don't think Lewis is ready to go back to—"

"I don't want Lewis to go with you."

"You don't?"

"I know you two are engaged, and I also know I supported the match. But after spending time with him here . . . something about him rubs the wrong way."

"It does?"

"I don't mean to disappoint you or disparage him, but there seems to be a certain . . . deficiency in his character."

"Such as?" She wanted him to say it plain.

"He puts himself before others."

Josephine hadn't realized she had been holding her breath until she let it out. "I know."

"You've seen it too?" Papa asked.

"I didn't want to see it. I did my best to ignore it, but . . ." She tried to think of a way to be generous. "He is not you, Papa. You have made me expect high standards in a man, and Lewis . . ."

"Falls short."

She nodded, feeling great relief at having it out in the open. "I thought you supported the match—Mother certainly does—so I left things as they were. But now . . . Would you prefer I was released from the engagement?"

He looked at her for a long moment. "I would."

She let his words sink in and was surprised when the notion did not cause sadness or pain.

Papa pulled her into an embrace. "You have always spoken your mind, Josephine. Although it sometimes gets you in trouble, I much prefer you be frank rather than suffer because you don't wish to cause offense."

She wondered how Lewis would react to the news. Even the thought of ending their betrothal made her stomach clench.

"Can you take us home, Papa? I'm sure Mother would so enjoy seeing you."

He shook his head vehemently. "There is no way I can leave. It will have to be someone else. Someone I can trust." He looked south toward the river, then took in a breath. "I know the man. Maguire. Hudson Maguire."

Josephine's heart beat double-time, but she dared not show her eagerness—or even acknowledge the emotion to herself. With a new breath she said quite calmly, "He *has* proven himself to be trustworthy. And a gentleman."

"I will ask him about it." He walked away as if he was intent on doing just that. But then he turned back. "If I were you, I wouldn't say anything to Lewis just yet."

Josephine nodded, and as she watched him leave, she felt the birth of a smile she had difficulty suppressing. Yes, they were leaving early, and yes, she would have to face the repercussions of bringing Nelly back home. But the fact that Hudson was going to accompany them to Washington?

Her reaction was surprisingly strong. And pleasant.

* * * * *

"What do you think?" the general asked Hudson. "Are you up to the challenge of escorting three females halfway across the country?"

"Well, yes, sir. Though I will say I'm a little stunned by the request. Didn't Simmons bring them out?"

"He did, but I have had a change of heart about him. I need someone I can trust with my most precious jewel, my Josephine." The general looked deep into Hudson's eyes. "Someone I can completely, absolutely trust to see her safely home."

Hudson got the message. "But don't you need me here? We're starting to lay rail tomorrow and—"

"Which only supports my decision to send my daughter home. I must also consider potential trouble with the Indians and the tension Josephine caused by taking the girl."

"Has there been more trouble?"

"Not yet. But I don't want to wait until there is. And by the way . . ." The general pulled out a wallet. "How much do I owe you for your payment to Miss Mandy?"

"It's not necessary."

"It is. The amount please."

"Five dollars."

The general pressed that amount into his hand, then another twenty. "For expenses. I need all of you on that train, heading east. Do you agree to do me this very large favor?"

"I do."

Hudson could think of nothing he'd rather do.

* * * * *

As soon as they finished the meal and Lewis left, Josephine broached the subject of leaving with Frieda and Nelly. "Papa says we are leaving tomorrow," she declared.

Frieda stopped her task of trying to run a comb through Nelly's hair. "So soon? We came all this way for such a short time?"

"Things have changed." She nodded toward Nelly. "Actually, the three of us are going back to Washington, where it is—" She left off the "safe" word and changed direction. "Because it is time."

"What's Washington?" Nelly asked as she played with a hairpin.

"It's where we live. Where you will live now."

The hairpin was forgotten. "But I like it here."

Like it? How can you like it?

"You will like Washington too. My mother and aunt are there and—"

Frieda interrupted. "What will they think of . . . this?"

They will hate it. "They always emphasize how we should help those in need."

Frieda shook her head. Josephine understood her hesitance and doubt, for it was her own.

She added the *pièce de résistance*. "Mr. Maguire will accompany us on our journey."

Frieda dropped the comb. "Not Lewis?"

"Not Lewis. Papa no longer trusts him."

"And he trusts Mr. Maguire?"

"Apparently." Josephine retrieved the comb and handed it to Frieda. "As do I."

Frieda gave her a familiar look. "If the general says so, I will trust Mr. Maguire. But that leaves the larger question."

"Which is?"

"Can I trust *you*?"

"Me?"

"I think you know my meaning."

She did.

* * * * *

While Frieda hung Nelly's now-clean dress to dry on the back platform, a freshly washed Nelly was at the window, looking outside. She was dressed in one of Josephine's nightgowns, the sleeves rolled high. Her brow was dipped in worry.

Josephine moved beside her. "What are you looking at?"

"Will they come get me?"

"Who?"

"Miss Mandy or . . . the sweet man."

Given the way she said it, Josephine guessed the man was anything but sweet. "What sweet man?"

Nelly shook her head and gave a little shudder. Then she looked at Josephine. "Was that Lewis fellow right? Do I belong to that man who paid for me?"

Josephine wanted to cry. She put her arm around Nelly and drew her head against her breast. "No one owns you, Nelly. And you are safe here with me and Frieda and Papa. We won't let anything bad happen to you."

"Or let anyone get me?"

Josephine's throat grew tight. "Or anyone get you." Just let anyone try.

Frieda stood, her work done. "Okay, girl. To bed with you."

Nelly climbed between the covers. "This is soft." She drew the sheet to her nose. "It smells like fresh air."

Josephine knelt beside her, looking into the face of not just *a* child, but *her* child. In spite of all Nelly had endured, there was innocence there. The knowledge that Josephine was taking Nelly away from anything that could further taint that innocence strengthened her.

She took Nelly's hands in hers. "Let's say prayers."

Nelly closed her eyes. "Now I lay me down to sleep . . . "

Josephine joined in, "I pray the Lord my soul to keep."

Frieda stood over them and added her voice, "If I shall die before I wake, I pray the Lord my soul to take."

"Amen," Nelly said with gusto.

Josephine was pleased—and surprised. "Who taught you that prayer?"

"One of the ladies. Miss Vera. She made me say it every night."

"Really?"

Nelly let go of Josephine's hands and turned on her side. "I'm tired."

Josephine stood. "You've had a hard day."

"So have you," Nelly said.

She was a smart little whip.

Josephine leaned down and gave her a kiss good night.

* * * * *

Josephine awakened in the middle of the night, but she wasn't sure of the cause. She lay still and held her breath, but the only sound she heard was Frieda's soft snore beside her.

But then . . .

There it was again. Voices. Soft, but *there*.

Josephine slipped out of bed and looked through the door to the main room that she'd left ajar, just in case Nelly needed them.

Nelly was standing beside the town-side of the railcar, leaning out an open window, talking to someone on the ground below.

Had the "sweet man" come to nab her?

Josephine burst out of the bedroom. "What's going on?"

Nelly jumped back from the window. "I'm just talking to—"

"*Who* are you talking to?" Josephine grabbed her parasol to use as a weapon, then looked out the window, ready to jab anyone who dared get close.

But then she saw it wasn't a man but a woman with black hair, a shawl wrapped close around her.

"It's just Miss Vera," Nelly said.

Vera of the bedtime prayer. Vera who'd brought Nelly's belongings out of the brothel.

Josephine dropped the parasol and stuck her head out the window. "What are you doing here in the middle of the night?"

"I couldn't sleep, thinking about the girl." She pulled the shawl tighter. "I was just seeing she was all right."

Josephine let herself take a fresh breath. Everything was fine. There was no threat in the night. "She is doing well," she told Vera.

Nelly nudged her way beside Josephine. "We're going to Washington tomorrow."

"All that way?"

"My father thinks it best."

Vera looked to Nelly. "You all right going so far?"

Nelly hesitated. "Is it very far?" she asked Vera.

Vera shrugged. "It's a ways." She looked at Josephine. "You take care of her, you hear? She's special."

Josephine was touched by her concern. "I will make sure she's safe."

"And happy. Make her happy."

"I will do my best."

Nelly turned to Josephine. "Can I go hug Miss Vera good-bye? Please."

"I suppose."

Nelly ran toward the door of the railcar and fumbled with the lock. Josephine helped her with the latch, and the girl ran into Vera's arms.

Together they rocked, and Vera kissed the top of her head. "It's good you get away, Nell. But I'll miss you something awful."

"I'll miss you too."

Then Vera let her loose and walked toward the town.

Josephine ushered Nelly back inside and helped her into bed. She was curious about Vera, but her questions could keep until the long trip home. "To sleep now," she said, tucking her in.

"Miss Vera's nice. I'll miss her."

"Maybe we can send her a letter when we get home."

"Really?"

Why not? Sending a letter to a prostitute was nothing compared to taking one into her home.

Chapter Eighteen

Nelly plopped on a chair, her arms crossed. "I don't want to go to Washington. I want to stay here."

Frieda busied herself repacking their trunk. "Don't be silly. There's nothing for you here—nothing you should want, at any rate."

"But some of the ladies are nice. Vera and Jenny. Not Miss Mandy so much, but she's busy with the—"

Frieda pointed at her. "Shush. We don't want to hear what Miss Mandy is busy with, nor do we want to hear about the *ladies* who are not *ladies* at all."

"They're ladies to me," Nelly said, swinging her legs. "They been nice to me."

"Humph."

Josephine had heard enough. Yes, she had met Vera last night, and yes, she had seemed like a nice enough woman, but she didn't even want to think of Nelly's life at Miss Mandy's. It only fueled her need to leave. "Come now, Nelly. It will be a great adventure. And when we arrive home, you will have a pretty room all to yourself, with my old dolls and toys, and I shall buy you some new dresses, and—"

Nelly's eyes lit up. "Can I have a corset with black lace on it like Vera and Jenny have?"

Josephine withheld a shudder. "You're too young to need a corset. Enjoy your freedom while you can. Now up with you." She handed her a small carpetbag.

Nelly began packing with all the enthusiasm of someone cleaning out a privy.

Josephine heard boots on the platform and expected Papa to come in. But then there was a knock.

Frieda went to answer it.

"Good morning," Lewis said. "I wondered if Josephine would like to go for a morning walk to look at the sunrise."

That was nice—but very unlike him. And very badly timed.

Part of her wanted to break their engagement now, before she left Cheyenne, and have it done with. But she dreaded the thought. She had secretly hoped she could leave without having to endure the confrontation just yet.

"Good morning to you too, Lewis," she said. She stepped aside to let him see what they were doing. "But I can't go walking with you, because we are leaving this morning. Going back to Washington."

His brow creased. "But I'm not ready to leave. I still have lots of photographs to take, especially now that they're going to start laying track again. . . ."

She couldn't do it. She just couldn't tell him yet. What if he tried to do something to keep them there? What if he tried to come *with* them as a means to get her to reconsider? "You aren't going, Lewis. We are." She hoped he wouldn't ask for specifics.

He pointed past her, to Nelly. "Is she going with you?"

Josephine stepped between Lewis and his view so she could speak with more confidentiality. "Her safety is one of the reasons we are going. I don't want Miss Mandy to change her mind, or have one of the men . . ." She hoped he wouldn't insist on more details.

"Three women traveling alone? How will you manage?"

Josephine resented his low opinion of her abilities. Who was the one who had run after the thief? "We will manage quite well," she said, deciding not to mention Hudson. "After all, this will be the second time I have made this return trip."

Frieda closed the lid on the trunk. "And we won't be—"

Josephine cut her off. "And we won't be foolish. We will be very careful." She flashed Frieda a look, and the woman looked away.

"But what about me?" Lewis said. "What about our wedding plans?"

She found the order of his concern telling. But Josephine didn't want to risk either Frieda or Nelly mentioning Hudson's name, so she motioned Lewis outside and led him a short distance away. "When we first return home I shall be busy getting Nelly settled, and—"

He stopped walking. "Settled? How can a girl like Nelly get settled back home? Do you really think your mother and aunt will accept her?"

No, she didn't, but that was a worry for another day. "I have to do this whether they accept her or not. I can't *not* help her, Lewis. Don't you understand that?"

He answered with a shake to his head before his words caught up. "No, I don't." He leaned close. "She's a whore."

Josephine felt the spark of anger rise, and she faced him. "She is a little girl who needs help. I believe I was placed here at this time and in this place to help her."

He laughed. "So you're the angel of mercy, swooping down to pluck a nothing-girl from a nothing-whorehouse in a nothing-town?"

The spark fanned into a flame, and she pushed him away, not wanting to be tainted by his boorishness. "If not me, who?"

"No one. Did you ever consider that? Maybe Miss Mandy's is her lot in life. Her place."

She stared at him, incredulous. And then Papa's words returned to her: *I much prefer you be frank rather than suffer because you don't wish to cause offense.*

It was the time to be brutally frank. "You are not the man I want to marry, Lewis. I am sorry, but our engagement is over."

He stepped back, as though her words had physical force. "Our engagement is not over. It can't be."

"It can be, and it is." She stepped away, ridding herself of his presence. "Good-bye, Lewis. Take care of yourself."

"But . . . what happened?" he called after her. "What did I do to cause this? And what happens now?"

Not knowing the answer to his last question, she kept walking.

* * * * *

You stupid, stupid man. You've blown everything.

Lewis strode away from the train, away from the town, walking onto the prairie without seeing or caring.

Why did Nelly ignite his anger and annoy him so much? The brat was the reason Josephine was leaving, the reason she'd called off their engagement.

Surely Josephine didn't mean it. And she couldn't leave. If she did . . . there would be no hope for reconciliation with him here and her in Washington.

She's leaving whether you like it or not.

His thoughts took another tack. With her gone, he'd have to work on the general, slip deeper into his good graces. He would wait a short while, then return to Washington with the father's blessings fortified. Josephine wouldn't refuse her father's wishes for them to marry.

Why had he let his mouth run away with him? He should have known better. The idea of that girl blending into the Cain household *was* a joke, but he should not have said so to Josephine. If he tried hard enough, he might even be able to muster up some pity for the little scamp. Hadn't he been through hard times himself? After he'd deserted the Union army for the second time, he'd had to run behind enemy lines to North Carolina to find his parents. It was either that, or get executed as his friend Smith had been.

As his father had been.

He stopped walking and closed his eyes, pressing his hands to the sides of his head, trying to rid himself of the memory of his fellow Union deserter being marched out, accompanied by a band and four men carrying an empty coffin. That Smith had marched along with them, helping to carry his very own casket, was something Lewis would never understand.

Twelve men with rifles had formed a line, and a chaplain said a few words and put a blindfold on him. Then Smith sat upon his coffin. He raised his hand two times, and on the third, held it straight in front of him.

The rifle shots roared and created a cloud of smoke. Smith fell back but was still kicking, so the shooters stepped up and put their guns right against his head and chest and shot some more.

Appalled and frightened, Lewis had fled into the woods and was sick. His insides spent, he curled up on the leaves and lay there a long time.

After Lewis had deserted the first time, he'd run into Smith hiding out in the woods. It was Smith's idea to re-enlist for the signing bonus, desert a second time, and enlist yet again. It was a good way to make a little money.

But then Smith had bragged about the scheme to the wrong person, and the man had turned him in. He'd gone to his death, arrogant to the last, the soldiers shooting him then mutilating his dead body with gun blasts.

It could have been me.

Lewis felt fairly certain that it *would* have been him eventually, had he not headed south. After two weeks of hiding out in haystacks and caves, he'd found his parents in North Carolina. There he'd joined his father's blockade running, working for the Confederacy. They ran their steamships—which had been painted gray to match the water—into Southern ports at night, sliding around the Union blockades. And his father had done more than that, spying for the South while feigning loyalty to the North. The situation was risky and complicated, but when it came down to it, Lewis hadn't really cared who won the war. A wise man made good use of his circumstances.

He had especially enjoyed the trips to the stunning island of Bermuda, where they stored the goods, until he and some fellow sailors brought yellow fever back to Wilmington. His mother had nursed him to health, but then she'd caught the sickness and died of it. He hadn't lied to Josephine about her death, though he hadn't mentioned that a third of the population of the city had also died from a disease he'd brought home with him.

He might as well have died too, for all the guilt he felt about it. But it wasn't all his fault. If his father hadn't gotten Lewis involved in the blockade running, none of it would have happened. Unexpectedly, his father accepted the blame. He was never quite the same after his wife died, which made him careless. He made mistakes.

And got caught.

When Lewis heard of his father's arrest, he'd rushed to the jail where his father was held. But he'd been too late to help him.

Lewis pressed his hands against his eyes to rid his mind of the most horrendous memory—that of a certain general giving the order to have his father hanged as a spy. With one nod, the hangman had pushed his father off the gallows. The snap of his neck was forever embedded in

Lewis's mind. As was the sight of his body twitching and gyrating until it was still.

That accomplished, General Reginald Cain had simply turned and walked away, as if the hanging had meant nothing. As if the death of Lewis's father was just another task for the day.

With both parents dead, Lewis had gone underground until the end of the war, only bringing with him a few mementos of his life *before*. He'd ended up in Washington. Working at Ford's Theatre the night Lincoln was shot marked a turning point for him, for his illustration of the event had brought recognition of his talent and the possibility of a new profession. And then finding out that General Cain lived in the city and had a pretty daughter . . .

That was when he'd decided to stay. He'd found work at the butcher shop to support himself while he devised his plans.

Without Mr. Connelly, I'd be on the streets. He saved me.

He sat upright. *Like Josephine saved Nelly.*

With a start Lewis recognized the parallel acts of kindness, yet he couldn't move past another fact: he had needing saving just as much as Nelly had.

They were both victims of bad circumstances.

Lewis pulled in a breath. "I am not like Nelly. I'm not. I've risen above my past."

To prove it, he pushed Nelly out of his mind and headed back to town.

* * * * *

Hudson tied his saddlebag shut. "That's it then."

Raleigh sat on his bed and pulled on his boots. "When will you be back?"

He hadn't really thought about it. "I suppose I could turn around and come back right away. My job is to see the ladies home. That's it."

Raleigh stood. "You *could* stop in Pennsylvania. See the folks and Ezra. See Sarah Ann."

He hadn't thought of that. Why hadn't he thought of that? "I suppose I could."

"Your enthusiasm is unconvincing."

Hudson glared at his younger brother.

"If you ask me—"

"I'm not asking you."

Raleigh began again. "If you ask me, it would be the perfect time to get in good with Sarah Ann again."

"She's the one who has stopped writing."

"Then see what's what. You can't chase after a second woman when you haven't let go of the first."

Hudson took his coat off the peg. "I'm not chasing after anyone."

"Only because you don't have to. The general's making it easy for you."

"He asked me to do him a favor."

"Convenient favor."

Hudson put on his coat and brushed some dust from his hat. "Take care of yourself, brother. And behave."

"You're the one who needs to be told to behave."

"I have been—and will continue to be—the perfect gentleman."

"That's no fun."

"Fun or not, it's who I am."

"You're a lovesick fool."

"I'm no fool."

"You're acting like one. You can fool yourself, but you can't fool me. You're in love with that girl. It's probably best you admit it."

But he didn't want to admit it. Not to Raleigh, and not to himself.

"She's engaged to Simmons."

"Then why isn't he taking her home?"

"None of our business."

"Right."

"Don't read something into it that—"

Raleigh walked away, shaking his head. "Foolish *and* blind. That's quite a combination, brother."

* * * * *

Josephine wrapped her arms around her father's waist. "I hate to leave you."

"I hate to see you leave," he said. "But it's for the best—for Nelly's best, and for your own. I am going to be incredibly busy starting today. I barely have time to say good-bye."

She hugged him all the tighter. "When will I see you again?"

He gently pushed her back and looked into her eyes. "It may be awhile, sweet girl. You have other responsibilities now, and we're heading over the mountains. We both have our work to do."

She fingered the buttons of his coat. "I never meant to be tied down like this. I—"

He tipped her chin upward, and none too gently. "You took that girl away from the life she knew, which makes it your responsibility to give her a better life. And don't go pawning her off on your mother or aunt either."

As if they would take her.

"But I'm too young to be the mother of a ten-year-old."

"Then be her big sister."

She saw Lewis running toward them. He was the last person she wanted to see.

"Josephine," he said, gasping for air. "I'm so glad I caught up with you before you left."

"Lewis, please . . ." She suddenly thought of Hudson getting settled in the car with Frieda and Nelly. *Please don't show yourself. Please don't let Lewis see you.*

"Good-bye, Lewis," she told him with as much firmness in her voice as she could muster.

"But, Josephine . . ."

Papa put an arm around Josephine's shoulders and led her toward the train that would take her east. Once on board, he gave her a final kiss. "I love you, daughter."

"I love you too."

He stepped back and made an arm gesture to the locomotive. The whistle sounded and the train began to move away. Josephine rushed to the window to wave.

Papa waved back, blowing her a kiss.

Lewis waved too.

But then the others waved their own good-byes.

Too late, Josephine realized that Lewis would see Hudson waving and—

She yanked his arm down. "Don't do that."

"Why not?"

"Because Lewis doesn't know you're the one taking us home."

Hudson headed toward the door of the railcar. He opened it and stepped onto the platform.

"What are you doing?"

"I don't have to be here. I can still jump down."

"No! Don't."

"Why not?"

The train was gaining speed. She had to say it. "I want you here."

"Do you?"

She put her hand on his arm. "I do."

He turned toward her, and on the narrow landing, he touched her waist. "I want to be here too."

Josephine felt a tingle at his touch. But then she spotted Lewis, watching them go.

Although she was glad she had ended it with him, although she was glad to have Hudson as their escort home, she couldn't help but feel sorry for him.

With a silent prayer that God would watch over him, she turned toward the railcar and went inside, letting the distance between them widen.

"Are you all right?" Hudson asked.

"I will be."

But when Josephine took one last look through the glass of the door, Lewis was gone.

As if he were never there.

* * * * *

Lewis pointed to the train as it pulled away. "Maguire?" He turned to the general. "What is Maguire doing on that train?"

The general walked in the direction of the railway office. "I asked him to go."

"With them? With your daughter?"

"And Frieda and Nelly."

Lewis had to rush to catch up with the general's long strides. "But what about me?"

The general suddenly stopped and faced him. "What about you, Mr. Simmons?"

He was taken aback. "She's my fiancée."

The general shrugged. Shrugged! "Has she spoken with you?"

Lewis played dumb. "About . . . ?"

"The truth of it, Mr. Simmons, is that I want my daughter to marry a man of courage and honor, and I am not sure you are that man."

This wasn't happening. He'd hoped he still had favor with the general. It was his only chance. "I am that man. What have I done to make you say such a thing?"

The general's right eyebrow rose, and he began ticking off points on his fingers. "Number one, you let my daughter and Mrs. Schultz run after a thief in Chicago."

"She told you about that?"

"Number two, during the shooting in front of the gambling hall, you hid in the store, leaving the women open to fire."

"I—I don't like shooting."

The general leaned closer. "And I do?" He eyed Lewis. "There's no shame in being afraid. Self-preservation makes us all want to run the other way. But thinking only of yourself? That's unforgiveable—especially where my daughter is concerned."

He began walking again, and Lewis hurried after him. "So *you're* saying our engagement is off?"

"That's up to my daughter." They reached the rail office. The general went in and closed the door, leaving Lewis outside.

Flummoxed. And seething.

It was all Hudson Maguire's fault.

And the general's.

He'd make sure both paid for their sins against him.

Chapter Nineteen

Josephine watched Nelly gripping the windowsill of the railcar, hunkered low so her chin rested on her hands.

"Is she scared or sad?" she whispered to Frieda. "She's been like that since we left."

Frieda took out her bag of knitting. "Maybe it's because she hasn't been on a train before. She came west on a wagon."

Suddenly, Nelly left her perch and pointed. "What's that?"

They all moved to the windows. For as far as they could see, hundreds of small mounds dotted the land like smallpox. And out of the mounds popped small tan animals. Many stood erect on their back legs and others scurried from one hole to the other.

"That's a prairie dog colony," Hudson said. "They dig elaborate tunnels connecting their underground homes."

A passenger they had picked up in Grand Island joined them. "There's twenty-five square miles of the tunnels on both sides of the railway."

"They're cute," Nelly said. "Can we stop and play with them?"

"You'd never find them," the man said. "They'd scurry underground. If it weren't for the sound of the train, you'd hear them squealing and whistling at us."

Josephine returned to her seat. "Why didn't I notice them before?"

"Maybe we came through in the dark," Frieda said.

Whatever the reason, she was glad to see them now. She was glad for anything that made Nelly happy.

The girl had been quiet since they left Cheyenne, glued to the window and the view. When they'd stopped in Grand Island to eat, she had even refused food. Hudson had bought her a sandwich anyway and taken it on board "for later." But there'd been no *later*.

Hudson stood beside Nelly now, discussing the prairie dogs, and Josephine had a flash of what the trip would have been like if Lewis had been their chaperone.

Lewis wouldn't have bought Nelly a sandwich, and he certainly wouldn't have shared a view with her. Most likely, he'd be sulking in a far corner of the railcar, his sketchpad open, which was his way of erecting a wall when he didn't want to be sociable.

She would have been worried about him *and* Nelly.

Nelly laughed and swatted Hudson in the arm. Then she turned to Josephine. "Can I have my sandwich now? I'm hungry."

Josephine got it out, and Nelly took it back to her seat. She tore off a bit and gave it to Hudson as they continued to talk.

Josephine amended her observation. If Lewis were along, they would all be miserable. But with Hudson here . . .

There was nothing to worry about.

* * * * *

Josephine was awakened from her dozing by the train screeching to a halt. She lurched forward, nearly hitting her head on the row of seats in front of her.

"What's going on?" was repeated by every passenger.

Suddenly, a railroad man ran by the car, yelling at them. "Everybody out! Now!" He pointed to the southwest. "Twister!"

An eerie finger of gray reached down from angry storm clouds. The sky had a sickly, yellow cast as lightning ripped through it, racing the tornado to the ground. Rain began to pelt the train, and some passengers scrambled to close the windows against it.

The inside conductor swatted a hand at their efforts. "Don't worry about that! Get off! Run toward that ditch. Lie down as flat as you can and cover your heads!"

"But we'll get soaked. Shouldn't we stay in—"

"Twisters devour trains and spit them out. You want to be spit out? Now go!"

Two dozen passengers from their car joined a throng of people running the fifty yards to a ditch. "Hold on to each other!" Hudson yelled. He picked Nelly up and pulled Josephine along, and she in turn held on to Frieda.

They lowered their faces against the rain, wind, and debris being hurled and swirled around them. *Please God, keep us safe!*

Once at the ditch, they fell into it, facedown. Josephine wrapped her arm around Frieda on one side and Nelly on the other, and she felt Hudson's protective arm spread over them.

It sounded as if a train were barreling down on them, yet she knew the train was stopped.

"Keep your heads down!" Hudson yelled above the wind.

Nelly whimpered beneath them.

And then it hit. The world moaned and wailed around them, a monster screaming at its prey.

It wasn't the only scream they heard, as the other passengers released their fear. Men, women, children—no one could be brave against nature's hellish fury.

Josephine's skirt whipped against her legs, and the rain felt like nails shot through the air.

"Please God, please God, please . . ." Her prayers melded with those of the others, a communal plea for mercy.

Then she heard the sound of metal straining and creaking. Was the train fighting its own battle against the storm? She wanted to see.

"No! Head down!" Hudson yelled.

And then, as quickly as it attacked, it retreated. Or moved on.

Josephine let herself breathe and felt Hudson's protective cover release her.

"Is it over?" Nelly asked.

"For us," he said as he got to his knees to look. "Unless it turns back on us."

He helped them stand. They were all soaked and muddy, with grass and leaves pasted to their bodies.

But they were alive.

Josephine threw her arms around his neck, and Nelly did the same around his waist. He opened his other arm to Frieda, and the four of them stood as one shaking, soggy, grateful mass.

"Thank God," Josephine said.

A conductor scurried among the people. "Are you all right? Anyone hurt?"

A few had cuts, but nothing worse than that. It was a miracle.

Only then did they turn to look at the train.

"It's still there!" Nelly yelled.

The sides of the cars were plastered with mud and debris, but they were intact.

"Everyone back on the train," the conductor said. "We'll stop in Omaha and let you get cleaned up."

As they slogged through the muddy ground, Josie looked to her left. "Wasn't there a shed over there?"

"Used to be." Hudson helped them board the train.

Everything was covered with muck and damp, but they sat anyway, Nelly huddled with Frieda, and Josephine with Hudson. He wiped a leaf from her temple. "I thank God you're all right," he said.

"I thank God—and you."

She leaned her head against his chest as the train began to move.

* * * * *

It took four hours for everyone to get cleaned up and boarded onto a new train heading east. According to the chatter, the only casualty was one missing valise. It was probably in Iowa by now.

"We could have stayed overnight in a hotel," Hudson said as the train pulled away.

But Josephine shook her head. "I just want to get home as soon as possible."

"Amen to that," said Frieda. "And again, Mr. Maguire, we can't thank you enough for getting us to that ditch. I swear we would have wholly blown away if it weren't for your solid anchor."

Their gratitude embarrassed him. "You've thanked me enough. In fact . . . could I ask a favor of you three?"

"Of course," Josephine said.

"We've traveled five hundred miles and have fifteen hundred to go. Plus, we've survived a tornado. Enough of 'Mr. Maguire.' Please call me Hudson."

When Josephine smiled, a dimple appeared in her right cheek. "And you can call me Josephine."

"And me Frieda," said Mrs. Schultz.

Then Nelly piped up, "You can call me anything but late for dinner." She giggled.

"Where did you hear that saying?" Josephine asked.

"Vera taught it to me."

Hudson tried not to think of what else Vera might have taught her. "I am very glad to call you Josephine, but . . ."

"But?"

"The name doesn't suit you."

"Oh?"

It was hard to explain, and he didn't want her to take offense. "Josephine is the name of a lady of society, and though I know that's what you were born into, I don't think that's who you are."

"Who am I then?" Her hazel eyes were alive with the challenge.

"You are more a . . . Josie."

She cocked her head and looked into the air, considering it. "Josie. I think I like that."

He was relieved. "It has spunk and vigor. Like you."

She nodded, and her smile cemented the transformation. "Then Josie I am."

* * * * *

The miles went on. And on. And on.

The ladies impressed Hudson with their patience. They hardly complained—and that surprised him. He'd expected Josie to grumble about the delay caused by the tornado, the food, the minimal facilities, the noise and soot in the depots, or the constant chatter of the other ladies seated at the far end of the car. Would they ever stop talking?

He was glad the four of them had commandeered two benches that faced each other, which made for easier conversation. Though there was *one* conversation they had avoided since leaving Cheyenne.

Hudson studied Nelly a moment. She was lying on the bench across from Josie and him, her head in Frieda's lap. Her eyes were closed, and she appeared to be sleeping.

It might be now or never . . .

He touched Josie's arm, pulling her attention from the window. "What are you planning for Nelly when you get home?" he whispered.

"I don't know," she whispered back. "I should have thought ahead when I got the notion to pull her out of there, but I didn't."

"You're impulsive," Frieda hissed.

Josie shrugged, then said, "I also never expected Papa to send me home. *Us* home."

"What will your mother think of her?"

Josie made an odd shudder, and Frieda shook her head in short bursts.

"That bad?"

"Worse."

This wasn't good. If the mother rejected her, where would Nelly go? "Is there a local . . ." He didn't want to say it out loud. "A home for her?"

"I'm sure there is," Josie said. "Or a boarding school perhaps."

"I doubt she can read," Frieda whispered.

"Then she will have to learn." Josie sighed. "Let's just pray an answer comes to us."

Frieda nodded, as did Hudson. Josie returned her attention to the view.

It was then Hudson saw Nelly open her eyes. She didn't move otherwise but simply looked at him. What had she heard?

Enough and too much.

What could he say? Or do?

She closed her eyes again, pretending to sleep.

Hudson closed his own eyes and prayed for answers.

* * * * *

Lewis didn't mean to end up in front of Miss Mandy's, but with Josephine breaking off their engagement, and then seeing Maguire on the train with her, and then the browbeating he'd gotten from the general . . .

The women were packing up to move on with the crews.

A pretty woman with black hair looked up at him. "Instead of gawking, you could help."

"I'm not gawking."

"Ogling, then."

He couldn't deny it. No man in his right mind could avoid looking at the women in their scanty attire. Lewis strolled over from across the street. "So you're heading out?"

"In a few days. The next big town is Laramie. It won't take the men long to get there, and where the men go, we go." She pointed to the row of crates the women used to sit upon while they showcased their wares on the porch. "Help me pry these open so we can pack stuff in 'em."

"And what'll I get in return?"

She stopped work and gave him an annoyed look. "Really? You won't help me just to help me?"

I suppose. He took up the pry bar and removed a lid.

"That's the way," she said. "As far as payment, we'll see how good a worker you are."

Lewis worked all the harder.

* * * * *

Her name was Vera.

After paying him for his help with the packing, she got dressed and said, "I do hope Nelly will be all right."

It took him a moment to understand who she was talking about. "She's better off anywhere but here."

She stopped hooking her corset. "Why would you say that?"

He sat up on his elbows. "Come on . . ."

"The girls and I love that little girl. Miss Mandy saved her."

"Saved her for what?"

She smacked him. "What kind of women do you think we are?"

He was confused. "So she didn't . . . work here?"

"No! At least not like that. She did our laundry and mended our clothes."

"That's not what Josephine and the general think."

She pulled a skirt over her head. "Everyone always thinks the worst. Nelly was living on the streets when we came through Council Bluffs. She'd be dead by now if it weren't for us. She was like a little sister."

"Then why did you let her go?"

She fastened the skirt in front, then twisted it so the placket was at the back. "Because she was growing up. There *are* a few men around here who've shown interest when they shouldn't."

The thought made him shudder. "That's disgusting."

"That man Sweetin is disgusting." She put on a blouse and buttoned it. "That's why it's good she's gone, and though Miss Mandy grumbles about it, and we all have more work to do now, I think she's glad too."

All dressed, she threw him his pants. "Now git outta here. I have more packing to do."

"You need more help?"

She put her hands on her hips. "You wanting to work so I'll pay you again?"

He shrugged.

"Go on. I'd rather do it myself."

* * * * *

Josephine looked around the Chicago depot. Memories flooded back. "There! Right over there is where we caught the thief."

Hudson looked in the direction she was pointing. "Caught what thief?"

"The one who stole my reticule last time we came through."

Frieda carried the tin of milk they'd bought. "If it weren't for Josephine and me, she never would have gotten it back."

No thanks to Lewis.

Nelly bobbled one of the apples, and Josephine saved it from the floor. "How did you stop him?" Nelly asked. "Did you hit him? Hit him hard?"

"We didn't hit him." Josephine started to laugh. "Actually, Frieda sat on him, and I poked him with my parasol."

"Really?" Hudson adjusted the stack of sandwiches so they wouldn't fall.

Josephine shrugged. "How else could we hold him until the police showed up?"

Hudson just shook his head. "That's my Josie."

She liked the sound of that.

"Now I know better than to rile you, don't I?" he asked.

"Yes, you do."

They boarded the train and set about eating. From his place by the window Hudson passed the sandwiches around. Ham. Again.

Frieda spread a napkin in Nelly's lap, then in her own. "I will say this trip is a much better experience than the last time."

"I bet," Hudson said.

She glanced at Josephine. "Not just because of the thief incident, but because of the difference in our escort."

Josephine was shocked that Frieda would bring up Lewis. Thinking of him, she looked down at her left hand and noticed . . . the ring.

"Ah!"

"What's wrong?" Frieda asked.

"I didn't give Lewis back his ring!"

As they passed the milk jug around, Hudson asked, "Give it back?"

She realized she hadn't mentioned the broken engagement to him. Actually, she'd hardly thought about it at all since they left Cheyenne. Didn't that prove it was for the best?

"I'm sorry," he said. "You don't have to answer."

She passed the milk to Nelly. "Right before we left Cheyenne, I ended our engagement."

"Why?" He shook his head. "Sorry. I'm prying again."

Josephine waved away his apology, and then she noticed the ruby bracelet that still adorned her wrist. "Oh dear. I need to give this back too."

"Let me see your jewelry," Nelly asked, standing up to get a better look.

Josephine extended her left hand across the space between them.

"That ring's really showy," Nelly said. "I bet it cost more'n a dollar." She sat down again.

Josephine pulled her hand back. "It probably did cost a pretty penny, but I don't need showy."

Frieda snickered.

Josephine flashed her a look. Frieda was diluting her point. "I *like* showy, but I don't need showy."

Why did she feel the need to stipulate in Hudson's presence?

"You can give the ring and bracelet back to Lewis when he returns to Washington," Frieda suggested.

Josephine stared at her hand, then tried to remove the ring. "My hand must be swollen. It won't come off."

"Just as well," Frieda said. "It's safer on your hand than loose in your bag. Wait until we're home."

It was good advice, and Josephine went back to eating. But when she brought her sandwich to her mouth, she caught another glimpse of the ring and lowered her hand so as not to see it. The memory of her last encounter with Lewis flew through her mind and made her shudder as if the wind of it were very, very cold.

Hudson touched her hand, his voice soft. "I'm sorry for bringing it up. I've upset you."

She shook her head. "It's all right. My thoughts and feelings are just a bit tangled at the moment."

"Regarding?"

"Lewis. And . . ."

"And?"

You. Even though she ached to say it aloud, she couldn't. *She* might be free of her romantic ties, but Hudson was not.

Josephine looked out the window, feeling envy for a girl named Sarah Ann.

Chapter Twenty

It was time to reboard the train heading from Pittsburgh to Washington, but Hudson couldn't move. He kept staring at the sign that read *Allegheny City*. He was only a few miles from home.

He should go there. He should see his parents and Ezra.

And Sarah Ann.

He took a step toward the sign, toward the track that would take him home.

But then General Cain's voice played in his mind: *I need someone I can trust with my most precious jewel, my Josephine. Someone I can completely, absolutely trust to see her safely home.*

He stepped back to his original position. He'd promised. And he'd never forgive himself if he left them and something happened.

But can you forgive yourself for being so close to your family and ignoring them?

"Hudson? Is something wrong?"

It was Josie. He shut his eyes against the sign pointing home, and found a smile.

Luckily, where Josie was concerned it wasn't hard to find.

* * * * *

As they neared Washington, Josephine's nerves began to dance in a syncopated rhythm. "I wish we'd had the chance to buy Nelly a new dress and coat. She looks like a ragamuffin."

"I look like a muffin?"

"Shush, girl," Frieda said, halting the near-constant swing of Nelly's legs.

Hudson stood and spread his arms. "Am I presentable? Or do you want to doll me up too?"

Actually, he was shabby by eastern standards. His boots needed a dozen coats of polish, there was a small rip in the knee of his right trouser leg, his wool coat was missing a button, and his rawhide vest—which had looked so appropriate on the prairie—looked primitive among the city folk on the train. And his brown, fur-felt Stetson hat . . .

The men around him wore top hats or derbies, long sack coats, checkered vests, and narrow trousers. Rugged boots were nowhere to be seen.

Apparently, with her delay, he made his own conclusion. "So be it. I am what I am."

Yes, you are. Which was one reason she was so attracted to him.

But then he contradicted himself as he added, "Out west I couldn't care less about my appearance, but the thought of meeting your mother and aunt has me worried."

"Don't worry another minute about them." *I will worry enough for the both of us.*

* * * * *

Nelly sat on her knees and stuck her head outside the carriage window. Her hair blew every which way.

"Sit down, girl, or I will never get a comb through your hair," Frieda said.

"No, let her see," Josephine said. The girl's enthusiasm for Washington sparked her own pride.

"What's that?" Nelly asked, pointing to a large square stack of limestone about a hundred feet high.

"That's going to be a monument to George Washington, but they stopped building it before the war."

"I suppose they had a few other things on their minds," Hudson said.

A few minutes later, Nelly let out a long "oooh." "Who lives there?" she asked.

"The president."

"Who's he?"

Josephine exchanged a glance with Frieda and Hudson. Nelly's ignorance was alarming, yet considering her background and childhood . . . president, king, or queen, what did it matter?

"President Johnson is the president of the United States," Josephine said.

"All thirty-seven of them," Frieda added.

"It's a fancy house," Nelly said.

"Actually, it's in a sorry state. The floor needs refinishing, and some visitors have even pinched tassels off the furniture or been bold enough to cut souvenirs from the draperies and carpets. Mrs. Lincoln bought some wonderful new furniture but despaired at how the public treated what was already there."

"I don't like that aspect of human nature," Hudson said. "People should never just take something because they want it."

Josephine nodded, yet she couldn't help letting her mind move from souvenirs to more personal subjects—and inclinations.

Frieda returned to the description of the president's home. "The First Lady is ill with consumption, so the president's daughter has been acting as hostess, and is overseeing renovations."

Josephine pointed out the window. "It used to have a greenhouse over there, but it burned down. I assume they'll replace it."

As the carriage moved them past the White House, Hudson asked, "It sounds like you've been inside?"

She was embarrassed by the truth. "A few times. Papa and President Lincoln were very close."

Frieda nodded and adjusted her gloves. "The Cains are a very important family here in Washington."

"Just one family among many," Josephine murmured.

"Oh posh," Frieda said. "The Cains can count themselves among society's elite."

Hudson sat back in his seat, suddenly quiet. Was he feeling intimidated?

Yes, she was proud of her family's position, but lately the importance of that status had waned. She wished she could think of something to say to make him feel more at ease. Instead, she changed the subject. "I certainly am glad I wired Mother and Aunt Bernice to tell them when we'd arrive. I'm famished."

"Me too," Nelly said, finally facing forward. "They won't have sandwiches, will they?"

Josephine pretended to be aghast, placing a hand to her chest. "But I told them how much you enjoyed ham sandwiches and asked them to make an enormous tray, piled high."

"No!" Nelly said. "That's all we've eaten the entire trip and—" Her panic changed to understanding as she studied Josephine's face. "You're joshing me, aren't you?"

"I am."

"Good." Nelly returned to the window. "Are we almost there?"

"Almost."

Josephine gave Hudson a reassuring smile—one he did not return.

She prayed her mother and aunt would be filled with God's grace. And good manners.

Although Josephine had sent her mother a telegram informing her that she was bringing along two guests, she hadn't given details about their identities. So as they turned onto the final block, her nerves tightened. Although she'd had days to think about it, she knew that nothing she could say would change the fact that Nelly was from a brothel. And then there was Lewis's absence, and Hudson's presence . . .

The first ten minutes would be the hardest.

It was just ten minutes.

Josephine turned to Hudson. "Mother is the leader of the duo. Up until the last few months Aunt Bernice rarely said a word, but now she is becoming her old self—whom I happen to like very much. But Mother can be difficult and often takes to her bed."

"I'm sorry she's ill."

"I didn't say that."

Hudson nodded with understanding.

Nelly made a face. "She doesn't sound very nice."

She isn't. "Nice or not, she is the mistress of the house and my mother. As such, I would like you to treat her with respect."

"But what if she's mean to me? Do I have to be nice then?"

"Even then."

"That's not fair."

No, it isn't.

The carriage stopped in front of their brownstone, and Dowd opened the door. "How good to see you, Miss Josephine. Mrs. Schultz." His eyebrow rose as he saw Nelly.

"This is Nelly."

"Your suit's fancy," Nelly said.

Dowd hesitated, then said, "Thank you."

Josephine saw Hudson unloading the luggage. "You don't need to do that. Dowd will see it's brought in."

Hudson looked at the butler, then piled the baggage on top of Josephine's trunk and carried it up the steps of the house. "I can handle it." He nodded at Dowd. "Thanks for the offer."

They all retreated inside, and Hudson set the luggage near the stairs and removed his hat. Josephine removed her capelet and bonnet, while Frieda helped Nelly with her coat, hurriedly removing it before Mother saw its deplorable condition. At least Nelly's dress was clean and mended. Frieda had seen to that after the tornado.

Mother and Aunt Bernice appeared from the parlor. Josephine rushed forward to greet them.

But there was only so much greeting that could be done.

Josephine stepped aside to find that Nelly had taken refuge in front of Hudson, making them a pair. She began her introductions. "Mother, Aunt Bernice, I would like you to meet Mr. Hudson Maguire, who has been kind enough to accompany us home, and—"

"I'm Nelly," the girl said.

Mother took in a breath. "Well then. Hello . . . Nelly."

Hudson filled the moment by extending his hand. "It's a pleasure to meet you, Mrs. Cain, and Mrs. . . . . ?"

Aunt Bernice actually blushed as she shook his hand. "Mrs. Miller. Lizzie and I are sisters."

"I can see the resemblance," he said. "You both have striking brown eyes."

Mother's face pulled in a strained smile, but she ignored Hudson's hand. She retreated into the parlor, leaving Aunt to say, "Please come and sit down."

The elder ladies took their usual chairs on either side of the fireplace, and Josephine sat on the sofa while Hudson stood behind her. Nelly rushed out of Frieda's care to sit beside Josephine.

Mother flashed a look toward Frieda. "Please take the girl upstairs."

Nelly burrowed into Josephine's side. "But I want to stay with you."

Josephine wrapped her arm around the girl and briefly considered gathering the others and leaving before things got worse.

Hudson saved the day. "Go with Mrs. Schultz, Nelly," he said, taking her hand and leading her toward the foyer.

"But . . ."

He put a finger to his lips, and she blessedly remained quiet and disappeared upstairs with Frieda.

Josephine wanted to feel relief but knew that Nelly's absence would not negate the need for an explanation.

"So then," Mother said. "Mr. Maguire, is it? I must say your daughter is very . . . willful."

"She's not my daughter, ma'am."

The two women exchanged a look. "Then who is she?" Aunt asked.

There it was. *The* question. "She is an orphan girl I took in," Josephine said.

"Took in?"

"In Cheyenne. Wyoming."

"What happened to her parents?" Aunt asked.

Her mother was a whore whom her father pushed down the stairs before shooting himself.

Hudson answered for her. "Both died. Life out west can be very difficult for even the strongest men and women."

Aunt Bernice offered a *tsk-tsk*. "I am so sorry. Lizzie and I know all about being alone, don't we, Lizzie? Time seems endless with no one to talk to but each other and . . . I am so glad you're back, Josephine."

Josephine was surprised by the long discourse. She knew Aunt Bernice was making social calls now, but she did not remember her ever talking so much. Where was the aunt who parroted her mother's comments with a single word?

"So my conversation is not enough for you, Bernice?" Mother's cheeks were flushed and her chin raised.

"I meant no offense to you personally, Lizzie. It's just that I think it's time to think of the future more than the past."

Mother's eyes flashed. "Perhaps you can forget Thomas and William, but I cannot and will not."

Aunt Bernice suffered a sigh. This was an ongoing battle, but it was refreshing to see a bit of her aunt's old personality come back to fight it.

Aunt moved on from the disagreement and turned her attention to Josephine. "You should be commended for taking the girl in. But why bring her all the way back here? Surely there are orphanages in Cheyenne."

"Surely," Mother added.

There was a tiny part of Josephine that wanted to blurt out the entire truth and be done with it. But before she could think too long in that direction, Hudson answered, "General Cain was the one who thought it would be best if Nelly came back with Josie and—"

"Josie?"

She had been so worried about how to explain Nelly that she had forgotten about Hudson's nickname for her. "Josephine seems too formal out west."

"Perhaps the West could use a little more formality."

Hudson continued. "There's another reason the general thought it best to bring Nelly back here. There have been some incidents with Indians, and with the track-laying starting up again and the general's responsibilities increasing—"

Mother interrupted. "What about his responsibilities here, to . . . ?"

Josephine noticed how Mother had left off the full phrase: *to me.* She couldn't blame her resentment, but she also couldn't imagine her father in this house again, taking up his old life. He had changed, and had truly become a man of the West.

As she looked around the room, she wondered if *she* would fit back into her old life again.

Before she could ponder her own transformation, Aunt gathered some newspapers from a side table. "I think the West is stimulating. All those brave people conquering new lands. I have been reading everything about it in the *Chronicle*."

Mother's head jerked to attention. "Speaking of the *Chronicle,* where is Lewis?"

Josephine wanted to look at Hudson but refrained. "He has remained behind with the railroad, working." She thought of something to add. "Don't you remember he went west because he had been hired to photograph images of the project?"

"Hired or not, he is your fiancé, and I would expect him to accompany you home instead of sending you to travel with—with—"

"Hudson Maguire, ma'am."

Mother huffed. "I know your name. What I do not know is your role in this journey. Why are you here?"

Josephine felt her anger rise. If Aunt Bernice had changed for the better, Mother hadn't changed a bit. "Mr. Maguire is here because Papa asked him to see us safely home. He is one of Papa's most trusted employees."

"I also served with the general during the war. He is a great leader of men."

"Hmm," Mother said. "Is it also your assignment to find an orphanage for the girl?"

"No, ma'am. I don't think that was the plan." He looked to Josephine.

"Nelly is my responsibility, Mother. I was the one who chose to save her from . . ." She was glad she caught herself before saying too much. "But it was Mr. Maguire who provided the funds to pay for her . . . care."

Mother's eyebrows nearly touched her hairline. "Funds? You paid for her?"

Josephine kicked herself. Why had she mentioned the payment at all?

Hudson explained. "At the time, some compensation to her previous home seemed appropriate."

"I thought you said there were no orphanages out west?" Mother said.

What now? *Please God. Tell me what to say.*

Mother continued. "Or was that a lie?"

As if he were an angel from heaven, Dowd entered the room and said, "Dinner is served."

Hudson stepped toward Josephine's mother and offered her his arm. She walked by it, but Aunt Bernice gladly stepped up. "Thank you, kind sir," she said.

He offered his other arm to Josephine. "There now. I am the luckiest man in all of Washington."

He certainly was the most gracious.

* * * * *

During the meal Josephine repeatedly thanked God for Aunt Bernice and Hudson. If it weren't for her aunt's sudden interest in all things "west" and Hudson's ability to tell a good story, dinner would have been a tense affair.

As it was, the food was served and eaten, and the dishes removed with little delay. At Josephine's request, plates were sent up to Frieda and Nelly. At first she had been upset that Nelly hadn't been asked to join them but came to feel it was for the best.

Once dinner was over, the older ladies retired, and Josephine and Hudson moved into the parlor.

It was odd being in the room alone with him—especially after all the chaperoned evenings she'd spent there with Lewis—yet it was exactly what she needed. She turned her aunt's chair and stretched her feet toward the fire. Hudson still stood. "Sit," she said, pointing to her mother's chair.

"Dare I?"

"It is just a chair."

"But I see you chose the lesser of the two thrones."

She had. Somehow she felt safer sitting in Aunt Bernice's chair. How cowardly was she? "You can pull another chair close, if you'd like."

He shook his head, angled Mother's chair toward the fire, and slowly descended into it, guiding himself with an exaggerated grip upon the padded arms. Upon contact he grimaced, then relaxed and sighed dramatically. "Phew. I wasn't burned up or turned to stone."

She laughed. "I'm sorry she is so ill-tempered."

"She's downright angry."

"She misses my brother."

"I miss my brother. Nearly every family in the entire country misses someone who was lost in the war. Her anger must stem from more than that."

"She doesn't like that Papa's gone."

"But wasn't he gone a lot during the war?"

"She didn't like that either. And then Thomas left to fight. He was her shining star."

"You shine a bit yourself, Josie."

She sighed. "In Mother's eyes I am a dull pebble to Thomas's glittering gem." The talk was depressing her. She looked to the windows. It was already dark. "Where's a good sunset when you need one?"

"It was there, we simply missed it."

"I never saw a sunset until I saw the one in Nebraska. Thousands of sunsets in my life, and they all happened without me."

"But now that you know . . . "

What did it matter? In the city there were no vast horizons, nor the ability to see the sun melt into the earth.

"Josie?" he said softly.

She blinked. "Sorry. I was feeling sorry for myself."

"Because . . . ?"

"I don't know."

"Yes, you do."

She looked into the fire, then at him. Both were full of comfort and warmth, flicker and flame. But as her gaze included the rest of the room— the room she'd known all her life—she acknowledged what was wrong.

"I am home here," she said, clasping the armrests of the chair. "But not here." She crossed her hands over her heart.

He placed his hand on his own heart and nodded.

Suddenly she began to cry. He hurried to kneel beside her, taking her into his arms. "I don't know what I'm doing," she said amid her tears. "I don't know what I should do."

He stroked her hair and whispered. "You will. We will."

She pulled back in order to see his face. "We will?"

He stood and drew her up beside him. "But not tonight. Let's go check on Nelly and get some sleep."

With a gasp she realized she hadn't even shown him his bedroom. "I am so sorry. You're probably dead on your feet, and I didn't even show you where you'll be staying."

"I know where I'll be staying," he said as he led her to the staircase.

When she gave him a questioning look, he paused and put his hand upon her heart.

His touch was barely there, yet she felt as warm as if he'd wrapped her in his arms.

Too soon he pulled his hand, away and they walked upstairs.

* * * * *

Josephine quietly opened the door to the yellow guestroom. Nelly was curled in a ball, looking tiny in the wide bed with the congregation of pillows and cushy covers looming around her. Josephine's childhood dresses were strewn on the chairs and window seat. Frieda must have gotten them out for Nelly to try on. Josephine felt bad for not thinking of it herself.

She adjusted a down coverlet over the little girl's shoulder. The poor thing. To be brought into the house and sent away like something offensive or inconsequential.

I should have insisted you stay in the parlor to talk. I should have insisted you eat dinner with us.

But it had been easier to let Mother shoo her away. Out of sight, out of mind.

Josephine stroked her hair. "Tomorrow I will do better."

Nelly opened her eyes and touched Josephine's hand. "I missed you."

"I missed you too."

"Tomorrow can I come downstairs?"

Josephine wanted to cry. "Absolutely. And we'll do something fun."

"Really?"

Josephine kissed her good night.

Really.

* * * * *

Hudson lay in bed, his hands clasped behind his head. He stared at the window, at the moonlight that bent and curved over the window seat and floor and foot of his bed.

He held his fingers in front of his face. He could still feel the beat of Josie's heart . . .

Then he abruptly made a fist. What was he doing? What were *they* doing?

The trip from Cheyenne to Washington had been like a dream. Each moment he'd spent with Josie was painted with exquisite detail in his memories, a masterpiece to enjoy for all time.

Yet this place was not for him. It wasn't for Josie either, but he knew it would be difficult for her to completely let it go.

She *had* spoken fondly of the sunsets they'd shared.

But Hudson didn't create the sunsets. They were God's doing, not his own. That he'd had the great privilege of sharing them with a girl like Josephine Cain was a gift he cherished, another portrait for his mental gallery. But that didn't mean they had a future together.

She's not bound to Lewis anymore.

But you're all but promised to Sarah Ann.

Josie had a position in high society. Hudson's family worked in a cotton mill and belonged to the invisible working class. To find a future with each other would require that some very high walls be breached—or torn down. Either way there would be a battle. And casualties. Victory would come at a price.

He turned on his side and forced his eyes to close.

Josie's image met him there in the dark.

A woman worth any price.

Chapter Twenty-One

Josephine sat at the dressing table so Frieda could arrange her hair. The tug of the brush was more forceful than usual, so Josephine stopped it with a hand and turned on the bench to face her. "Please tell me what's wrong before I end up bald."

Frieda smacked the brush against her palm. More than once. Then she said, "I know I've always taken on the role of governess, and I don't mind taking care of Nelly. What I object to is your ignoring her all last evening."

"I know," Josephine said. "I was wrong."

Frieda looked surprised at the confession, but she still had more to say. "Nelly is not a piece of luggage to be unpacked and set aside."

"I know that too. I have already made amends and promised her we would do something fun today."

"You did? When?"

"Last night before I went to bed."

"Oh. Well then."

Since they were on the subject . . . "Yesterday I was so overwhelmed, dealing with Mother's rudeness and the tension of being home."

"What did she say about Nelly? What did you say?" Frieda leaned close. "Did you tell her where she'd been living?"

"We simply said she was an orphan."

Frieda sighed. "Good."

"For now, at least."

Frieda made a turn-around motion, and Josephine returned to her place, facing the mirror. "So where are you two taking her today?"

"We two?"

Frieda pointed the brush at Josephine's reflection. "Hudson isn't a piece of luggage either."

No, indeed, he was not.

"I thought I would show them some of the city."

"That takes care of today, but what about tomorrow and the next day? What are you going to do with her? And him?"

"Hudson will be wanting to head back. His assignment is complete."

"This was not just an assignment for him. That's clear to anyone with eyes and ears."

There was no use denying it. "Nelly and Hudson. What *am* I supposed to do with them?"

"Perhaps you should ask them what *they* would like to do."

That *was* an option. And yet, "What if I don't like their answers?"

Frieda raised her hands and gazed toward heaven. "God? Are You listening to this? Make sure these three very confused people do what's right, for everyone's sake. And Yours."

Amen.

* * * * *

They sat at the breakfast table, waiting. Josephine saw Nelly eyeing the scones. The smell of eggs and bacon coming from the chafing dishes on the buffet was intoxicating.

"Do you think Mother's coming down?" Josephine asked Aunt Bernice.

Aunt glanced toward the stairs. "You know she rarely misses a meal . . . except if she decides to be indisposed."

"Decides to be?" Hudson asked.

"She has frequent . . . ailments."

"Has a doctor been called?"

"They see nothing wrong." Aunt leaned toward him and whispered, "I think she gets bored."

"So is she *bored* this morning?" Josephine asked. "The food is getting cold."

Aunt nodded, then lifted her arm. "Dowd, please serve. And start with Miss Nelly."

* * * * *

"What is this?" Nelly asked, holding up the hoop and the stick.

"It is a game my brother and cousin used to play," Josephine said. She tried to demonstrate on the marble floor in the foyer. "You balance the metal hoop upright, then roll it forward with the stick." She tried to do it, but the hoop fell to the floor with a rattle.

"Here," Hudson said. "Let's go outside, and I'll show you how it's done."

"So you are an expert?"

He smiled at her. "I believe I am."

"This, I must see." She followed them outside, where Hudson soon had the hoop rolling down the walk at a tremendous speed. Nelly ran beside him, her long hair flying, her laughter returning with the breeze.

It was quite a sight seeing the little girl in one of Josephine's childhood dresses, running alongside the grown man wearing a rawhide vest and Stetson, in upscale Washington. A well-dressed couple was forced to step out of the way. When they approached, Josephine nodded. "Good morning."

They responded politely, but as soon as they passed, Josephine ran in the direction of the fun. By the time she caught up, Nelly was taking her own try at it—quite successfully. "Stop at the end of the street!" Josephine called after her.

"She's a quick study," Hudson said, a bit out of breath.

"You are a good teacher. Did you and your brothers play this often?"

"Not often enough. We didn't have much free time as we worked in the cotton mill for twelve hours a day, six days a week. " He held up a hand, his fingers splayed. "Believe it or not, these fingers used to be small enough to fit into the small crannies of the weaving machines to fix them. Me and my best friend, Andrew Carnegie, nearly got them cut off a few times, but—"

"You worked in a factory as a child?"

"I started out when I was only seven. Andrew and I were bobbin boys for a dollar a month."

Josephine thought about the dollars she spent on trinkets without a second thought.

"There was a gentleman in town, Colonel Anderson, who owned hundreds of books. But on Sundays, he let us boys borrow them. We lived for Sundays."

"And your family still works at the mill?"

"My father worked his way to supervisor. My brother Ezra works there too. And Sarah Ann's been a spinner for years."

They shared an awkward silence. Then Hudson looked down the street, toward Nelly. "We'd best catch up with her. I have more I can teach her."

And me.

* * * * *

After their outing with the hoop and stick and some time spent at a nearby park, Hudson waited in the parlor while Josie helped attend Nelly's fresh wounds.

While trying to toss pebbles through the moving hoop, the girl had fallen and scraped her knee and palm. He felt bad about it, but Nelly shrugged it off and wanted to play more. Josie was the one who'd insisted they return home.

Hudson strolled around the room, waiting for them to come downstairs. Playing with Nelly brought back good memories of home.

But also sad ones. Being in a room like this one with its fancy draperies at the windows, thick patterned carpets, paintings in gilt frames, and breakable bric-a-brac on every surface made him mourn what his mother would never have. She earned money by sewing at home, but the only item in their house that was remotely pretty was a teapot she'd brought over from Ireland. And even that had a chip in the handle.

Not that fancy things were necessary, but they did give him a feeling of stability, safety, and satisfaction.

Yet *satisfaction* wasn't the right word. . . . What he felt was hard to pinpoint. He didn't care if he owned such frivolities, but there was a certain sense of fulfillment in being around them, as if their very presence were an assurance that the bigger concerns of survival were under control and the harsh realities of the world couldn't touch him here.

He opened an oak humidor and let the aroma of fine tobacco waft over him. He removed a cigar and held it beneath his nose, drawing in the smooth aroma of aged wood, leather, and spice.

To sit in such a room and enjoy a cigar . . . would he ever live in such a house? Did he want to?

Josie expected to live in such a house.

"A-hem."

He turned to see Mrs. Cain in the doorway.

"My husband is very protective of his cigars. They come all the way from Cuba."

"Of course." Hudson returned the cigar to the humidor and closed the lid.

When she entered the room, he felt the need to flee. But to where?

"Please sit down, Mr. Maguire. I must speak with you."

Dread tightened like a vise. She was a bitty thing, standing barely to his shoulder, but she had a presence that evoked tension and rigidity, like a harsh judge who held the balance of his life in her hands and found great pleasure in her position.

She took a seat in her chair, and Hudson sat in the seat she offered nearby. Aunt Bernice's chair. He noticed the mourning brooch at her neck and imagined it held a lock of her son's hair. She smoothed the skirt of her black dress, then placed her clasped hands in her lap. It was time for business.

"When are you leaving us, Mr. Maguire?"

It wasn't the question he'd expected. "I suppose as soon as Josie— Miss Josephine—is fully settled with Nelly."

Her eyebrows rose. "Settled with Nelly?"

He shouldn't have brought it up. Nelly was Josie's issue, and as far as he knew, nothing had been decided regarding the girl's future.

He sidestepped the subject. "As soon as your daughter indicates she no longer needs my services, I'll return to my work on the railroad."

"I would like you to leave today. I don't approve of your influence on her."

He didn't understand. "Influence? I'm a friend who made sure she traveled in safety. I don't—"

"You are not a suitable match for my daughter."

Her supposition surprised him. "We're not . . ." He didn't finish the sentence to prevent stepping into a lie.

"Even in the short time I've seen you, I sense your attachment to her."

It's that noticeable?

"As I hope you know, Josephine is betrothed to Mr. Simmons. Wedding plans have commenced, and I will not have your presence place those plans in jeopardy."

There were a hundred things he wanted to say. He wanted to tell her that Josie had already broken the engagement with Lewis. He wanted to tell her about her own husband's comments against the man. He wanted to tell her about the instances when he himself had witnessed Lewis's true character. But he knew she wouldn't believe him.

"To put it bluntly, Mr. Maguire, you are not my daughter's equal."

"I never said I was."

"What does your family do?"

Here it comes . . . "They work in a cotton mill near Pittsburgh."

She spread her hands as if that was the end of the issue.

And perhaps it was. Whether or not he had feelings for Josie, *there* was the crux of it. He came from poor Irish stock who were lucky to have a few extra dollars left over at the end of the month, while Josie—Josephine—was an Irish general's daughter who had never considered the cost of anything and felt comfortable dining with presidents. The only thing they had in common was their family's country of origin.

Mrs. Cain rose from her chair, causing him to also rise. "I believe there is a two o'clock train headed north."

He wanted to argue with her but knew his words would ring hollow. If he couldn't convince himself, how could he convince her?

And so he nodded, then left the room and hurried upstairs to gather his things.

Once his saddlebag was ready, he paused a moment to let his heart stop its awful pounding. Should he step down the hall, knock on Josie's door, and tell her good-bye? Tell Nelly good-bye?

He could imagine the scene—a scene that would do no one any good nor change any facts.

He'd leave a note.

He sat at the desk, found paper, pen, and inkwell, and wrote his heart. He placed the note on the bed, his fingers lingering on its words.

Then he slipped down the stairs and out the door.

* * * * *

Her scrapes bandaged, Nelly sat at the dressing table while Josephine and Frieda played with her hair—which was actually quite thick and had a nice natural wave. The girl opened a jar of face cream and rubbed some on her cheeks. "Ooh, Vera and the ladies would love this."

"I make it myself," Frieda said. "Cook hates it when I'm in her kitchen stirring up a batch, but I appease her by giving her some."

Next Nelly removed the lid on a glass powder jar. As she reached for the puff, Josephine said, "Careful now. I don't want powder all over. Just a little is enough."

Nelly carefully removed the puff, dabbed it on her face, then held it to her nose. "Smells pretty."

"It's lavender."

"Vera would like some of this too."

Josephine had heard quite enough about Vera. "We will have to check out the schools nearby. The Grayson School takes girls, and—"

Nelly swiftly turned around on the bench, causing Frieda to lose hold of the braid she was creating down the back of her head. "I don't want to go to school. I already know how to read."

"You do?"

Nelly nodded with emphasis. "Vera and Jenny taught me." She picked up *A Tale of Two Cities* that was perched on the edge of the vanity, and opened to the first page. "'It was the best of times, it was the worst of times, it was the age of wisdom, it was the age of foolishness, it was the e . . . ep . . . '"

Josephine looked over her shoulder. "Epoch."

"What's that?"

Josephine had to think a moment. "Age, era. Time."

Nelly nodded and continued. "'It was the epoch of belief, it was the epoch of incred . . .'"

"Incredulity."

"'It was the season of Light, it was the season of Darkness, it was the spring of hope, it was the winter of despair, we had everything before us, we had nothing before us, we were all going direct to Heaven, we were all going direct the other way.'" She closed the book with a *thwack* and looked up. "See?"

Frieda clapped. "Very good, child. Quite impressive."

"I can do my numbers too," Nelly said. "Miss Mandy taught me. She's good at numbers and counting money."

I bet she is.

Josephine turned the discussion back to the matter at hand. "There is more to an education than reading and numbers. You need to learn how to be polite and—"

"I say please and thank you."

"Yes, you do."

"Vera taught me—"

"Yes, you do," Josephine repeated. "But at school you will also learn how to paint watercolors and play a piano."

"Why would I want to learn that?"

Josephine was flummoxed. What had either of those skills done for her?

Frieda laughed. "She's got you there." She motioned Nelly to turn around and went back to the braiding.

"I suppose we can think about that later. We'd better go downstairs. Hudson is probably bored silly waiting for us."

They passed Mother on the stairs. "Have you seen Mr. Maguire?" Josephine asked.

"I believe he is gone."

"Gone where?"

Mother continued to the landing. "Back west, where he belongs."

"What?"

She shrugged. "His mission was complete. You have been returned home safely." She walked down the hallway toward her room.

He can't leave!

Josephine rushed up the stairs after her. "But what did he say? When did he go?" *Why did he go?*

Mother cocked her head and looked to the ceiling. "I suppose he said 'good-bye.' As far as the time of his leaving, I have no idea."

"Do you want me to run after him?" Nelly said from the stairs. "I can run really fast."

Frieda stood behind Nelly and put her hands upon her shoulders. "There will be no running after," she said.

Why not? I don't want him to leave.

Mother continued down the hall. "It is for the best, Josephine. Such a man does not fit into our lives."

That's when Josephine knew her mother had something to do with Hudson's departure. "What did you do to him? What did you say?"

"I did what any mother would do. I protected my daughter— a daughter who is betrothed to marry a fine gentleman who *does* belong in our family."

Josephine suffered past images of Lewis's bad behavior and downright cowardice. "Lewis is not the man you think he is. Hudson is a far better—"

"You gave your word. You will marry Lewis Simmons."

"But I don't want to marry—"

"If you will excuse me, I am feeling a bit tired." She opened the door of her room and closed it with a *click*.

Josephine stood at the door and yelled, "I'm tired too! Tired of you trying to rule my life! You don't know Lewis and you don't know Hudson. You—"

Frieda motioned Josephine away. "Come now, Liebchen. She's not going to listen to you."

"She has no right—"

"She has every right. She's your mother."

"But she doesn't know either one of them."

Suddenly, Nelly came running out of the guestroom where Hudson had been staying. "He left a note!" She ran to Josephine's side, the note waving in her breeze.

Josephine read aloud:

My dearest Josie,

Again I say the name suits you. Josie is the name of a modern woman who knows her own mind. And yet you are also Josephine, a lady of society, with ties to a family legacy of wealth and privilege. I don't begrudge you either, but neither will I make you choose between your roots and another kind of life that may not be to your liking. Or in your best interest.

Since our feelings have not been fully expressed, it is best they remain in our hearts.

Just know that I shall always care deeply for you, dear Josie. And in my absence, I wish you all happiness. May God protect and guide us both.

Yours always,
Hudson

Josephine felt as if she had been struck. "Mother told him to leave! It's her fault!"

She ran down the hallway toward her mother's room, but Frieda caught up with her. "Stop. It will do no good."

Josephine felt her heart beating in her throat. "It will make me feel better."

"But it will solve nothing."

"What is there to be solved? He is gone and I am here."

"Let's go after him," Nelly said.

And there it was. "Yes," Josephine said, running back in her room. "Let's pack and catch him at the train station."

But then she heard a bell ringing. And ringing. Frieda looked down the hall to see where the noise was coming from. "It's your mother. She's in need of something."

"That's for certain," Josephine said, as she kept packing.

But then Aunt Bernice raced past their door, as did Audrey, Mother's maid. Josephine heard a lot of commotion. "Go see what's wrong," she told Frieda with a sigh. "Though if she is suffering, it probably is the result of her guilt and manipulation."

Frieda left the room. But then Josephine saw Audrey running past the doorway to the stairs and heard her ask Dowd to send for the doctor.

Josephine snickered. Mother certainly knew how to create drama.

But when Frieda returned, her face was pulled in genuine concern. "They think it's her heart. When she went into her room, she collapsed."

Concern mixed with doubt. Was Mother really hurt, or was it a ruse to gain Josephine's attention and create a diversion from the awful thing she did in sending Hudson away? Yet Josephine didn't have time for delay. Hudson had a head start to the train station, and she had no idea when the train was due to leave. If they didn't go soon, he would be gone.

And then what?

Aunt Bernice ran to the railing overlooking the foyer and yelled down to Dowd, "Did you send for the doctor?"

"Yes, ma'am."

She ran back to Mother's room.

With a sigh, Josephine followed.

* * * * *

"All aboard!"

Hudson took one last look around the depot, hoping to see Josie rushing up to stop him. She would run into his arms and say, "Don't ever leave me. I love you."

And he'd pull her close and kiss her, right there in public. But neither one of them would care because they would finally and truly be committed to each other.

It was a ridiculous fantasy, but it was one he'd nursed since purchasing his ticket. Alternating with the dream were prayers asking God to bless their feelings and make it all work.

Somehow.

He climbed the steps leading to the railcar, and with one last glance, accepted the fact that she wasn't coming.

Hudson told himself *so be it,* but the fissure in his heart exposed the words as bravado.

Josie . . . what am I going to do without you?

As the train gained speed, he let the rhythm of the rails lull him into nothingness.

It was better than feeling the pain.

* * * * *

The doctor drew them into the hall and spoke in a concerned tone. "It appears she may truly have suffered some irregularity of the heart."

Aunt gasped. "Will she recover?"

"She should," the doctor said. "It seems mild." He looked directly at Josephine. "There was some confrontation?"

Instead of trying to explain it or even qualify their exchange, she simply said, "Yes."

"There's to be no more of that. At least not until she feels better." He handed Aunt a vial. "Some laudanum to help her sleep. Otherwise, just let her rest and eat as she wishes." Again he looked at Josephine. "I know your mother very well, and I know she can be difficult and melodramatic. I don't know what went on between you two, but I ask you to leave it alone for a few days."

Leave alone that she sent away the man I love?

He was waiting for her response. "Yes, Doctor."

Aunt left to see him out. Josephine returned to her room and endured the stares of Frieda and Nelly.

"Are we going after Hudson now?" Nelly asked.

"We can't. Not for a few days."

Nelly plopped on the bed, her lower lip in a pout. "That's not fair. Every minute we sit here, he's gittin' farther and farther away."

You think I don't know that?

"Or," Frieda said, "are we staying for good?"

That was the big question. "If we leave, it means we are going out west. Is that where you want to go—permanently?"

"Permanently?" Frieda repeated. "As in forever and always?"

Josephine wasn't sure how to answer. Impulsively, she wanted to say, *Yes, absolutely. We have nothing to keep us here,* but realistically, the thought of starting over in a wild town like Grand Island or Cheyenne was frightening. Papa had ordered them to leave because of the surrounding danger. And what would they do there? *Was* she a modern woman like Hudson said in his note? Or would she always be a woman of society, finding her comfort by living in affluence and following convention?

Was she Josie or Josephine?

Nelly raised her hand high. "I vote for the West."

"I am not taking you back to Miss Mandy's. Ever."

Nelly climbed off the bed and wrapped her arms around Josephine's waist. "I don't want that. I want to be with you. And Mrs. Schultz. The three of us, together."

Josephine pulled Nelly's head to her chest and kissed her hair. "Frieda? What do you want?"

Frieda plucked hairs from a brush, her eyes focused on her task. Then she stopped. "I guess it comes down to this. You and I have been joined together since you were born, so as the Bible says . . . 'Whither thou goest, I will go; and where thou lodgest, I will lodge: thy people shall be my people, and thy God my God.'"

Josephine extended an arm and drew Frieda into their circle, three females, determined to conquer new worlds.

Wherever they were.

* * * * *

Pittsburgh.

Hudson stood in the depot, in the same spot where he'd stood on the way to Washington, staring at the sign that read *Allegheny City*, facing the same decision he'd faced then.

Do I go home and see my family, or do I get back on the train?

He closed his eyes and let the sounds of the busy depot fall into a buzzing background. *God? What should I do?*

Two words entered his mind, causing him to open his eyes: *Finish this.*

Finish what? His trip west?

No.

He knew what the words meant.

And so he left the westward train behind and boarded another one.

Toward home.

Chapter Twenty-Two

Hudson paid the innkeeper for his room. For as much sleep as he'd gotten, it was a waste of money. Plus, he'd awakened with a cough. How many coughs had his family suffered from working in the dusty conditions of the mills? Spinners lungs, they called it. That's why his mother had quit the mill and started sewing at home. Yet the conditions there weren't much better. Bitter cold in winter, stifling in summer . . . but at least she didn't have to be on her feet all day.

In truth, Hudson could have gone home last night but had lost his nerve. After not hearing from Sarah Ann in months, after choosing to remain in Cheyenne over the winter, he wasn't sure what he would say to her or his family, and even more, wasn't sure what he wanted them to say. Would they treat him like the prodigal son coming home? Or would they hold his absence against him?

He passed the docks on the north shore of the Allegheny River and turned onto the street where he grew up. Two towering rows of three-story tenements blocked out the sky. The smells from each building's communal privy wafted onto the street, making the memories of the aromatic bunk cars seem like perfume.

Although it was barely dawn, workers streamed out of the tenements. And then . . .

"Da!"

Hudson's father turned and blinked as though not believing his eyes. Then he ran toward his son with open arms, embracing him and clapping him on the back. "Yer here!" Da let him loose to show him off. "Look, men! Me boy is home agin!"

"I'm just visiting."

Da pulled back. "Visiting? You been gone forever, and you come back only to visit?"

Other workers called out to Hudson as they passed on the way to the mills. He'd known many his whole life.

He changed the subject. "How are Mum and Ezra?" He hesitated. "And Sarah Ann?"

Da pointed to their building. "Go inside and greet yer mum. We see you tonight. Surely you be staying that long."

Did he have a choice? He nodded.

"I be seeing you then." He smiled. "Good it is to see you, boy."

Da joined the other workers, the mass of them like a stream of tadpoles swimming upstream, doggedly flowing against the odds.

As he entered the darkness of the tenement he wondered after Ezra. He and Da always walked to work together. Where was his brother?

He climbed the stairs to the second floor and walked down the dim hall. Babies cried behind paper-thin walls. He reached their apartment, with a painted 5 on the door, though the bottom curve of the number had flaked off. He paused a moment, taking a deep breath. What would Mum say to him? A fit of coughing made his presence known, and the door opened.

Mum's eyes grew wide before she pulled him into her arms. "Oh my dear boy. You be here! You be back."

He didn't contradict her but let himself be drawn inside. Little had changed. There were six mismatched chairs around a square table, with a bed in the corner that Ezra had shared with John. The cots that Hudson and Raleigh had slept on were gone, and in their place was a chair strewn with Mum's sewing. A stove in the corner was used for cooking, and the walls were covered with makeshift shelves holding crockery and pans. His parents' bedroom was the only other room.

Mum put a hand to her head, smoothing loose hairs. "I look a fright, I do. You shoulda sent word you was coming." The familiar Irish cadence of her voice made Hudson feel at home.

"I didn't know, and you look lovely—as always."

"Ah you," Mum said, pulling out a chair. "Would'cha like some coffee?"

"Don't make anything special."

"I have some left from this morn'. And some soda bread too, if it please ya."

Although he didn't feel up to either, he let his mother flutter over him. She finally sat down across the table from him. "How are ya? Things go bad out west?"

He realized she also thought he'd come home to stay. "Not bad at all. We're laying track across the Wyoming Territory now. I'm just here for a visit."

Her once-beautiful face grew old again. "A visit?"

"I'm sorry. But there's still much work to do, many miles to lay."

"Your letters mentioned Indians and wild towns. . . . I donna see why you want to be 'round such things."

It's better than being around poverty and a job that leads nowhere.

It was time to ask the question that had brought him here. "How is Sarah Ann? I need to see her."

Mum looked away, then rose from the table, returning with the dress she was making. "I be making quite the name for me handwork. This dress is for the butcher's wife. See the tiny stitches?"

"They're very tight and straight," he said. But he wouldn't let her off so easily. "Can I see Sarah Ann after work? I—" He suffered a fit of coughing that forced him to double over. Mum brought him a glass of water, but his throat felt raw from the hacking.

"You lay down now, boyo," she told him, leading him to Ezra's bed. "I make ye a compress for yer chest."

"Sarah Ann . . ."

She ignored him.

But why?

* * * * *

"You should go check on your mother," Frieda said, as she brushed through Josephine's hair.

"I will. And I did check on her in the middle of the night. She seemed to be resting well. Too well."

"Hush. You should be happy she's all right."

"I am. Absolutely. But I am also unhappy that her episode prevented us from going after Hudson."

"At least we can catch up."

"That's the only reason I'm not tearing my hair out." She spread face cream on her cheeks. The subtle scent of vanilla always made her inhale deeply, wanting more. Then suddenly she remembered Nelly using some of the cream the day before, saying, *Vera and the ladies would love this.*

And it hit her. Hit her hard.

Josephine grabbed the jar of cream and spun around on the bench to face Frieda. "*This* is what we can do out west to make a living. We can sell your face cream to the women."

"Sell? It's not good enough to sell."

"So it's good enough for me, but not good enough for the Veras of the world, or the pioneer women?"

"Well . . . when you say it that way."

Nelly climbed off the window seat where she had been reading. "The powder too. Remember the lavender-smelling powder."

"I don't make that," Frieda said.

"But we could buy it and bring it with us to sell at a profit." Josephine began to pace. "What other items would women buy from us?" She stopped at her dressing table and pointed from one item to another. "Perfume atomizers, powder puffs, brushes with pretty backs, combs—both functional and decorative, nice-smelling soaps, toothbrushes and powders, mirrors, hairpins, ribbon, lengths of lace . . ."

"Handkerchiefs," Frieda added. "And maybe some collarettes or lace fichus that can fancy up even the dullest of dresses."

"And shawls," Nelly said. "Vera and the ladies like pretty shawls."

Josephine's mind swam with ideas. "Frieda, retrieve a paper and pencil and make a list."

"Can we really do this?" Frieda asked as she looked through the desk. "We don't know anything about selling."

"Reticules!" Josephine added. "And parasols. Not as fancy as my peach one, but some that will keep the harsh sun off their faces. And hats. Not just frivolous hats like the ones I wore, but hats that combine function with beauty."

"Now we're milliners?"

"We will be whatever we need to be."

Frieda was furiously writing the list, which allowed Josephine a moment to ponder their lack of sales experience. "It wouldn't have to be a real store—not at first," Josephine said, working through the issue out loud. "We could have a store that travels like the saloons and gambling houses do."

"And Miss Mandy's," Nelly said.

Josephine let the comment slide. "Eventually we can settle in a town that suits us, and wait for the trains to start running back and forth on a regular basis. Our business would grow. It's inevitable."

Frieda stopped writing. "If we do this . . . it means we *are* leaving here forever."

Although they had all said as much the night before, those decisions had been born from frustration and the desperation to catch up with Hudson. But to have a plan and a purpose, to start something brand-new . . .

She was finally ready to answer. "Yes, it means we are leaving here forever."

They shared a moment of silence. Then Nelly said, "Wow."

Frieda and Josephine shared a look before bursting into laughter.

"What?" Nelly asked.

Josephine pulled the girl to her side. "You expressed the moment perfectly."

Frieda was looking over the list. "I can make some more face cream, but where do we buy so many jars, and the other products?"

The overwhelming dilemma found an answer in two words. "Rachel Maddox."

"Who's she?" Nelly asked.

"My good friend, whose father owns Hanson Mercantile. He likes me and has known me my entire life. He will sell me the items at good prices, and if our store takes off, he might even connect me with his suppliers."

"You're confident," Frieda said.

"Yes, I am."

She had never felt so sure of anything in her life.

* * * * *

Josephine walked toward her mother's room to check on her, but she met Audrey coming out. "How is she?"

"Fine as can be. Your mother recovers from illness faster than anyone I've ever known."

Maybe because she was never sick in the first place. Josephine kept her opinion to herself.

"You're going out?" Audrey asked, looking past Josephine to Frieda, and Nelly carrying her hoop and stick.

"For a bit. If you have things attended to here . . ."

"She's fine. Go on then."

The coast made clear, Josephine hurried the others along just in case Mother decided to have another relapse.

* * * * *

The three females entered the park near the Maddox residence with the plan that Frieda and Nelly would spend time there while Josephine had a conversation with her friend about their store idea. Nelly wasted no time in racing down the sidewalk with her hoop. "You'd better hurry and catch her," Josephine said to Frieda. "I will be back soon."

She then turned toward the row of stately homes that edged the park, hoping that Rachel was home and available for an impromptu visit.

As she passed the house of the Maddoxes' neighbor, the man of the house came outside. When he saw Josephine, he smiled a greeting. "Miss Cain. How wonderful to see you again."

"Police Chief Brandon," she said with a nod. "It's nice to see you too."

"I heard that you've had some adventures with trips out west."

She wondered what the Washington grapevine had picked up about Nelly and Hudson's presence here. "I have. It's an exhilarating place."

Oddly, he looked directly at her left hand. "Are you still engaged?"

Although she wasn't, she didn't want rumors to take flight. Remembering the ring she still had not removed, she offered proof by removing her glove and showing it to him. Let him draw his own conclusions.

But instead of offering the typical quick glance and smile, he did a double take. "May I see?" He examined it intently. "This is an emerald?" he asked.

"I believe it is."

"If I may?" he asked, clearly wanting to take her hand. When she nodded, he tipped her hand this way and that, making her uneasy. "It is a very intricate setting."

"Yes, it is." She pulled her hand away.

With a blink, he moved his attention from her hand to her face. "What is the name of the lucky man again?"

Oh dear. Yet she couldn't backtrack now. "Lewis Simmons."

He nodded once, then tipped his hat and bid her good day.

The exchange was a bit strange, but she pushed the thoughts aside for another time. The task at hand pressed her toward the Maddox home. The butler answered the knock and informed her that Rachel was available for a visit.

She stepped inside and said a prayer.

* * * * *

Josephine flew out the door of Rachel's home. She found Frieda and Nelly on the far end of the park, sitting in the grass, looking for four-leaf clovers. When Nelly saw her, she came running. "Look! Frieda says it's good luck."

Josephine rolled the stem of the clover between her fingers. "Indeed, for I have just had some very good luck."

Frieda held out her hand, wanting assistance to stand. When she was stable and her dress brushed smooth, Josephine continued. "Rachel thinks our store is a wonderful idea and is certain her father will help in whatever way he can."

"How marvelous."

"She is going to his office right now to ask him whether we might purchase goods at a discount—she mentioned twenty-five percent."

"That would be very generous."

"It gives us twenty-five percent profit when we sell the items."

"Yet we *could* charge more than the regular price," Frieda said. "Western goods are costly."

"I will consider it," Josephine said. "Yet I want to provide a service to western women as well as make a profit. I'm sure there is a middle ground." She held out her hand to Nelly. "But all that is for another day. Let us return home and wait for Rachel to contact us."

"Then what?"

"Then, we go shopping."

"I've never really been shopping," Nelly said. "I'd go look at the stuff in Mr. Benton's store, but I never had any money."

"But didn't you earn . . . ?" Josephine couldn't take the question any further.

Nelly shook her head. "Miss Mandy said room and board was my pay."

Josephine couldn't even think about it. She put her arm around Nelly, and they strode down the street. "Then shopping will be a special treat. For soon we are going to buy out the store in order to create our own."

* * * * *

Hudson sat on the floor, fixing a chair leg.

Mum stood next to him. " 'Tis so nice to have you here, boy. I am ever so glad ye feel better, and I mightily appreciate yer help. Your da never has time for repairin' things."

"Ezra could help."

"I'm supposin' he could." She pointed toward the bedroom. "After you be done fixing that chair, could ye hang another shelf?"

Why not?

He heard voices outside and feet on the stairs. Mum rushed to the pot of soup on the potbellied stove. "Never you mind," she said. "Your da's home. He'll be so happy to talk to you."

Why didn't she mention Ezra? He lived here too, didn't he? Was he okay? Hudson righted the chair and stood.

And then his father was there, rushing through the door to embrace him. He smelled of hard work and wool. "I thought o' you all the day and was fairly itching to get home. I be so glad yer here, I am." He stepped back to see his face. "I talked to the boss, I did, and you can take a job on the line, take up where you left off."

Hudson shook his head. "As I said this morning, Da, I'm not staying. There's still a lot of track to lay. I want to see the railroad through until east connects with west." He looked toward the door, waiting for his brother. "Where's Ezra?"

Da glanced at his wife. "You didn't tell him?"

She shook her head. " 'Tis yours to tell."

"They be coming over," Da said.

"They?"

He nodded.

And then there was a knock on the door. Da answered it, and Ezra walked in—with Sarah Ann. Hudson gave his brother a strong handshake and looked to his girl. She had gained a little weight—which was becoming on her. She had always been so slight a stiff breeze could blow her over.

"Sarah Ann." He held out his hand.

She looked down and kept her own hands clasped in front of her.

When Hudson looked back at his family, every brow was furrowed. "What's going on?"

Da looked at Ezra. " 'Tis your responsibility. You be on with it."

Ezra put his arm around her shoulders. "Sarah Ann and I fell in love and got married. We're expecting a baby in the fall."

Hudson felt as though his breath had been knocked out of him. "But . . ."

Finally, Sarah Ann met his eyes. "I know I said I'd wait for you, but then you stayed away so long, and . . . well . . ." She looked up at Ezra.

Hudson expected to be angry. But he wasn't.

He was thankful.

He offered his brother his hand. "Congratulations."

Relief washed over Ezra's face. "You're not upset?"

"Not so long as you're both happy."

Sarah Ann took a tentative step forward, then kissed Hudson's cheek. "Thank you."

Mum whooshed out her breath, her relief palpable. Then she picked up the spoon and stirred the pot. "Now that be settled, let's eat."

* * * * *

What now?

After Sarah Ann and Ezra left for their apartment, after Da and Mum went to bed, Hudson was left alone in the main room, the room he used to share each night with three brothers.

John was dead.

Ezra was married.

And Raleigh was out west laying track.

Sarah Ann—the girl he had planned to marry—was married and expecting a child.

And Josie, the woman he . . .

Loved?

She was unavailable. Her mother had made that perfectly clear.

So now what?

Hudson turned on his side and closed his eyes.

God? What should I do?

Chapter Twenty-Three

"I will take six of those brushes with the matching mirrors, ten regular combs, and . . ." Josephine looked at the selection of decorative combs for dressing hair. "And four sets of these."

The clerk at Hanson Mercantile was nearly giddy writing down the order, while two other clerks scurried around gathering the items as they were purchased.

"What about these?" Nelly asked as she ran her fingers through the lengths of ribbon that hung from spools on a rod.

"Perfect," Josephine said. "We will take the ribbon."

"Which colors?" the clerk asked.

"All of them."

My, this was fun.

* * * * *

They walked back home, with Nelly racing ahead with her hoop and stick. The clerk at Hanson Mercantile assured them the goods would be delivered within the hour.

"You spent a lot of money," Frieda said. "Are you sure it will be all right with your mother?"

"No, but it will be all right with Papa."

"But your father doesn't know about your idea. Maybe you should have sent him a letter or telegram."

She probably should have, yet that would have taken time, and Josephine didn't have time to waste. She wanted to purchase the goods and board the train heading west in the span of a few days.

"What are you going to tell your mother when everything arrives?"

Josephine hesitated, for she knew a confrontation was inevitable. "It will come to me."

She hoped.

Aunt Bernice was waiting for them when they arrived home. She'd found some toys for Nelly that had been her son's. "You try to flip the ball into the cup, like this." With difficulty, Aunt accomplished the task, though she lunged forward to do it, nearly knocking over an urn.

Suddenly, Aunt stopped the playing and looked toward the stairs. "Lizzie!"

Mother was being helped downstairs by Audrey. Aunt swept toward her, full of solicitude. "I am so glad you are finally up, sister. How are you feeling?"

"Better," Mother said, as she crossed the parlor to her chair. "No one came to visit me this morning, so I had to come downstairs to see if you had all abandoned me."

Josephine stepped forward to take her scolding. "I'm sorry. We had some errands to do, and—" She heard a wagon stop on the street out front and turned toward the window.

Nelly ran to see. "It's here!"

"What's here?" Mother asked.

Aunt moved beside Nelly, pulling the curtain aside. "A Hanson Mercantile wagon? Josephine, what have you been up to?"

Josephine stood between them and said a quick prayer for the right words. "Frieda and Nelly and I are going back west to start a store catering to women's needs. The goods being delivered are the inventory."

Silence.

Aunt Bernice was the first to speak. "What is the name of the store?"

That was her first concern? Josephine laughed. "I have no idea."

"Nelly's Store," Nelly said.

"Not Nelly's Store," Josephine said.

Frieda shook her head. "I certainly don't want my name on it."

"Which leaves you, Josephine," Aunt said. "Josephine's Dry Goods?"

"Emporium," Frieda said.

It was a good word. "Josie's Emporium."

For the first time, Mother spoke. "Don't be ridiculous."

"I don't think she is ridiculous," Aunt said. "I think it is a splendid idea, and a splendid name." She moved to the foyer where Dowd was accosting the deliverymen.

He looked very confused. "Where should I have them put all this, Miss Josephine?"

Good question. "Perhaps in the dining room? It won't be there long. We will be leaving in a day or so."

"Leaving?" Mother asked.

Hadn't she heard anything? "Going back west. To start a—"

"What does Lewis think about this? Does he approve of a working wife?"

"Lewis is not the man you think he is, Mother."

"What does that mean?"

It was time she knew he truth. "He has shown himself to have . . ." How could she put it? "Less character than we thought."

"Oh, I see what is going on," Mother said, nodding. "If you think your father and I will allow you to marry that other man, you are wrong."

"If you are speaking of Mr. Maguire, the man *you* sent away . . . you should not disparage him in any way, because you don't know him. Nor do you have the right to tell me I can't marry him."

"So you *are* planning to marry him?"

If only she knew . . . "At this moment, I am not planning to marry anyone." Josephine couldn't believe she had said that. Was that really her intent—to marry no one?

Mother pointed to her hand. "You are still wearing Lewis's ring."

Yes, she was. Then Josephine remembered the police chief's odd reaction to it. Something wasn't right about it, and in that moment, she knew she needed to find out what.

A deliveryman came forward, his hat in his hands. "All through, miss."

Josephine asked Dowd, "Do you have something for their trouble?"

Dowd gave the men a few coins.

As the door closed, Mother laughed. "You lack a few coins to pay a gratuity, yet you bought out the store? Where did you procure the money for all this?"

"Papa has given me an allowance for years."

"That you have spent."

"Occasionally, but I also saved." *Some.* "Mr. Hanson agreed to sell on credit."

"Cains do not buy on credit."

This one does. "I know I will be able to sell all these goods, and when I do, I will send Mr. Hanson what I owe him—and order more."

Aunt Bernice unwrapped a bolt of blue fabric that was dotted with a dainty floral. "I can imagine women liking this piece."

Mother walked a few steps toward it, then eyed it as if it were soiled. "It is nothing more than a simple cotton."

"Women out west don't need silk and velvet," Josephine said. "Functional fabrics are best—but pretty fabrics."

Aunt opened another bolt of a tan calico with red flowers. "This would make a nice camp dress."

"What do you know of camp dresses?" Mother asked.

"I may prefer finer fabrics now, Lizzie, but you may remember George and I weren't always wealthy. I have worn my share of simple dresses." She rewrapped the bolt and turned to Josephine. "I don't want you to worry about paying the bill, Josephine. I will be happy to see it paid."

"Bernice!"

"I have the money, Lizzie. And what good is it doing me just sitting in the bank? The world is changing, and I want to be a part of it. I am keen on Josephine's store and want to be its first investor."

Josephine was stunned—and moved. She embraced her aunt and whispered in her ear, "You are marvelous."

Aunt whispered back, "So are you."

Never would Josephine have expected Aunt Bernice to be an encourager or a supporter. Since William's and Thomas's deaths, Josephine had always tossed her into the same box as her mother: disapproving, staid, and dour. The she-bears. To see Aunt so full of enthusiasm was an unexpected blessing.

Frieda found the box of jars and said, "Dowd, would you please take these to the kitchen for me? I have some face cream to cook up."

"Face cream?" Aunt said.

"No one is going to spend money on Frieda's face cream," Mother said.

"I met some Mormon women who would love it."

"Mormons? You met Mormons?"

Josephine sighed. "Yes indeed. I met all kinds of people you wouldn't approve of. Mormons, Indians, ex-slaves, Confederate soldiers, gamblers, prosti—" She stopped and looked at Nelly.

Unfortunately, Mother perked up. "You were saying 'prostitutes,' and then you look at the girl?"

Josephine kicked herself. To have kept the secret so long, only to let it out when they were on the verge of leaving . . . But since they were leaving, what did it matter?

"I took Nelly away from a brothel where she was working."

Mother gasped. "She was a prostitute?"

"Yes," Josephine said.

"No," Nelly said with a shake to her head.

Josephine whipped toward the girl. "No?"

"Oh no. I weren't one of them. I just did their laundry and washed the dishes."

Josephine ran to her, grabbing hold of her upper arms. "Really? That's all?"

Nelly was clearly taken aback. "I guess I scrubbed the floors too." Then her eyes grew large. "You thought that I . . ." She shook her head. "No, no. The ladies would never make me do any of . . . that."

Josephine pulled her close, her relief palpable. "Thank You, sweet Jesus! The thought of Nelly . . ." She couldn't put it into words—and luckily, there was no need.

Mother strode toward them. "You said you were an orphan."

"I am. I was living on the streets when the ladies took me in."

"This is . . ." Mother looked toward Audrey. "I am not feeling well. Help me upstairs."

After she left, Josephine wasn't feeling very well herself. "I shocked my mother. On purpose."

Aunt looked through another crate of goods. "Perhaps she needs a little shocking."

Josephine couldn't believe what she was hearing.

Aunt looked up and swatted the air. "Oh stop your worrying. She will be all right. Come show me what you bought for Josie's Emporium."

Josie's Emporium. She had to focus on that.

Chapter Twenty-Four

Hudson heard his parents stirring, getting ready for another day.

After spending four days at home, fixing every broken item in their apartment—including some fixits done for the neighbors—and listening to their talk of work at the mill, he was more than ready for the day. For during the night, he'd made a decision.

He folded his clothes into his saddlebag and buckled it shut. Then he waited for his parents to come out.

Mum came first, tying her apron. She blinked when she saw him. "Best of the morning to you, boyo. You be awake early. I know we *have* to be up, but you . . ."

"I have to be up too. I have a train to catch."

She sighed a mother's sigh and took his face in her hands. "You could stay."

He shook his head. "I couldn't. I can't."

"How long you be west this time?"

He hesitated, then said, "As long as it takes for God to show me His plan."

"Be we part of that plan?"

He noticed the sunburst of wrinkles around her eyes that made her look old. Yet her eyes were still full of life and vigor. "You will always be a part of the plan, and a part of me, and maybe . . . would you ever like to move west and start over?"

He expected her to say no, or to laugh at the notion. Instead, she said, "Perhaps." Then she wrapped her arms around his waist, and he held her close.

Actually, he hated telling his mother a half truth. But it couldn't be helped. He *was* going out west again.

But first, he had to travel south. Southeast, to be exact.

* * * * *

Frieda had to walk double-time to keep up with Josephine. "Slow down!"

"I can't slow down. I want to leave on the afternoon train, and we have a lot to do."

Frieda grabbed her arm and pulled her to a stop. "Exactly. Which is why we should be back at the house, helping pack the goods into crates. At least I should be back there."

She was right, but Josephine had no choice but to bring her along. "I can't very well go to the police station by myself, can I?" She linked her arm in Frieda's and walked.

"I still don't understand what you hope to gain by this."

It was very simple. "The truth."

* * * * *

As he fluttered around her, it became evident Police Chief Brandon rarely had ladies in his office. After getting Josephine and Frieda settled, he returned to his chair behind the desk. "Twice in a few days, Miss Cain. To what do I owe this honor?"

For the first time since putting it on, Josephine pulled her engagement ring from her finger. "This."

He held it between his beefy thumb and forefinger. "Your ring." He cleared his throat and set it on the desk between them. "Is there some problem with it perhaps?"

"You tell me." When he hesitated, she persisted. "The other day, you gave the ring extra scrutiny. I wish to know why."

"Are you certain of that?"

Her stomach flipped. Was she? She nodded.

He turned his chair around to a pigeonhole cabinet behind him. He found what he was looking for and retrieved two papers. One was a drawing. He looked at it a moment, then handed it to her.

It was a drawing of her ring. At the bottom was the name *Tiffany and Co.* She had heard of that New York jewelry establishment. Mother had a necklace designed by them.

Designed by them.

She picked up her ring and compared it to the drawing. There was no doubt the one was the result of the other. So Lewis had exquisite taste. Or . . .

"Why do you have a drawing of my ring?"

"Because it was reported stolen by a Mrs. Benjamin Troester."

"Oh dear," Frieda said.

Josephine was mortified, yet there was nothing that could make the moment less painful. She set the drawing back on his desk and placed the ring on top of it. "Would you please see that Mrs. Troester's ring is returned to her?"

"Of course," he said.

Humiliation propelled her to stand. "I assure you I had no idea it was stolen."

"I know you didn't. But . . . when I saw the ring, and you mentioned your fiancé's name, I looked into him and . . ."

"Yes?"

"There's more?" Frieda asked.

"I'm afraid so. It turns out your Lewis Simmons is actually Lewis Simon."

Josephine sank to the chair. "I don't understand. Why would he change his name?"

He brought forward a page for her perusal. It was from the United States Army. The words blurred. All except one.

"Deserter?"

"Apparently he deserted and rejoined the army for the signing bonus. More than once. Twice that we know of."

"Once a coward, always a coward," Frieda said.

None of this made sense. "Lewis said he spent the war in Europe, studying art."

Chief Brandon shrugged. "Apparently he was lying."

"He said his family had a fine house in New York and—"

The chief shook his head. "His father, Archibald Simon, was hanged as a spy. He pretended to work for the North while blockade-running for the South. . . . He was hanged on your father's orders."

Josephine gasped.

The chief continued. "I don't know what happened to the mother, as there is no record of the family beyond the war."

Lewis said she died of yellow fever.

Maybe she did. Maybe she didn't.

Josephine pressed a hand to her forehead. Everything she had known and believed about Lewis was a lie.

"I am so sorry, Miss Cain. I didn't want to tell you, and yet . . . he is not someone a woman of your station should marry, whether you love him or not."

His mention of love made her bristle, and she raised her chin. "Love should be freely given, and it should be based on honor and truth. Since Mr. . . . ?"

"Simon."

"Since Mr. Simon has chosen to falsely insert himself into my family, I have no choice but to assume that his motives were far from pure, and his supposed love for me was a farce to be played out toward a profitable end."

"Or revenge," Frieda said.

Josephine looked at her.

"Think about it," Frieda said. "*Your* father orders *his* father hanged. Was Lewis getting close to you to somehow hurt your father?"

It was too much to take in. Josephine extended her hand to the chief. That it was shaking couldn't be helped. "Thank you, Chief Brandon. I think this concludes our business."

"Best of luck to you, Miss Cain."

She had to set him straight on that. "There is no such thing as luck. God arranged for our paths to cross in order to give me His assurance and the truth, and so I thank Him, and you. Good day."

Josephine assumed Frieda followed her out to the street, but she didn't dare dally or look back.

There would be no looking back.

* * * * *

Once home, Josephine went up to her room and quietly shut the door. Although she was teeming with anger, humiliation, and grief, she didn't react as she had done in the past when confronted with disappointment: with a tantrum or sulking. Instead she crossed the room with slow deliberation, feeling the gentle sway of her skirt, hearing the subtle rustle of her petticoats, conscious of the beat of her heart.

She removed her hat and placed it on her dressing table with the care reserved for a piece of delicate sculpture. Then she sat at her desk, chose a single piece of paper, and turned it in a writerly direction. She took up the pen and removed the lid from the inkwell. She took a cleansing breath and began the letter as she always began it: *Dearest Papa.*

But then she stopped. What should she tell him? Everything or nothing? There seemed little possibility of anything in between. She couldn't tell him about her sudden idea to start a store without telling him about Lewis's deception—and warning him of Lewis's possible revenge. Nor could she tell him about the latter without mentioning that she had fallen in love with Hudson Maguire—who had recently been sent away by her mother.

In the last few days, the high and low points of her life had converged, changing it completely. Truth was deceit, old love was proved false, new love was out of reach, and her future had been moved from an eastern city to a western plain. A life of mindless privilege, where she was expected to accomplish little, had transformed into a life of hard work greatly dependent on her own abilities and determination.

Yet for the first time in her life, Josephine felt a surge of exhilaration at the possibilities that were within her grasp. Her future was not destined and designed by others, but would be molded and fashioned by herself.

For the first time in her life, she was in control. Before the war, she had only thought she controlled her life. Whatever she wanted she could acquire through charm. Yet that wasn't really control. It was manipulation. Papa was the one in ultimate control of everything; Josephine had simply learned how to maneuver his wishes to match her own.

And then Lincoln's assassination and the deaths of the boys had mocked her so-called control, showing her that she had no say in any of it. What she wanted didn't matter.

Did it matter now?

She moved her gaze from the page to the window. It had not been her choice to be duped by Lewis, drawn into a relationship based on lies and, she was beginning to believe, some diabolical plan. It had not been her choice to fall in love with Hudson, a man who was beyond the image and description of any man she had ever met or expected to meet. And now he was gone, sent away by her mother because he didn't fit into a nice, neat box. Where was Josephine's control in all that?

It seemed that love, which was intimate and invisible, was beyond her control, while the choices of starting a store and moving west—choices that were pragmatic and social—were hers to do with as she wished. Hers to control.

But you are not fully in control of any of it, Josephine.

She sucked in a breath, hearing the inner check. "No, I am not," she whispered. "You are."

And so she set the pen in its holder and clasped her hands, leaning her chin against them. *Father God, You are leading me on a journey into the unknown. Thank You for the path ahead and the choices You have placed before me. Help me make the right ones.* She opened her eyes, finding it hard to say the final words that begged to be said.

To have achieved control only to relinquish it? It was like being given a gift and being asked to give it back.

A gift. A gift had been *given* to her.

And then she knew that every door that had opened—and closed—had been orchestrated by the Almighty. He had been leading her on this journey from girl to woman, from socialite to merchant, from easterner to woman of the West. She had walked through the doors, but they would never have opened if it hadn't been for God, who was working toward a bigger plan for her life.

He deserved her gratitude, her worship.

And even more than that, her surrender.

With a nod she closed the deal, mentally handing the gift back to the Giver.

Take control of all that is before me, Lord. It is Yours.

As am I.

* * * * *

Josephine and Frieda checked a list of the boxes of inventory to make sure each one bore the *End of the Line* designation before it went out the door and onto the wagon that would accompany it to the depot. It was odd to see those words, because they seemed the opposite of what Josephine felt. The destination where those boxes and trunks were going—where she was going—was not the end of the line, but the beginning of something new. It was exhilarating.

And terrifying.

They both looked up when they heard Aunt Bernice on the stairs, giving directions. "Make sure my trunk has the same destination designation as the others. I wouldn't want it to end up in Minnesota when I am going to Wyoming."

What?

Josephine and Frieda stepped into the foyer just as two men reached the bottom of the stairs with Aunt's trunk. She swept down behind them. Upon seeing Josephine, she touched her hat and said, "Is it too busy? I packed some simpler ones, but I thought this would do at least until we reached Omaha."

"Omaha?" Josephine asked.

"That *is* where the new railroad begins, yes?"

"Yes, but . . ."

Nelly rushed down the stairs behind Aunt Bernice, a carpetbag held against her chest. "Isn't it wonderful Auntie is coming with us?"

Josephine let the new "auntie" designation pass. "You are coming west with us?" she asked.

"If you will have me."

Frieda clapped her hands beneath her chin, her opinion obvious.

It wasn't that Josephine didn't feel the same joy. It was the suddenness of the decision that gave her pause.

Aunt stepped forward to explain, taking Josephine's hands in hers. "I am too young to sit here and while away my life. I want to start over too." She let go of Josephine's hands and peered toward the door. "When I lost George in the first days of the war, and then lost William in the last, I thought my life was over." She looked back at Josephine and smiled. "But it is not. Your visits out west inspired me to think of the future. I had no idea what that meant until you shared your idea about a store. And . . ." She held out her arm and Nelly found her place beneath it. "And until you brought this little jewel into my life." She flicked the end of Nelly's nose. "She needs a new start, and so do I. And so we will all go together and take the West by storm."

"All?"

They looked up the stairs and saw Mother standing there.

"I am going west too, Lizzie. Why don't you come with us?"

Josephine inwardly repelled the idea.

Luckily, Mother said, "Don't be ridiculous. My home is here."

Aunt put her hand on the newel post at the bottom of the stairs. "What is a home, Lizzie? It is not a building and a few pieces of furniture. Home is being with family—which includes Frieda and Nelly. Our family is going west, and your husband is already there. Come with us and be part of it."

Mother's right hand gripped the banister. Her mouth tightened. "I cannot."

"Cannot or will not?"

Although the last thing Josephine wanted was to have her mother come along, she felt it was her duty to make the argument for the trip. "I hate the idea of your being alone in this house."

Mother's eyes bore into Josephine's. "I have always been alone in this house."

Josephine took a step back as if she had been slapped. Was that really how she felt?

Aunt was direct. "Listen to me, Lizzie. I have lived in this house since William was killed. I have spent every day by your side, acquiescing to your preferences. I found comfort in your companionship, but to hear that you felt nothing in my presence? You are either heartless or a liar. Which is it?"

Mother's breathing turned heavy, but then her gaze fell upon Nelly. She pointed at her. "Those clothes belong here."

It took Josephine a moment to switch her focus. Mother was worried about Nelly's clothes? The absurdity of it spurred her out of her pain. "Those clothes were my clothes. As such I can do what I want with them, and I want to give them to Nelly."

"As you wish."

With those three words, Mother turned and ascended the stairs. A few moments later they heard her bedroom door close.

They looked up after her. That was it?

"I'll give the clothes back," Nelly said.

Her offer broke through the moment. "You most certainly will not," Aunt said. "Now then. We have a train to catch."

Josephine couldn't pull her gaze away from upstairs. She hated to leave like this. She loved her mother. She didn't always agree with her, but she loved her.

What was uncertain was whether her mother loved her.

Aunt tied a ribbon beneath Nelly's chin and adjusted her bonnet. "Come now, ladies. Let us be off."

In a flurry they moved to leave. Josephine was the last out.

"Miss Cain?"

She turned to see Dowd, ready to close the door behind her. "Don't worry about your mother, miss. We'll see to it she's all right."

On impulse, she embraced him. "Thank you."

"Godspeed, Miss Josephine."

As the carriage pulled away, Josephine took one last look at the house where she had been raised. A parade of memories filed past: of her and Thomas playing checkers and singing around the piano; of spending time with Papa in his study, not caring what was said, but taking full joy in his company; of Frieda teaching her how to dance before her first cotillion—which she never attended because the war began. Even Dowd had a place in her memories, as she always used to tug on the tail of his coat and giggle, receiving a wink in return.

Where was Mother amid the memories?

Ah. There she was. Peering back at Josephine from the shadows, a spectator rather than a participant. Perhaps Mother was right. While the rest of the family had lived in the house *with* her, Mother had chosen to live here separate and alone.

Then, with a glance, Josephine saw her mother at an upstairs window, watching them leave. But when Josephine waved good-bye, the lace curtains fell back into place.

So be it.

* * * * *

As the train sped north, Josephine leaned her head against the windowpane, deep in thought.

And prayer. *Please keep us safe. Keep Mother safe. I worry about her alone in that house. Please make this all work out. I feel responsible for—*

Aunt put a hand on her arm. "Are you all right?"

"I don't know."

"Are you questioning your decision?"

Josephine was surprised when she shook her head no without a second thought. "I made the right decision to leave. But it's such a huge step."

Aunt looked across the aisle at Frieda and Nelly playing rock, paper, scissors. "For all of us."

"I know, and that's—"

"That's our choice. Our happiness is not your responsibility."

"Indeed it's not," Frieda said, joining in the conversation. "And mark my words, I intend to be deliriously happy."

"Me too," Nelly said.

"Me three," Aunt said.

Josephine's first thought, that it wouldn't be that easy, was overridden by a smile. "We are the four musketeers." She thought of d'Artagnan's cry. "All for one, one for all!"

"What are musketeers?" Nelly asked.

"Oh, my dear girl," Aunt said. "They are characters in a book that is all about adventures. I will have to read it to you."

"I can read it by myself."

"Of course you can."

Their laughter was a balm.

* * * * *

Hudson stood in front of the Cain residence. On the train he'd had plenty of time to think about what to say to Josie. Winning her over was not the issue, as he truly believed she cared for him. And now, there was the bonus that his obligation to Sarah Ann was severed. He was free. And so was Josie. Mrs. Cain was the problem. For in the short time he'd been gone, Hudson's financial and social prospects had not miraculously been transformed. Yet didn't she want her daughter to be happy? He would focus on that. For he knew he could make Josie happy. Maybe not rich, but happy.

He removed his hat and ran a hand over his head. His heart beat in his throat and he whispered a prayer. "Please, God. You sent me here. Make it work out."

That said, he strode up to the door and knocked. The butler answered.

"Hello, Dowd. Is Miss Josephine at home?"

Dowd looked confused. "No, Mr. Maguire, she's not. She's on a train heading west."

"West?"

"Yes, sir." Dowd looked toward the upstairs hall as if checking for ears. "She and the little girl, and Mrs. Schultz, and even Mrs. Miller."

"Aunt Bernice went too?"

For the first time, Dowd smiled. "Miss Josephine ignited a mighty spark among them."

"Dowd! Who's here?" called Mrs. Cain.

The butler lowered his head and stepped back, fully opening the door. "Mr. Maguire, ma'am."

Hudson turned his hat in his hands. "Hello, Mrs. Cain."

She descended the stairs. "I thought you left."

"I came back."

"Why?"

"I came to see your daughter."

"You are too late. She went west. They all went west."

"So I heard."

"She is starting a store."

"A store?" The idea surprised him. "A real store?"

"Is there any other kind?"

"I suppose not, but—"

"Do not ever doubt she can accomplish it, Mr. Maguire. What my daughter sets her mind to, she makes happen. If that's all . . ." She moved as though to return upstairs.

"When did they leave?"

She turned back to him. "On the two-o'clock."

It only took him a moment to realize, "We must have passed each other on the tracks."

Mrs. Cain let out a *humph*.

"Is something funny?"

"So goes the story of my life." But then she pointed toward the depot. "The next train leaves within the hour."

"Thank you, Mrs. Cain."

Her brow drooped. "Take care of my girl, Mr. Maguire. Tell her . . . tell her I love her."

"I'll do that, ma'am. I promise."

She nodded, and the door closed between them.

Hudson ran toward the station.

PART THREE

Go confidently in the direction of your dreams.
Live the life you've imagined.

—HENRY DAVID THOREAU

Chapter Twenty-Five

"Josephine, look!"

They all turned toward the window. A large herd of antelope raced the train, keeping up with it. The engineer let go a shriek on the whistle, making the animals run faster. The train picked up speed.

"They are keeping up with us," Josephine said.

"Astounding," Frieda said.

"And breathtaking," Aunt added. "I would never see anything like this back in the city."

Josephine was relieved and surprised that Aunt Bernice had taken such a liking to everything "west." It was as if the West was an old friend she hadn't met until now.

After six or seven miles, the antelope finally gave up and veered away from the track. Nelly sat with her nose to the window and waved to them as the train surged forward. "They didn't lose," she said. "They just gave up."

"Giving up *is* losing," Aunt said.

Josephine did a double take. "I've never thought of it like that."

"It's the only way to think of it. 'Let us run with patience the race that is set before us.'" She gave Josephine a pointed look. "We are in this race together, niece." She nodded at Frieda. "'A threefold cord is not quickly broken.'"

"Hey," Nelly said, leaving the window behind. "Three? I make four."

Aunt nodded once. "All the better."

* * * * *

The train pulled into the Cheyenne depot. It seemed a thousand years had passed since Josephine had left with Nelly and Frieda. And Hudson.

Where was he now?

She suspected he was at the end of the line, back at work. After being so rudely sent away by her mother, was he trying to forget her? Or did he still have feelings for her?

She certainly had feelings for him, deeper now than ever before.

Josephine had thought about him mile after mile, minute after minute. The notion of seeing him again kept her awake, and when she closed her eyes she imagined different scenarios of how their first meeting would come about. In doing so, she gave others the impression she was dozing.

But she wasn't dozing. She was daydreaming.

And praying. She had honed her prayers to a few words that mimicked the rhythm of the train. *Let us be together, let us be together . . .*

"We're here!" Nelly popped out of her seat. "The very first thing I want to do is see Vera."

That pushed thoughts of Hudson aside. "You will not see Vera," Josephine said. "We cannot risk going back to Miss Mandy's. Or even close to that place."

"I agree," Frieda said.

"As do I," Aunt said. "Though I am rather curious about such an establishment."

"Aunt!"

"I have never seen a brothel before."

"And you shan't see one today."

Nelly sank onto a bench. "It's not fair."

Josephine pulled her to standing. "Come now. First, I need to check for a wire from Papa. When I sent the letter, I asked for him to leave a response in Cheyenne."

They stood in line to exit the railcar. Frieda stood behind Nelly, a hand on her shoulder. "I do wonder what he thinks about the store idea, and all three of us returning."

"He doesn't know about my coming along," Aunt said.

What would Papa say to that?

That he was angry Josephine was rebelling against his directive by coming back?

That he didn't want Nelly in this wild place?

That with Aunt Bernice along, he worried after his wife, left alone?

And by the way, a *store*? What made Josephine think *she* could start a store in the first place, and out west in the second?

She stepped off the train and headed to the depot office. Whatever Papa said, she would take her licks.

She deserved them, each and every one.

* * * * *

"Read it aloud," Aunt said.

"'Surprised by your letter. Proud of you. Try Laramie for store. Ask for Adolf Richter.'"

"What's Laramie?" Frieda asked.

The railroad employee pointed west. "Next big town. Fifty miles." He raised an eyebrow. "Laramie's a wild place."

"Wilder than Cheyenne?"

He shrugged. "As regular folks come to both places, they'll settle down. Eventually. Last I heard we got two hundred kids here. Talking of building a school for 'em."

"That sounds promising," Aunt said.

"Lots of promises going around." He nodded toward a table nearby. "Sandwiches for sale. Train's leaving soon." He pointed at the telegram. "Want to send a reply?"

She took up a pencil and tried to condense her swimming thoughts into a few words: *On to Laramie. Trust me. I love you.*

Josephine was asking for his trust.

Did she trust herself?

* * * * *

The train came to a halt in the middle of nowhere. Everyone looked out the window, trying to see the cause of the stoppage.

A nice man who'd been on the train since Omaha took charge. "I'll go see—"

But a conductor came into the car. "Sorry for the delay, folks. But the Dale Creek Bridge has some restrictions. When it's windy out . . . you don't want to be on that bridge when it's windy as it sways a bit."

"A bit?" Josephine asked.

"You shoulda seen the workers building it. I ain't never seen men so scared. They added some steel cables, but it still ain't fit for crossing when there's more than a breeze. Yet it's the tallest such bridge in the entire world. Worth looking at, if you want to get out and stretch your legs."

"How long will we be delayed?" Aunt Bernice asked.

The conductor smiled. "If you get God to tell you His plans for the wind, let me know and I'll tell the watchman."

"The bridge has a watchman?" someone asked.

"Watching for wind and fire from the locomotive's sparks. Wood trestles don't take kindly to neither."

Frieda shuddered. "I'm not sure I want to cross such a bridge in the best of weather."

"Then this'll be the end of the line for you. No other way to cross."

The passengers filed out of the cars and walked toward the locomotive, shielding their faces from dust blowing in the gale-force winds. There was another waiting train ahead of them.

And then they saw it. A massive trestle bridge spanned a canyon, rising over a hundred feet above a creekbed. It was five times as wide as it was high.

The passengers didn't stay outside long, as the wind made it hard to even stand.

There was nothing to do but wait.

* * * * *

The wind didn't bother Nelly. She was outside, hopping from stone to stone on the rocky soil. But then she stopped and pointed east. "There's another train pulling up behind us!"

Dozing, Aunt Bernice opened an eye. "You would think they'd figure out a better way to do this."

Josephine agreed. Although it had only been a few hours, the wind still hadn't let up. A few enterprising men from the nearby hamlet of Dale Creek had brought some food from car to car, charging exorbitant prices that Josephine had refused to pay. But now, as her stomach growled, she wished they would come back. One of the perks of having a new train arrive might be another chance to buy something to eat.

The passengers from the newest train began to stroll past, seeking their own look at the bridge. As usual, it was a contingent of regular-looking people, railroad workers wearing much-worn clothes, cowboys with dust on their boots, soldiers heading to man the next fort to protect against the Indians, and fancy men who looked like they were aching for a way to take other people's money.

But then she saw a brown Stetson and thought, *That hat is just like Hud*—

Josephine sucked in a breath. "Hudson!"

She rushed out of the car and ran to him.

* * * * *

Hudson looked up and saw a woman running—

"Josie!"

He met her halfway, and she flew into his arms. He swung her around, the wind of his emotions forcing him to make an extra circle.

Then he gently lowered her to the ground. But they didn't let go of each other, keeping hold in a fierce embrace. He whispered in her ear, "I don't dare let go lest you're a figment of my imagination."

"I am real," she whispered back. "And I am really here. We are both here."

Finally assured that it was safe to let her go, he gazed upon her bright eyes and delightful freckles, then took her face in his hands. "I feared I'd never see you again."

Her eyes welled with tears. "Mother had no right to send you away."

"I went back for you," he said.

"To Washington?"

He nodded. But that could wait.

Right now all he wanted to do was hold her.

And never let her go.

* * * * *

The couple was joined by Frieda, Nelly, and Aunt Bernice. Hudson kept his arm around Josie as he talked. "To say I am shocked to see all of you is an understatement. Your mother said you were starting a store?"

"We have the goods with us, at least enough for the first go-round," Josie said. "Women's items like face cream and ribbons and toiletries and—"

"All the luxuries of home."

"Even some toys," Nelly added.

"I commend your entrepreneurial spirit." He looked down at her. "I always knew there was a fire in your belly. I just didn't expect it to spark Josie's Emporium."

"Neither did I."

He had so many questions. Personal questions—and explanations. He tipped his hat to the other ladies and said, "If you don't mind, I'd like a little time with Josie."

"Don't mind a bit," Aunt said. "We—"

A boy ran toward them from the front of the train. "There's a man taking photographs up ahead and selling them. You can have your picture taken by the canyon."

Many passengers took the bait and headed forward. But then Josephine said, "Lewis? Do you suppose it's Lewis?"

Lewis Simmons was the last person Hudson wanted to see.

Josephine took Hudson's hand and led him forward. "Come on. If it is him, I have something I need to do."

"Need . . . ?"

She gave him a single nod. "Need. Come with me."

Hudson felt sorry for Lewis Simmons.

* * * * *

The wind whipped the drapery that Lewis pulled over his head in order to see the scene to be photographed. More than once he'd had to collect his tripod from the dust and set it right again. Logically, he should call it a day.

Yet to have captive customers with nothing to do but spend money until the train was allowed to cross the bridge . . . he'd be a fool to let the opportunity pass. Money was money. That was why he'd already traveled to the end of the line to take pictures, and had come back for some more of the bridge. As Rosewood had predicted, the railroad was his best customer.

He gripped the drapery and looked through the lens. The subjects were a motley crew of workers, most wearing the leftovers from their Union Civil War uniforms. But motley or not . . .

"Hold it. Hold . . ." He held the cover off the lens, counted, then put it back on. "Done."

The men let out the breath they'd been saving. But just as Lewis removed the plate for developing, he heard his name.

"Lewis! Lewis Simon."

Simon?

He turned toward the voice.

Toward Josephine.

His stomach clenched as he saw her stride toward him like an oncoming storm. He pasted on a smile until he saw that she was accompanied by Hudson Maguire.

Lewis put the plate in its box and stepped away from the group of potential customers. He needed whatever was going to happen to happen away from prying eyes and ears.

Simon? That was the clincher. Somehow she'd discovered his real name, which begged the question of what else she knew.

He held out his arms, trying to act as though nothing was wrong. "Josephine! What a surprise to find you out here in the middle of—"

She stopped ten feet away and held up her left hand. "See this?"

There was nothing there.

NANCY MOSER

"The ring you gave me? I don't have it anymore, because it's now back on the finger of the woman you stole it from."

Lewis glanced at the crowd that had gathered, then moved to take her arm. "Let's go talk about this alone."

She stepped out of reach. "You don't appreciate public humiliation? Well, neither do I. How do you think I felt when I found out that you— my one-time fiancé—are a thief, a fraud, and a deserter?"

The ex-soldiers who'd just had their photograph taken stepped forward. "Deserter? What's this about, miss?"

Lewis wanted to flee, but his feet were leaden. The knowledge that the truth was about to demand payment caused the moment to lengthen, as if his sins would be given extra time and attention as part of his punishment.

Hudson put a hand on her shoulder. "Josie, don't. Not here."

"Why not here? He certainly had no compunction leaving the Union army, only to join again for the signing bonus." She stared at him. "How many times did you play that game, Lewis? Two? Or was it more?"

The urge to flee spurred him to pack up his equipment. "That has nothing to do with you."

She put her hands on her hips. "Nothing to do with me? The woman you were going to marry? How about the fact that your name isn't Simmons but Simon? Don't you think I should have known your real name?"

An army soldier in full blues stepped forward. "If what you say is true, miss, then this man needs to be tried for theft, desertion, and fraud, maybe even treason against the Union."

Josephine let out a little laugh. "Like father, like son, right, Lewis?" She turned to the crowd. "His father was hanged as a spy after working both sides of the war for profit."

The faces of the soldier and the ex-soldiers hardened, and two of the roughest men started toward him. Their eyes promised pain.

He dropped his equipment and ran toward the bridge. Away from the trains. Away from accuser and jury.

Away from judgment.

* * * * *

Hudson took Josephine's arm. "What have you done?"

"Told the truth," she said. But her throat was dry and her heart beat too fast.

"Let's go get 'im," an ex-soldier said. He looked to the officer. "Hanging is what's due a traitor, right?"

"That's right, but . . ." The officer stood before them, blocking their progress. "The proper thing is to bring him to Fort Russell and let those in charge dole out justice."

One man pointed to the bridge. "There's plenty of trestles to hang him from. Save everyone the trouble of a trial."

What have I done? Josephine stepped toward the men. "Please don't kill him. I didn't mean—"

The officer faced her. "Were you speaking the truth about him?"

"Yes, but—"

"Then he needs to face the consequences."

"But—"

The whistle of the first train shrieked and a conductor walked toward them. "All aboard!"

While creating her own whirlwind, Josephine hadn't noticed that the wind had died down.

Hudson walked toward the conductor. "There's a man who's run away from the group. We need to wait for him."

He glanced over his shoulder. "Saw a man running over the bridge. Yelled after him, but he kept running."

"That must be him!" Josephine said. "We need to pick him up."

"We can't go more'n four miles per hour over the bridge. If we see him on the other side he can run to catch us."

"But if he's not there?" *If he's run away?*

"Then God help him." The whistle shrieked again. "All aboard!"

She tugged on his sleeve. "How far is it to Laramie from here?"

"Twenty miles." His face softened. "Sorry, miss, but I can't hold up hundreds for one man who got a bee in his bonnet. He can walk to Laramie. Or catch the next train coming."

The others got on the train, but all Josephine could do was look west, across the bridge. *Lewis, I'm sorry. I shouldn't have had it out with you in front of everyone.*

"Josie," Hudson said from the steps to the car. "Come on. We'll try to spot him on the other side."

Reluctantly, Josephine boarded. She heard passengers talking about the exchange but ignored them. She went to a window and opened it as wide as she could, leaning out in order to look for him.

"Get yerself back in the train, miss," a conductor said as he walked through the car. "Going over the ravine is precarious enough without you upsetting the balance. Besides, many a mighty man has got sick looking down."

She sat, and Hudson sat beside her, locking her in by holding her hand. "Lewis will be all right. He's a survivor. He got through the war without a scratch, didn't he?"

"But war back east is not the same as the open plains and mountains, lands full of Indians and wild animals and—" She shuddered, unwilling to think about the dangers that lay beyond the tracks. She pressed a hand to her forehead. "I shouldn't have attacked him like that, right in front of everyone."

"You'd been lied to. He was *not* the man you thought he was."

She appreciated Hudson trying to make her feel better—and she did. A bit. But the truth remained. "We're to show mercy. We're supposed to forgive. 'Vengeance is mine, saith the Lord.' God's, not mine."

He kissed her fingers. "Feeling angry isn't a sin, Josie. And yet, acting on it like you did . . ."

May God forgive her.

* * * * *

Lewis hid behind a rock outcropping and watched as his train moved across the trestle, and shortly after, Josephine's train. His only hope was to grab on to that last train and ride to Laramie. He had no idea which passengers had witnessed Josephine's tirade, but he had no choice. Get on that train or die in the wilderness. It was nearing dark. He'd seen the blackness of the night out here. He'd heard the howling of the coyotes.

He'd even seen bands of Indians on the horizon, watching the trains as they passed. Just a few weeks ago Indians had attacked a construction party at the bridge, killing two and injuring four others. He'd also heard of men getting scalped and shot straight through with arrows, left for buzzards and critters to pick their bones clean.

He *had* to catch that last train or he'd die.

When the second train passed, he saw Josephine at the window, looking for him. Her concern seemed genuine. He couldn't believe that she'd been the one who'd done the digging into his past. It had to be Maguire's doing. Had to be.

The second train moved on, and the last train started its pass over the bridge. It was only three cars long. He waited until the second car passed, then burst out of his hiding place and ran toward the final car. His left ankle screamed as he ran, but he kept going. The train took up speed. He reached for the handle of the stairs, missed, then ran some more and grabbed it, swinging up onto the steps. Other passengers must have seen his plight, because they came out on the landing and helped him up.

"That was a close one," the man said. "You miss your train?"

"Almost," Lewis said. Then he settled into the back of the passenger car, hunkered down, and willed himself to disappear.

For now.

Chapter Twenty-Six

"Laramie!" called the conductor. "All off for Laramie!"

Lewis didn't waste any time but slipped off the back of the train before it was completely stopped. He hurried past the depot, away from all those who would accuse him.

He had a destination in mind. Only one person in the entire world would understand and give him comfort.

Two men were hanging a sign above Miss Mandy's new establishment—a permanent place this time. No more pulling up stakes every time the railroad moved on. Laramie was a town of thousands. There was a sense of permanency here. Unlike a lot of the railroad towns, people thought this one would stick.

He passed the men and went inside. The lamps were being lit, and one of the girls recognized him. "Now there's a loyal customer."

"Where's Vera?"

She nodded to the back. "Where she always is."

He started in that direction, then stopped. "Is she alone?"

The girl smiled. "For now."

He only paused a moment at the curtain that divided Vera's space from the hall. Then he pulled it aside.

She was lying on her side, reading a book. "Back from the bridge so soon?"

He took off his hat and hung it on a hook, then sat on the bed, his head hanging low. "I've had a hard day."

Vera set the book down and moved beside him, pushing his hair behind an ear. "What happened?"

He shook his head. "You don't want to know."

"You know you can tell me anything."

Vera was the only person in the entire world he could talk to. He turned sideways, bringing a bent leg onto the bed. "I had a run-in with Josephine."

"I thought she was in Washington."

"Not anymore. But the trains were backed up on the east side of the bridge because of the wind, so her train caught up with mine, and . . . and she attacked me."

Vera raised an eyebrow. "Attacked?"

"Verbally. I was taking photographs, making good use of the opportunity to make some money, and she came barreling toward me, screaming that I'd stolen the engagement ring I gave her, and calling me a deserter, and—"

She held up a hand. "You stole her engagement ring?"

That seemed beside the point. "I couldn't very well afford one to her liking. She's a pampered rich girl. I did what I had to do." He tilted his head to the side. "I always do what I have to do. That's how I get through hard times."

She studied him a moment. "Hard times like the war?"

He nodded.

"So you *are* a deserter?"

He wished he hadn't brought that up. "Of a sort. I wasn't alone. There were many of us who joined the army, ran away, then joined up again for the signing bounty."

"That's awful."

He was shocked by her reaction. "It was *smart*. It was a way to get through the war alive."

She stood and moved her book from the bed to a dresser. "Did you ever fight in battle?"

"Why would I want to do that? I didn't care if the South had slaves or whether they even formed their own country. My father said smart people could get rich in wartime." He grinned. "Once I left the Union side, I worked with my father for the Rebs. We didn't get rich, but we were getting by far better than the poor slugs who died for nothing."

She faced him, her jaw hard. "My brother was one of those poor slugs who died."

He expelled a breath, then took another. "You didn't tell me that."

"We don't usually spend our time talking."

And he shouldn't have talked now. He went to her, stroking her soft shoulders.

But she recoiled, moving to the doorway, pulling the curtain aside. "Out. I want you out of here. Now."

She had to be kidding. "Come on, Vera. You've done business with worse men than me."

"The thieving I can forgive, and maybe even the desertion and the treason. But saying that my brother was a poor slug who died for nothing ... Even I have my limits." She pointed to the hall. "Out. Now!"

She was throwing him out for a few wrong words? "I'm sorry, all right? I can't leave here. I have nowhere to go. The soldiers from the train will be looking for me, and I don't have a cent. My wallet was with my equipment, which is still back at the bridge, and—"

She pushed past him to the dresser, plucked a few coins from her jewelry box, and pressed them into his hand. "Here. Take it. But don't come back. Move on to some other town. Some other whorehouse."

Miss Mandy appeared in the doorway. "Is there a problem?"

"I want him gone," Vera said. "And don't let him back in. Ever."

The madam nodded once. "It's best you go, Mr. Simmons."

"Don't you want to hear my side?"

"In my house there is only one side, the side of my girls. Go on now."

He couldn't believe this was happening. He left the brothel and looked up and down the street for the soldiers from the train. He didn't see any of them. Maybe he could get himself a room; once they all moved on, he'd be safe. Give it a few days and he'd go back and retrieve his equipment—if there was any of it left.

It all depended on how much money she'd given him. He paused in the street and pulled out the coins. Three, four, five dollars ...

Suddenly, he heard a loud sound and felt a sharp sting to his chest. He touched a hand to the pain and felt something wet.

It took a moment to comprehend.

I've been shot? No. That can't be.

But then the pain gained ragged teeth. His thoughts spun and his legs gave out. He fell to his knees. Then to the ground.

A man carrying a smoking gun strode over and snatched the money from Lewis's hands.

"Thank you kindly," he said.

Lewis Simon closed his eyes.

And died.

* * * * *

As Hudson, Frieda, and Nelly saw to the task of getting their baggage off the train and onto a wagon, Josephine continued her plea with the soldier. "But Sergeant, someone has to go back to the bridge and pick up Mr. Simmons. He just got spooked."

"The guilty often do."

Aunt Bernice added her two cents. "But to leave a man in the wilds is inhumane."

The sergeant scuffed a toe of his boot in the dirt. "Now there's a word we could debate." He looked at Josephine. "Do you really want me to go after him, miss? 'Cuz if I get him, it won't be to save him, but to take him into custody for desertion and a slew of other charges. What it comes down to is that his odds at living are better on his own than with me."

A man came toward them, removing his hat. "Begging your pardon, ladies, Sergeant, but the man you're looking for might already be here."

"Why do you say that?" the sergeant asked.

"Just as we got over the bridge back there, a man jumped onto the last car. Didn't say anything but made himself scarce, hunkered down in the back row. Someone said he was the man who'd been taking pictures."

Relief swept over her. Josephine looked toward the last train. "Then let's go talk—"

"He's gone, miss. Got off the train before it was even stopped. Jumped on, then jumped off."

The sergeant gave her a knowing look. "The guilty run."

He was right, of course, but Josephine was relieved just the same. The thought of Lewis out in the dark . . . it was her fault he'd had to run. If something happened to him, she would never forgive herself.

* * * * *

Josephine was forced to leave the problem of Lewis behind. It was dusk, and they needed to find Adolf Richter per Papa's instructions.

After some inquiries, they were sent to Richter's place on Second Street. The Fill 'er Up Café was sandwiched between an empty building on a corner and a hotel. The smells from inside were enticing.

"Can we eat?" Nelly asked.

Josephine was hungry too, but, "First things first. Let us talk to Mr. Richter."

"Then we eat?"

"Then we eat."

They entered the café, which contained five mismatched tables. Everyone looked up when they came in the door. "I am looking for Mr. Richter?"

A man stirring a pot on the stove looked up. "*Ja*. Dat's me."

"I am Josephine Cain. My father—"

He handed the spoon to a young girl. "Do *not* let it burn. I be right back."

He ran a hand through his hair and removed his apron. "The general's daughter. I been waiting for you. Come, I show you your store."

"My store?"

"It not *mine*."

Her store. It sounded so odd. "Is it far?"

He chuckled. "Ten steps."

He led them to the empty building next door. Inside, he lit an oil lamp hanging on the wall, then turned toward the room. "There is top floor you live in. Being on corner, traffic *ist gut*."

They heard a gunshot, and everyone looked to Richter.

"Sorry to say, you must get used to gunfire. At least till gang of outlaws . . . *getötet*." He made a cutting motion beneath his chin.

"Outlaws?" Aunt asked.

"They wild bunch who steal for fun, shoot first, ask later." He held up a hand, touching his fingers as he named them. "*Der* Kid, Big Ned, Ace Moore, Con Wagner, and . . ." He touched his fingers again, mentally going through the list. "*Und* Big Steve. *Böse* Menschen. Evil men, up to no good."

"Why doesn't the sheriff do something?" Josephine asked.

"Likely because there isn't a sheriff," Hudson said.

Richter touched his nose. "There was *ein Bürgermeister*, but he quit after three weeks because of threats. And then the city treasurer ran off *mit* the city money." He leaned forward and lowered his voice. "Do not speak too loud, but there is talk of making vigilante committee to take care of riffraff."

"Oh dear," Aunt said. "Maybe we shouldn't have come."

"I not mean to scare you. We need people like you in Laramie. It just so new it not right yet."

Indeed, having thieves and murderers running loose sounded far from right.

"Anyway," Richter said, spreading his arms to show the room. "Place not much, but is enough, ja?" Then he looked at Josephine. "What you say, *Fräulein*?"

She was speechless. It was a large room, sixteen by twenty. The wood smelled new. There hadn't been time enough for it to be built since she'd made her decision to start a store, so how . . . ?

Richter leaned close to Hudson. "Is she liking, or not?"

"Oh, I am liking," Josephine said. "But how did it happen so fast? I just sent my father a letter and cable and—"

"When General Cain want something, he get it done."

"But he only got the letter a few days ago."

"I know nothing about letter, but I get wire saying you coming, and to find you space for store. Blast the cost, it said."

Josephine looked at the space with added appreciation. "He bought this for me?"

"Bought it from me for you. I to make Fill 'er Up more big, but your *Vater . . .*" He rubbed his fingers together. "Gave me money so you have it."

Aunt Bernice moved to the window. "We could display all sorts of goods here." She looked back at Richter. "But we need some tables and shelves."

"Plenty of men look for work," he said.

"I could help," Hudson said. He crooked a thumb to the left. "It's a good location. Not far from the depot, and you'll earn business from the café and the hotel."

Josephine strode to the front, looking out at the Freund Gun and Ammunition shop across the street. Not the best neighbor, but she couldn't be choosy. "I will have to order more items for travelers," she said.

"And maybe I could make some *Stollen* and *Springerle* to sell," Frieda said. "And *Spätzle*."

Richter's eyes grew large. "*Köstliche deutsche Küche?* Mmmm. *Ja, bitte.*"

"Richter," Frieda repeated, giving him a long look. "My husband was *Deutscher.*"

His eyes lit up. "*Ich bin aus München. Woher kommt er aus?*"

"He was from Hamburg. My name is Frieda Schultz."

"*Freut mich, Fräu Schultz.*"

"*Mich auch, Herr Richter.*"

Josephine followed the gist of the exchange and was shocked to see Frieda blush.

Was Richter blushing too? He tried to cover it up by pointing to the wagon outside. "Let us unload. By the by, what is name of place?"

"Josie's Emporium," she said.

"*Sehr gut.*"

Ja.

* * * * *

Hudson left the women all talking at once as they made plans about the store. He was happy for them. Proud of them. To start from nothing in a strange place. To finish something that just days ago had been a dream.

You should be so brave.

He should be. Which was why he walked back to the depot. He had some things to clear up.

He stepped into the telegraph office, but the man was just closing up for the evening.

"Need something?"

"I have a wire to send."

"I'm closed."

Hudson played his ace. "It's to General Cain at the end of the line. It concerns the arrival of his daughter in Laramie."

The man sighed and nodded. "That girl's been the subject of more'n one wire from here to there and back." He returned to his desk and took up a stub of a pencil. "First off, what's yer name?"

"Hudson Maguire."

"Mc-Guire?"

He spelled it for him.

The man wrote it down, then said, "Let's have it."

"Josephine arrived Laramie safely. Store perfect. I am coming to EOL to ask question."

The man looked up. "Why doncha just ask it now?"

Hudson shook his head. "It needs to be done in person."

The man grinned and winked. "Think he'll say yes?"

"I sure hope so."

* * * * *

Hudson returned, only to find all the women but Josie gone from the store. As it was dark, he tapped on the glass so as not to scare her.

She was sitting on the floor, armed with a pencil and piece of paper.

"Where are the others?" he asked.

"I sent them to the hotel." She flapped the paper in the air. "Look at this list of things we need to set up, and this list of more things we need to sell." She pointed to the ceiling. "There's not a stitch of furniture up there, so we'll need beds first thing. Frieda is serious about making food to sell so we'll need a stove of some sort." She held out a hand, and he helped her to her feet. "We have decided to put a counter over here with a small table and four chairs, just in case someone wants to eat a bite before they leave. I was thinking of changing the name to Josie's Emporium and Café, but Frieda doesn't like the sounds of that, just in case no one likes her food, and she doesn't want to fully compete with Mr. Richter." She finally took a breath. "What?"

He laughed, totally delighted by her enthusiasm. "It's as though you were always meant to do this."

She considered this a moment, then strode to the front window, looking out at the dark. Lamplight shone from down the street where the saloons' business was just starting. "That is silly, of course, because there is no way I *should* be doing this, thousands of miles from home, in a wild place that has just decided to become a town."

He put his arm around her waist. "You didn't know, but God did."

Her eyes glimmered in the lamplight. "Do you really think so? Do you really think this is part of His plan for me?"

He nodded. *For us.* But he kept those two words to himself until after he spoke with her father. "It feels right, doesn't it?"

"Alarmingly so."

"Feeling peace is a pretty good indication you're on the right road."

"Is it?"

"That's the way I've always found it."

She wrapped her arms around his waist, leaning her head against his chest. "I feel peace about us too."

He wanted to propose right then, but he also wanted to do things right. So he only said, "Me too."

She looked up at him, clearly wanting more.

In place of words, he gave her a smile.

And a silent promise.

Chapter Twenty-Seven

When Josephine felt Aunt Bernice slip out of bed, she greedily spread her limbs into the empty space. The bed in the hotel was barely made for one, much less two.

Aunt groaned, and Josephine opened her eyes enough to see her press her hands against her lower back and arch it. "Not as comfy as our beds back home, is it?"

There was no need to answer, and Aunt moved to the window. She pulled back the width of fabric that sufficed for a curtain, drew up the sash, and stuck her head outside for some fresh air, looking right and then left.

And then she gasped. Her movements were quickly rewound. "Don't look. You don't want to look."

Which, of course, made Josephine *have* to look.

She shouldn't have.

Putting her head out the window and looking left, she saw a man hanging by his neck. Dead. Just half a block away.

"Is he a bad man, or a good one?" Aunt asked.

"Does it matter?" Josephine hurriedly put on her clothes. "We can't let Nelly see him."

Aunt nodded with sudden understanding. "How are we going to stop her?" she asked. "He is right . . . there."

It would require a two-point attack. "Get dressed and go to Nelly and Frieda's room. Keep them there. Above all, keep them away from the window."

"What are you going to do?"

"I'm going to get him taken down."

Once dressed, Josephine went to the hotel's front desk and looked for someone, anyone, in charge. She spotted a man sweeping the floor in a back room and marched toward him. "Sir?"

He looked up as though surprised anyone was up at this time of day. "Yes?"

Josephine pointed outside. "There is a dead man hanging outside."

He nodded once. "That's the Kid. Those of us on the vigilante committee strung him up around midnight."

Why hadn't she heard anything? That was beside the point. "I have a child upstairs, and I do not want her exposed to such a sight. I want him taken down."

He shrugged. "That's not possible, miss. Not till he serves his purpose."

"Which is?"

"To warn his friends to get out of Laramie or we'll do the same to them."

"But . . . but he looks so young."

"That's why he's call the Kid." He leaned on his broom. "Don't have no sympathy for 'im. He and his cronies run the Bucket of Blood. They lure customers in, get 'em drunk, rob 'em, and kill 'em. They toss the bodies in a wagon and haul them outta town for the coyotes to eat."

She shuddered. "That's despicable."

"Which is why the good men of Laramie are banding together to get 'em outta here, one way or another. We're setting up for a showdown." He pointed a finger at her. "But it's a secret. I advise you to keep the knowledge to yerself."

She took a step back. "I want nothing to do with any of this."

"As a shop owner, you might change your mind about that. We're taking care of the scum for the good of the town." He gave her a final nod and went back to sweeping.

Josephine went upstairs to Nelly and Frieda's room, where she found Aunt Bernice brushing Nelly's hair.

"I'm hungry," Nelly said, "but Aunt Bernice says we can't go eat."

The three women exchanged a glance. They couldn't very well stay in this room all day. But how to get Nelly from here to the café without seeing the dead man?

Fast. Do it fast. "I think we *can* go eat," Josephine said. "In fact, I say let's race. The first one all the way into the café, touching the counter, gets something extra."

Nelly rushed to the door of the room. "I can run really, really fast."

Josephine stood beside her. "So can I. Ready. Set. Go!"

She and Nelly hurled themselves down the hotel stairs. At the door, Josephine let Nelly run ahead of her and hurried from behind, pressing the girl into the café. Nelly slapped the counter. "I won!"

Josephine didn't have to pretend to be out of breath. "Yes, you did." She pointed to a table just as Frieda and Aunt Bernice came in. Frieda looked a little green.

"What you eat, *Damen*?" Richter asked.

"What is there?"

"We have eggs and bacon."

"And?" Aunt asked.

"Eggs and bacon."

Hudson walked in the door. "Make that five orders," he said, pulling an extra chair to their table.

She looked at him with questioning eyes and nodded in the direction of the hanged man.

"I saw," he said.

"What did you see?" Nelly asked.

"I saw that you won the race. Congratulations, speedy."

He was a gem.

* * * * *

After breakfast, they shielded Nelly and walked from the café to the store. There was plenty to keep them all busy.

"We need something to use as a counter," Josephine said.

"Let me see if I can scrounge up some wood, some nails, and a hammer," Hudson said.

"I'll come with you," Nelly said.

"No!" the women said all at once. Their smiles were strained.

"We need your help here," Aunt said.

Just then a man came in with a stack of newspapers draped over his arm. "Newspaper? Just a penny."

Hudson handed him a coin, and while the others sorted through the goods they had brought from home, he and Josephine looked through it. On the front page they found a column called *Last Night's Shootings*. "Really?" Josephine said. "They have so many deaths that they must list them in a special column?"

"Apparently," Hudson said as he read. Then he sucked in a breath. "Oh no."

"What?"

He pointed at one name on the list: Lewis Simmons.

She snatched the paper from him. "Lewis? He was *killed*?"

Aunt and Frieda came close. "What are you talking about?"

She handed them the paper and stepped away, needing room to air her guilt. "It's all my fault. If only I hadn't yelled at him in front of everyone, he would be alive."

"You can't know that," Hudson said.

"I *do* know that." Memories of Lewis's humiliation were scathing. She had taken such pleasure shaming him, letting her own pain fuel her tirade. "I blindsided him," she said. "There was no way for him to defend himself."

"Because you were telling the truth," Aunt said. "He was guilty of each and every point."

"But I didn't need to share it with the world, in earshot of those soldiers." She didn't wait for more comfort, for she didn't deserve it. She strode out the door and entered the café. Richter looked up from pouring coffee. "Who handles the burials around here?" she asked.

He stepped away from his customers. "If you want Kid get proper burial . . ."

She shook her head vehemently, having forgotten about the Kid. "My friend was shot yesterday, and I want to make sure he gets a Christian funeral. Who do I talk to?"

"*Herr Doktor.* Doc Grant."

"Where is he?"

He pointed down the street. "Turn at corner, on right."

Thankfully, as she passed the place where the Kid had been hanging, he was gone.

As was Lewis.

* * * * *

The four women and Hudson stood at the grave of Lewis Simmons. "Will you say a few words, Dr. Grant?" Josephine asked.

He took out a worn Bible and flipped the pages until he found the verse he wanted. "'The Lord is my shepherd; I shall not want. He maketh me to lie down in green pastures: he leadeth me beside the still waters. He restoreth my soul: he leadeth me in the paths of righteousness for his name's sake. Yea, though I walk through the valley of the shadow of death, I will fear no evil: for thou art with me; thy rod and thy staff they comfort me.'" He snapped the Bible shut and looked to Josephine. "You want to say something, Miss Cain?"

What should she say? The man she had thought she knew was a stranger to her. And yet . . .

"I loved him. Once." But had she? Or had she used Lewis as much as he'd used her? She took a fresh breath and repeated the words. "I loved him once. In my own way." She wiped away a tear. "He did not deserve to die like this. May God bless his soul."

The others nodded, and Nelly laid a sprig of wildflowers on his grave. Josephine felt guilty for walking away, but what else was there to say or do?

Suddenly, Nelly sprinted away from the group. "Vera!" She wrapped her arms around the woman's waist.

"Who is she?" Aunt asked.

"Nelly's friend." Josephine strode toward her, and Vera looked nervous. She touched her hair as if checking it, then wrapped her shawl around herself like a shield.

"Hello," Josephine said.

Vera had a charming smile. A relieved smile. She nodded a greeting. Nelly pointed to the grave. "That man died."

Vera looked at Josephine. "I knew that man." Then her face crumpled. "He died because of me."

Josephine couldn't have been more surprised if Vera had said she was president of the United States. "Why do you say that?" she asked.

Vera glanced at Hudson, Aunt Bernice, and Frieda, who were standing close by. "Can you and me talk a minute?"

This would be interesting. "Of course." She laid a hand on Nelly's shoulder. "Go join the others. I will catch up with you."

Nelly was reluctant and gave Vera another hug. "I'm so glad you're here. We're here too. We're starting a store."

"Are you now?"

Nelly joined the others, leaving Josephine and Vera alone. "Can we get away from this awful boot hill?" Vera asked. "There are too many fresh graves."

And there were. The land was dotted with heaps of freshly dug earth.

Vera pointed ahead. "There's a nice rock grouping ahead. I go there sometimes to be alone and think."

Josephine's first reaction was unkind. She went there to *think*? But she walked with Vera to the rocks and each found a seat. The silence was awkward. They were from such different worlds.

Vera took a deep breath and pointed to the mountains nearby. "It's so beautiful here. Peaceful." She nodded toward the town. "So unlike that place."

"We saw a hanged man this morning."

"The Kid. A bad seed for certain. I wouldn't be surprised if he was the one who shot Lewis."

This was news. "How do you know?"

"I don't. But he and his gang are responsible for at least a dozen graves." She sighed and picked up a pebble, moving it from one palm to the other. "We're all hoping the vigilantes will get 'em. Though that won't stop another bunch from coming in to make trouble."

"You are so matter-of-fact."

"It ain't called the Wild West for no reason."

"Then why are you here?"

Vera raised a neatly plucked brow. "I could ask you the same question. A store? Pardon me for asking, but what do you know about running a store in a town like Laramie?"

Josephine considered defending herself, but for some reason, could not. "Not a thing."

Vera laughed. "The West makes a lot of people do things they've never done before."

Josephine wondered if Vera's profession was included in that statement.

But Vera moved on. "Lewis came to me yesterday afternoon, all upset about your run-in at the bridge."

"He told you about that?"

"He told me about a lot of things." She threw the pebble away and brushed her hands as if brushing away the *things* Lewis had told her. "He was one complicated man." She snickered. "But aren't they all."

"I wouldn't know. I haven't known many men—" Her words carried a meaning she hadn't intended, and she felt herself blush.

"Don't worry. I know what you meant. And truthfully, I haven't known much about many men neither. They usually aren't fond of talking deep about things."

It was Josephine's turn to laugh. "My father likes to fix things."

"They all do, honey. But don't hold it against them. It's their job."

"And what is our job? As women?"

Vera thought a moment. "To love and nurture them in spite of their fixing."

Josephine adjusted her bottom on the rock. "You said Lewis died because of you? That's not true. He died because of me—because of my public tirade against him."

Vera shrugged. "You lit the spark, and I fanned it into a flame."

"What did you say to him?"

"I told him to get out and never come back." She hung her head. "He said my brother was a poor slug who died for nothing."

"What did he mean by that?"

Vera stood and looked to the east, her shawl pulled tight around her. "He was talking about all soldiers who fought in the war." She turned back to Josephine. "I'm sure that not every soldier—on either side—totally believed in what he was fighting for. They risked their lives because it was their duty to fight for a cause. Lewis was a coward who fought for no one but himself."

"My brother died too," Josephine said softly.

Vera's forehead crumpled, and her eyes filled with tears. "They didn't die for nothing. They didn't."

Josephine went to her, and the two women embraced, rocking to the rhythm of their common sorrow.

* * * * *

Aunt Bernice swatted Hudson on the back with a towel. "What are you doing, staring out the window? She'll be back."

"She's talking to Vera," Nelly said. "I hope they like each other. They're both nice ladies."

"Hush, girl," Frieda said.

"Well, they are."

Hudson turned his back to the glass. "I need to leave town."

They all stopped working. "You can't leave Josephine now," Aunt said. "She will be heartbroken. She cares for you so much and—"

He raised a hand to stop her words. "I'm not leaving for good. And I care for her too. I need to go to the end of the line, to find her father and . . ." He grinned. "You know."

Aunt Bernice gasped, then encased him in a hug. "I'm so happy for both of you."

"What?" Nelly asked. "What's going on?"

Was Nelly old enough to keep a secret?

"Tell me!" she said.

He put his hands on her shoulders. "I am going to General Cain to ask him for his daughter's hand."

"Why do you want her hand? Doncha want all of her?"

They all laughed, and Hudson pinched her chin. "Yes, I do. But I want to ask the general for her hand in marriage."

"Oh," she said, finally understanding. "She didn't say nothing about you two getting hitched."

"That's because I haven't asked her yet."

Frieda pointed a finger at Nelly. "It's a secret. Josephine can't know anything about it until Hudson comes back and formally proposes."

Nelly looked to Hudson, and he nodded. "It's very important she not know anything about why I've left or what I'm planning to do."

"All right."

Hudson blinked. "That's it?"

Nelly made a disgusted face. "You want me to promise on a stack of Bibles and cross my heart and hope to die?"

"That won't be necessary."

"Good. 'Cuz I can keep a secret as well as any of you. Just you watch."

He was counting on it.

* * * * *

Comforted by her talk with Vera, Josephine was eager to get home.

Home? Did she really consider the store home?

It was all she had since she'd burned her bridge back in Washington. She had cut her ties with that old life, and the old Josephine. In a way, Lewis's death provided the nail in that coffin. Now it was time to move forward with the store and with the family she'd brought with her.

And Hudson. Oh yes, with Hudson.

Turning onto Second Street, she remembered seeing the body of the Kid. Was he being buried in the same cemetery as Lewis?

She shook the discomforting thought away. Happy thoughts. Positive thoughts. That was the plan.

Josephine found the door of the store open to the nice day. Hudson had just finished building a narrow table to use as a counter, and set it upright.

Nelly saw her first, and pointed. "Look! A real table."

"It's a piece of art."

Hudson wiped the top with a rag. "It's a table."

From the other side of the store, she saw Aunt Bernice and Frieda with the sleeves of their dresses rolled up. They were setting a shelf on some new brackets on the wall. "Voilà!" Aunt said. "A shelf. The first of many."

Nelly flitted between them. "Auntie even cut the board herself."

Aunt flexed her arm. "I am stronger than I look."

"I think we all are," Josephine said. She took off her hat and began to roll up her own sleeves.

But then Hudson came close. "Can I speak with you alone?"

Josephine glanced at the ladies, but they looked away, as if they knew what he was going to say.

What *was* he going to say? By his demeanor it couldn't be good.

Hudson led her outside, around the corner. Then he faced her. "First off, let me tell you how much I care for you."

"Uh-oh," she said. "A preamble like that can only lead to something bad."

He smiled. "It's not bad, it's just . . ." He took a deep breath and let it out with a huff. "With Lewis dying, and all you must be feeling . . . would you prefer I went away for a bit?"

"I probably should want you to leave, because you are one of the main reasons I broke things off with him. He provided all the other reasons, but meeting you was the spark that started everything." He looked stricken, and she hurried to say, "But I don't want you to go. I have been waiting my whole life to have you here."

He smiled. "To have *me* here, when we only met a short time ago?"

"To have someone like you here, with me." She looked past him toward the cemetery. "I should be crying over Lewis's death. I should be mourning, but I'm not. What is wrong with me?"

"Would you feel better if you were wailing and keening over him?"

"No."

"From what I've seen, grief is personal. It's not something you can plan or force. No one can tell you that it's right, or enough, or too little. Let yourself grieve as you need to grieve, and forgive yourself the rest."

She looked into his eyes, his deep brown eyes that were so full of compassion and wisdom. "How did you get to be so smart?"

He shrugged.

She took his hand and started to lead him back to the store. "Wait," he said, halting their walk. "I *am* going to leave town—for a short time."

"But I want you here."

He squeezed her hand. "I want to be here. But I need to leave Laramie and go to the end of the line. I need to finish . . . something. I'd also like to see my brother."

"How long will you be gone?"

He pulled her close and looked down at her. "Not a minute more than necessary."

"A whole minute?"

"Not one second."

She could accept that.

* * * * *

Josephine turned over in bed and faced the window and the dark night outside. Just a few blocks away lay the body of Lewis Simmons—or Simon. Whatever his name was.

Hudson had told her to grieve in her own way. What was that way?

She had cared for Lewis. She had him to thank for getting her out of the family home. They'd shared some good times together.

But had any of it been genuine? Or was it all another lie?

All facts pointed to his wanting to marry her for shameful reasons—either for money or revenge for Papa's part in his father's death.

But how did he hope to gain revenge? What would have happened after they married?

It didn't really matter. He was gone. Dead.

Was he in heaven?

She pulled her pillow into an embrace and prayed for his soul.

And her own.

Chapter Twenty-Eight

"Well, look who's here in Utah. Mr. Maguire. Back for the final push, I see. How handy to miss the tunnel and bridge work of the mountains."

Under the scrutiny of the general's gaze, Hudson felt his face grow hot. "Nice to see you again, sir."

The general sat back in his chair, eyeing him. "So then. Is it you I have to thank for my daughter's idea of starting a store?"

He smiled. "No, sir, I'm happy to say I had nothing to do with that."

"Too bad. I think it's a marvelous idea." The general laughed and lit a cigar. "Relax, Maguire. I'm just chaffing you." He pointed to the chair on the guest side of his desk. "Give me an update on Josephine."

Hudson told him about Josie and the store. And the run-in with Lewis. And finally, his death.

The general sighed. "It embarrasses me to have been duped by him."

"We all were. It was Josie who dug into his past and discovered the truth."

"Josie?"

"Sorry, sir. It's a name I've given to her."

He considered it a moment, then shrugged. "It does suit her. And it's nice to see her stepping up to find the truth. She's showing a strength I didn't know she possessed."

"I think it's a strength *she* didn't know she possessed."

"Well said. At any rate, many thanks for being there for her during this rough time."

"Actually, there's more." Hudson confessed that his tardiness was also due to a short stay in Allegheny City. "I felt the need to settle some of my own family business."

The general let a cloud of smoke settle between them. "And was it . . . settled?"

His tone suggested he remembered Hudson's long-ago mention of a girl back home. "Yes, it was. I've cut my ties and . . ." With the chance to state things plain, he was suddenly tongue-tied.

"You want to marry my daughter."

Relief wafted over him. "I do, sir. With your permission."

"I guess you need to thank me for sending you back east as her escort. Love born on a train ride?"

"Actually, it was born on the prairie, during a sunset."

His eyebrows rose.

"During the one-hundredth meridian celebration. I was enjoying a sunset and your daughter joined me."

The general nodded. "Powerful thing, sunsets."

All tension left him. "Yes, they are."

"When were you wanting to propose?"

Here was the clincher. "I know we're getting to the end of the line—"

"The meeting of the Central and Union railroads is set to happen at Promontory Summit, Utah, second week of May."

A few weeks. "I should get back to work then."

"You'll do no such thing."

"Sir?"

"I have a thousand men to do the work of the railroad—especially since we're offering triple-pay during this final stretch. Plus we've taken on hundreds of Mormon subcontractors. But I only have one daughter. Your job is to make her happy."

This was going far better than he could have imagined. "I'll do my best, sir."

The general stood and held out his hand. "Then consider this my blessing." After they shook hands, he pointed to the door of his office. "Now go. Get her. Love her."

"Gladly, sir."

"But do me one favor."

"Of course."

"Bring her back to the end of the line, to Promontory. There, the West will be connected with the East. The vision of a few and the hard work of many will culminate. I'd like you and Josephine to be here to witness that. Actually, bring the other ladies too. They deserve to be a part of the celebration."

Hudson felt his throat grow tight. "We'd be honored, sir."

"As I am honored to gain you as a son-in-law."

Hudson shook his hand again, then rushed to jump on the next eastbound train.

If only he could fly.

* * * * *

Gunshots!

Lots of them.

Josephine ran toward the window to see what was going on just as Mr. Richter burst in the door and pushed her back toward the others. "Stay back!"

Aunt took Nelly under her arm. "What's happening?"

"Housecleaning."

When they gave him quizzical looks, he explained. "The Kid's gang meet their match. Five hundred citizens say *genug!* and have it out at Belle saloon." He paused to look at each female and seemed hesitant to say more.

"What?" Josephine asked. "What don't you want to tell us?"

"There be big necktie party today."

"Necktie?" Frieda asked.

With another glance at Nelly, he made a subtle pulling motion by his ear.

"Oh," Frieda said.

"You're gonna hang 'em?" Nelly asked.

Aunt Bernice gasped. Josephine hated that Nelly knew of such things, and that she could mention them in such a matter-of-fact way.

More gunshots caused them to retreat even farther into the store. Mr. Richter headed out.

"Be careful," Frieda told him.

He gave her a wink. "I come get you when coast clear."

Frieda gazed after him. "I hope he'll be all right."

Josephine arranged some crates to use as chairs and was glad for the chance to change the subject. "Are you sweet on Mr. Richter?"

Frieda looked to the floor. "That's absurd."

"Why?" Aunt said. "You are of the same age. He seems to be an honorable man, and you're a virtuous woman."

"What's virtuous?" Nelly asked.

"Good. Respectable."

Nelly nodded. "You *are* virtuous."

Frieda's face turned red. "Thank you for your kind words, but it's hard to think about a future with a man. I set aside that part of me decades ago."

"For me," Josephine said. "To raise me."

Frieda put a hand on Josephine's knee. "A life well-spent."

"But your life's not over," Aunt said. "It is just beginning."

Josephine remembered something Frieda often told her. It was time to return the favor. She took Frieda's hands in hers and said, "Who loves you best?"

Frieda blushed. "You do."

"Which is why I want you to be open to happiness, wherever—and whomever—it comes from."

They heard more gunshots and shouts, and men ran past the window toward the saloon. Josephine walked forward to see.

"Come back here!" Aunt demanded. "There is a time to be brave and a time to be wise."

Josephine stopped short of the window and returned to the group. A memory came back, making her laugh.

"What's so funny?" Frieda asked.

"I remember on the first trip out here when I was on the steamboat heading up to Omaha, I was afraid of the branches in the water. How silly that was."

Aunt nodded. "We have all grown stronger and braver—because of you."

Josephine shook her head. "You are all strong and brave in your own right."

"If we were, it was deeply hidden. Don't you understand it is because of you and *your* strength and courage that any of us are here, having this glorious adventure?"

Josephine laughed nervously as the sounds of the battle continued outside. "I'm not sure if a shootout is glorious."

"Maybe not," Aunt said. "But if it weren't for you, I would be sitting in that horrible chair by the fire, getting my ribs poked by the springs, having yet another cup of weak tea."

"And I'd be washing laundry till my skin was raw," Nelly said.

"And I'd never have the chance to sell my face creams to the public," Frieda said.

Their words made her teary, and her heart swelled with love for them. "So you think you'll be happy here?"

Aunt looked to the other two. With their nods she answered for all three. "We are happy now."

Josephine looked at the disarray of the store—which might not be a success, and realized that she was happy too. Right now. Amid the chaos in and out of the store. She reached for the hands of her aunt and Frieda, and Nelly joined the circle. "Let's thank God for each other."

"And new opportunities," Aunt said.

"And new friends," Frieda said.

"And another good lunch over at the café," Nelly said.

Together they laughed. And prayed.

As the gunshots flew.

* * * * *

The first thing that greeted Hudson when he returned to Laramie was the sight of four men hanging by the neck.

"What happened?" he asked the station manager.

"We took our town back."

"So these were outlaws?"

"Of course. The rest skedaddled out of town."

"Will they come back?"

"We'll be ready if they do. Just got ourselves a new man in charge, Sheriff Boswell."

He was so matter-of-fact about it. To realize that all this had happened in the time Hudson was gone was testament to the determination of Laramie to survive.

But then his thoughts turned to Josie and the women, and he hurried toward the store.

It was dusk, and the streets were growing dark. But through the window of the store, a lamp glowed. He went inside and immediately saw Aunt Bernice, Frieda, and Nelly.

"Where's Josie?"

"Hello to you too," Aunt said.

He was being rude. "Yes. Sorry. Hello. But is she all right? I heard about the fighting and—"

"She is fine. We all are."

Nelly pointed to the west. "She's out looking at the sun."

"At the sunset," Frieda corrected. "She needed some time alone. I told her no, with all that's happened she shouldn't go out, but she wouldn't listen. She's getting so headstrong out here. Must be the air."

"She's *getting* headstrong?" Hudson asked.

Frieda chuckled.

"Actually, I know for a fact Josephine wouldn't mind the company," Aunt said. "That is, if your visit with the general was successful . . ."

He ran out the door.

* * * * *

Josephine drew her shawl tightly around her shoulders. The evening was cool but tolerable. But whether the air blasted with heat or driving snow, she'd had to come.

The past few days had been eventful. The shootout had to be included in the events, yet it measured a far second when compared to the joy and satisfaction she had gained during the talk with the women in her life.

To discover they were happy here, were eager about the future, and were relieved to be away from their previous lives filled her to bursting. Because of that joy, she had sought the solitude and grandeur of the sunset, for only its beauty could rival the beauty of the love and gratitude she felt in her heart.

The sun dipped below the ridge of the Medicine Bow Mountains, its rays radiating to heaven amid blue and pink clouds.

Josephine pressed a hand to her chest, overcome by the sight. She spoke her prayer out loud. "Thank You for bringing me here. Thank You for the wonderful women who have come with me. And thank You for—"

"Josephine Cain."

Josephine whipped around and saw Hudson standing nearby. Overcome by happy tears, she ran toward him, and he toward her, until they met in a joyous collision.

He lifted her completely off the ground until her face was even with his. Then he pressed his lips against hers. "Thank You, God, thank You," he kept repeating amid his kisses.

She nodded, adding her own silent prayers of gratitude. How could life be so good? What had she ever done to deserve such happiness?

He gently let her slide down until her toes touched the ground. But then he continued his own downward movement until he was perched on one knee. He took her hand in his. "Josie, I adore you. Would you do me the honor of becoming my wife?"

It was the question for which she had only one answer. "Yes. Oh please, yes!" She took his face in her hands and gave him one tender kiss. But when she bent forward to embrace him, they toppled over amid much laughter. Fully fallen, she lay on her back, and he raised himself to an elbow to peer down at her.

He ran a finger along her cheek. "You've made me the happiest man in the world."

Then he kissed her again and again, as the sun gave way to the stars.

Chapter Twenty-Nine

As the train moved through steep canyons, ran next to rushing rivers, and crept over rickety bridges, Josephine had one thing on her mind— and his name was Hudson Maguire.

Yes, they were heading to the momentous celebration at Promontory Summit, Utah, where the Union and Central Pacific lines would merge. Yes, they were carrying Thomas Durant and a bevy of other dignitaries to see history in the making.

But with Hudson's marriage proposal, Josephine's world had grown very small. It wasn't that the work of thousands didn't matter, or that the vision of those who had imagined the connection of the East and the West was inconsequential.

The sun, the moon, and the stars, the heavens and the earth, all paled with the knowledge that Hudson loved her, as well as the astounding breadth and depth of her own feelings for him. A line from *Romeo and Juliet* said it best: *Did my heart love till now? forswear it, sight! For I ne'er saw true beauty till this night.*

"Did you say something?" he asked from the seat beside her.

Had she said the words aloud? Or had they seeped from her pores, as if her mind, soul, and body could no longer contain their essence?

She intertwined her fingers through his and offered him a smile that in no way expressed her joy.

He bumped her shoulder with his. "Soon," he whispered.

That their thoughts were already as one should have surprised her. But didn't.

Frieda got out of her seat and stood beside them in the aisle. "Did you two even notice the bridge had washed out back there? That they had to get crews to repair it?"

Josephine smiled at Hudson. "What bridge?"

"Did either of you notice when the train was held hostage in Piedmont until Dr. Durant paid a portion of back wages?"

"What wages?" Hudson said, his eyes only on her.

Frieda sighed and threw her hands in the air. "Carry on."

Gladly.

* * * * *

The next time the train slowed, it was for the best of reasons. The passengers lined the windows, marveling at the crowd that had already gathered.

But the best view was outside, and so the cars quickly emptied. Looking ahead to the track were the mighty symbols of the dream: two locomotives, a few yards apart, head-to-head like two bulls readying for a final fight.

Yet the fight was over, the battle won.

Dr. Durant left the other passengers behind, rushing to claim his congratulations. He shook hands with a dozen other dignitaries, some from the Central Pacific, and some from his own Union Pacific line.

Josephine had little care for those men. There was only one person she longed to see.

"Josephine!"

"Papa!"

His embrace was full of his usual strength, and yet she could feel more power within his arms and torso. With good reason. He had guided the work crews over 1,086 miles.

"Reginald," Aunt said, giving him her own embrace. "We are so proud of you."

He spread his arms. "Me and a few thousand others."

Then a young man ran toward them. "Hudson!"

"Raleigh!"

Hudson made the introductions, then told his brother, "Josie is my fiancée."

His only sign of surprise was the raise of an eyebrow. "It's about time I met you proper," Raleigh said. "I've heard enough about you—starting the first day you two met."

The family reunion was interrupted when an argument broke out at the base of the two locomotives. Papa listened a minute, then rolled his eyes. "Durant is arguing with Leland Stanford, the head of the Central Pacific, over who's going to give the first blow to the final spike."

"Arrogance," Aunt said.

"Exactly," Papa said. "But come close. We have been waiting for your train to arrive, so I expect the ceremony will commence rather quickly."

They—along with hundreds of other dignitaries and workers—moved toward the two facing trains. A few speeches were endured, then two ceremonial spikes were presented: a silver one from Arizona, and a gold one from California.

A telegraph wire was attached to the maul that would set the final spike. "It's supposed to signal the final blows to both coasts," Papa explained.

Then Stanford and Durant each swung at the spike, but laughter erupted as the men missed their mark. It seemed appropriate somehow.

Sitting close by, there was a frenzy as a telegraph operator tapped a message, then stood for an announcement. "The wire on the maul didn't work, but I've sent word that we are D-O-N-E!"

The crowd erupted with cheers, and Papa lifted Nelly high into the air. Then the two locomotives—the Central Pacific's "Jupiter" and the Union Pacific's "119"—inched toward each other. Engineers from each locomotive stretched forward with bottles of champagne to christen the trains.

Josephine noticed Papa staring at the scene. She found her way under his arm and looked up at him. His eyes were brimming. "You did it," she whispered.

He nodded. "The country has been forever changed."

"And linked together."

"It was President Lincoln's dream," he whispered. "I wish . . ."

Josephine leaned her head against his chest and watched the merriment. The mention of the president brought a flood of memories of the night of his assassination. The country had changed on that day too, the bitter culmination of a horrible Civil War. But now men from North and South, ex-slaves, and new immigrants from China and Europe had left their pasts behind and worked together to achieve this enormous task that defied logic and probability.

As Hudson came to join them, Josephine left her own past behind, and thought of another hopeful future.

"Papa?"

"Yes?"

"Can Hudson and I marry here? Today?"

She looked to Hudson and received his nod. "I agree," he said. "I can think of no better day than this one."

Papa smiled. "Nor can I. Let me find a preacher."

When he walked away, Josephine was faced with the reality of her request. "We are going to be married. Now. Right now."

Hudson laughed. "You were never one who liked waiting."

Especially today. Especially when it came to becoming Hudson's wife.

* * * * *

Josephine didn't know more than a handful of the people gathered at sunset on the tenth day of May 1869. But even if she had personally invited each one to their wedding ceremony, she would not have been aware of their presence.

Her eyes were on Hudson, and his were on her.

Before the preacher began, she noticed dust on the shoulders of the man's suit coat and mud underneath his fingernails. But his well-worn Bible was sign enough that he was a man worthy of the task.

"Do you, Josephine Genevieve Cain, take Hudson Lee Maguire to be your lawfully wedded husband?"

"I do."

"I'm not done yet."

There was a titter of laughter.

"Do you promise to have and to hold from this day forward, for better or for worse, for richer, for poorer, in sickness and in health, to love and to cherish; from this day forward until death do you part?"

She hesitated, not wanting to get it wrong again.

"Do you?" he repeated.

"I do!"

The preacher repeated the words for Hudson, who never took his eyes off of his bride. "I do too," Hudson said.

"What God hath joined together, let no man put asunder. And so, I am proud to pronounce you husband and wife." He nodded to Hudson. "Go ahead, man, kiss your bride."

"Don't mind if I do."

When his lips met hers, Josephine heard a cheer go up—or was it an angel chorus? For she felt as though God Himself approved of their union. For He had brought them together. It was the one fact that Josephine would forever embrace.

And then there was one other fact . . .

"I love you," Hudson said as they walked arm-in-arm through the crowd.

"I love you too."

* * * * *

This is indeed a great event of the world. It is one of the victories of peace—a victory grander than those of war, which leave in their track desolation, devastation, misery, and woe. It is a triumph of commerce—a triumph indicating free trade as a future law of our nation.

—THE REVEREND DR. VINTON, TRINITY CHURCH, NEW YORK CITY
MAY 10, 1869

Author's Note

Dear readers,

Thank you for coming along on the journey of Josephine Cain. She and I both appreciate your interest.

Even though I hail from Nebraska, I knew very little about the Transcontinental Railroad when I started—and only half of it when I finished. There's so much to learn and too little time and too many pages to get it all read and included in the book. And I only covered part of the Union Pacific's story heading west from Omaha, Nebraska. There's a whole other set of circumstances and stories that belong to the Central Pacific heading east from Sacramento, California.

Many of the events in Josephine's story actually happened. To name a few: General Cain was inspired by Union Brigadier General Jack Casement, who was hired to run the Union Pacific crews with his brother, Dan. Casement was responsible for inventing the unique bunk cars. The Indian visit where they had a tour and dinner on the train was true. As was the mock war dance and battle at the 100th Meridian celebration; Lewis's memories of his friend Henry Smith's execution; the influx of Mormons heading to Utah; the attacks on both sides of the Indian issue; the deaths of nearly two thousand in Wilmington, North Carolina, from Yellow Fever brought back from Bermuda by blockade runners; the lynching of "The Kid" and his outlaw gang in Laramie; as well as the condition of the Dale Creek bridge. And Hudson's fellow bobbin-boy, Andrew, mentioned in chapter 21, was future billionaire and steel magnate Andrew Carnegie, who worked in the Allegheny City cotton mills. Colonel Anderson, the book-lender, was real, and inspired

Carnegie to construct 1,700 public libraries across the country so anyone could have access to books. One act of kindness led to so much good.

I tried to include as many facts as possible, but alas, there were many, many facts I had to leave out (or else you'd be reading a book of a thousand pages or more!). Plus, in order to have a proper romance I had to condense time. The actual time span for the building of the railroad from Omaha was June 1865 to May 1869. Rails were being laid in California as early as December 1863. Fremont and North Platte, Nebraska, were the towns the Union Pacific wintered in the first and second winters, Cheyenne was the spot where they hunkered down during the *third* winter, and they stayed at Evanston, Wyoming (on the Utah border), during the *fourth* winter. Laying 1,086 miles of track took nearly four years. Or should I say, *only* four years considering the hardships and challenges the crews encountered along the way.

How many men worked on the railroad? It's hard to say, as men came and went. But it is known that Chinese immigrants were the prominent work force on the Central Pacific line heading east, while the major ethnic group working for the Union Pacific were Irish (like Hudson). Add men of every background, character, and ethnicity, and tens of thousands of men worked on the project. Many died along the way.

As for what came next? The following is paraphrased from a PBS timeline of the project: By 1880, the Pacific railroad carried $50 million worth of freight annually. It served as an artery for 200 million acres of settlement between the Mississippi and the Pacific. The Plains Indians were scattered to reservations, and a little over one thousand buffalo remained of the millions that once populated the grasslands. A trip between San Francisco and New York, which once might have occupied six grueling months, only took a few days.

Progress always comes at a high price. That price is what continues to capture my interest in all things historical. Those who came before us left everything they knew to take a chance on the unknown. Would I be so brave? I'm not sure.

If you'd like to do further research, there are many good resources. Here are a few: AMC has a very interesting, frank miniseries called *Hell on Wheels* that details the life in the transient towns that followed the railroad. Season Three started last August (2013). Eugene Arundel Miller has three books that detail the construction in Nebraska, Wyoming, and Utah, which include ways for you to personally visit the sites along the railroad's path. *Empire Express* by David Haward Bain has a very detailed account of all sides, and *The Journal of Sean Sullivan* by William Durbin is a fictional diary of one young worker. All the books provide many photographs and illustrations to help bring the history alive.

Like Josephine in this book, I pray that you enjoy the journey of *your* life, and recognize God's plan along the way. May you find love, happiness, courage, a deeper faith, and your unique God-given purpose.

Blessings,
Nancy Moser

Discussion Questions

1. How was Josephine's life changed by a world event—the assassination of President Lincoln? What world events have changed your life, and how?

2. Josephine desperately wanted to escape her family's house of mourning. Was she being selfish or do you empathize with her? How do you think she should have treated the situation?

3. Would you have been the sort of person to want to go west? Would you go as a worker, a pioneer, a tradesman, a farmer, a soldier, or . . . ?

4. The nineteenth century was a time of immigration. Where did your family come from? When did they immigrate to the United States (or have they always been here)? Why did they leave their homeland? Did they thrive here?

5. In chapter 12, as Josephine is heading out to Cheyenne with Lewis, Frieda says, "The Almighty is very adept at getting people to the right place at the right time." When have you experienced God getting you to the right place at the right time?

6. Josephine was impulsive, yet sometimes her impulses led her in the right direction. What do you think about her choice to take Nelly away from Miss Mandy's? How would you have handled the situation?

7. What do you think about Josephine's sudden choice to start a store out west? What nudges occurred that led her in this direction?

8. Do you think Josephine ever loved Lewis? Did he ever love her?

9. In chapter 24, "Josephine felt a surge of exhilaration at the possibilities that were within her grasp. Her future was not destined and designed by others, but would be molded and fashioned by herself." Have you experienced such a crossroads in your life? What decision did you make as a result?

10. Josephine realizes that her journey has been mapped by God, and so she surrenders her future to Him. What moments in your life do you recognize as God-moments, leading you toward surrender and full trust in Him?

11. Because Josephine's journey involved taking risks, the lives of Frieda, Nelly, and Aunt Bernice were forever changed. Are you a risk-taker? Whose lives have your risks affected—and how? If you aren't a risk-taker, are there any instances in your life when you *wished* you would have been more courageous? How would your life have been different? How can you be courageous *now*?

12. Near the end of the book, Hudson talks to Josephine about grief: "From what I've seen, grief is personal. It's not something you can plan or force. No one can tell you that it's right, or enough, or too little. Let yourself grieve as you need to grieve, and forgive yourself the rest." What have been your experiences with grief?

13. What do you think will happen to Josephine and Hudson? Nelly? Frieda? Aunt Bernice? Vera?

About the Author

 NANCY MOSER is the best-selling author of more than twenty novels, including Christy Award–winner *Time Lottery*; finalist *Washington's Lady*; and historical novels *Mozart's Sister, Just Jane,* and *Masquerade.* Nancy has been married for thirty-eight years—to the same man. She and her husband have three grown children and four grandchildren, and they live in the Midwest. She's been blessed with a varied life. She's earned a degree in architecture; run a business with her husband; traveled extensively in Europe; and performed in various theaters, symphonies, and choirs. She paints canes, kills all her houseplants, and can wire an electrical fixture without getting shocked. She is a fan of anything antique—humans included.

WEB SITE: nancymoser.com

BLOGS: footnotesfromhistory.blogspot.com and authornancymoser.blogspot.com

PINTEREST: pinterest.com/nancymoser1 (Check out my boards! I have a board for *The Journey of Josephine Cain* that shows some of the real photographs and fashion pertaining to the story, as well as a board on 1860s fashion, History That Intrigues Me, and many others that involve history, fashion, and antiques.)

FACEBOOK AND TWITTER: facebook.com/nancymoser.author and twitter.com/MoserNancy